DIRTY MONEY

TERRIBLE PEOPLE

Published in the UK in 2020 by BryherHouse Publishing

www.bryherhousepublishing.com

Hardback ISBN: 978-1-8382583-3-7
Paperback ISBN: 978-1-8382583-0-6
.epub eBook ISBN 978-1-8382583-1-3
.mobi eBook ISBN 978-1-8382583-2-0

Cover design and typeset by Spiffing Covers

DIRTY MONEY

TERRIBLE PEOPLE

CALUM KERR

PREFACE

He could feel his heart hammering. It was the only thing he could feel. Random memories scrolling across his mind. Lights flying over a river; Scott's restaurant in Mount Street; a huge iMac screen covered in numbers; a tiny data key. Running in Richmond Park at dawn with mist on the lake. The grunts of rutting stags. A line of cocaine; a police station. Passports without names and a piece of paper that had travelled the world. A carafe of vodka, and a boat full of booze.

Darkness. But then a tiny faint light in the corner of his eye, getting wider, getting brighter. "So here comes death," he thinks; all panic and fear gone, a great sense of calm. The light became whole but his body had gone. Just sense remained. He sleeps or dies. But later; minutes or hours. A voice.

"I think you are waking up." It was a pleasant voice. A woman's voice with a slight Scottish accent. It reminded him of someone on TV. Someone small. Someone knitting and listening. Small yet strong. Someone to trust.

"You have been in a very bad way but we are taking good care of you. Try to open your eyes." The glare was painful but he could make out a shape, framed by whiteness.

Cool grey eyes gazed at him; full of concern and care. Half glasses. A surgical mask and hair tucked into a plastic cap told him hospital. The smell of antiseptic confirmed it. Clean and cool. And the sight of her hand moving to touch his forehead sent him back to his childhood. He was safe. He felt tears in his eyes but nothing more.

"The thing is," she said, "we have had to use quite a cocktail of drugs to help you and I know you will be feeling a little strange. Blink your eyes if you can understand what I am saying."

He blinked once.

"I'm going to try and give you some water. Is that OK?" He blinked again. Small hands offered a beaker with a straw. He sipped.

"Try and talk to me," she said.

"I can't feel anything at all. Where am I? What is going on? What is wrong with me?" he croaked.

"My name is Sadie and I'm your surgeon. I am going to look after you and I don't want you to worry about a thing," she replied. "But I have to tell you that as the drugs wear off you are going to feel some discomfort."

The pain in his eyes started to recede and little by little he got to grips with the situation. He could see but couldn't feel a thing. It was as if his body had gone. And he understood that he had had a major accident.

He couldn't move a muscle. All he could see were white tiles, white walls, white light and Sadie's steady eyes. And then she spoke:

"I need you to stay calm. I need you to listen to what I am saying and to understand what I am saying. Let me repeat. In a few moments, the drugs are going to wear off and you are going to feel some discomfort. There may be more discomfort ahead and it may not be an easy journey but I promise you that I shall be with you every step of the way. Are you OK about that?" More tears of relief fell from his eyes but he still couldn't move his hands to wipe them away.

"Thanks," he mumbled as he slipped back into wherever it was that he had been before.

"Wake up, it's a beautiful morning" was the next thing he heard. Sadie was with him again, resting her hand on his forehead and the bright white ceiling again framed her calm face as she watched the blood pressure meter.

"110 over 90; not bad given your condition," she announced. "In a little while you will get some feeling back into your body.

"I need to explain some things to you. I shall leave you hooked up to these instruments as we will need to monitor your heart as well as your blood pressure and other stuff. Is that OK?"

"Yes," he murmured, attempting to smile.

"Feeling and the ability to work your muscles will return over the next hour or so and as I said there may be some discomfort. Hang in there; I shall be back shortly," she said as she left the room.

He found that he could move his head but could only

see upwards to the white ceiling and the bright lights, but he knew something wasn't right. His heart sank and then started hammering again. This wasn't like any hospital he'd been in before. There was a knock at the door. A woman walked in wearing a surgical cap and gloves. She must be the doctor, he thought... except she was only wearing a white bra and pants. She knelt beside him and talked quietly.

"When the feeling in your body returns and you are able to look around, you will see that you are in a bathroom and are lying naked in the bath. Your hands are tied behind your back and your feet are tied to the taps. You will pee in that bath, you will probably shit in that bath. You will probably cry, scream and bleed in that bath. The certainty is that you will die in that bath. How much pain you suffer is entirely up to you." His confusion turned to terror. He knew what this was about and he knew there was no escape. He was going to die in this bath.

"My clients have told me that they have very reliable information that you know the whereabouts of a data key which contains something that is important to them; that belongs to them. And they want it back. They have promised me a lot of money to get it. If I succeed I shall be paid that money; if I fail they might kill me. Or worse. Those are the rules. But I have carried out a number of similar assignments over the years and the fact that I am here suggests that I am good at this job. The reason I am telling you all this stuff is not like in a movie when the villain explains his master plan to make the story complete before the hero breaks out of his chains and saves the world. The reason is that you need to understand absolutely that I am a professional and that you are going to die. Full stop. I could kid you that once I had the data key I would let you go but I know you wouldn't believe me. Anyway, I want us to have an honest relationship; albeit a short one.

"Let me tell you, this house is in the middle of nowhere. This bathroom is pretty much soundproof. You are in the bath because these things often turn messy and baths are easier to clean than floors. They can also be useful for other reasons as you may discover. The reason I am dressed like this and exposing my grey old body is that as far as I am concerned you are already a dead man lying in a bath. And dead men can't see. More important, I can burn all I am wearing swiftly. Because when you give me what I want you are going to die, and cutting up bodies to dispose of them neatly always makes a mess."

Without any warning, he was sick. Lying in the bath sick. Sick all over his chest and his body. The woman rushed to his side; moving his head to prevent him chocking; wiping his mouth and cleaning his body. Getting a plastic beaker and throwing water over him before offering him a sip.

"Take it easy please," she whispered. "If you die too soon, so might I. So, this is what is going to happen. You are going to tell me where the data key is then I shall kill you. If you tell me now, it will be a pleasant death and you will be spared a great deal of pain."

His head was full of fear and confusion. If he told her where the data stick was he knew that one of the few people he loved would be killed. No way could he do that. How could he find a way out of this?

"Untie me; let me out of here. People will be searching for me. You are in serious trouble. This is just fucking crazy!" He tried to shout but the words came out as a desperate whisper.

"Don't be stupid. No one is coming to your rescue. No one knows where you are – not even my employers. As soon as you tell me what I need to know and I verify your information, I shall administer the best cocktail of drugs you can imagine. And you will die. Quietly, pleasantly, painlessly.

"Think about it for a while. Sleep on it. I know you must be exhausted. But dream on this. If you don't tell me where the key is tomorrow morning I will have to hurt you. And I am an expert in hurt. I'm a trained doctor and I know how to use drugs, I have a plethora of drugs, that is why you have no recollection of what happened to you yesterday. I'm also a very experienced interrogator – in my world that is a euphemism for torturer. I like to use tools as well as chemicals. And you know what, I enjoy it – it gets my juices flowing. That's why I call myself Sadie.

"So, if you do want to play silly buggers that's OK with me. I have a week to get the key, I already have a down payment of £50K and look forward to when – not if – I get another £50K for handing it over. Anyway, in previous projects like this I have found that the time spent getting my deliverable to the client is often reduced if I provide a little 'amuse-bouche' before I say goodnight and sleep the sleep of the innocent. I shall be back in a mo."

When the drugs had worn off, he could feel the pain in his feet where they were bound tightly to the taps. He was lying on his back with his arms tied beneath him and they were hurting him even more than his feet. He was naked, incapable of movement, and a space where his memory used to be. What to do? What to do? He tried pushing at whatever was tying him up but it just increased the pain. No give whatsoever and anyway he felt his strength was as distant as his memory.

Then she was back in the room holding what looked like a leather pouch.

"You may not know this but the best secateurs in the world are made in Japan. And the best secateurs in Japan are made by Hiryu. Have a look," she said, taking them out of the pouch. "Hand forged by Yasuhito Tobitsika at Toshibo. They have slightly concave blades for a finer and cleaner cutting action. I understand that Monty Don loves them. Do you know of him? He does Gardener's World along with his dog; can't remember what his name is. Nigel, I think. What a silly name for a dog. I think he had a nervous breakdown or something; Monty that is, not the dog. Actually, I think he has several dogs but it's Nigel that gets the screen time.

"Bunny Guinness also loves these secateurs She's the posh, rather sexy lady who used to be in Gardener's World; don't know where she is now. And I love these secateurs as well. But unlike those two tree huggers I'm not a gardener on TV. I am a surgeon – specialising in pain – not vegetables. Although I have to admit that some of my patients end up like vegetables sometimes!" She shrugged.

"Anyway, before we get too sophisticated I just want to put down a marker by pruning one of your toes. Try and keep still as the more you move the more it will hurt. Let's see: This little piggy went to market this little piggy stayed at home and this little piggy… Oh, wait a moment!

"I have been taught by a master. Sadly, he is no longer with us. But his death was painless; just like yours will be if you behave. One of the many lessons I learned from him when I started this career was always to use the correct tools for the job. I nearly forgot! Of course, these secateurs will remove a toe swiftly and cleanly but that's not really the purpose of the exercise; is it? Have a look at this: a miniature saw made by Bakuma in Tokyo.

"This lovely instrument is designed for pruning bonsai trees. Very sharp. But it may take a little time to saw through the bone. Bound to be very painful but if you pass out I will wait for you to recover before continuing the surgery. The thing with Japanese saws is that you pull rather than push – this creates a narrower cut so it uses less effort. And creates exquisite pain." As she spoke she tapped each of the toes on his naked right foot lightly. And then she paused, resting the tiny saw on his little toe.

"Look, just the lightest stroke, just a feather-like stroke and I'm almost through to the bone..."

CHAPTER 1

"Sky, why don't you tell them to just fuck off?" asked Freddie. "Just tell them they are confusing you with someone else. Someone who gives a shit what they think. I mean, who the fuck do they think they are? Why do you care? Ignore them. And pass me that joint."

"Oh yeah; like I could do that? You can't imagine. They're like, exams are important, very important. No exams equal no prospects equals no money. They're like: you drink all the time, you drink too much all the time, we know you take drugs – don't say that you don't. We worry about you. It's like we think you should act your age, get real… It's…" Sky's voice faded away as she passed the joint to Freddie and searched around in the darkness for the near-empty bottle of vodka and the next sentence.

It was about midnight. Hot and humid. Sunday approaching Monday. Thunder in the distance. No moon, no stars, no breeze. Devices all down except Freddie's iPad streaming something that sounded like an old Jay-Z album through the wireless speakers on the deck. The almost finished candle's flame hardly flickering. Thick air; dark sky.

They were at the bottom of Freddie's parents' garden

on the Thames in Chiswick. The procession of planes on route to landing at Heathrow had almost finished. Just a few stragglers punctuating the sounds of the river rustling the weeds beneath the decking as the black, high tide started to run out. They were all wasted. Drinking in Duke's Meadows, back to Freddie's parents' place. Wine, vodka, coke and weed. Sky had nearly passed out earlier but she was wide awake now.

"What else, Sky? What else don't they like about you?" murmured William. Although he had heard it all before, he liked to wind her up. A bit like listening to a familiar tune, even one you didn't like. And William liked Sky; he liked her more than anyone else in his life. In fact he thought he loved her. They had known each other for years and she was there for him when he needed her.

"I'll give you a fucking list," she muttered. "They don't like my hair, my piercings, my music, my choice of mates, the fact that I get up late and don't eat fucking breakfast. They don't like my shoes, my ripped jeans, my smoking, my Facebook page, my Twitter, my ringtones, my music and the fact that I don't give a shit about all the things they keep on about."

"You already said music," said William.

"Fuck off you!" grunted Sky. "It's like they just don't get it. Like they don't get me. Like they don't like us. They are just so fucking straight it's unbelievable. Just the other day I got a bloody lecture. Actually, more like an interrogation or whatever. It's like 'We need to talk. What time did you get in last night? Who was with you? We know you were with someone. It's just not right at your age; you need to grow up.' Blah fucking blah. I mean, why the fuck can't I do what I want to do?"

"Well, you know what babe?" said William. "I'm not too sure your kids are wrong about those ripped jeans. I mean how old are you? Fifty? Is that really a good look?"

And he passed what was left of the joint to Freddie. Who then stood up, walked to the edge of the deck, took one last drag, threw it in the water, unzipped his jeans and pissed into the river. That stopped Sky for a moment.

"Ugh Freddie, that's just disgusting. How could you do that?"

Freddie laughed, "What do you think I'm going to do, walk all the way up to the house? I'm finding it difficult to even stand. Anyway, what the fuck is that?"

There were lights approaching them from the river, two, three, four, five of them. Slowly, hovering about six feet above the water, moving a bit sideways and then up and down. They came closer and closer until shapes could be seen. People walking on water? What! No! Paddle boarding in the middle of the night, using head torches to see their way, riding the out-going tide as it took them towards Chiswick Bridge.

"Fucking hell," said Freddie. "I thought I was tripping but I've never seen that before. In the middle of the night. What time is it, anyway?"

Sky picked up her phone. "It's almost twelve and I've

got a text from Lizzy. She wants to know where we are."

"Tell her it's too late," pleaded Freddie. "Don't tell her you're here. She was out of her head when she wandered off this afternoon. She will have put that down for a while and now she will be up to God knows what. Tell her to chill. Please!"

"OK," Sky said as she texted rapidly. "I'll also tell her we've run out of everything and that you are being boring as usual. And that you don't give a stuff about the hassle I'm getting from my kids."

"You know what you should do about those fuckers, Sky?" said Freddie. "You know what you should do? You know what you should really do? Tell them not another word. Tell them that if they ever criticise anything about you again you are going to cut the fuckers out of your will. And you're going to cut their precious kids out as well."

"Let me tell you: one of my boys from wife number one – the Armenian one – is about thirty, acts like he's ninety. When I was leaving their house last Christmas he leant into the car and said, 'Dad, Rula and I would really appreciate it if you could act a little more like an adult when you come visit' – 'come visit!' –arsehole! She goes, 'We know Christian' – Christian; I've got a grandson called Christian! – 'smokes, but suggesting the two of you pop outside for a cigarette implies that smoking tobacco is normal behaviour when we all know that this is not the case in this day and age.'

"I just told him to fuck off and get a life. I also told him that his grandfather smoked and drank from age fifteen and died with a smile on his face and a glass of Scotch nearby at the age of ninety-one. Glenmorangie seeing as you ask. Which he didn't. I told him that his grandmother died a few weeks later in her sleep. I reminded him that they left this fuck-off house, worth millions, to me. And I told him that unless he loosens up and gets off my case, he will not be getting anything, let alone this house, when I shuffle off this mortal coil. And nor will poor old Christian and the rest of the litter!"

William's phone pinged.

"It's just Stan letting me know he's outside."

"What? Why?" Freddie asked.

"Unlike you, I'm still working a bit and have to do a presentation at 10 am tomorrow. And I know you too well, Freddie. You will go up to the house, come back with more booze and more blow and the next thing we'll be seeing is the sun coming up on Monday morning."

"I don't know why you keep that chap," muttered Freddie. "He's like a poodle hanging around waiting for a chocolate drop or a rub on his nose. I've heard him call you 'boss' for Christ's sake!"

"He's just polite, is all. And I don't know what I'd do without him. Yes, he drives me. But he also does all the gardening and fixes stuff. He's good with wood and electrics and other things that need doing around the place and the buy-to-lets. Anyway, Sky do you want to come along and he can take you home after he drops me off?"

"No thanks darling. I'll take my chances with Freddie."

CHAPTER 2

If you were driving west out of London towards Heathrow Airport and beyond, the A4 dual carriageway is only interrupted by one roundabout – the Hogarth roundabout. So called because it is near a house once occupied by William Hogarth, a famous English painter printmaker and satirist of the 18th century.

The dual carriageway swings to the right and traffic heading south swings to the left. What most drivers never notice is a small exit immediately to the left. This is Church Street. And it leads to the River Thames and one of the most attractive streets in London – Chiswick Mall. On the left-hand side of this quiet road are lovely houses – most have large and private gardens at the back. At the front is the river. And between the river and the road are the front gardens of these houses.

Inside one of the best houses an alarm sounded: "Good Morning. Good Morning! Wake up Mr West!" William's hand found his iPhone and Kanye stopped.

5.30 am. Monday morning. Sun was already shining all over the floorboards and rugs. He woke feeling full of energy and optimism in spite of less than five hours' sleep. Something programmed into him over the years. He rolled out from under the duvet; through the dressing room and into the bathroom. As he used his electric razor he read the news on his phone and checked for emails. Then into the dressing room which had three fitted cupboards. One for work uniforms, one for social and one for sports. Opening the sports door, William selected black running shorts, white technical t-shirt and white socks. Then downstairs to the kitchen where he took some blueberries out of the fridge to bring them up to room temperature, and into the hall where there was a cupboard with the same three sections; this time for shoes.

Within less than fifteen minutes of waking, he was out the door, switching on his Garmin 205 GPS and heart monitor, taking it easy, careful not to go too fast too soon. Conscious that his joints, tendons and muscles got damaged much more easily than back in the days when he used to race for fun as well as just running as he did now. He jogged the first few minutes past houses like his, some with smaller gardens by the river, others with back gardens reaching up to the side road between the houses and the busy A4 beyond. He revelled in the smell of the grass that reflected some rainfall in the night. He stepped up the pace on the riverside pavement approaching Dukes Meadows – the day's agenda sorting itself in his mind. Keeping his heart rate to around 140.

A working day, so William's run was a quick five miles. As he ran back along the towpath on the south side he looked across the river to Freddie's garden and thought he could see sunlight reflecting on the bottles and glasses left on the deck. He then ran over Chiswick Bridge and back towards Chiswick Mall. He took a quick detour down Riverside Drive to his allotment, opened the padlocked gate, went to his plot, unlocked the shed and took out his fierce-looking asparagus knife. It was about eighteen inches long with sharp serrations at the end. Ideal for the purpose. He cut a dozen or so spears, wrapped them in some kitchen roll and put them in a paper bag. Then, carrying the bag, he jogged home for some stretching and a shower.

CHAPTER 3

Getting dressed for business was a long-standing routine for William. Possibly an obsession. To say that he liked to be well organised would be a major understatement. Part of his philosophy was to eliminate unnecessary decisions of any kind. He wanted a life of simplicity, not complexity. And the older he got, the more simplicity he sought; in all elements of his life, including relationships,

His business wardrobe was organised by shirt colour: blue and white. All the shirts were Brooks Brothers with button-down collars. William decided on blue for today: M&S boxers, blue Pringle socks – sorted in pairs so the logo would be on the outside – blue Brooks Brothers slacks, and a casual Armani jacket. There were also watches, a Cartier Tank watch for formal meetings and a Roadster when things were more casual. Today it was the Roadster and he swiftly clicked off the brown strap he had worn over the weekend and swapped it with a restrained blue one to go with his shirt. And then spectacles; off with yesterday's brown, on with today's blue.

William's dressing room was a tribute to his mother whose household motto was 'A place for everything and everything in its place'. Getting dressed took about five minutes unless a tie was required; this seemed to take longer as it could be weeks before he wore one, by which time he had almost forgotten how to tie it. And he only had two ties; one for the blue shirts and one for the white. Touching the photo of Ryoko on the dressing-room wall and feeling the familiar hollow in his stomach he went downstairs for breakfast.

If he chose to use public transport rather than being driven by Stan, William would walk along the river to Hammersmith, catch the tube to Green Park and the Jubilee line to London Bridge. He often reflected that this journey was the worst part of his day until he hired Stan full time. Today he chose the tube and, as usual, he felt really good using his Freedom Pass. He knew it was ridiculous but it was a great feeling. A feeling shared by all his pals; no matter how rich they were. By the time he got to London Bridge station and was strolling down Tooley Street and turning left into More London Place, he was feeling and looking the part of a senior person in a firm that employed over 250,000 people in about 170 countries – DPK, the largest of the 'Big Three' global accountancy practices.

As a partner, William had been self-employed and had been required to resign when he reached sixty. But his reputation and contacts were some of the best in the business, so he had been asked to carry on as a contractor working whenever required. Dealing with important clients, helping with big pitches and mentoring key employees. He only tended to work four or five days a month. But at £3,000 a day, that worked out at around £150,000 – almost as much as his pension.

CHAPTER 4

The huge reception space in DPK was extraordinary. Massive modern art, an atrium rising twelve floors to a glass roof. As usual it was buzzing with people and energy. Today, one of the huge plasma screens was welcoming about a hundred graduates who were all talking at once as they milled around, waiting to be summoned to their induction meeting.

William walked up to the reception desk and handed over the paper bag of asparagus to the grey-haired lady on the left. She didn't need to open it.

"Thank you, William. Picked this morning?"

"Of course, Grace. Enjoy!" Then, as he often did, he wandered over to chat with a couple of the bright, excited people. He always enjoyed hearing what they had to say but sometimes the noise made it difficult to hear.

First up, according to his name badge, was Pradymayor Gupta. "Welcome to DPK. I'm William. Where will you be working?"

"I shall be in ITAAFS," he replied. William had long since given up keeping up with the abbreviations used in the firm and had no idea or interest in knowing what this collection of letters meant. So, as usual, he asked another question.

"What is your particular area of interest?"

"Big data and blockchain," was the reply.

"Excellent, excellent. Big data. Big data! Our footprint in this space is limited. Too limited!. Here is my card; let me know if I can be of any help to you at any time in your DPK career."

Blockchain, thought William. I still don't really understand how that works. Am I getting too old for this stuff and do I care? It only took a second for him to realise that he did.

Ten minutes later, at precisely 10 am, William walked into a huge room with about a dozen round tables, a hundred voices and a sea of colour. As he walked up to the lectern the noise settled down. He waited a while until the room was silent. And then he talked from his head and his heart. No notes. No hesitation. He really enjoyed talking to groups

"Hi, I'm William West. You can call me William or Will. For the next couple of hours we will be talking to you about what you need to do to be successful inside the firm. But first, congratulations and welcome to DPK. The reason I'm congratulating you is that in the UK we recruit about 10,000 graduates each year from about 75,000 applicants. So, you're special. Here are some facts about you. There are ninety-two of you here; fifty-four per cent female, forty-three per cent male and three per cent transgender. Ninety per cent of you have a university degree with forty per cent having achieved a first. We have eleven nationalities in the room and the capability of speaking twenty-six languages fluently. For eighty-five per cent of you this is your first career role but seventy-three per cent of you have been employed or completed internships previously. So, how do things work around here? What are the secrets of success?"

William spoke fluently and answered questions for about an hour and a half and as he was close to finishing, his phone vibrated in his pocket. He wondered who might be calling him as he carried on talking about the importance of creating a personal brand, sharing some stories of amazing success. He wasn't reciting corporate bullshit. He really believed that DPK was special. He knew DPK was special; the people, the processes, the technology and the culture. Countless times over the past twenty years he had witnessed people doing remarkable things, doing the right things; and never putting profit in front of principles. But William was about to discover that he was wrong. And he was going to pay a terrible price.

CHAPTER 5

William was planning to have lunch with a senior partner, Lionel Lamb; known by the partners as 'Two Lunches' or 'Lionel Lunch' due to his famous habit of having two lunches one or two or maybe three days a week. The first, early one Lionel would attend, was a typical DPK event with clients and colleagues. They may be offered a glass of wine or a beer. Most often not. And there would be a serious purpose. The second would be the opposite. The late lunch was the kind of lunch that meant it would be unwise – or even impossible – to return to the office. Lionel was the number one rainmaker in the UK firm and they were meeting to discuss a pitch to a major UK insurance company. But when William called his voicemail there was an anxious message from Gill Littleton.

"William, please call me as soon as possible. We have a serious problem. I can't talk about it now." He called her back and they arranged to meet at the bar in Baltic near Southwark tube station. The lunch with Lionel didn't happen and everything changed.

Gill Littleton was a high flier that William had been mentoring since she joined the firm ten years ago. She was assertive, ambitious and articulate. She was also extraordinarily technically competent, having qualified as an accountant higher and younger than anyone else in her year. On top of all of this, unlike most aspiring partners – who happily sacrificed health for money – Gillian was a keen runner and gymnast. And, unlike William, she didn't spend her off time getting drunk with pals who should and did know better.

The call from Gill was out of character. And William was worried. What could this mean? He knew she was under pressure with the work at Kutzevenia Bank. Mark, the partner responsible, had gone off sick a few days ago and she was leading the team of six people carrying out the annual audit. They would all be working really hard, maybe sixty hours a week, going through the KB accounts which DPK would need to sign off very soon. And the bank was one of the firm's recent audit wins and one of the largest clients – operating in seventy-five countries and paying fees of around $160 million a year.

The bar was empty when William arrived. He ordered a 10 ml carafe of Belvedere vodka, requested a short glass with ice and diet tonic on the side and took a table near to the restaurant. Gill arrived almost immediately and ordered a coffee as she passed the bar. They air kissed, William took a sip of his ice-cold vodka and raised an eyebrow. "OK. What's the problem?"

"It's not a problem. It's a nightmare! The team moved to the wealth management bit of the bank this morning. It's based in Mayfair. Very posh. They focus on rich

Russians living in the UK and most of the staff are Russians themselves. I got in late as I had a dentist appointment and as soon as I got there, Felicity Strange came up to me and started whispering. Apparently, there had been a bit of a mix-up. They were expecting us next week. Very strange as we'd all been given passes for the Mayfair office when we left Canary Wharf on Friday.

"Felicity told me that she got to the bank about eight this morning and all hell broke loose. A complete shitstorm. Lots of shouting in Russian. She's one of the Russian speakers but their accents were quite hard for her to understand. But a few words like 'clean up' and 'lock' came through loud and clear. Anyway, she showed her pass and explained in English why she was there and things got a bit better. But there was still an unpleasant atmosphere; people rushing around all over the place. Felicity told me that when she was looking for the kitchen or somewhere there would be coffee, she nearly stepped on a couple of passports in the corridor. She opened one, she doesn't know why. She just said she wondered why it was there. Anyway, it was blank! She opened the other one and it was blank as well! She didn't know what to do but decided to drop them back on the floor and go and find the kitchen. She's a bright girl, she knows that blank passports should not be lying around."

"Oh God," whispered William. "Are you sure Felicity wasn't mistaken?"

"Yes, I'm sure. You don't imagine things like that. You

don't make up stuff like that. Anyway, Felicity is made of stern stuff. Jolly hockey sticks sort of girl; eventing, skiing, rock climbing, kick-boxing, all that sort of thing. If she said she saw it then she saw it."

"Actually, I know who you mean," said William. "I had a coffee with her a while ago. Yep, she's the real deal."

William took a sip from his vodka and carefully topped up the glass from the carafe before speaking. "Jesus Christ; Russian bank, Russian wealth management, Russian millionaires or even billionaires and blank passports. We both know that this looks like money laundering or maybe illegal immigration or even both. And we know what we need to do; inform the client service partner. Who is it?"

"It's Mark Lawson and he's off sick."

"Can you talk to him anyway?"

"Yeah, I'll try," she replied.

"Who is the partner responsible for the global account. Do you know him?" asked William.

"Well," said Gill, "I have spoken to him on conference calls a couple of times but haven't met him. He is the big cheese, the wonder boy who joined the firm in Moscow last year and won the audit for KB. $160 million each year for five years. This is the last thing he will want to hear. And no evidence. Just the word of Felicity versus a bloody great big audit client. And bang goes my career!"

"It doesn't have to be and should not have to be. What I suggest is that you get another coffee or a stiff drink or whatever and let me think about what we might do about this," said William, trying hard to keep his voice calm and confident. Even though he walked the walk and talked the talk he always worried that one day people would realise that he wasn't as smart and competent as they thought he was. And maybe this issue was going to expose him. He had to pull himself together.

When Gill came back to the table with a glass of wine he sat back, making sure the bar was still empty and spoke slowly. "My thoughts aren't in any specific order: one; you need to speak to Felicity and explain that we are looking into this situation and she must, must, must not discuss it with anyone else, even if someone comes onto them appearing to know something about it. Two; call whoever it is at Kutzevenia Bank in Canary Wharf who knows about the confusion this morning and confirm all is now sorted. And three; forget all about it. The only person who actually saw this is Felicity so there is nothing that you and Kathy can add to this. You have done the correct thing and escalated the issue. It's now my problem. What I am going to do is talk to a couple of pals in the firm and get some advice. But I shall do this on a no-names basis. I'm not going to notify our Risk Management team at this stage even though that is a golden rule. I'll get back to you as soon as I can. In the meantime, business as usual?"

"I'll try," replied Gill.

CHAPTER 6

William called Lionel that evening and laid out the problem. Lionel was silent for a few seconds. "William, this could be a storm in a tea cup or a veritable gale. I suspect the latter. Put it another way, it's got the makings of a cluster fuck. What you need to do now – and I mean now – is contact Partnership Protection. Now. Immediately."

"Now? It's 10.30 at night!"

"Not a problem, old chap. 24/7 service. I happen to have the number. Got into a small problem myself a while ago and they sorted it out. Very discreet. Very effective. I have the number somewhere. Should have it on speed dial. Here you go."

"What exactly is Partnership Protection?"

"Well I guess you will find out in the morning. But basically it is a team which steps in when shit happens. And with over 250,000 people working in about 170 countries you can be sure that happens pretty often. Getting people out of jail for paying bribes – or for not paying bribes. Sorting out high-profile matrimonial disputes – aka chaps fucking their secretaries; right up to journalists seeking to expose elements of our operations. Or should I say, expose fake news. My sense is that they are the epitome of the iron hand inside the velvet glove."

William called the number and went straight to voicemail. He left a message explaining he had a problem that he would like to discuss and that Lionel Lamb had suggested he make contact. Within ten minutes he received a text. 'George Price. 9.30 am tomorrow. Technical Support 3, Lower Ground Floor More London office.'

CHAPTER 7

It was unlike William to be anxious but as he took the lift down to the lower ground floor he had no idea what to expect. He saw a door on his left with a long list of offices including one marked Technical Support 1,2, 3. Using his pass to open the door he found himself in a brightly lit corridor and realised that in spite of all of his years in the firm he had never been down here. There were doors to the left and doors to the right marked as 'First Aid', 'Faith Room 1', 'Contemplation Room', 'Faith Room 2', 'IT Peripherals', 'IT Support', 'Bike Store', 'Garage', 'Gym', 'Showers male', 'Showers female', 'Showers other', 'Courier', 'Post' and then, after turning some corners, 'Technical Support'.

Using his pass again, William opened the door and found himself in another corridor. 'TS 1' was on the right, 'TS 2' on the left and 'TS 3' facing him at the end. When William used his pass yet again to open the door, he was in a small room facing a man in a three-piece suit, white shirt and quiet tie sitting at a desk with nothing on it other than a laptop.

"Good morning George," said William.

"Actually, I'm not George," was the reply as the guy

looked at his laptop. "Right on time for your meeting, Mr West. Would you mind leaving your bag here and also your mobile phone? It's just standard procedure. Thanks." He opened a door to a large conference room. Sitting at the table was an overweight man with grey crew-cut hair. William walked in and shook hands. George's grip was firm, his palms dry and he met William's eyes with a friendly smile.

"William West. The living legend. Mr Consistent. Never late, never in a hurry, never stressed, wears a uniform, knows everyone that matters in the market. Good to meet you! Have a seat and let me explain what we do here. Then, if you want to, you can share the issue that seems to be troubling you. First off; I am, as you know, George Price and I have been a partner of the firm for ten years. Prior to joining I was in the military and the police. I'm in charge of the Partnership Protection Team which covers the UK and about sixty other countries. There are a couple of other teams looking after the rest of the world. We all report directly to the chairman of the firm.

"The teams deal with issues that could cause material, financial or reputational damage to the firm. And the range is considerable. Sometimes we can resolve issues with an email or telephone call. Sometimes we find ourselves having face-to-face conversations with senior government ministers and board directors. Needless to say, everything we do is highly confidential – hence this office. It may not have any windows but the door behind me has direct access to the garage which is important to some of our clients. So, do you want to tell me about the problem?"

It did not take long to tell the story and George did not say a word; just looked William straight in the face and made the occasional note.

"Have you discussed this with anyone else?" he asked.

"Only Lionel Lamb, who suggested I make contact."

"OK we know Lionel. Have you not contacted Risk Management?"

"No."

"Why not? It's mandatory."

"Well I'll do so immediately if that is your advice."

"Have you contacted the partner responsible for the audit?"

"No; he is off ill."

"What about the partner responsible for the bank itself?"

"No."

"Why not?"

"I don't have any evidence."

"Is it possible that this Felicity Strange might be making this whole thing up?" asked George. "I mean it wouldn't be the first time that someone might be looking to lift their profile by getting their name in lights. Demonstrating how they get in early, reporting things that need attention – as a result getting attention. What do we know about her? Let's have a think about that."

"No, that cannot be right," replied William. "I know

her well."

"So," said George. "Seems you have made up your mind. How well do you know this lady? Let's think about that as well."

William went straight home to Chiswick Mall feeling a little, but not much, better. George seemed very professional but there was something about him that William thought was unnerving. After dwelling on it he got it. George was there to protect the partnership, not to protect him. This had been implicit in everything he'd said. And he wondered what pressure they might put on Felicity to convince her she'd imagined the whole thing. After all, it was just a couple of passports she'd found, not a suitcase full of cash. But at least the problem now belonged to George.

CHAPTER 8

Wednesday morning and William saw Stan trimming the edges of the lawn even though they already looked perfect.

"Could you run me down to the station later, please Stan? I want to catch the 1.14. But I'll come back under my own steam so nothing for you to worry about this evening. Tell you what, though, I've got to be at the Hilton Park Lane by 9.30 tomorrow. It doesn't matter if I'm a little late; what time do you think?"

"I'll pick you up at 8.30, that should be OK," was the reply.

William first met Stan about two years ago when the man rang the bell one afternoon and tried to sell him some useless household products which he was carrying in a rucksack. He had an official-looking badge and an official-looking ribbon. William was not impressed with his story and was about to close the door on him. But he thought for a moment and instead asked him a question. "If you sold all that stuff today, how much money would you make?"

Stan replied, "I get half of what I sell so, maybe ten or fifteen quid if I'm lucky."

"Tell you what then," William said, "how about I pay

you fifteen quid to help me out with a job I'm about to do? Then you get the money but keep the products."

"What kind of job?" was the response.

"Helping me sand down these railings," was the answer.

Apart from complaining that William had bought the wrong grade of sandpaper, Stan worked quietly and industriously, sanding down about twice as many railings as William and doing an excellent job. By 5.30 the job was half-finished and William asked Stan if he could help again tomorrow and offered the minimum wage – nine pounds an hour. The answer was yes. Over the next couple of days, Stan finished off the sanding and applied two coats of paint to the railings, which now had a new lease of life. One thing led to another and Stan became William's odd-job man. He could apply himself to almost anything: driving, painting and decorating, carpentry, gardening, plumbing, brick work and cleaning even the highest windows on the house. When they talked it was usually about work and football. But over time William managed to coax out Stan's history – bit by bit. It wasn't a pretty story.

Stan was the youngest of four brothers brought up in Camberwell. "When Camberwell was real like; not like now. We all got into a little trouble; thieving like, two of my brothers 'went away' for a while. And I could see it coming down to me. So, I applied to join the army. Big mistake, at first. Fucking hard. But I learned a bit about a lot and was starting to enjoy it. Then I went to Afghanistan. And I knew what hard really was. One tour and I was out of there. Back in the world most of us didn't know what the fuck to do. Thought about going back to the sandpit and the ragheads. But then I got a job as a driver for a casino. Gold mine. Great tips from the winners, most of the time sitting around and reading. Got to know London in the end but thank Christ for GPS.

"A new manager rocked up and replaced me with his boyfriend. No money, no job; later on, nowhere to live. So I ended up in my eldest brother's fuck-off place in Chelsea. Magic. Girls, booze, blow, coke, pills, whatever. I knew he wasn't kosher but what the fuck; it was a great billet. All I had to do was drive him around, make some deliveries and make sure all his people were on the straight and narrow; you know, like not going self-employed or falling in love with the product or becoming careless. Actually, most of them were up to something naughty; I was only firm where necessary. Trouble was, one of the old hands did get careless and got charged. The fool grassed me up to get a reduced sentence. So there I was; done for a kilo of coke with intention to supply. First offence. Two years. Out in one. As for the fool? Haven't seen him since. Nor my brother. I'm out of all that now. But how do you get a job when you have been away? That's why I was trying to flog that stuff when I rang your bell."

Like Tina his housekeeper, William now thought of Stan as part of the team. He lived rent-free in a studio in the basement of one of William's two houses that he rented out near Turnham Green tube. Large houses by any standard; nine flats in total. All very smart. Stan was the caretaker, along with all his other responsibilities. He was now employed by William at £15 per hour and even had a pension. Freddie told William frequently that he was wasting his money and that Stan was not to be trusted but William disagreed. "No more Addison Lee bills; they were costing me God knows how much each month. No more Pimlico Plumbers coming here or going to the flats at ninety pounds an hour. No tenants phoning me in the middle of the night. And no other tradesmen ripping me off and putting muddy footprints on the carpets!"

When William walked into the kitchen, Tina was putting some shopping away. Pointing to the kitchen table she said, "Stan brought this asparagus from the allotment this morning and I'm sure you will find something sensible to do with it. I got everything on your list as I came in today but the cost of this stuff just keeps going up. I just don't know how people manage with children and all."

"Well", said William, "if the going gets so tough that we can't afford to eat, I suppose I'll have to take in lodgers. It's not as if there isn't plenty of room here!"

CHAPTER 9

William's house was built in the 18th century, enlarged in the 19th century, updated in the 20th century and refurbished by William just five years ago. It was a ridiculous house for one person. Starting from below ground level, there was a cellar which had been tanked in order to keep it completely dry, even when the Thames water table rose at the highest of the high spring tides. And there were two rooms down there. One containing the main store of William's wine. The other, all the junk that was in the attic when it was refurbished. William hadn't looked at it since.

Above the cellar was the lower ground floor. Two windows below street level letting in a lot of light. This was Tina's domain. And sometimes Stan's. There were four rooms. The largest contained the utilities: washing machine, dryer, a sink, two large fridges; one devoted entirely to drinks. Appliances, brushes, brooms and loads of cupboards including William's gun cabinet. There was also a cupboard full of tins with a safe built into the wall behind it. William had no secrets but he cared about privacy. Especially when it came to his money and his drugs. Then there were two connected rooms: a small bedroom and bathroom. William had no idea why this facility was created but now and then it was used by Stan. The final room had no daylight at all, had a combination lock and was used to store the paintings and other art that was not currently displayed in the house. On the ground floor, there was a huge kitchen, and a dining room which opened up onto the garden, a cloakroom and another room at the front of the house which William sometimes used as a reading room.

At the back of the garden was what looked like a New England Shaker-style cottage with clapboard painted in a muted green. The ground floor was given over to a shower room on one side and William's garage on the other. Upstairs was his office with large windows facing the garden and house. He had a glass desk with a twenty-seven-inch iMac and a red leather Charles Eames lobby chair. Also a small meeting table with four chairs. In the corner was a wet bar and fridge. There was no clutter in the room; nothing on the table, nothing on the desk apart from a keypad and mouse.

The first floor of William's house was really special. A wonderful living room at the front with two floor-to-ceiling windows looking over the river. A little annex where drinks could be prepared, and a sixty-five-inch Samsung Frame TV flat against the wall and currently showing a John Piper print. There many other wonderful limited-edition prints, paintings, rugs and furniture combined with a huge window looking over the garden at the back.

On the second floor was William's bedroom with another two windows looking over the river. His dressing room was bigger than most peoples' living rooms. And it led into a wet room. Black and white tiles. White walls, with black waterproof-framed black-and-white photos of jazz legends – Miles Davis, John Coltrane, Charlie Parker, Ella Fitzgerald and Louis Armstrong. Black-and-white tiles on the floor. A massive shower with jets from the sides and a very long bath. Thick white towels and an aroma of Aqua Di Parma Colonia cologne, shower gel and body lotion.

The next floor contained two bedrooms and two en-suite bathrooms and the attic that was now a guest suite with a bedroom, bathroom and living room. Keeping all of this clean and tidy plus washing and ironing kept Tina working from ten in the morning until five in the afternoon four days a week; sometimes even longer.

CHAPTER 10

Stan was waiting outside the house in the black Mercedes S Class at 1 pm. The 1.14 pm train to Waterloo was dead on time and pretty empty so William was able to read his Kindle without any distractions. But his mind kept going back to those passports. There was no question about it. Someone in the bank must be up to some sort of identity fraud. And it was very unlikely that it was going to be all down to one individual. The more he thought about it, the more worried he became. As auditors, DPK had to notify the authorities of any suspicions; not doing so was a criminal offence. Even delaying for a couple of days could mean you ended up with a prison sentence. He shuddered; what a way to end his career

The tube from Waterloo to Bank arrived at the platform the same time as William. And less than ten minutes later he was getting into the lift that took him to Coq D'Argent on the roof of the building. Emerging from the lift, there in the garden, in the shade of a large umbrella, sat Lionel with a glass in his hand and a bottle in an ice bucket on the table.

"Thank God you are here, William. I have been gasping for a drink. I've had a terrible morning and a dry lunch. Dry conversation, dry wit and bugger all but water to drink."

After some chat about DPK gossip, William looked around to see if anyone was within earshot then said, "I met the guy in Partnership Protection on Tuesday. Haven't heard from him since. He seemed pretty laid back about the whole thing. But I'm not. We all know what the rules are and we are all exposed. Me, you, Gill and Felicity, the girl who picked up the passports. We all know we should have reported this. What should we do?"

"Stay calm for a few more days would be my advice, old chap," replied Lionel. "These people know what they are doing. They are not about to hang anyone out to dry. But just to be on the safe side, I'll have a chat with a couple of pals over a no-names no-facts lunch.

"By the way William, changing the subject, how is your pal Freddie? His name cropped up the other day. I gather he is on gardening leave."

"Yes. Something to do with offering some coke to a client."

"Jesus Christ," replied Lionel. "If he wasn't such a rainmaker he would be out on his ear."

"Agreed. He just rocked up in the desk facing me a couple of years ago. And you know how it is. Unless the person facing you is a complete bore, the chances are they become your new best friend. It happens almost every time we have some sort of desk reorganisation. You know, 'Good morning. How was your weekend?' soon turns into

'How about a drink' and 'What is the problem?' 'How was the meeting?' 'How come that twat is still a partner?'.

"Anyway, Freddie wan't a complete stranger. Team drinks, water cooler chat, you know how it is. But we specialise in different markets so never really talked that much. And he was always talking to other people, it's the kind of bloke he is. He's larger than life. When he's in the room you know he's in the room. It's not that he's huge – although I guess he's about 6'3" and quite fit – it's just something about him. I mean, who would expect to meet an accountant with charisma – incredible charisma. Like a rock star, for Christ's sake! No question, he is a good-looking bloke with a sort of battered-about face, an innocent expression and dishevelled but expensive clothes. But it's not that. He has a kind of attitude – he's always laughing and joking. Never anything other than foot to the floor, full on.

"But I have got to know him quite well as he lives near me in Chiswick and we have quite regular drinks and dinners. He's single as well as me. Interestingly, I bumped into one of his ex-colleagues a while ago. And I discovered that Freddie has a very interesting background. He joined the Royal Navy after a pretty mediocre degree at St Johns and after a while he passed through qualifying for the Special Boat Service with a very good reputation. Needless to say, there was no information about what happened over the next few years; they are just like the SAS in that space. Seems he left on good terms and joined

Control Risks; again, he never talked much about what he did there. But his next job involved broking kidnap and ransom insurance in the Lloyds market, so no prizes for guessing that it would have involved negotiating hostages and all that goes with that. Then he arrived at DPK on partner track working in the London market.

"First day we are together, this screeching noise starts from his empty desk. It's the ringtone of his phone. 'Screech, screech, screech!' I recognise it but can't place it. Then I get it. The shower scene in Psycho: 'Screech, screech and screech!' You know what I mean – violins screeching as Janet Leigh is stabbed by Anthony Perkins – blood on the shower curtain and around her feet. The sound stops when Freddie strolls over and picks up the phone and wanders off. 'Sorry. Wife number three,' he says when he gets back. Freddie's constitution is extraordinary. And so is his sex drive. Awesome. He behaves like a school boy who has just discovered sex. If he looked behind – which he doesn't – he'd see a pile of train wrecks. Including the ex-wives.

"I got to know him much better when we spent an evening together. We were in my booth at Balthazar and on our second bottle. Yes, Lionel I would like a top up. Thank you. I asked him about wife number one. He goes, 'We had two girls and as they grew up we sort of grew apart. I wasn't completely faithful, to be honest. Actually, not at all faithful. She is still well pissed off and lurking around looking for more money. Her ringtone is the theme from

Jaws. As for wife number two, she was after my money and I didn't have any left after the divorce. Bitch. Her ringtone is Kanye West – 'I ain't saying she's a gold digger but she ain't fucking no poor ni… person of colour!'

"Wife number three. And Lionel, you will not believe this. You couldn't make this up. Now it's late. And we are both pretty hammered. But I remember the words as if it was yesterday. He goes, 'She was twenty-eight, I was fifty-five. Lasted six weeks. Just as my daughters were getting used to the idea of a stepmother that was younger than they were, she walked out on me.' I asked. 'Was it the age difference?' He said, 'No. I mean that could have been a factor. But the real problem was she found out I was shagging her mother.' He said this as if having an affair with your mother-in-law was kind of no big deal. Like catching a bus or something! I was almost speechless. 'Her mother? You were having an affair with her mother! When? Why?' He sat back and took a thoughtful sip of wine. 'Not long after the honeymoon. She was really up for it, mate.'

"So that's Freddie and the ex-wives. They cost him serious money. But he doesn't just collect expensive ex-wives. He collects expensive cars – six at present – expensive shotguns (the most recent Beretta came in at ten grand), expensive watches and cameras – 'no idea how many old chap'. But all in all, he's a good bloke and I hope it works out for him in the firm."

William arrived home from lunch at about five, lay

down on the huge sofa in the living room, put his 'Old Quiet Songs' playlist on the server and fell fast asleep. When he woke up he asked himself, "What would Ryoko suggest?" When she was alive she always came up with the right idea and a decision formed in his head. He called the Partnership Protection number and left a message saying he would like to see George as soon as possible. Within five minutes he received a text: 'Same time, same place tomorrow.'

CHAPTER 11

At 9 am William was back in the basement and shaking hands with George. "William," he said. "We have been doing a little research and discussing this issue at the highest level. The decision is that we will contact HMRC. But before we do so we need to sit down with this Felicity Strange just to verify that she is solid. Is that satisfactory from your perspective?"

"Yes," replied William. "As you know, she is in Gill Littleton's team and I'll get Gill to fix it up. Best to ask her to come along as well, as the grad might find it a bit intimidating."

Gill, William and Felicity met George at 11 am the next day. Felicity looked a little nervous but still imposing in a dark grey skirt and jacket with a white blouse. As George got up to shake hands her five feet and ten inches plus heels matched his height. "So, Felicity, sounds like you have had a bit of an adventure. Good of you to come and discuss it. Anyway, before we get to that, why don't you tell me a bit about yourself."

"Of course," she said. "I am twenty-four years old and single and I was born in Leatherhead. My father was in the army and then became a property developer. My mother was an eye surgeon."

"When you say 'was' does that mean they are both retired, Felicity?"

"I'm afraid not. My dad died of a heart attack many years ago and my mother died last October."

"Brothers or sisters?"

"No, I'm an only child."

"So," said George, "I've had a look at your file and can see you are an exceptional person. A first at Magdalen and lots of sporting achievements at the same time. Quite an unusual combination. Do you still get the time to stay fit?"

"Yes, I do. I'm lucky that I have never needed more than five or six hours sleep so I can be in the gym or running most mornings."

"Clearly we were fortunate to hire you," said George. "Tell me about your time at DPK."

"I've been here about eighteen months, I'm working hard to qualify quickly. I'm attached to the Financial Services audit team and enjoying most of the work. I've got a good network of colleagues and have made some firm friends."

"All good," said George. "Anything you want to say, Gill? If not, let's cut to the chase."

Gill shook her head.

George continued. "OK Felicity. I know you have been through this already but take me through Monday morning from start to finish. Please don't miss out any details, no matter how unimportant they might seem to you. I need to understand exactly what happened. And you need to understand that if we take this forward you will have to go through this many more times; perhaps in front of a judge and jury."

Felicity was now completely composed. Gill had explained to her that this was bound to happen, she had a very clear recollection and had been thinking about how she would present the facts of the matter. But William didn't like the way this interrogation was going. He felt that George was on the verge of bullying Felicity but decided to let things run for the time being.

Felicity cleared her throat, looked George in the eye and spoke.

"I understand. Here it is: I woke up at 5.15 am on Monday morning. I live in a mews house near to Belgrave Square. It used to belong to my parents but they gave it to me some time ago to avoid inheritance tax. It was a lovely day. I walked up to Hyde Park and met up with my personal trainer. We worked out for an hour and I was back home about 6:45. I showered, had breakfast and walked to Mount Street which is where the team was tasked to start the wealth management business audit. I got there at 8.03. I looked at my watch as I swiped the security pad.

"There was a staircase in front of me, pictures on the walls, expensive carpet. It's a very posh place. I walked up to find someone who could tell me where we were to set up. On the landing at the top there were two doors; one marked reception. The door was closed and locked but my pass opened it. There was no one around but then a guy appeared who looked at me as if he had seen a ghost. He was about thirty, quite good looking, smart suit. Just what you'd imagine a private banker would look like. He asked me something in Russian but I didn't understand it. It was quick. Then he asked in English, 'Who are you, who let you in? What are you doing here?' I showed him the pass and said 'DPK. To do the audit.' He snapped, 'Stay there' and rushed off.

"I could hear some shouting in Russian. This time I could understand some of it. They were swearing a bit and I heard a couple of words: 'Clean up', 'Lock up'."

George interrupted. "Are you sure those were the words you heard, Felicity?"

"Yes I am. My Russian is pretty good. I spent half my gap year there and had no problems. In fact, I think it is better than my French, Spanish and Mandarin. Anyway, a different chap came to talk to me and explained that they were expecting us the following Monday and he asked me to wait while they sorted out some space for us. He asked me how many were coming and I told him there would be five of us and the work should not take longer than a couple of weeks. I was looking at my phone when the guy came back. It was 8.35. He took me to an office which was fine. I set up my PC and went looking for the loo and somewhere where there might be coffee."

"Hold on, Felicity. Do you always wander around client premises with impunity?" asked George.

"Yes, we do," was the reply. "We are auditors. Shall I continue?" George nodded.

"I couldn't find coffee or the loo so I went out the door and across the landing and through the opposite door which also opened with my pass. I turned right down a corridor and as I turned right again I saw two EU passports on the floor. I thought someone might have dropped them. I picked them up and opened one. It was completely blank. I opened the other one and it was the same. I didn't know what to do. I dropped them as if they were red hot and scuttled back to the team space. When Kathy arrived, I told her what had happened. She asked me where the passports were and then went off to find them. When she came back she said that they weren't where I had said they were. That afternoon, Gill took me for a coffee and I told her what had happened. She said I should not discuss it with anyone and I told her that I had mentioned it to Kathy."

"Kathy? Who is Kathy?" asked George.

"Kathy Stobart. She's Felicity's team leader," replied Gill. "I have spoken to her and she understands that it is vital that these events are highly confidential."

George made a note. William frowned; this was the first time he had heard this.

"Felicity, that is very helpful. I know you know that this is a tricky situation but you can rest assured we will deal with it professionally and swiftly," said George. "In the meantime, you have done all the right things and all

I can ask is that you continue to ensure that you don't share your experience with even your closest friends. That includes any flatmate, boyfriend and your parents."

"Thank you, George," said Felicity, coolly. "As I told you, my parents are dead and I don't have a boyfriend or a flatmate."

The three of them left the building and walked along the river. "What do you think of George?" asked William.

"Very professional," responded Gill.

"I'm not so sure," suggested Felicity. "There was something about him that I didn't like. Something that I didn't quite trust. I mean, he didn't say anything about what the next steps would be."

"That's a good point. I need to have another chat with him in a couple of days," said William. "And, you know I also have my reservations. Anyway, Felicity why don't you go home now and come back in to work on Monday. I think you could do with some time off. See you later. And Gill, you and I need to have a chat. Let's get lunch somewhere."

CHAPTER 12

William and Gill walked down Shad Thames and managed to get a table outside in the sunshine at the Chop House.

"Why didn't you tell me about Kathy?" asked William.

"I'm sorry," replied Gill. "I meant to tell you but there has been so much on my mind. Anyway, Kathy is very experienced and discreet. I can guarantee that. By the way, how come you know Felicity?"

William smiled. "It must have been four or five years ago when she came in as an intern. As she mentioned, her father died some time ago and her godfather took his responsibilities very seriously. He was a partner in the mergers and acquisitions sector who I knew quite well and he asked me if she could come into my team for a couple of months.

"It has to be said that I didn't know her very well or rate her too highly, especially because she seemed to take a lot for granted and to lack energy, enthusiasm and commitment. So, on the last day of her placing I sat down with her and gave her some feedback. Basically, I told her she would need to lift her game if she got a chance to come back after her degree. And I asked her what she had planned in the meantime. She told me she wanted to get a first, that she wanted to row for the college, that she wanted to travel for a year and learn Russian and Mandarin and do some other things that I can't remember. I gave her a piece of paper and got her to write down her objectives.

"Anyway, eventually Felicity did join the firm and called me about a year ago and asked if we could have a coffee, which we did. And she handed me back that piece of paper. The paper had travelled the world, was creased almost beyond recognition but I could see a tick against each objective. Class act! She has a great future ahead of her, and I hope this passport thing doesn't get in the way. Talking of that, have you been in touch with Mark Lawson?"

"No, I haven't," replied Gill. "No response to my voicemail, no response to my emails and no response to my text. I decided not to mention the problem; if he is really ill, I don't want to worry him with it. I will speak to HR on Monday if he hasn't responded. It's so unlike him. Anyway, I have to get back over to Mount Street and check on the troops before close of business. Some of the poor buggers will be working over the weekend and I have to go in there on Sunday to update the CEO of the wealth management business. Don't ask me to pronounce his name!"

CHAPTER 13

The rain was hammering on the roof of the black cab, the windows were misting over and the wipers were unable to cope with the deluge. The thunderstorm had taken the pedestrians along Oxford Street by surprise and they were huddling in every doorway or rushing into the nearest shop to escape the pouring rain. Peter Carby was oblivious as he struggled with his thoughts. Had he made the right decision? Is it too late? He could tell the driver to take him back to Hampstead, he could collect what he needed and head for Heathrow. No one knew about his flat in Nice, he had some money and he doubted anyone was going to invest a lot of time to find him. But if they did? He didn't want to think about it. He had only met Jorge once; on that occasion he was invited to dinner, during which he had to watch a man killing someone's wife. She screamed for three hours before she died.

Should he keep going and tell Frances what had happened? His stomach was churning, his hands were sweating and shaking. That conversation could also put his life at risk; it probably depends on what mood Jorge is in when he hears the news. He just didn't know what to do.

"What number Guv?" Peter could hardly hear the

cab driver over the drumming rain. For some reason, the words of an old pop song came into his mind: Should I stay or should I go?

He closed his eyes and made a decision. "Number 55 on the left up there, please."

His coat was soaked, his hair flattened and his glasses smudged in the minute or so it took him to get from the cab to the small, modern office block. There was no one at the reception desk. He walked straight to the lift, touched his card to the reader and pressed floor 11. His legs felt weak, he tried to dry his sweaty hands on his trousers. He wiped his glasses. It wasn't too late to stop the lift. Then it was too late.

"Passports? Fucking passports? Fucking blank passports? Blank fucking blank passports lying around on the fucking floor! Just waiting for some fucking bean counter to pick them up. Jesus fucking Christ, Peter. How could this happen? Tell me again!"

"Well, as I said, there was a mix up about when the auditors…"

Frances stood up and looked down at Peter.

"I suppose that's alright then. Maybe we could have that engraved on our tombstones! 'There was a mix up about the auditors.' Not that we are likely to have tombstones. Thanks for this fuck-up the best we can hope for is a quick death and our bodies in one piece before we die. Is there anything you can tell me that might help me avoid that? Do we have any leverage at DPK?"

"We do have some leverage at DPK and we do have some information. We have the name and address of the woman that arrived first and discovered the passports. We also know that DPK have not yet notified the police or HMRC. They haven't even told their risk management people. We also know that the partner responsible for the audit is on sick leave."

"What about our own people?"

"We have two guys in the loop at Mount Street. Andrea and Steve. They are solid. I am ninety-nine per cent they will stay solid. But it might make sense to transfer them out of there in case the police or HMRC start asking questions. The key point is that there is no evidence. Maybe Jorge will be OK with that."

Frances frowned. "Peter. Let's get real here. Jorge is not a rational human being. He is completely unpredictable. I have no idea where he is in the world. He could be finishing breakfast or about to start dinner. He could be negotiating with our clients, raping a ten-year-old boy in front of his mother or finishing a long lunch in the trendy restaurant next door. In any event, I need to call him immediately. If he hears about this fuck-up before he hears from us we shall be history. So fuck off and I will call you when I have some news."

Peter spent the afternoon wandering around the West End, worrying and drinking. He knew that when Frances called him there was no guarantee that she would be telling him the truth about her call with Jorge. All he could do was to hope for the best. And the best was what he got.

"Good news, Peter. Jorge was in a good mood. I chose not to ask why. Needless to say, he was pretty pissed off about the passports. But it seems he doesn't wish to punish either of us if we can ensure that the matter is closed off quickly. His instructions are that the woman who found the passports disappears as soon as possible and that the two guys in Mount Street are transferred and taken care of. Can I assume you can deal with these issues?"

"Of course."

Frances put her elbows on the desk and looked Peter in the face. "Let me be clear. Let me be completely fucking clear. This issue needs to be dealt with immediately. No loose ends. Now piss off and don't get back to me until everything is sorted."

CHAPTER 14

Peter was in the Mount Street office first thing the next day and asked Andrea and Steve to join him in a meeting room. Both of them looked very nervous when they arrived. He tried to reassure them.

"Guys, as you know we have a problem with a couple of passports. It seems pretty much inevitable that at some stage DPK will inform HMRC and that HMRC and/or the police will come here and start asking questions. As a result, we think we need to transfer you somewhere out of reach until the problem goes away."

"How come the problem will go away?" asked Andrea, looking worried.

"It's a question of evidence. There isn't any. Just one person's recollection. Trust me on this. But we need to move quickly. I have arranged a secondment for you both to our Northern Cyprus office where you will be safe from UK jurisdiction and I am making arrangements for you to move tomorrow."

"Tomorrow?" asked Steve. "What is the urgency?"

Peter frowned. "Guys, you know what we have been doing here. You know why you have been receiving shedloads of cash as well as your salaries. If the police turn up tomorrow and start looking at your lifestyles you will be in deep trouble. Anyway, you are both in the company apartments in Finchley; it's not as if it's complicated. The plan is that we collect you and your things tomorrow morning, take you down to Poole harbour, nip across to Cherbourg in a privately owned Sunseeker and then a train to Paris and a flight to Cyprus. No chance of anyone knowing where you have gone. And you can come back when things have settled down."

Steve seemed to relax a bit but Andrea was very concerned. Leaving in twenty-four hours, avoiding passport control. Paris? Cyprus? She wished she had never got involved. What if she couldn't get back to the UK? Could she go to prison? After all, no one had been hurt. Maybe she should go to the police?

Peter seemed to read her mind.

"Don't worry, Andrea. In six months maximum you will be back here safe and sound. Trust me; it's a better deal than a prison sentence and a criminal record. And let me explain something. Our ultimate boss is a ruthless man with even more ruthless clients. If you go to the police and end up in prison, he will be willing and able to have someone in there take your life."

Andrea couldn't believe what she was hearing. Her head was buzzing, she wanted to speak but couldn't. She swallowed, shook her head and started crying.

CHAPTER 15

Andrea and Steve talked long into the night. Both of them had misgivings but going to the police seemed a step too far. After all, Cyprus wasn't the end of the world. They decided to tell friends and family that that were being seconded to the Paris office for a few months rather than mentioning Cyprus, and started packing. Neither of them had much stuff.

An SUV arrived at 10 am and they arrived at Poole harbour in the afternoon. Peter was waiting for them and helped them with their luggage. The Sunseeker took their breath away; it looked like it was about seventy-feet long and when they got aboard it was incredibly luxurious. Plush white leather seats, expensive looking floors and a bar.

Steve sat down. "Wow, this is more like it. I could get used to this."

"How about a glass of champagne?" asked Peter.

"Yes please!" chorused Steve and Andrea. And after another glass they were both finally feeling relaxed. They looked at each other and smiled.

The first couple of hours went very smoothly. There was a captain and three crew members on the deck. Peter was sitting back with a glass of champagne and looking completely relaxed. Not a cloud in the sky, not another boat in sight, then the Sunseeker slowed down.

Andrea was the first to react. Was there a problem with the engine? She didn't think so; the captain didn't look troubled, although she could sense some sort of tension around the boat. It seemed he was just waiting for something. Steve was also looking around but couldn't see anything on the horizon. Then he noticed that Peter was holding a gun.

"Guys, I'm sorry about this. I know it's a cliché but I am just following orders."

Steve knew it. He knew that he had thought about this and chucked it to the back of his mind. He hadn't been able to confront it. And now it was too late. He looked at Andrea; she was already on her knees and crying. She looked up at Peter and begged.

"I promise you, we promise you! We won't ever tell anyone about it. Promise you. Promise you!"

The Sunseeker was gently rocking. There was silence. Peter just shook his head. Steve dived at him, grabbing him around the waist, reaching for the gun. Peter just stepped back and smashed the gun on the back of Steve's head. Andrea piled in desperately and Peter's fist hit her in the throat and she fell down on top of Steve.

"Do the bloke first," said Peter as the two deckhands walked in. "I'll keep an eye on this one. She scratched my fucking face."

Five minutes later the deckhands returned. Andrea gasped. "Where is Steve? What have you done to him? Where is he? What are you doing to him?"

Neither of the men replied. They simply picked her up from the floor and dragged her outside onto the deck. She looked around. Steve was nowhere to be seen. But just a few feet away she saw a pile of black chains with an anchor attached. She knew immediately what had happened to Steve and what was going to happen to her. She fell on her knees; the sun was shining, no clouds in the sky. It wasn't fair. She hadn't done anything wrong.

The men were trying to wrap the chains around her body. She twisted and turned. Biting them, scratching them; trying to poke her fingers in their eyes. They started breathing heavily and grunting but finally they got it done. Her arms were trapped to her sides. She wailed as they picked her up, she was still wailing and crying as they took her to the side of the boat and she didn't stop until her body went into the water.

CHAPTER 16

Peter's journey to Wells Street was very different to his last one. The sun was shining, the traffic was flowing, his mind was free from worry and even the cab driver's chat wasn't annoying him. As usual there was no one sitting at the reception desk of number 55; as usual he left the lift on the 11th floor. What was unusual was that Frances smiled at him when he arrived.

"So. Tell me all about it, Peter. Your call was reassuring but I would like the details. Tell me about the boat trip."

"It went smoothly although they both put up a bit of resistance at the end. Can't really blame them when they worked out what was going to happen."

Frances licked her lips. "Tell me more."

"We were about ninety minutes out of Poole. The depth gauge showed over a hundred metres. We took the bloke out on to the deck, wrapped an anchor chain around his waist and threw him over the rail. He was still stunned from a bang on the back of his head so there was very little drama."

"What about the girl?"

"That was different. When she saw the bloke was gone and the other anchor chain lying on the deck she immediately lost it. Shouting, praying, screaming and wailing. Lashing out, kicking and biting. The guys took almost ten minutes to get the chain on and she was still kicking and wailing when she went into the water."

"Did you get the videos? Jorge will want to see them. And so will I."

"Sure. They are on this data stick. Enjoy!"

"Don't push your luck, Peter. What about their stuff? And what about the woman who spotted the passports?"

"Their stuff went overboard with plenty of ballast. As for the woman," Peter looked at his watch, "she is dead and buried."

"Are you sure?"

"Yes. I am very sure."

Chapter 17

The first thing Felicity felt when she woke up was a wetness down below, spread out underneath her, along her legs and up her back. It was cold and it smelt of urine. As things became clearer, she remembered coming back home after her run and then the courier ringing her bell. She remembered him saying he had a package from DPK and him holding it up so she could see the logo on the envelope through the little window in her door. She had a vague recollection of the courier pushing her backwards when she opened the door and then noticing another man behind him. Then she felt a sharp pain in her arm, then nothing until now. She was lying on the floor of the backseat of a car. She wasn't tied up or gagged. She could hear two voices, one of them with poor English, and talking about football. Maybe a club called Paris Saint Germaine? It was black outside. She couldn't see any street lights, or headlights. But no, there were some lights, sweeping towards and past, and gone with the sound of the engine, evaporating in time along with her hope.

She could smell urine, cigarette smoke, petrol and vomit. There was a vile, acidic taste in her mouth that told her she'd been sick. She felt petrified. Her heart sank. This had to be connected to those passports. She decided to stay still and pretend to still be unconscious. She heard, "two-hundred-million euros. No chance." Her heart sank deeper. It was beating faster than any physical effort she had ever experienced. She felt panic. Claustrophobia. What was this about? It couldn't be about a couple of passports, could it? Then they mentioned another name: Neymar. Who was he? Then she heard a name she recognised, FC Lokomotiv Moscow. Was all this connected to football? False passports and football? She felt dizzy, as if she was drugged. Whatever she had been drugged with was still in her system and she surrendered to it thankfully.

Felicity had no idea what time had passed when her eyes opened again. Nothing had changed. The noise from the car, the smell and the question.

"Why can't I fuck her?" said one man.

"I've told you; we are professionals. At least I am," said a man with a gruff Russian accent. "This is about doing a job. It's not about fucking around. So, tell me exactly what you are going to do when we get there. Repeat exactly what I have told you." The reply sounded sullen, even bored. TV crook dialect with a London accent.

"OK mate. You will stop the car. I get out and take all the plastic sheeting from the boot and the three petrol cans. I then lay the plastic on the ground where you show me and start digging the hole. I make sure that all the earth I dig out goes onto the sheets. The hole should be deeper than my waist and about six feet long."

Felicity couldn't believe what she was hearing. They were going to kill her and bury her. She was helpless and petrified.

The man with the London accent continued.

"When the hole is finished she will kneel down and I will hit her head with the spade until she is out of it. Then we put her in the hole, pour over the petrol and when she is burnt up we fill up the hole and then bury the plastic in a different place. OK?"

"OK. Not all OK!" was the gruff response. "You need to slide the shovel underneath the topsoil and put it to one side so that it can be put back afterwards. Don't you listen to anything I say?"

"If I can't fuck her and I'm doing all the digging, then why aren't I getting as much money as you?" asked the other man.

"Let me explain: I am the one with the contract, I'm the guy that knows the client. I'm the guy that knows where to put the body where it won't be found. I'm the guy who hired the car. And I am the professional. I am the guy that makes people vanish. Forever. You are the hired hand. The client doesn't even know you exist. You will get four grand just to do some gardening. That's how it plays. Now shut up."

"So, when do we get the money?"

"I have it here in my jacket pocket and I'll give you your share when you've done your job. Now just shut the fuck up; we are nearly there."

Felicity heard all this and her panic just rose and rose. Grave, shovel, petrol. Jesus Christ. Her life was going to be over before it had started and no one would know what happened to her. Could there be a way out of this? She wasn't tied up: maybe she could fight her way out. Forget that; this wasn't a movie. What about her phone? Slowly, gently she moved her hand towards her pocket.

"I think she's woken up," came a voice from the front; the voice with the London accent.

"Give her another shot."

Felicity gasped. Was this it? More drugs? Maybe that would be the end. Was she going to die in the car, soaked with vomit and urine?

"Oh shit; I think I dropped the syringe in the house or in the street," was the reply.

The man with the Russian accent shouted, "You fucking idiot…"

"Oh no, here it is in the footwell. But it's empty."

"Alright. We are nearly there and she's not going to be a problem."

CHAPTER 18

Lying there, listening, quaking, shaking, shivering, holding back tears of despair, Felicity held on to this conversation as a tiny piece of light, like a pinhole in a dark sheet. She thought about what might happen to give her the slightest chance of escape. And she made a decision. If she was going down, she was going down fighting. No matter how big these men were, no matter how ruthless and strong, she was going to take them on.

The car stopped, the passenger door opened and one of the men got out. She heard a gate or some sort of barrier being opened. The car moved forward and stopped again and she heard whatever it was close. The man got back in and the car moved forward slowly. It rattled and rumbled along what felt like a rough track. Time passed… The track seemed to become even more rocky and Felicity noticed that daylight was breaking and she could make out a bit more about her situation.

She couldn't stop the shaking. Tears came to her eyes, there was a coldness flowing through her body. How could her life end this way? How unfair! Would anyone know what happened to her? Who would care? Then, for no apparent reason she thought of Rachel – her kick-boxing coach and her question every time they met. "Do you want to be a never been or a heroine?" "Heroine!" Better to die fighting than sniveling, even though she couldn't stop sniveling.

The car stopped. The men got out, locked the doors and she heard the boot open and close. Time passed. She heard nothing, but couldn't stop trembling and imagining what might be happening, what was going to happen. They were going to dig her grave, smash her head until she died and burn her body. No one would find her; no one would know what happened to her. Her life was over. The door opened and hands pulled her over the folded down front seat, lifting her out, banging her head on the roof and dropping her on the ground. Some birds were singing. She wished she knew what kind of birds they were. She was never going to know. She looked again at the sunlight filtering through the trees. Dappled shade. Why not just go with the flow? No one's going to miss me.

The taller man, the guy that seemed to be the boss, looked at her. "It's over for you. We want to make it quick." They walked her over to the edge of the clearing where she could see a pile of earth and petrol cans beside a hole. "Take me, fuck me; do what you want. Please don't kill me. I don't want to die! Please!" She knelt down in front the taller man, as if in prayer, pleading. "Please, please. I can give you money. I'm rich. I could give you a hundred-thousand pounds." And then she leapt, pushing the guy backwards into the hole. And she ran. Out of the clearing into the wood. She ran virtually blind with the low sun flickering through the trees. And then she was out of the trees and into a ploughed field, racing across the furrows never looking back. Feeling the earth getting heavy on the running shoes she was still wearing, instinctively using her arms to propel herself forward, raising her knees high, lowering her shoulders, heading for the gate in the far corner as if it was the finishing line in an ironman event. Her pace was increasing, her breathing was regular on the last straight. She felt freedom. What to do? Where to go?

She was still running, bleeding, panting and petrified. Just keep running seemed the answer. But she could hear thumping steps behind her. And she could see one of the men over to the right, on course to cut her off from the gate, so she veered left towards some woods. Maybe she would find somewhere to hide? Maybe she could find a road or some people? Maybe just outrun these guys? Why not? She made it to the woods and a small path. She could hear the men not far behind, crashing through the bushes but not gaining on her. She was breathing very hard now, legs still feeling strong but heart pounding like she had never experienced before. But the noises from behind seemed to be quieter. She was pressing ahead. She was winning. And then she tripped.

Chapter 19

Hands were on her almost immediately. She was picked up, punched in the face, punched in the kidneys, punched in the chest and the back. Dragged by her hair and then lifted and carried back through the woods. The dawn chorus sounded around her as if nothing had happened. In broken English, a gruff voice said, "This could have been painless for you. Now it will hurt."

She was back by the hole. Just dumped on the ground like she was already a dead body. Her running gear was ripped, her whole body ached, her head was whirling. She had no sense, no plan. But she could hear the men arguing. Then a loud noise, a clang, a crunch and a body falling. A voice. "You told me I am worth less than you. Worthless? So here you are, in the hole with your head smashed. I get to fuck the girl. You get to be burned alongside her. I get all the money. No one knows I was involved."

Felicity stayed still, pretending to be out of it. Footsteps approached. She felt a kick in the stomach. She grunted. "Stand up and take off your clothes." She stayed still. "If you don't do as I say I will drop you in that hole, pour petrol over you and burn you alive." There was the sound of a cap being unscrewed and then the smell of petrol.

In the clearing, at dawn on a perfect English day. Bird song and the smell of petrol. For some reason, an image floated into her mind: her horse Hector, at Burleigh, flying through the air as she cleared the highest jump. Invincible.

She stood up and took off her ripped t-shirt, her bra, her shorts and briefs. She was naked, apart from her trainers. "Lie down," he said as he started to undo his belt. And the moment he lowered his trousers she bolted and gained some precious seconds. This time she headed back down the track that she guessed led to the road. This time there was only one person chasing her. And she knew she could outrun him. Naked, bruised, battered and bewildered. Hysterical. Adrenalin flooding her system, she powered forward.

She kept running towards where she knew the road must be. Invincible! It was now broad daylight, she looked desperately to see if there was anyone around that might be able to help her. And she started thinking about what she would do without clothes or phone or money when she got to safety. There was a bang and something flashed past her head. And then another bang and something hard hit her in the back. She kept running but somehow her legs were no longer driving her forward. She stumbled. She fell and all was black.

Felicity woke to the smell of petrol. She was lying in the hole on top of a dead man. His chest was covered in blood. She could hardly breathe. She could see the feet and lower legs of the other man as he showered her with petrol.

It was in her hair and in her eyes. A match struck and fell nearby. Blue flames in an instant. Her foot exploded with immediate agony. The man emptied another petrol can. She leaped up and grabbed his leg to try and pull herself out of the fire pit. He kicked her in the face. She fell back, her legs alight. She tried again, clawing her way upwards, digging her feet into the side of the hole. Her arms now alight, her back alight. She managed to grab his foot. He kicked again, she screamed, she shrieked, she howled in agony. The flames engulfed her. And at last she died.

CHAPTER 20

Friday night was date night for William. Stan was collecting Diana from her flat in Hampstead and bringing her to meet him at Le Caprice for dinner at 8 pm. William was having an early drink at Freddie's and then sharing an Addison Lee into the West End. As usual, Freddie was on fine form. "Sharpener for you William? I know it's not yet six, but who cares? Let me guess: large Sipsmith vodka and a splash of tonic over three ice cubes?"

Some cool jazz on the stereo, some cold drinks and friendship led William to ask the question. "Freddie, what is happening with you and the firm? Have you fucked up seriously or is it a minor infringement?"

"It depends on your perspective, I suppose," was the reply. "I think the problem is that previous offences might be taken into consideration. I accept that I do have a bit of a record. Anyway, let me explain and you can tell me what you think. By all means top up that glass while you listen to my tale of woe. And do the same for me please.

"It won't surprise you that this started with a woman. No ordinary woman but Ruth Reed who joined from HSBC about six months ago. To cut a long story short, we met and one thing led to another. There is a surprisingly sexy person underneath those modest clothes and haughty disapproving glances. Anyway, for some reason she thought our relationship was what she called 'exclusive' and when she discovered it was far from that, it was like There Is No Fury, etc. etc. And she grassed me up to the firm about the amount of coke I was using and my suggestion that she might like a line or two. So, William, what do you think?"

"Guilty as charged but a suspended sentence or DPK Community Service as maximum punishment would be my view," replied William. "And I guess you are doing the suspended sentence now. Are they blocking your drawdown?"

"No."

"So I reckon you are quids in and guess that the moment you make some rain, or pop up to solve some problem, all will be well. Speaking of problems, I may have an opportunity for you involving a banking audit where the partner looks like he will not be carrying on. When we first met, weren't you the UK audit partner for a small Russian bank? And more to the point, I know you speak Russian as well as Japanese and Spanish.

"The most senior person on the audit at the moment is Gill Littleton and the client will want to see a partner on the scene and so will Risk Management. Even if it's just to shake a few hands 'til the man gets back. And, to be fair, to make sure this piece of work gets finished in time. Let's have a think about that. Might be some sort of path to some sort of redemption.

"Anyway Freddie, what were you up to today?"

"I went to West London shooting school this morning to hit a few clays with Lizzy. She is getting pretty good. Tonight, I'm taking her to eat at Chutney Mary."

"Are you two becoming an item?" asked William.

"No, not really. But we enjoy ourselves both in and out of bed and neither of us has anything else going on."

"Oh really," said William. "That's a first. In fact, I don't believe it. What about that child you were with last week in the Crown and Anchor?"

"Unfair, William. That's below the belt. That was Lesley and she is a teacher. She's twenty-six and very grown up!"

"Below the belt is very apposite, Freddie. It's where most of your thinking takes place. Fifty plus and still a teenager. How on earth did you find her?"

"Actually, I met her at the boxing gym under the arches at Kew Bridge. I was sparring with the coach. She was hammering away at the speed ball and distracted me for a moment. She's pretty fit. Then that fucking coach caught me on the nose and it spurted blood. He didn't care, just told me to get out of the ring. She stepped in, grabbed the first-aid box, took out a cotton swab, poured on the epinephrine and gently pushed it up my nose. Then she wiped the blood off my face with a tissue. Obviously, I had to buy her a drink to say thank you!"

William smiled. "Very romantic. Freddie Findlay and

a fit Florence Nightingale. What could possibly go wrong!"

CHAPTER 21

The car dropped Freddie off at Chutney Mary and a few minutes later William was at his table in Le Caprice. Diana had texted that she would be there shortly so he ordered two glasses of champagne. She arrived at the same time as the wine. Tall, slim, elegantly casual; she was the sort of woman that attracted attention wherever she went, from both men and women. She looked a good deal younger than William and he knew many people wondered how it could be that she was with him rather than a younger and better-looking man. William had no such concerns.

They had met about two years ago, three years after William's wife Ryoko had died. He wasn't looking to start any new relationship. He couldn't imagine doing so. But he found himself next to this extraordinary lady at the bar in Cecconi's. It was the only seat available when he arrived and ordered a glass of Gavi de Gavi. He'd been at a quite intense board meeting and felt like a drink and an opportunity to catch up on emails before heading home. The barman knew William, by face if not by name, and as they exchanged a few words the lady interrupted very politely and asked for another glass of wine. Somehow, they started talking. She ran a marketing agency and her clothes, her Chanel handbag and Cartier watch suggested it was a successful business. They talked about this and that and shared another couple of glasses. William, tentatively, asked if he might have her number and she delved into her handbag and finally found a card which she handed to him. He reciprocated and left.

William called and asked Diana out to dinner a few days later, but she suggested drinks instead and mentioned that she had something important that she wanted to discuss. They met at 5.30 pm in Claridge's bar. William suggested a bottle of something crisp and cool. Diane surprised him. "Just a glass for the time being, if that is OK. And let's think of this evening as speed dating. So, William give me your elevator pitch, say, ten floors. That's about thirty seconds."

"OK. I'm in my sixties, single. Quite well off, live on the river in Chiswick. I'm pretty much retired but have a small portfolio of work including a retainer from DPK – one of the big three international accountancy firms. I love to run, walk, work, cook, grow vegetables, read, go to movies and the theatre, get wasted with my pals, travel – particularly to warm places in the winter. I'm also trying to write a book about financial services. How about you?"

"I'm not going to tell you my age but I'm single, live in Chelsea. I hate running but like long walks. I also go to the gym. I enjoy the theatre, dance and travel. But my business takes up most of my time. That's fine with me because I really love what I do." She raised her glass. "Cheers."

"So," asked William, "what exactly is it you do that you enjoy so much? What is it that you market?"

"I'll give you three guesses," was the reply.

"OK, something to do with fashion?" Diana shook her head. "Property?" Another shake. "Without wishing to be sexist, is it beauty products?"

Diana smiled. "That's close. But not quite correct. I'd better explain. I market women. Actually, men and women. But mostly women. Basically, I run a very up-market escort agency. And when I say escort I mean exactly that. The ladies and gentlemen that work for me are paid to be escorts, not hookers; although there is no rule that prevents them from doing more if they wish to. The point is that I run a legal business."

William was disappointed to say the least, as he assumed Diana was looking for a client. "That's cool but I'm not in the market."

"Did I say I thought you were?" was the frosty response. "However; I do have a proposition. Why don't we have another glass of wine and I'll explain."

Diana's proposition was simple. She liked the look of William and would like to start a relationship. But she wasn't looking for a conventional relationship; she was looking for an unusual but mutually enjoyable relationship. She might have other similar relationships or she might not. Dates would cost a significant amount of money. Discretion would be guaranteed and both parties could terminate the relationship at any time. So a deal was done.

Chapter 21

William really enjoyed the relationship, not only because of the excellent sex but also the conversations. Diana was amusing and a great listener. What's more, there were no commitments. And that suited him perfectly. He was still in love with Ryoko.

CHAPTER 22

Dinner at Le Caprice was lovely as usual. But Diana sensed that William was not on top form.

"Will, what's worrying you?"

"Nothing," he replied.

"Well, that's bollocks. I know you well enough to see something is on your mind."

"Yeah OK, you're right," said William. "It's a work thing. And I don't know what to do. When Ryoko was alive and I had a problem I could always ask her what to do. She was very wise, with a sort of Zen mentality that helped me make the right decisions. She was calm and thoughtful, she often knew the characters involved which was helpful."

"When did you get together?" asked Diana.

"Almost exactly twenty years ago. I was speaking at a small conference and I noticed her immediately in the audience. She came up to me afterwards to say thanks for the talk and we had a brief chat. Afterwards, when I was leaving there was an absolute downpour and I didn't have a brolly. But I saw a cab nearby with its light on so I ran over and threw myself in. And guess who was already in there?"

Chapter 22

"Ryoko!" Diana replied.

William laughed. "No, the conference organiser! But we shared the cab to Green Park tube and she told me that Ryoko was an international tax partner at Freshfields and that was all I needed to know."

Diana put down her knife and fork. "So, William, what happened next?"

"I called her, we dated, we fell in love, we married and fifteen years later she died. So now I can't ask her for advice. I can only ask myself: what would Ryoko do?"

William couldn't stop the tears forming in his eyes as he thought of her, remembering some special times, picturing her on beaches, and watching plays and movies and operas together. But he knew he had to pull himself together and wiped his eyes with his napkin.

"Sorry Diana. It's Friday night and I'm feeling sorry for myself. I think I've bottled up my feelings for too long and then one word or one memory just turns on the old waterworks."

Diana gestured for the bill. "Don't worry about that, William. But let me ask you this. What advice do you think Ryoko would give you at this moment?"

"I don't know."

"Well I do. She would tell you to forget about the problem until Monday morning, and take this lady back to her flat."

CHAPTER 23

Saturday night was another date night. But this time a blind date night. William was tired and not particularly hopeful. In fact, he was wishing he hadn't agreed to go to the dinner. For the last couple of years, friends, colleagues, even recent acquaintances, had been trying to fix him up with someone 'suitable' but he just wasn't interested. Tonight, it was his friends Lorna and Alex who lived a couple of miles away on the marina at Chiswick Quay. Apparently, one of their friends had recently moved to London and had been invited to dinner.

It was a beautiful summer evening but he still felt despondent as he walked the two miles to the marina. The house faced west so the deck outside by the water was full of sunlight when he arrived at 7.30. He was immediately introduced to a strikingly attractive woman called Ina – Ina Maclean – a friend of Lorna's from university days. She was Scottish; tall, slim and athletic looking, freckled, with red hair and green eyes. She was wearing faded blue jeans and sneakers with a pale silk blouse. William thought she was stunning and with Lorna and Alex busy in the kitchen, it wasn't long before they were getting on like a house on fire.

Eventually and inevitably Ina asked, "William, what do you do?"

William replied sheepishly, "Not very much actually. I'm a kind of partner at DPK. How about you?"

"Actually, I've spent the last ten years at RBS and was number two to the finance director. But I'm starting a new job on Monday with a Russian bank as the finance director of their UK business."

"Blimey, that sounds exciting or maybe daunting. Which bank?" asked William, hoping it would be one he didn't recognise. "Kutzevenia," was the reply.

The other two guests arrived. The dinner was delightful. Lorna and Alex were great hosts. Very relaxed. Ina and William stayed on for coffees and more drinks sitting outside with Lorna and Alex, talking about everything from Brexit to Trump and even Love Island. Ina and Lorna were fans. William had never watched the programme; he thought he knew enough about it to nod from time to time without looking patronising. But Ina's mischievous smile made it clear she wasn't fooled. He couldn't help smile back to acknowledge the truth. And there was something intimate about that moment. Something he had missed for many years. Something that didn't exist with Diana.

CHAPTER 24

On Monday morning, William was having a relaxed breakfast until his phone pinged with a message from Gill: 'Please call me asap.'

William called.

"Christ almighty," she gasped. "The police have called. Mark Lawson, the guy running the Kutzevenia audit, the man who we thought was ill, has committed suicide. And they want me to identify his body. They haven't been able to trace a relative but, apparently, his last call on his phone was to me, which is why they called. I can't believe this. I can't believe this; I can't handle this. One thing after another! And another thing is that Felicity hasn't shown up at KB in Mount Street so I guess that that George bloke has scared the shit out of her!"

"What the fuck!" William's mind almost exploded. What the hell was going on? Why would this man have killed himself? It must be something to do with the bloody blank passports. He took a deep breath and spoke quietly. "Let's calm down. What exactly did the police say to you?"

"They said that he has a cleaner that comes in every Friday and when she arrived last week and let herself in there was a note on the dining room door telling her not to enter and to call the police. Well she did open the door and there he was – dead."

"Did the police tell you how he did it?" asked William.

"No, they didn't go into any detail apart from the fact that it was suicide. They have been spending the whole weekend trying to find a relative to confirm the identity and ended up looking at his phone records. And now they want me to identify the body. I'm not sure I can handle this. Apparently he's in a mortuary at Hammersmith hospital and they want me to get over there at four this afternoon."

"I tell you what," said William. "I'll collect you and run you over there and take you home afterwards. Some moral support; you know what I mean. They might even let me come in with you. Where will you be?"

"More London."

"Fine. Stan and I will be there at two-thirty."

"This is going to be dreadful, terrible. I've never seen a dead body," said Gill later as Stan finally found a parking space at Hammersmith hospital. "I don't know how I am going to handle it." William nodded, not sure there was anything he could say that would help. Gill continued. "The lady I spoke to said there would be someone waiting for us outside the mortuary who would look after me. God knows, it's hardly likely there will be a big sign." But they did find a small one, and they followed other signs which finally led to the place.

Waiting outside was a tall, smartly dressed woman who introduced herself as Detective Constable Jane Delany. "You must be Gill," she said. "Sorry to have to bring you along here. And who are you?" she asked William.

"Just a friend to provide support," he replied. Looking at Gill, the policewoman smiled and said, "I know, I look like a younger version of you-know-who. Someone who is a DCI not a lowly constable." Gill smiled. William was mystified. "What do you mean?"

Gill explained. "This Jane looks like Jane Tennyson."

"Who is she?" asked William.

"Helen Mirren, Prime Suspect; surely you recognise her? Haven't you seen it? Good God William!" Gill laughed, the tension of five minutes ago gone.

But then Jane said, "We'd better get on, you can come too William or would you rather wait outside?"

"No, I'll come along."

Jane opened the door and they walked along a bleak corridor and through another door into a surprisingly pleasant room with armchairs and a table with some magazines. They sat down and waited nervously. William found his palms sweating and his heart beating faster. In his entire life he had only seen one dead body and that was Ryoko's. He grabbed the arms of the chair and tried to breathe normally. Gill's face was white, he could see her hands shaking. Jane came back into the room followed by a man in a white coat carrying a folder. Gill got to her feet and tried to pull herself together.

"Hello, I'm Doctor Hughes. Thank you very much indeed for coming along. I'm sure this must be very upsetting but it won't take long. Now let me explain that what is going to happen here is not like anything you have seen on TV or in the movies. Apart from unusual circumstances no one needs to view the body nowadays. All I'm going to do is to ask you to look at some head and shoulders photographs and tell me if you recognise anyone. If so, please identify him. However, I should warn you that the photograph is a little shocking, owing to the fact that the deceased died of asphyxiation. So, would you be kind enough to sit down at this table. And you sir, please sit over there."

Gill sat down and the doctor put the photos face down in front of her. "There is no hurry; please take your time." Gill turned over the first photo. It was black and white, very close up and frighteningly clear. Even though she had never seen a dead person it was obvious that this man was dead. She didn't recognise the face. Nor the second one. The third was Mark Lawson.

"Yes," she said, "that is Mark Lawson."

"Thank you very much indeed," said the doctor. "That's all we need." Picking up his papers, he left the room.

"Good. Thanks Gill," said Jane. "We were confident that we had the right ID but we do need to be one-hundred-and-one per cent sure. Anyway, I've prepared a couple of documents for you to sign and then you are off the hook. And all I have to do is take this stuff back to the station and I'm off the hook until tomorrow as well. But here is my card. If you have any questions or concerns about today, please don't hesitate to call me."

CHAPTER 25

William and Gill navigated their way through and around the hospital and back to the car. "Where are we going?" asked Stan.

"Head towards Shepherds Bush Green, please, and we will have a think. What do you think?" asked William turning to Gill.

"I don't know about you but I need a drink. In fact, more than one drink. I know it was just a photo but it was horrible," was the reply. "OK how about coming back to my place and Stan can take you home afterwards?" suggested William. "Let's make the most of this weather, sit by the river, watch the boats and try to forget all of this for a while."

Gill sat in the swinging chair in the riverside garden as William fetched the drinks: a full ice bucket, two glasses, a bottle of Sipsmith vodka, a bottle of Sipsmith gin and some cans of diet tonic.

"Help yourself; that way you will get it just like you like it. I'm always being accused of making drinks too strong," he said, as he filled his glass with vodka, leaving room for just a splash of tonic. They sat in silence. A pleasant silence. Two people with a thirty-year age gap but joined together by several years of challenging projects and comradeship.

"Poor old Mark. Let's raise a glass to him," said William, mixing himself another drink. "I read this thriller a few years ago where a bloke killed himself by suffocating himself. It was horrible. And very simple. He used a Harrods carrier bag, some plastic twine and some olive oil. He sat down, opened the bottle and put it within reach by the chair. He then put the bag over his head and tied a knot. Then he quickly tied the twine tightly above the knot and finally poured the olive oil on his hands and smeared them all over the bag so he couldn't have undone the knot himself or torn the bag even if he'd wanted to. DIY asphyxiation!"

"God, William, that's macabre. You don't suppose that's what Mark did?" asked Gill. "And why? Why did he kill himself? Last time I saw him he was fine. Talked about a holiday he had planned in September. We fixed a date for my appraisal, for God's sake. We joked about the new car he had just bought – a 911. I accused him of having a mid-life crisis and he said it was a late-life crisis. It's only just sinking in how unhappy he must have been. What an act he was putting on. Perhaps I am so pre-occupied with myself and my team that I just didn't notice. Maybe if I had, things might be different."

"Maybe, but maybe not," said William. "Don't beat yourself up. As Daniel said to me earlier about the passport thing, we are where we are."

"Yeah, but…"

"Yeah, but what?"

"But what if?"

"What if Mark had found something going on in the bank? Maybe he saw some blank passports himself or saw something in the files that the firm had been auditing? By the way, have you still got the text he sent you?"

Gill looked at her phone and checked her old texts. There it was from Mark, the morning he died. She read it out loud. 'Sorry Gill. Won't be able to make it on Monday. Feeling sick. Mark.' Seems straightforward to me, William. It's clear he was under stress as it's not his usual style. Normally, he ends his texts ATB meaning 'All the best' but none of that here."

"Well, maybe he didn't send it," said William.

"Christ, William. Don't start suggesting that Mark was murdered. Why would you even want to think about that?"

"OK. I was just saying; just thinking. Maybe trying to help you shed the feeling that you were somehow responsible for his death. Anyway, whatever. Mark is dead but the passport clusterfuck is still alive and kicking. And talking about kicking, I have kicked it upstairs. George, Daniel and Colin Ballantyne from Risk Management. HMRC are bound to get on the train soon and the suicide of poor old Mark will be a sideshow at best." Then William paused. "The key thing is that the two of us stay tight as gloves on this thing. Who knows where it might go?" He decided to change the subject. "By the way, are you going to call that cop, that Jane?"

"What do you mean? Why would I call her?"

"Well, she gave you her card didn't she?" William replied with a smile.

"Yeah, well that was just in case I needed some support."

"Precisely," said William. "And I could see the kind of support that you might like to get!"

"What are you talking about William?"

He raised an eyebrow and smiled. "How long have I known you? How many of your girlfriends have I met? I know your type and I could see the instant chemistry. Love at first sight?"

"Absolutely not. Lust at first sight maybe. But we shall see!"

"Shame about that, Gill. Shame she is batting for the other side. I always fancied Helen Mirren," said William. "One for the road?"

CHAPTER 26

William felt a weight lifting off his shoulders when he arrived for his meeting with Daniel at eight o'clock the next morning. He wasn't surprised to find that George and Colin Ballantyne had also been invited. Daniel kicked off the meeting. "We are all up to speed on where we are and I think we are all agreed that we now have to escalate this issue; hence Colin is here. Colin, what are your thoughts?"

"Well the first thing I want to say is that I fully understand why you have delayed putting me into the loop," said Colin. "But I am not happy about it. Basically, you didn't trust me on this. No one is to blame for this; you need to trust me and I need to be seen as trustworthy by you. I will do my best to address the latter and I expect you guys to address the former. Are we clear on that?" Nods all round.

"My recommendation is not complicated. We inform HMRC, which I intend to do after this meeting unless anyone here wants to go on record as disagreeing." Colin looked around the table and continued. "I will explain to HMRC that we needed to be sure that this Felicity Strange was credible before contacting them and that we have now completed that process. I will also tell them that the tragic sudden death of the client service partner disrupted our normal governance processes. Any questions or comments?" No one spoke. "Excellent! William, could you ask Felicity to call my office so that I can meet up with her, please. Are we all done? Thank you, gentlemen."

Colin and George stood up.

"Actually Daniel, could I have a quick word?" asked William.

"Of course, and see you later gentlemen," was the reply.

"I know it's none of my business, Daniel," said William, "but who is going to take over from Mark as the client service partner for Kutzevenia?"

"Why do you ask?"

"Well," replied William, "it's not my problem but after the upset of the team arriving in Mount Street and Mark's death, we need to put a credible partner in very quickly. And I was thinking about Freddie."

"Sorry William, but did you say Freddie? Freddie! Fuck off!"

"Yes' I did," said William. "And with some purpose. He would be highly credible given his experience. He speaks fluent Russian. And if there is anything a bit shady about that place he will sniff it out."

"Sniff it, William, or snort it?" was the crisp response.

"OK Daniel, it's your call. It was just a thought."

CHAPTER 27

While Daniel and William were discussing Freddie, the man himself was sitting in a traditional Japanese Hinoki hot tub having previously washed and rinsed himself under a shower that was almost as hot as the water in the tub. The wooden floor, the steam, the smell of the cedar wood and the silence created a timeless and totally relaxing experience. He sighed quietly. After a few minutes, there was a gentle knock on the door which then opened slightly.

"OK if I come in?" asked Lesley.

"Of course," he replied. "It's your bathroom. You can pass me that towel. I love this tub but I guess it's getting quite late. And I actually have some work to do today!"

In Lesley's flat there were no chaotic cutlery drawers and too-full-to-close wardrobes. No miscellaneous objects. No pots and pans and crockery on shelves in the kitchen. No recipe books. In fact, no books at all. Lesley always read on her Kindle. No TV, she watched on her MacBook. Just two pictures in her living room; a signed Barbara Hepworth print and a copy of 'The Wave'; the iconic woodblock print by the Japanese artist Hokusai. Plus, a sleek sideboard and some shelves with nothing on them. Freddie found it very strange indeed given that his house was crammed; not only with his possessions but also with those his parents had left behind.

After an hour's yoga on the balcony, Lesley came into the kitchen, her singlet damp and her skin shining with light perspiration. Over coffee they chatted about the weekend and agreed that she would drive over to Freddie's house after work which would be convenient as she was rowing first thing and her club – The Tideway Scullers – was less than a mile from him. They also decided to have supper at Annie's, his local restaurant. Having settled that, Freddie grabbed his overnight bag and set off to More London and Lesley went for her shower and started getting her things together for school. She also packed for the weekend; she hadn't yet committed to leaving anything at Freddie's. And, more to the point he hadn't suggested she should.

That evening, Freddie took a cab to The Delaunay in Aldwych where he was having dinner with his old pal Rod Gladstone. They had joined the Royal Navy at the same time and served on the same ships until Freddie applied to, and finally joined, the Special Boat Service. After discharge, Rod became an estate agent in a posh West End firm and Freddie, after a few adventures, finally ended up as a partner in DPK. Rod beamed when Freddie arrived, drinks were ordered and then food.

Freddie finished his starter and said, "Rod, I need some advice about my house that I want you to sell. It's ridiculously too large for me and it needs quite a bit of work. The question is, do we sell it as is, or do we do it up first? And there is another issue: apart from some substantial payments into a trust fund for the grandchildren, I was the sole beneficiary of my parents' estate. And in addition to the house, I've got about one-point-five-million pounds in the bank. That sounds great. That is great. But the house was valued at seven-point-five-million and the total inheritance tax was about three-point-five-million pounds. Can you believe it? Needless to say, I didn't have it! The most I could scrape together, including the one and a half in the will, was about two-million pounds. So, I had to take out a mortgage for one and a half. The interest is killing me, so selling the house seems sensible. Is that right?"

"I'm afraid so, Freddie. That's pretty much the size of it. But you must have been coining it in for God knows how long. Where has all the money gone?"

"Another long story, Rod. But to be brief: three divorces, fast cars and fast women, classic shotguns, watches and cameras. And to quote George Best, 'I wasted the rest of the money!'"

Rod laughed. "God Freddie, you never change. But classic cameras? Anyway, let's get another bottle and consider what's best to do."

Rod put on his serious estate agent face and spoke. "Your house must be very valuable. I can't remember it exactly but it's pretty huge. Five bedrooms?" Freddie nodded. "Four bathrooms. Loads of space." Rod smiled. "You would be surprised how few houses of substance sit on the north bank of the River Thames looking south. There will be no difficulty selling it. And in my professional opinion, the best option would be to do so without doing it up. It's some time since I last visited you but I can remember the place clearly. The cost of a significant makeover would be over a million pounds. And there is no guarantee that a potential purchaser would like what you have done.

"I think we should market your house as an opportunity to create an even more wonderful property and to add value to it. My guess is that we look for a private buyer and price it around ten-million. The view, the garden, the pool, the dimensions and the location, Hartington Road, Chiswick, which is one of the Golden Postcodes. It's a great proposition. And I'll give you mate's rates – or at least a little discount!" Freddie beamed at Rod.

"Thank you, old chap. As I am now a client, I think the least you can do is buy me a glass of Calvados later on."

CHAPTER 28

The house in Islington North London looked like all the houses in the terrace. But unlike most of the others it was not divided into flats. The attic in particular was unique. It was soundproof and the walls were coated with shiny white tiles like a bathroom. It also had a large skylight, and the afternoon sunshine had poured through the glass to create a hot and glaringly bright space. Sadie Cowley was hanging from a wall; spreadeagled with her hands and feet tied to the rings. She was naked and her body was glistening with sweat. She couldn't move her head; her runny nose was pressed into the tiles. She could feel the sweat down her back, in her hair, on her face and between her breasts. She was naked and trembling with excitement. Her body was taut and waiting for the next sting of the whip. She would know when it was coming as the woman holding it behind her always took a breath before bringing her arm back and striking. Just enough for exquisite pain, not enough to cut the skin. Sadie had never felt more alive as she wondered where it might land. High on her back? Low on her thighs? She heard the intake of breath, the swish of the whip and felt the sharp sting on her shoulders. She squealed and shouted, "Red", the word agreed to command her dominatrix to stop the punishment.

Later on, at home in the shower, she used a harsh flannel to clean off the cold wax from her chest and breasts and stomach, remembering the pleasure and pain when the hot wax had been dropped on her. And she smiled as she dried herself and remembered the killing that had earned her this treat. The woman had been very noisy, shouting and screaming until her mouth was filled with her bloody silk blouse. Then Sadie had injected her with a heroin and fentanyl cocktail and watched her eyes fluttering for a few seconds until they stayed open. What a wonderful moment that was. What a wonderful morning.

She had arrived at the gates at about nine o'clock. The drive in front of her was about a hundred yards long with perfect trees and manicured grass on both sides. The huge house at the end looked like something she had seen in a Country Life magazine in her dentist's waiting room. She pressed the bell and put on a meek smile. She guessed what the woman in the house could see on the CCTV. A little old lady with a little old lady's car. Grey hair and a little hat.

"Hello. How can I help you?" The voice was charming.

She had looked straight at the camera with a shy expression. "I'm from the local Women's Institute and wondered if I might have a word with you."

A slight hesitation. "Of course." And the gates opened.

When she had driven to the house and parked the

car, the lady was in the doorway with a welcoming smile on her face. She looked exactly like the picture Sadie had been sent. Mid-forties and rather glamorous, with silk pyjamas and some sort of cashmere dressing gown. She smiled. And Sadie smiled back. Then she had reached into her bag. "If I could just show you this…" as she pulled out the cosh and hit the woman on the side of her head.

It was later on when the woman had started getting noisy that Sadie had decided to put her to sleep. Then the work started. She had taken the dildo out of her bag and used it roughly on her victim. She wanted it to look like rape. Then she had taken out the used condom and poked the dildo into it until she was sure some of the semen would stick. Then back into the previously glamorous lady to leave a present for the police. At the very least it would be a diversion. She smiled.

But thinking about it; she thought that maybe it wasn't fair. The young man from the agency was quite pleasant and the dinner was OK. But the sex was second rate and it was clear that he wasn't really turned on by her mature body. It was a fit mature body! Anyway, if his DNA was not on the system and if he had an alibi all would be well. Of course, if he had no alibi and his DNA was on the system then he would be facing some serious time. 'Serves him right for saying I reminded him of his mother,' she thought as she tidied up and dressed the scene, deleted and unplugged the CCTV and got into her stolen old lady's car.

Later on, when she was in bed, she thought back to the killing in the morning and the session in Islington that afternoon. And, as always, she wondered why she enjoyed inflicting pain and receiving pain so much. She knew it had something to do with her older brother and how much it hurt when he raped her so many times when she was a child. Or maybe it was the excitement when she killed him after her thirteenth birthday party. Her first kill. And the jury agreed it was self-defence.

CHAPTER 29

William got a call from Gill. She sounded anxious; again. "I went around to Felicity's place last night. It's in Belgrave Mews, very posh, very quiet, near Belgrave Square. I rang the bell a couple of times but no reply. I looked through the letter box but couldn't see anything. I tried her phone and couldn't hear it ringing. As I was standing there, a bloke was letting himself into his house and looked at me as if I was a thief or something and I explained I was looking for Felicity. He didn't know her but he pointed to a Mini convertible and said it was her car. So, wherever she has gone she hasn't driven anywhere."

"God," replied William. "I don't blame her for wanting to get away from all of this but Risk Management will be well pissed off if our key witness has done a runner. Text her and tell her we need her back at the big house pronto."

"There's another thing," said Gill. "Guess who called me last night?"

"Helen Mirren junior or whatever her name is?" replied William. "And let me guess; she needs to talk over a couple of things and she thinks it would be a good idea to meet in a pub rather than in the station. In other words, you have clicked!"

"Clicked. What do you mean by clicked?"

"What I mean is that this is a date not police business. Enjoy!"

William was invited to another meeting in More London for the following day. Daniel was there. George was there. Colin was there. Gill was there. He felt a bit uncomfortable; he couldn't work out why. Maybe it was Colin. He looked a bit nervous. Anyway, as soon as everybody was sitting down, and before anyone else spoke, Gill looked around the table and said, "Felicity seems to have vanished. I have texted her and called her numerous times. I went to her house yesterday and her car is still parked outside but there was no response to the doorbell. I'm worried about her."

"Sure," said George. "You are worried about her. That does not surprise me, Gill. I know how close you can get to your female colleagues. But putting that aside – for the present time – let me tell you all what I'm worried about. I'm worried about HMRC wading into one of our largest clients with allegations of blank passports and Christ knows what else, only for us to tell them that the only person who actually claims to have seen the passports has done a runner."

"So, what do we do?" asked Daniel.

"You know, the first thing I think we should do is to clear the decks," said William.

"What the fuck do you mean by that?" asked Daniel.

"What I mean is that we need to be sure we are all going to work together as a team. Like we are on a boat together and we need to trust each other," said William.

"Of course," said Daniel, "that's how it is. That's how it always is."

"So," said William, "what's the 'Gill, I know how close you can get to your female colleagues' comment George? Could you put that on the deck right now please? What did you mean by that?"

"Come on, don't get your arse out of gear, William. I was just saying!"

"Enough," said Daniel. "Dial it down, George. And Gill, please forget about his statement for the time being but bring it back to me later if you see fit. Now, can I repeat my question please? What do we need to do next?"

"Have we notified HMRC yet, Colin?" asked George.

"Not at this time," was the reply.

"So, we have some options?"

"Possibly."

"What do you mean?"

"Well," replied George, "without Felicity we have no evidence of anything so why don't we just forget about it."

"The answer to that option is simple," replied Colin. "We have to report any suspicions; not to do so is a criminal offence. And we do have our suspicions, don't we? It's almost two weeks since we first heard about this. It's several days since I was informed. We know Felicity told her immediate superior – Kathy? – about the passports and Kathy will be expecting to hear something."

"She's already concerned about Felicity's whereabouts," added Gill.

"OK, "said Daniel. "My view is that we inform HMRC today. I'm sure I don't have to remind you that the firm was fined two-point-five-million pounds a couple of years ago when we failed to report our suspicions about the Dubai money laundering. And now, of course, we are talking individual fines for relevant partners. That is us. Colin, do you agree? How about you William?"

Both said yes.

"George?"

"I don't agree," he replied. "We are putting a hugely important relationship at risk."

"Maybe," replied Daniel. But there is only one reason for blank passports in a bank. And that is money laundering. So, step one, I'm going to speak to Wendell today, as head of Global Financial Services he needs to be in the loop. Step two. Colin, you will make an appointment with HMRC, say Friday or next Monday. Step three, William and Gill, try and chase down the elusive Felicity please."

"Just one last thing," said Daniel. "As you know, Mark Lawson, who was running the Kutzevenia audit, has sadly passed away. Clearly we need to replace him asap and I have decided to ask Freddie Findlay to take over – for the time being at least." Eyebrows were raised, glances exchanged. But no one chose to challenge Daniel's decision.

"Want a lift to Mount Street, Gill?" asked William as they waited for Stan. "That would be great," she replied. "It will give us a chance to talk about step three. Find Felicity. As if it was that easy." In the car Gill summed it up. "Parents dead, no brother or sisters, no relationship, at least that's what she told George. Where do we start?"

"I've been trying to remember the name of the partner who asked me to arrange the internship," said William. "I'll see if I can get his contact details from my PC and follow up."

"And I'll talk to a couple of people who were in the same intake as she was to see what they might know about her," said Gill. "By the way, what do you think about Colin?"

"I don't know. He seemed uncomfortable. He doesn't fill me with confidence, that's for sure."

Gill snorted. "Uncomfortable? He looked scared to me!"

"Of course he is," replied William. "He heads up Risk Management and it looks like we are at risk of getting into some serious shit!"

Gill glanced at him then looked out of the window. It was clear to William that she wasn't impressed.

CHAPTER 30

"Stan, head to Chiswick please," said William after they dropped off Gill. He felt drained even though it was only ten o'clock. He also felt depressed; but he couldn't put his finger on why. He needed cheering up and called Freddie. "Hello mate; are you around for a bite to eat at lunchtime?"

"Is the Pope a Catholic?" was the response. "See you at the Old Ship at 12.30?"

"Done," said William. The pub was almost empty on a weekday, unlike the very different atmosphere on sunny Saturdays and Sundays. He ordered two large vodkas with ice and one tonic and took them upstairs to the terrace overlooking the tow path and the river. Looking to his right, he caught sight of Freddie cycling towards him. He waved, Freddie waved back and a couple of minutes later he was at the table. "Is that for me?" he asked pointing to the glass on the table. "I'd rather have a beer, I think."

"Just as well," replied William. "They are both mine. And you can bring me up another one, please."

Freddie came back, beer in one hand, vodka and crisps in the other. "So, what's new, old chap?"

"What's new is that you are paying for lunch," William replied.

"That's so unfair, mate. Here I am in somewhat straightened circumstances and you're putting the knife in," said Freddie, trying to look distressed.

"Well," said William. "When I tell you what's new I think you will thank your lucky stars that you're sitting here rather than The River Cafe down the river. Because you're now in charge of the Kutzevenia Bank UK audit. So, make the best of this weekday lunch; it will be the last you get for the next couple of months."

"What's the catch?" asked Freddie. "To say that Daniel Goor is not my greatest fan would be the understatement of the year. It's like saying Donald Trump is a bit of a loose cannon."

"Well, there is a bit of a catch and I'll come to that later. But I think the real reason is that they can't find anyone else who speaks Russian and has the right credentials."

"Will I be back on full pay and rations?" asked Freddie.

"I don't see why not," said William. "So, let's finish these drinks and go downstairs for some lunch."

They got a table out of any earshot, ordered food and wine and William laid it out. "I'm going to let you into a secret that only Daniel, Colin from Risk Management, Gill Littleton, a guy called George from Partnership Protection and a graduate trainee know."

"Oh Christ!" Freddie interjected. "Partnership Protection, Risk Management and that creep Colin? I've had more run-ins with that lot than you can shake a stick at!"

"You don't have to worry about that, mate; it's all history, I think. I hope. Anyway, this is where we are." And William took Freddie through the whole thing, from the passport on the floor, to Mark Lawson's suicide, Felicity's absence and the meeting that morning.

"Suicide, disappearance?" said Freddie. "Sounds like the curse of Kutzevenia to me. Seriously, you know me. I've been around the block enough times to disregard conspiracy theories but looking at it from where I'm sitting this could be a very serious situation. What if Mark's suicide was faked? What if Felicity has been threatened or even worse? What if this hotshot Russian partner who won this audit isn't altogether kosher? You know, when I worked for Control Risk I encountered some very scary people who made a great deal of money without too much fuss. Washing that money was their challenge. We are talking billions not millions. One organisation actually managed to set up some banks whose sole purpose was laundry. They didn't take prisoners, if you know what I mean."

"Well it's not your problem, or mine, Freddie, so I really wouldn't worry. Handling the audit, managing the client, keeping your nose clean – and I mean that literally not metaphorically – is all you need to do. What's more, Gill Littleton is on top of things at the bank and HMRC will be involved in a few days. So, if all goes well, in a couple of weeks you will be the DPK prodigal son."

William continued, "By the way, I met the new Kutzevenia finance director a few days ago. She actually starts this coming Monday so I guess you will meet her next week. Hands off please."

"Will do, William, and seriously I'm truly grateful for your support here. I don't know how you swung it. What I do know is that you are a true friend. And I won't let you down. Let's try and get together with the gang over the weekend. Maybe Alex will be taking his boat out."

CHAPTER 31

"Wake up Mr West." William was wide awake as usual. Friday morning. Not a cloud in the sky. He went off for a run and was back by eight. The start of the weekend as far as he was concerned; a date with Diana at Scotts that evening to look forward to. In the meantime, the book beckoned; so, he walked over to his office, sat down, and got on with it. Lots of research, lots of words and it was lunchtime before he noticed it. A quick lunch and he was back at the screen for another three hours before he felt he had done enough. Shaved, showered and smart, William enjoyed a sharpener of Grey Goose before getting into the car.

"Lights on amber, Stan. How are you and how are things going with the flat?"

"I'm good," said Stan, "and the flat is going well. Do you know when someone might be wanting to look at it?"

"Sorry no, but I'll call the agents on Monday to see if they have any prospects," replied William.

"Anyway Stan, we will be leaving Scotts about ten thirty and coming back to the house. After that, the weekend is all yours."

"Thanks boss" was the reply.

When they arrived at the restaurant, William noticed a very imposing building nearby with 'Kutzevenia Wealth' written on a brass plate by the front door. The last sort of coincidence he needed but he was determined not to let it spoil his evening. And he also noticed Diana; already sitting at a table outside and looking absolutely lovely.

"Darling, darling," he said, and gave her a kiss on the lips but was careful not to smudge her lipstick. A waiter was immediately at their side asking, "A drink Mr West?" and William felt it would be a wonderful evening. Afterwards they had coffee outside with a glass of Pinot Noir, watching the orchestra of Bentleys, Ferraris and all manner of expensive cars arriving and departing in Mount Street. They saw one driver leaving his Bugatti in the middle of the road with the door open and walk straight into the restaurant.

Stan arrived at about 10.15 pm and Willian asked for the bill while watching Stan have a joke with the doorman. Then he saw a man in a hoodie brush past both of them, pick up his pace and grab his phone from the table, then speed off towards Chandos Place. Stan rushed past, moving very fast indeed. The doorman came over to see if William was alright. "I'm fine," he said.

"How about you Diana?"

"I'm glad it was just your phone; my handbag was within reach as well. That would have been a disaster. Replacing a phone is really just an inconvenience, now all the stuff is in the cloud."

The front of house manager popped his head through the doorway. "I'm terribly sorry about this, can I offer you a brandy on the house?" William looked at Diana.

"How about a couple of glasses of that Pinot Noir?"

"Why not?" was the answer.

Their glasses were almost empty when Stan finally returned and proudly passed over William's phone.

"I chased him down to Berkeley Square, down Bruton Street up Bond Street, then into Dover Street and I caught him in that alley that leads to the back of the Holiday Inn. We had a bit of a scrap. Didn't take long. In the end he saw sense, dropped the phone and ran off. I was too tired to carry on chasing; in fact, too tired to do anything other than limp back here."

"Thank you so much Stan," said William. "Let me show you where the gents are and you can clean up. Don't worry about us; we are happy to wait."

"What a character that chap is. What a hero!" said Diana. "All of that for a phone. I hope you are going to give him a reward."

"Indeed I am," replied William.

Stan came back and drove them both to Chiswick Mall.

Diana used the guest suite to sleep, bathe and change when she stayed over. That was part of the unwritten contract. In fact, it was a reminder of the contract.

It was about ten o'clock in the morning when she arrived in the kitchen. William had already been for his run, showered and dressed in a polo shirt and chinos. He poured fresh orange juice, and made scrambled eggs and toast for both of them. Afterwards they took their coffees and sat by the river.

"You seemed in much better form last night, William," said Diana. "Actually, I mean last evening. No issues with our nights. But you were very quiet when we went to Caprice last week. Something was troubling you. Is that all fixed now?"

"More or less," he replied. "Actually, it's all been kicked upstairs but I still have one problem. I've lost a girl."

"You have lost a girl, what on earth does that mean?" asked Diana. "That's a hazard in my business but I didn't think it happened to accountants. What's happened to her?"

"I've no idea," said William. "No one has a clue. She seems to have no friends or relations, I'm trying to contact some people who might be able to help but I've had no joy so far."

They sipped their coffee in silence. "William, do you know what pensions auto-enrolment is?"

"Yes I do."

"Well," said Diana, "I'm doing it for my staff at the moment."

"I see. Do you need some help with the forms?"

"No William, I do not," Diana replied a little sharply.

"In fact, I may be able to help you in your search for your lost girl. Let me explain. I only have a few staff and as you can imagine, some of them, in fact most of them, lead lives which are somewhat unconventional. And like your missing girl they tend not to have close-knit families or friends.

"Anyway, the other day I got a call from one of the girls asking me about something called a 'designation of beneficiary' form. You fill it in so that if you die they know to whom to give the pension fund you have built up. She couldn't think of anyone; but that's another story."

"Diana, you are not just a goddess you are a genius!" William exclaimed. "My missing girl will have filled in such a form and it will lead us to someone close to her. Someone that she might have gone to. Excellent. Thank you."

"It's a pleasure William, and thank you so much for last night. A lovely dinner with some excitement at the end. And I'm not just talking about the phone theft. Sadly, I must go and get my stuff as I have a car arriving in a few minutes."

CHAPTER 32

Saturday morning and William had nothing to do. He was perfectly relaxed about being on his own; in fact, he liked his own company. So, when the text arrived from Sky – 'Hi Wills. What are you up to? I'm bored. Can I come over later?' – he thought twice before replying 'Yes, I'll cook dinner'.

Sky was William's oldest friend They had met at a mutual friend's wedding, hardly knew anyone there, got completely hammered and one thing led to another. They had stayed together through thick and thin. She was an ex-model, ex-actress, ex-chef, ex-God knows what else and now living in Richmond on the very substantial benefits of being the ex-wife of a very successful football agent. She was one of those people that light up any room they enter; long legs and short skirts, walking as if she was still on the catwalk. She looked aloof, but she was a bundle of fun; unless she was talking about her children. She arrived with a suitcase in one hand and a bottle in the other hand.

"Come on in," smiled William.

"So, what's for supper?" asked Sky. "And more to the point, it's 6.30 and I'm parched. In the meantime, stick this in one of your many fridges and make me a Belvedere

Martini if that isn't too much trouble. I see you already have a glass in your hand!"

Martini made, bottle stowed, they walked up to the living room. The view was fantastic. Sun going down, tide going out, people walking down Chiswick Mall, runners on the other side of the river, rowers gliding with the tide or straining against it. An old friend, a cold drink, food and wine shortly and the possibility of who knows what. William would remember this moment for as long as he lived. Dinner was great. But the thing about Sky was that she always had drugs. First-class drugs. Not economy-class drugs. Not business-class drugs. But first-class drugs. And tonight, after dinner it was coke. Snorted, massaged and used inventively. William did not go for a run the next day.

Freddie texted when Sky and William were still in bed. When he finally had a look: 'Game on. Alex is taking his boat up river. You need to be at Chiswick marina at 11.30 to catch the tide.' Sky got a similar text. They decided they could make it and Sky phoned for a cab to come immediately so she could go home and "put on my boating outfit". William had breakfast in his dressing gown on his own then changed into his own boating outfit of t-shirt, shorts and deck shoes, took a couple of bottles from the fridge and cycled the two miles along the tow path to the marina. As usual, he was the first to arrive.

"Morning skipper; hope you've got some room in

your fridge for these two."

"Thanks, Will, just pass the bag across and climb in. Be careful, we don't want anyone getting wet before we have even left port," said Alex.

Freddie arrived with Lesley. She was wearing jeans, a t-shirt and trainers. He was wearing what he always wore when not working; almost exactly what he wore when he was working. The suit was swapped for brass-buttoned blazer and grey flannel trousers. The shirt was identical to his business shirt but he wore no tie. The concession to boating was a pair of well-worn Green Flash tennis shoes.

Sky arrived, kitted out as if she was about to saunter up the gangplank of an oligarch's super yacht in Monte Carlo harbour and she climbed aboard like a seasoned sailor.

"Morning all. What's the plan, skipper?"

"We are going to cast off now. I've just texted John and he is by the lock," replied Alex.

"William, could you get on the pontoon and keep the bow from hitting it. Sky, could you untie that rope and hold onto it until I say?"

William jumped aboard as Alex reversed the boat slowly away from the pontoon and the other boats and used the bow thruster to turn. The marina was quite a crowded space and Alex was a very careful skipper.

The lock gates were already open and they entered, followed by another, smaller boat. Immediately the back gate was closed, water rushed in and in a couple of minutes the front gates opened and they were in the river.

"Right guys," Alex said, "pull up those fenders, tidy those ropes and let's get going. The plan is to go up stream with the tide, moor up at the Barmy Arms, have a beer or whatever, use their loos – I don't want you using mine – and come back with the tide when it turns. Then we will have some more food which Lorna will get ready. How does that sound?"

"Wonderful," said Freddie. "And Sky, do you want to come down and powder your nose?" asked Freddie, stepping down into the cabin and ignoring Lesley's puzzled then shocked face. Alex put on 'Revival', Eminem and Beyoncé started singing 'Walk on Water'. On the way back, it was a singalong with Shirley Bassey.

CHAPTER 33

William got home at about five and was woken by his phone. It was an unknown number. "William West."

"Hi William, sorry to bother you on a Sunday afternoon. I'm Bonnie Bailey. Executive assistant to Wendell. Are you free to talk?" William was stunned. Wendell was the global boss of DPK Financial services.

"Yes indeed", he replied. He was pretty sure this was about the passports but why was Wendell calling him?

"Well," said Bonnie, "Wendell has asked me to arrange a face-to-face meeting for the two of you as soon as possible. It's in connection with a large audit account where I understand there is an important issue to be discussed. He'd like to make it this week if possible and I wondered if you could maybe meet him in Bermuda as he is visiting some clients there and playing some golf."

"Actually, I could get there for Wednesday or Thursday," replied William.

"That's grand. Shall we say Thursday at two? Wendell is staying at The Hamilton Princess and suggested you meet there. Is that OK?"

"Sure," said William. "Could you email me his mobile number and your contact details in case there is a problem?"

"Will do, William. Have a nice day. Sorry, I forgot your day in England is pretty much finished. Oh, sorry, one more thing: Wendell asked me to say that he would appreciate it if you didn't mention this meeting to anyone else. Anyone at all. Bye now."

William made himself a drink, sat down and pondered. Why a face-to-face meeting? Why so urgent and why confidential? But he wasn't altogether surprised; it had to be about the bank. And he knew that he was closer to Wendell than anyone in the UK firm, having worked with him and mentored him during the five years that he had been seconded to the New York firm back in the nineties.

Apart from receiving Christmas cards, William had not had any contact with Wendell since he had flown over to William's retirement party. And they had precious little time to talk then. So he was looking forward to seeing his protégé again. But he didn't expect there would be much time for casual conversation this time either. He got straight on the BA website and booked a business class seat for the 2.20 pm flight to Bermuda on Wednesday with a return on Friday morning.

On Monday morning William went to More London in search of Human Resources to see how he could get sight of the pension form that Felicity should have filled in to designate the person who would get the fund should she die. He discovered that Human Resources was now called Talent Management and was in a completely different building on the More London estate. He finally got to see someone who informed him that all pension administration was outsourced to a firm in Newcastle.

Undeterred, William called the administrator who told him he needed authorisation from the DPK Pension Department which was based in the building which he had just left. Finally, he found someone who wanted to help. A young, enthusiastic apprentice; one of the many DPK employees who had decided to start work rather than going to university after obtaining good grades. Her name was Sharon and she recognised William from a presentation he had given shortly after she joined the firm.

He explained the problem without going into details and she was happy to call her opposite number in Newcastle. William went off for a much-needed cup of coffee and a sandwich from the staff canteen. Twenty minutes later he was back with Sharon. She beamed and handed him a piece of paper: "The designated beneficiary is Benjamin Cook, 60, Bath Mews, London W2 6FB. He is down for one hundred per cent of the benefit. Relationship is defined as 'Friend.'"

"Thank you so much Sharon, that's really helpful. Do drop me a note with a feedback request."

Progress at last thought William and called Gill and left a voicemail. Gill called back later and agreed to check out this Ben Cook and meet up with William at the bar in the Beaumont Hotel at six. She was there when he arrived. "There is good news and bad news, William. The good news is that I have just met Ben. The bad news is he has no idea where Felicity might be, he hardly knows her."

"What? The death benefit is four times her salary. That would be something like two hundred grand. So why the hell was she planning to give him all that if she died?" asked William.

"She isn't," replied Gill. "It's not for him. It's for her horse!"

"Her horse? What fucking horse? Is he taking the piss? Come on Gill," whispered William, not wishing to raise his voice in the quiet bar.

"Actually, it's all straightforward," said Gill. "Felicity owns a horse and it's stabled near Hyde Park. The stables are owned by this Ben guy's parents and it seems that she rode out with him quite often and formed a friendship. When she was filling in her pension forms she had no idea who to put down as beneficiary so she put down Ben and told him the money should be used for looking after the horse."

"God," said William. "You couldn't make it up. Are you sure he was telling the truth? Did he know anything about her at all?"

"Nothing," was the reply.

"OK," said William. "If I don't get anything useful back from the guys who knew her godfather – and that's looking increasingly unlikely – I'll suggest to Colin Ballantyne that we contact the police and tell them that Felicity is missing. She must have had an accident or something. She may be seriously hurt, they will know what to do. Talking of police, when is your meeting, or should I say date, with Helen Mirren junior?"

"It's this Thursday," replied Gill, "and I hope it's a date."

"I look forward to hearing all about it. Shall we have one for the road?" William asked, gesturing to the waiter.

"There is something else I need to tell you, Gill. And I'm not sure how you are going to take it," said William. He plucked up his courage as he knew that Gill, along with many others, thought Freddie was an accident waiting to happen and a serial womaniser.

"As you know, we have to replace Mark Lawson and Daniel has decided that Freddie is the man."

"Freddie! You are joking. 'Fucking Freddie', as he is so aptly described by the young and pretty as well as the desperate and well worn. Why on earth would Daniel choose Freddie?"

"Well," replied William, "he has excellent Russian, he has run a global banking audit before. He is a great networker and will keep the client happy and he's available. There are two other reasons. First, we have no one else with those credentials. And second, I suggested it."

"Why?" asked Gill. "Just because he is an old friend?"

"Yes and no. But I think he deserves one more chance."

"Well thanks for the honesty. But make sure you tell him to keep his hands off the team. Not a problem for me as he knows I'm gay. So at least Fucking Freddie won't be trying to fuck me."

"Want to bet?" asked William. "Only joking... or maybe not! By the way Gill, purely by coincidence, I met the new Finance Director at a dinner party recently. Her name is Ina, I can't remember her surname. I didn't get around to telling her about my role in DPK but I guess that doesn't really matter. Anyway, she was good fun but I have no idea what kind of Finance Director she might be."

William's phone pinged. "That will be Stan. Do you want us to drop you off in South Ken?"

Later that evening William received a text from Daniel: 'Wendell on board, the Moscow partner advised and unhappy, Colin's meeting with HMRC fixed for Thursday.' William replied to all. 'No luck re Felicity. Should we report as missing person?'

Almost immediately, both George and Colin texted to say not yet and Daniel texted his agreement. 'Why?' thought William. 'Why would these three guys be so unconcerned about a missing graduate trainee? Has the firm become this callous?' He knew it was really none of his business but he remembered that lunch with Felicity and that scruffy piece of paper with her objectives and achievement scribbled on it. And he felt certain that she would have contacted him or Gill if she was able to do so.

CHAPTER 34

Thursday morning and William packed his case carefully in just the way that Ryoko used to do for him before a business trip. Out of the blue came the pain, the sorrow and some tears. The memory of her in a hospital bed, bravely cheerful. Passing over a list of things he needed to know. How to run the washing machine, how to fill the water softener and the dishwasher. Reminding him that Tina would be coming in more often so not to worry about anything.

The case was a proper leather case, not one of those boxes on wheels. Behaving as if Ryoko was watching, he used tissue paper to prevent creasing, and added in another suit, two shirts, a t-shirt, shorts, gym stuff and swimming trunks, underwear, etc. Nothing that needed to go in the hold. Stan arrived exactly at midday and they arrived at Terminal 5 at twelve-thirty.

Thanking Stan, William passed him an envelope. "Thank you again for the other night Stan. I owe you. Here is a bit of a payback."

"Don't give it a second thought boss. I'll be here on Sunday to meet you from your flight, and have a safe journey," was the reply. William once again thought how lucky he was to have Stan at his side and reminded himself not to take the chap for granted.

The flight was on time, William had a light meal, put his seat back and his nap lasted three hours, not the normal forty minutes. A cup of coffee before landing and he felt top notch. Almost first to leave the plane, with no luggage to collect and no queue for taxis, he was checking in to the Hamilton Princess by seven-thirty. He went straight to bed, knowing that he would be waking up very early and keen to think things through before meeting Wendell. Sitting back on his soft pillows he checked his emails. One response from the DPK people he had approached. No one had any idea about what had happened to Felicity's godfather but there had been talk of him going to live in Spain. One email from Gill: 'The word has got out about Freddie. It's horrifying. Some of the girls are wetting their pants, others are putting on extra pants. I'm meeting him first thing Monday in Canary Wharf and he has suggested the whole team have a heads-up in the office at the back end of the day. At least that seems sensible!' William replied: 'Off the grid until Monday.'

The meeting was in the sitting room of Wendell's suite. They hugged each other and sat down at a table in the corner of the room.

After the usual pleasantries, Wendell said, "So William, lay this out for me please. Daniel has given me the headlines but I want the full story, including where we are now."

William poured some iced water into his glass and laid it out, from the passports on the floor to the disappearance of Felicity. "And there's one last twist to this Wendell. Mark Lawson, the UK CSP for Kutzevenia and leader of the audit team, has committed suicide."

"Well that's inconvenient to say the least. Do we know why? Is it connected?"

"No idea," replied William. "But I guess it has not come as a surprise to you, nor has anything I have said since we sat down. What's going on Wendell? Why the meeting? Why the urgency? Why the secrecy?"

"The reasons will be clear shortly, William. But first I need to tell you something. This job, my job, being responsible for global financial services in over 150 countries and over 100,000 people is a big job. And it's a privilege to be doing it. But the scale is challenging. I can't get to see all the partners. Well I might be able to see them from a stage, but you know what I mean. So, I have to trust them and trust the culture to be sure we are all pulling together in the right direction. But here's the thing; it's an impossibility. It is inevitable that some people, some partners will do the wrong thing, mostly by accident. But sometimes by design. And the same goes for our clients."

"Is this about Kutzevenia Bank or the bigger picture?" asked William.

"Kutzevenia is the bigger picture," replied Wendell. "And William, you have to help me with this. I need to introduce you to someone else who also needs your help."

Wendell stood, walked across the room and opened another door. A very short, thin man wearing a white shirt with a blue tie, blue Bermuda shorts, white socks and highly polished black shoes came into the room. "Hi William, my name is Peter Payne," he said softly. "I am an executive in the US Federal Reserve. My current area of responsibility is money laundering. For a number of reasons, I am based here in Hamilton. For the past three years we have been investigating Kutzevenia Bank. You are now their auditors. You have some suspicions regarding their London branch. We have our suspicions regarding the whole organisation. We think they are aware of our interest. We managed to get one of our agents into the bank at a senior level. We think his real role was discovered. It looked like suicide but we think he may have been murdered."

William couldn't believe what he was hearing. Mark's suicide, if it was suicide. Felicity's inexplicable disappearance and now the Federal Reserve and murder. What had he got himself into? It was a nightmare.

Peter Payne continued. "I took the liberty of recording your conversation just now. May I share it with my colleagues?" William looked at Wendell who nodded and replied, "Yes."

"Then please sign this release form. I also have another form which I would like you to read. It is a non-disclosure agreement and it is very specific. You may not discuss this conversation or any future conversations with the Federal Reserve with anyone other than those agreed with us. This includes official bodies such as the UK HMRC as well as DPK colleagues. We are not one hundred per cent confident they are secure. You will see the exceptions suggested by Wendell are Gill Littleton and Freddie Findlay as they are the two senior people on the audit team and we will need their help. If, of course, they are prepared to give it. And on that last point you can also opt out if you wish.

"All we are looking for is anything that looks at all suspicious. We don't want you to take any unnecessary risks. No snooping off piste or anything like that. But think on it carefully. When you do so, think about Felicity's disappearance. And Mark Lawson's suicide. Here is my card. Please put the number in your phone, don't use my real name and give my card back to me. Feel free to take as long as you like to decide what you want to do. This is important but not urgent. Feel free if you want to discuss it. If you fax back the form I'll assume you are committed and we can then discuss how exactly you might be able to help. Thanks for your time, William. Thanks for arranging the meeting, Wendell. Good afternoon to you both." He shook their hands and left.

"Wendell, what have you got me into?" asked William. "We aren't secret agents. We are accountants, for God's sake."

"Agreed," replied Wendell. "But I wouldn't have taken it this far without thinking about it very carefully. Let me explain my thinking, then you can challenge. To be honest, I'm not sure what we should or could do to help. But the first reason is this: if you decide not to take this further then DPK will be seen as trying to help the Federal Reserve, albeit unsuccessfully. And believe me, that's not a bad thing. Second reason, as auditors we have the opportunity and, actually, the duty to look into this. Third reason, our partner who sold the audit to Kutzevenia and continues to run the relationship. He is a new partner. We have to consider – I stress consider, no more than that – he might be part of the problem. And if that is the case it would be good if we understood the position before anyone else. The final reason is this: money laundering is not just a technical crime. It's the process that is used to confirm the result of crime, usually drug related. Call me old-fashioned but I would like to help the Fed because it is the right thing to do. Here ends the sermon. What do you think?"

William grimaced. "OK. I'll try and meet up with Freddie and Gill to get their initial reactions and get back to you early next week. Just one question: do you think the Fed guy meant what he said about Felicity and Mark?"

"I'm afraid so," replied Wendell.

CHAPTER 35

William had supper on the plane back to Heathrow and slept like a log until they had about an hour to run. Stan was waiting by the M&S shop near to the arrivals gate and all was well until the M25 and then the M4 heading into London. Both were jammed at that time of day. But William was relaxed and used the time to sort out his calendar: A pow-wow had been arranged in More London on Monday at ten for Colin to brief Daniel, George and William on the HMRC meeting that had taken place the day before. Gill and Freddie were having a team meeting, also on Monday, to get everyone up to speed on where the Kutzevenia audit was against plan, to ensure the Mount Street and Canary Wharf teams were joined up and to see where they were against the budget.

By the time he got home all was sorted plus several other issues and it was agreed that Gill and Freddie would come to lunch the next day at one. William sent a separate note to Gill asking her if she could come earlier at 12.30. He also texted Tina to see if she would be able to help with the lunch. She called and was happy to help.

At about twelve, William received an email from Gill's personal account. 'Looking forward to seeing you tomorrow. Drinks with Helen Mirren Junior were very worrying. Mark's death is now being treated as suspicious. Apparently, the post mortem revealed some bruises on his arms. The cops went back to the house and had a good look around and also had another look at the photos that were taken. By the way, a carrier bag was used, just like in that book you mentioned. Gruesome! Washing-up liquid rather than oil to make everything slippery, plus string and scissors on the floor. No note. But apparently that isn't suspicious in itself. What did concern them were several details.

'It seems the note on the door was written on Pages but Mark had Office on his MacBook and every document on file was in Word. And around the estimated time of death he had booked a ticket for La Bohème at Holland Park Opera for the following Friday. Apparently, the cops are pretty upset about all of this as they thought the case was closed and now it's more work. They haven't a clue where to start. This is not looking good. See you tomorrow. G.'

William sat back in his seat for a moment, then got up and made himself a drink. 'This is not looking good' was the understatement of the year. And his thoughts immediately turned to Felicity. His stomach fell, his heart started racing, his head whirled. He just knew that he would not be seeing her again. And he felt fear. What the fuck was going on and what about Gill? Were they in danger? How could they get themselves out of this?

His simple life had turned complicated in the space of a couple of weeks. This wasn't his problem. Why not simply disengage? He decided to see how the chat with Gill and Freddie went, what transpired on Monday and what, if anything, HMRC were going to do and then decide what to do. Then he had another thought and emailed Lionel to see if he was free any time Monday. 'Of course, old chap! Late lunch, do you?' was the reply. William called Balthazar on the special number, booked a table for 2.30 and made himself another drink.

CHAPTER 36

William took his breakfast out to the back garden on Saturday. It was a truly lovely warm day and the garden was in great shape. Lawn cut to perfection, flowers exactly where they should be. The rill making exactly the right sound. He reflected how lucky he was and reminded himself not to take this life for granted. But the passport thing threw a shadow across the whole scene and he really didn't know what to do. But of course if Freddie and Gill were clear they didn't want to increase their focus on money-laundering possibilities during the final few weeks of the Kutzevenia audit, then the problem would go away. So the last thing he needed to do was to persuade them to commit.

Gill arrived at 12.30 exactly and that was typical. Like William she was never late. It was one of the many things he liked about her. They went through to the garden and sat down at the table. "How was the date? Where did you go?" asked William.

"We went to a pub in Askew Road. It's near where she lives and it was pretty good."

"That's interesting. A pub near where she lives. How convenient. Did you go back to her place?"

"On a first date, as if!" replied Gill. "Actually, yes!"

"Anyway, you got my email and you know there are more important things to talk about. They think Mark was murdered. Could it be connected to the passport thing?"

"I think it might well be. This is getting very serious and I'll tell you what I've been up to when Freddie gets here but before he does, how are you getting on with him? Is he being professional in the role?"

"Actually, pretty well. He understands the process, he's quite an expert in wealth management businesses which is good because it's not my specialist subject. So far he has been completely professional, he's met the key players at the bank, including the new finance director, he's got up to speed on progress to date and already reviewed the work in progress. There've been no signs of any inappropriate behaviour. So far!"

"That's good," said William. "That's very good." And as he said it Freddie emerged from the house, followed by Tina carrying some nuts and pretzels. "Afternoon all," he said. "Good to see you Gill, William. When I signed on for this work I didn't know it would involve meetings at weekends but I gather we are being compensated with a lunch from Tina and that ice bucket looks promising as well."

William poured him a glass, topped up his and Gill's glasses and thought about how he might explain the situation they were in.

"I was summoned to Bermuda to meet Wendell on

Thursday."

"You what? Why?" asked Freddie.

"He was there for some client meetings. He wanted to talk to me about the Kutzevenia thing and we were joined by a chap from the Federal Reserve, who wanted to talk about it as well; they have been investigating the bank for a couple of years. Wendell was aware of this and alerted them to what had happened this side of the pond."

"Why you? Why not Daniel or Colin or that odious partnership protection man?" asked Gill.

"Wendell and I go back a long way; ever since I was working in New York. It seems to me that he thinks there might be someone in the firm that's involved. I don't know why. He wasn't specific, he just told me not to trust anyone other than you two. But I'm not sure you should be grateful for that."

William stood up and moved the parasol. The sun had shifted and it gave him a moment to think a little more.

"William, why should we not be grateful?" asked Gill.

"I bet I know why," said Freddie. "They want us to snoop around and see if we can find some more blank passports or do some other sort of spooky stuff given that our only witness seems to have disappeared. And as I told William a while ago, money laundering is big business. We are talking billions of dollars here, which means we are talking about guys who don't give a fuck about collateral damage."

"You're right there, Freddie, the police now think

Mark was murdered and why would anyone murder him and make it look like suicide?" said Gill.

Freddie smashed his drink down on to the table. "What the fuck!"

"Exactly," said William. "Freddie you have nailed it. But Wendell and the Fed just want us to keep our eyes open, they are not expecting us to take risks. Unnecessary risks to use their terminology! And Wendell understands that it is unlikely we will uncover anything. But just agreeing to help will position the firm well in the eyes of the Fed."

"Excuse me, William," called Tina from the doorway. "Eat in twenty minutes!"

William thought this was a good time to take a break, picked up the empty bottle of Chablis and collected a replacement from the fridge in the kitchen. He opened it swiftly, topped up the glasses, and looked at Gill and Freddie.

"In reality, we would be looking at the anti-money-laundering governance anyway so what are they actually asking us to do?" asked Gill. "I'm not willing or able to go sneaking around the client site. It would be unprofessional to say the least, possibly illegal and from what you said Freddie, downright dangerous."

"So that's a yes," joked Freddie. "Seriously, we are both on the same page."

"Well I'm not going to give you my view until we have talked some more," said William opening the new bottle.

"But I will say this. I think it is probable that Felicity is hiding because she has been threatened or that she has come to harm. In either case, we should consider if there is anything we can do sensibly that might lead to some justice for her without putting ourselves in any danger."

"You know what?" said Freddie. "I have an idea. There is something we could and should do, and I'm surprised that none of us have thought of it. We need to look at Mark's PC."

"That's right!" said Gill. "We know the police have his personal MacBook but we need to access his work one. If it's not in his house it will be in his locker at MLP. We have the team meeting there on Monday and I'll go get it."

"Could I do that Gill?" asked Freddie. "You will need partner authority to gain access and I can do that. I also know a guy who is in the Forensic team who spends most of his time breaking passwords and I imagine that Mark will have followed procedure and protected confidential folders. Maybe you could have a closer look at the shared space on the Cloud?"

"Yes, that makes sense," said Gill.

"OK," said William. "I'm meeting with Daniel and the others Monday morning. By the back end of the day we will have Mark's PC, we will know about HMRC, so shall we fix a meeting on Tuesday?"

CHAPTER 37

William arrived in the meeting room on the 10th floor of the office just before ten. Daniel arrived shortly afterwards followed by Colin and George.

"So, Colin, how did it go with HMRC?" asked Daniel. Colin spoke in his usual tone of voice, which sounded like a vicar reading a sermon. "Well, there were a couple of chaps. First off, they were more than a bit miffed to say the least about our delay in contacting them but I don't think they will be taking it any further. Second, they were quite candid and told me that Kutzevenia was of interest to them, for a number of reasons – which they chose not to specify. When I explained about the blank passports they got pretty excited but did their best not to show it. In fact, both of them were pretty expressionless for the whole meeting and they took copious notes.

"When I told them that the grad was missing they asked a load of questions about her. Thanks for the note George, it was very helpful. They think it is a matter for the police and said they would be seeing them immediately after the meeting. They also said that they would get a warrant and have someone enter the grad's house to see if she was there. They were equally miffed that we had not reported her missing to the police already. They would like to meet you, William and Gill Littleton and I said that would be arranged. I'm not sure what the next step after that will be but I expect we will hear something from them by the end of the week. I wrote up a full account of the meeting over the weekend and it will be in your inbox now."

"Did you get the impression that there is an active investigation of Kutzevenia?" asked Daniel. "Couldn't really say," replied Colin. "They gave nothing away apart from saying the bank was of interest. But I guess all banks are of interest to HMRC so I wouldn't read too much into that. One thing I should mention is that their standard procedure is that we provide a SPOC and that will be me."

"SPOC?" asked George.

"Single point of contact," replied Colin. "They don't want to be communicating with a gang of people."

"OK," said Daniel. "That is helpful. William, if our calendars work, could you meet with me after your meet with HMRC? I'd like to hear how it went. And Colin, I assume you will be present when they come here?"

"Yes of course," he replied.

CHAPTER 38

On Tuesday, Kanye woke William as usual. The room was chilly. The air conditioning was going at full blast and his glass of water was ice cold. The Dark Sky app on his phone forecast twenty-eight degrees by lunchtime with a ten per cent chance of heavy rain later. When he left the house for his run he was sweating within a few minutes and he decided on just five miles. He was walking by the end of it and texted Stan to let him know that some driving would be needed that day, although all he had planned was the meeting with Gill and Freddie wherever and whenever worked for them. And he got an email an hour or so later suggesting meeting at Isabel in Albemarle Street at four o'clock. Then he got a text from Lorna with Ina's phone number and he realised that with all the other stuff going on he had forgotten he had asked whether Ina would mind her sharing it with him. So, he now knew that Ina would like him to call her but would that be a good idea given the audit relationship? And did he want to start a new relationship? It could get complicated. Was now the right time?

The car was cool on the journey to Isabel and the heat hit

William hard as he stepped out. Mercifully the place was cool. He had only been there once before when it was very busy, but at that time of day there was only one couple seated; they looked like they were finishing a very long lunch. He chose a table near the window which had plenty of space around it and ordered a glass of Bandol rosé. His view was that one can drink Bandol at any time of day, even four o'clock in the afternoon. Gill arrived and ordered the same.

"God, that walk from Mount Street. I'm dripping," gasped Gill. "And what is this place? It's achingly cool. I bet it's bloody expensive. How was the meeting yesterday? What happened with HMRC?"

"Tell you what," said William, "let's wait for Freddie to get here before I go through the details but three quick things. First, they want to speak to both of us. Second, they are arranging for the police to enter Felicity's place. And third, they were a bit pissed off that Felicity had not been reported as missing and that DPK hadn't reported the passport incident. But Colin seemed sure they wouldn't be taking it further. He's a cold fish that guy. And I'm not sure I like him. "Anyway, how was the team meeting yesterday and how was today so far? All good?"

"I think so," replied Gill. "The critical path is Freddie. His is the head on the block. He is going to have to sign off on this audit when he wasn't even present for the first six weeks. That's a lot of catching up to do but let me say this, he's a very quick learner and works his socks off. Not just down in the detail but also up with client team. He's quite an operator. I may have misjudged him."

"Time will tell," said William.

Freddie arrived, scruffy and sweaty. "Sorry to be late but I have made some progress. But first things first. What are we drinking?"

"It's a Bandol," replied William and asked the waiter for a bottle and another glass. "Anyway, Freddie, tell us about the progress."

"I met up with the head of facilities where Mark's team normally hang out and she opened up his locker. She made me turn my back when she put in the release combination, as if she didn't trust me!"

"Can't imagine why that would be," said Gill, rolling her eyes.

Freddie chose not to react. "Anyway, his PC was in there together with the usual junk we put in our lockers. She handed me the PC and put all the rest of the stuff into a DPK carrier bag that was in there. Then I called Sparks."

"Sparks?" asked William and Gill, almost in unison.

"Sparks yes, Simon Parks. He is the bloke in Forensics I mentioned. He's called Sparks because he used to be a lighting engineer in movies and on TV and that was the nickname they used in those days. He is one of the good guys and when I explained I was taking over from Mark he told me to bring the PC down and he would reset the password to give me access."

Freddie took a large gulp from his glass.

"He had a quick look at the PC, plugged it into the intranet and within a few seconds we were in, with a new default password and an instruction to change it immediately. Apparently, people are always forgetting their passwords and they do this stuff every day. Needless to say, it is senior staff like us, William, that are the main culprits, probably because we have so much more on our plates than the younger people. Anyway, getting in was the easy bit. Like most of us, he has folders, and folders within folders and folders within those folders. But unlike us he follows the rules and has all of the main folders password protected. Sparks says accessing these folders could take some time. It seems that after the standard technology has exhausted all the typical passwords, the firm uses a Cray supercomputer to do the heavy lifting, and even though that works 24/7, it's mainly focused on data integrity issues and the development of algorithms. There is a queue to get usage. He reckons maybe a week or so wait."

Freddie looked at his glass and lifted the bottle, held it up to the light and gave a theatrical look of disappointment. William motioned to the waiter who nodded. The place was filling up.

Freddie continued, "After I left the PC with Sparks and set off to meet you guys I had a quick look in the carrier bag with all the rest of Mark's stuff. And I found a couple of data sticks. They are bound to be encrypted and put in the queue if I hand them over to Sparks so I've had a think and have an idea. One of my pals back in the day owes me several favours and now maybe is the time to call one in."

"What do you mean by that, Freddie?" asked William.

"Well, entrée nous, when I was at Control Risks things were not always controllable; particularly when you were in unknown territory. My pal was a boffin, an expert on cyber stuff and got in a bit of bother. I hauled her ashore if you know what I mean."

"I haven't a clue what you mean, Freddie," said Gill.

"I'm not sure that matters," William interrupted. "What are you proposing, Freddie?"

"I'm suggesting that we give these data keys to my pal to get un-encrypted rather than to Sparks. And not just to save time. Let's not forget we have been told to trust no one and who knows what might happen to the stuff on the PC. And let's ask ourselves a question: if something important is on those sticks, why? Why not in a folder on the PC?"

"But – and it's a big but Freddie – if we have been told to trust no one, why should we trust your pal?" asked Gill.

"Because, back in the day, I saved her life," replied Freddie.

"What?" asked Gill.

'It's a long story. I'll tell you about it sometime. No big deal."

"OK, I'm happy if you are, William," said Gill.

"OK Freddie, let's go with it," he replied.

"Shall I get Stan to help us go west?"

"Maybe another glass of this excellent Bandol whilst we wait?" suggested Freddie.

"That's very kind of you," replied William. "And you will find out just how kind when you get the bill."

CHAPTER 39

Stan dropped off Gill first, then William and finally Freddie who let himself into his parent's house on Hartington Road. He took off his shoes, put on his slippers, went into the kitchen, drank two pints of water from the tap and went for a swim in the pool. After he had showered and changed he walked down the garden to the summerhouse by the river and pulled out the bottom drawer of the dusty old cabinet. It was full of stuff; string, plant labels, instructions and spares for the lawn mower, candles, a CD, some batteries, a couple of croquet hoops, a box of matches and an empty half bottle of Scotch. He put all of this to one side and reached into the empty space behind it until his fingers encountered a carefully constructed space. There was a small bag and a much larger bag. He pulled out the small one, opened it, took out a phone, disconnected it from its permanent charge and put the drawer back in place.

It was still light. Freddie walked back up the garden to the house, picked up the data sticks and put them in an envelope. Then he sent a text. After locking the door, he opened the garage door, took out his bike and headed towards Kew Bridge. He walked the bike under the bridge and along the towpath then sat outside the One Over the Art pub for a few minutes before pushing his bike up to the main road and riding to Brentford where he sat outside the Holiday Inn and made a call. It was succinct: "I am here". Twenty minutes later, dusk. An indistinguishable figure walked past and, without hesitating, took the envelope from Freddie's fingers and walked on.

CHAPTER 40

When William got home, he signed the Fed document and faxed it to Peter Payne. And, even though he knew it was only early afternoon in New York, he was still surprised to get a call just ten minutes later.

"William, it's Peter," said the soft voice. "Glad you're on board. You guys need to meet one of my colleagues at the London embassy asap. I'll text you a number. Text it with your preferred time. My colleague will be available 24/7."

William called Freddie, then Gill. They decided on 5.30 pm on Friday. William sent the text. Within a couple of minutes came the reply. 'Done. Ask for John Britney when you get to the embassy.' William forwarded the note to Gill and Freddie, made himself a drink. 'Perhaps I'll call Ina,' he thought, picturing her in his mind. He called and it went to voicemail and he took a deep breath

"Hi Ina, it's William West. Hope all is well with you. It was good to meet you at Alex and Lorna's dinner and Lorna was kind enough to give me your number. I hope that's OK. I was wondering if you would like to meet up again. Maybe a lunch or a brunch next weekend, or the one after, somewhere convenient for you? Just call me back when convenient. All the best." He spelt out his number and email clearly and slowly before ending the call.

The next morning, after breakfast, William went over to his office, opened all the windows to let in the cooler air. Almost immediately his phone rang. it was Colin.

"William, hi. HMRC want to meet with you and Gill at 3 pm on Friday at More London. Can you do that?"

"I can do it; just need to check with Gill."

"Thank you William." The phone went dead.

William spent the next couple of hours looking at his investments. They didn't really interest him that much or give him any pleasure. He knew he was wealthy, but so what? He had no partner to share it with, no children or grandchildren who could look forward to an inheritance and nothing he needed to buy for himself. He looked at the portfolio as if it was someone else's money. He still felt that he didn't deserve it and one day someone would realise that this was true. He really wasn't the man that people thought he was. He had just got lucky.

By lunchtime William's inbox was empty and so was his stomach. He walked over to the house. The rain had stopped and Stan was cleaning the windows. He had a brief chat about the meetings on Friday and the cricket score and went down to the Old Ship for a sandwich and a glass of wine. As soon as he was upstairs and settled outside his phone rang. His heart jumped. "Hi Ina, how are you?" he asked.

"How are you?" she replied. 'Where are you?"

"Well I'm on a sort of balcony overlooking the River Thames with a glass of crisp cool white wine in my hand patiently waiting for a smoked salmon sandwich."

"Well lucky you! I'm in Canary Wharf with nothing to eat and a less than zero chance of a drink before eight o'clock. But talking about food and drink, yes, I would like to meet up and lunch would be great. I could do this Saturday or the following Sunday."

"Let's do this Saturday," replied William enthusiastically. "Whereabouts do you live? I don't want to drag you across London."

"I'm renting in Marylebone at the moment so anywhere central works for me."

"How about Balthazar in Covent Garden?" he asked.

"Great. I've been to the one in New York but not here. Is it the same?" Ina asked.

"I guess so," said William. "I think a restaurant critic, maybe A. A. Gill, said it was an English version of an American version of a French brasserie! I've not been to the New York version so we can compare notes! One o'clock good for you?"

"See you there, William, and enjoy your lunch."

CHAPTER 41

Gill and William arrived at More London at 3.15. The receptionist on the tenth floor told her the room was number twenty-one and when they opened the door Colin was there already and texting away energetically. Eventually the receptionist opened the door and in walked the man from HMRC who was introduced as Mr Croft. Gill took an instant dislike to him; she had no idea why. Perhaps because of his appearance; tall, he seemed to be looking down on her, and grey, as if he was an omnipotent family relative from her past. She couldn't remember who. She noticed his fingernails; too long and a bit grubby. All in all, he was an unpleasant package.

Colin stood up. "Gill, William, let me introduce you to Malcolm Croft."

"How do you do? Please call me Malcolm. Pleased to meet you both and thank you for taking the time to meet me," he said in a smooth Scottish burr. "If you have no objection, I will cut to the chase. There are two areas I wish to cover this afternoon. The first could be described as the story so far. The second as the plan going forward. I propose we commence with the former." Then he sat down, brushing the seat beforehand as if the already immaculate

DPK furniture might be covered in biscuit crumbs.

"As you both know, where there is any suspicion – any suspicion at all – that a client may be in some way committing or planning to commit a financial crime such as money laundering, it is a criminal offence not to report this to an appropriate person within the organisation as soon as possible. Colin is that appropriate person within DPK. You chose not to notify him of your suspicions for several days and at this time you are both liable to prosecution. However, HMRC is minded to defer such action and, possibly, wipe the slate clean should you provide us with some assistance. And this brings me to the second area I wish to cover. Any questions so far?"

Both William and Gill shook their heads.

"Needless to say, there is much that I cannot or do not wish to share with you. But let me expand on what I mean by assistance. The bank that you are auditing and that you suspect may be involved in some illegal activity has been of interest to us for some years. As you will know, it was originally established by a very low profile but immensely wealthy Russian oligarch, namely Sergei Kutzevenia and floated on the Russian stock exchange about five years ago. But he remains a very influential shareholder and, we believe, he exerts a good deal of control over operations and strategy. To put it bluntly, we believe it is possible that he may be using it to launder some of his own money and that of a number of other people, including individuals subject to UK taxation. To be even more blunt, we want you to ensure that no stone gets unturned during your audit and that you keep your eyes and ears as open as possible. We shall of course be talking to Freddie Findlay as well, given he is now running the audit and I have no reason to believe that he will not be unwilling to help. In fact; precisely the opposite. So what do you both think about this?"

"Sounds like blackmail to me," said William quite nonchalantly. "But we would be lifting the drains up on anti-money laundering in any audit. The thing is that we can't do anything too pro-active; there's a team to consider and they would catch on pretty quickly."

Malcolm raised his bushy eyebrows and stared at them both. "Oh really?"

"Yes," said Gill. "We can't go back again and dig deeper; they would want to know why. And I would not be able to do it personally as that would raise a red flag as well. However, if Freddie is on board we might be able to work something out. Obviously, if he isn't on board I won't be able to do anything."

"Don't worry about that. He will be on board."

"I think Gill and I need to have a chat about this and get back to you on Monday," said William.

"No need for you to call me, just let Colin know," replied Croft. "He is the single point of contact. We can't be doing with every Tom, Dick or Harry calling us any time they feel like it."

"Don't you mean every Tom, Dick or Harriet? Or is

sexism permissible in HMRC?" asked Gill without a smile. Her initial impression had been proven right.

"One other thing before I go," continued the man from HMRC. "If either of you are not willing or able to perform the small service requested by us, then I would strongly recommend that you consult solicitors. And I would suggest that you pass this recommendation on to any colleagues that were aware of your suspicions but also chose not to immediately inform HMRC. Thank you for your time. Colin?" Colin rose, having said nothing since the introductions and left the room.

"What a pompous arse!" Gill stood up as soon as the door closed. "Who the fuck does he think he is? Schoolmaster, nanny, secret agent? 'We can't be doing with every Tom, Dick or fucking Harry?' What is that all about?"

"You know what that is all about?" replied William. "They have us by the short and curlies. At least for the time being. We could easily find ourselves completely fucked. Probably through a fine; we are definitely in the wind. And they also have something on Freddie. No surprise there. But you know what makes it even more complicated? We now have two clients. The Fed in the US and HMRC here. Do we join them up? Do we try and play them off? More important, why are they not joined up? Anyway, Stan's in the garage downstairs and we have to get to the US embassy in Nine Elms and pick up Freddie on the way, then meet this John Britney bloke by five-thirty.

Should work out OK"

CHAPTER 42

"When Gill entered the garage her jaw dropped. It was full of Bentleys, Porsches, Ferraris and all manner of supercars.

"Just as well this lot is hidden away in the basement," said William. "If clients could see this they might not be so quick to sign off engagement letters! Only partners are entitled to park here and there is a long waiting list for a space; which, incidentally, costs two-thousand pounds a month. But there is some sort of scheme which means it's tax deductible."

Stan was just outside the garage and they set off for Nine Elms. William sat back in his seat thinking about the meeting.

Gill interrupted his thoughts. "Let me repeat myself. We now have two clients, plus an actual client with Freddie in charge of the audit, a threat of criminal prosecution, a potential murder not a suicide, and a missing grad. What else could possibly go wrong?"

William's phone rang. It was Colin.

"Hi William. Bad news I'm afraid. When I went downstairs with Malcolm he told me that the police had entered Felicity's house. No sign of her. And more worrying, her handbag, phone, purse, credit cards and everything that one would take when going away were all present. In other words, they think it likely that she has been abducted as a result of the passports. They are now going through a great deal of CCTV and will keep me informed. I thought you should know as soon as possible. I don't think there is anything we can do at this end. Perhaps you could think about what, if anything, we could say to her colleagues."

"Thanks Colin," was all William could say before closing the call and telling Gill what he had been told.

"Oh my God! Poor Felicity. Why would anyone…? Of course, it's obvious. It must be the passports. What a fucking nightmare. What are we going to do? Mark, Felicity, who's next on the list? Kathy? Me? You? Do we need protection?"

"God knows but somehow I doubt it. All we have is hearsay evidence which is worth sweet FA in court. But I will call Colin in the morning and see what he thinks."

"Should we tell John Britney?" asked Gill.

"Let's see what Freddie thinks, we are almost there."

Freddie was sitting outside The Black Dog pub near Vauxhall tube with a pint in his hand. He put it down and got into the front seat next to Stan.

"Bad news, Freddie," said William. "Looks like the grad – Felicity – has been abducted. The police have been into her house and all her stuff is intact. It can't be a coincidence, it has to be connected to the passports."

"Christ! I told you that these sorts of people don't play around. Now you know that I wasn't exaggerating. First Mark, now her. We need to be bloody careful if we are going to get involved."

William nodded his head. "I'll tell you more after the meeting but getting involved is probably a necessity for Gill and me. The alternative is a prosecution from HMRC. I think we are nearly at the embassy, do you think we should tell this guy John Britney whoever he is?"

"Don't see why not. At least we can give him something to think about."

Stan parked as close to the embassy as possible, which was about half a mile away. The landscaping was attractive but designed to ensure no vehicle could get close and maybe cause damage. The place was a fortress, albeit a very modern one.

As for the building, Freddie was quick off the mark. "What the fuck? What a monstrosity. What's that stuff all over the walls? Oh, I get it, it's security maybe to prevent high tech eavesdropping or a sniper. God, you couldn't make it up. Where the hell is the entrance?"

CHAPTER 43

As Gill, William and Freddie approached the embassy, they encountered an armed US marine standing by a path leading to what looked like some sort of moat. "Can I help you folks?"

"Yes indeed," replied William. "We have an appointment with Mr John Britney at five-thirty. Our names are West, Findlay and Littleton."

The marine reached into his pack, opened up an iPad and pressed a few buttons. To William's amazement he saw a photo of each of them. The marine put the iPad away, gave a broad smile and said, "Please follow me."

They passed straight through a security check, completely bypassing a huge queue of people, and into the largest reception any of them had ever seen. It had glass stairs leading to an indoor garden. They looked in amazement as they were led to another desk. "Guests for Mr Britney," said the marine. "Have a great day folks." He marched off.

They stood to have their photos taken, passes were handed over and they were told to go over to the lift and up to floor eight. When the door opened, they were confronted by a small black man in a wheelchair.

"Welcome to the United States of America! You are now on foreign soil, or should I say carpet. I'm John and I know who you guys are. Follow me."

He pressed a button on his chair, wheeled round, and sped off down the corridor. William found himself almost running to keep up but then relaxed. All three of them strolled towards the door where the man was already waiting.

The room contained a table big enough for more than a dozen people with views across the Thames. The three of them sat near John, who had positioned himself at one end with his back to the river.

"Help yourselves to water or coffee. I know it's teatime and you Brits like tea but as mentioned, you are on US soil," he grinned. "Thanks for coming. My colleague Peter Payne sends his regards to you, William, and we are both grateful that you are willing to provide us with some help. Clearly this is all confidential but you should know that some very senior people in our administration will be made aware of your contribution, and there will be reciprocation to DPK, whatever the outcome. We will have a special relationship."

William smiled to himself and thought, 'Well he would say that wouldn't he!'

"Gill and Freddie, can I assume that William has explained where we are at and what we want to achieve? Anyway, let me recap: we are in no doubt that the Kutzevenia Bank is engaged in industrial-strength money laundering in Russia, Europe and the US. We are pretty sure they are busy in much of South America and Mexico as well. But we have no proof. Our objective is to get some proof wherever it can be found and we think that the UK branch might be where we can find it. Clearly, we are exploring many other avenues and Wendell has been kind enough to suggest some other senior DPK colleagues in other jurisdictions. As William probably told you, we are not involving your global client service partner as there is a possibility that he may be part of the problem.

"My focus is on the UK and this is where I can use your help. All I ask is that you look for clues. Anything, anything at all that might be suspicious let me know. If you can follow up that would be great. But I'm not asking you to take any risks, not just for your personal safety but because we don't want these crooks to know for sure that we are onto them. Is that clear?"

"Yes, it is," said William. "But we do have a question. Are you working with HMRC? If not, why not?"

"We aren't because we are not sure we can trust them. The amount of money involved is stratospheric. A bribe to a civil servant of ten-million pounds would be insignificant to these people. By the way, where are you with HMRC?"

William frowned. "Our risk management partner has informed them, albeit quite late in the process. They have asked the three of us to help. We are considering our options. They have some leverage because Gill and I broke the rules by not informing them of our suspicions immediately and that's a criminal offence in the UK."

"Thanks for telling me that. Could you let me know swiftly what you decide please? And I now have a question for you. What news of the girl that saw the passports?"

"The police and HMRC think she has been abducted," said Gill quietly. "They have been into her house and nothing is missing. Her phone is there, her credit cards, her handbag, jewellery; it's all there. We think it has to be connected to the passports. What's more, your colleague may have told you that the partner running the audit, Mark Lawson, committed suicide. Well, the police are now treating his death as suspicious. It's all very worrying."

"I have to tell you that I'm saddened but not shocked. Freddie, I know a little about your military history and I imagine you have dealt with some pretty terrible people."

Freddie frowned. "Yes I have but let's not go there at the moment. What I can say is that in my experience ninety-nine-point-nine per cent of the civilised population treat human life as extraordinarily precious but point one per cent would be willing to terminate it without a second thought – provided the price was right. And you would be surprised how low that price might be. I've already touched on this with William and Gill and let me state my position. I'm happy to help if it saves these guys from being prosecuted by HMRC. But we need to be realistic. The chance of us getting evidence without red flags being raised are not great. And I'm not going to put myself at risk or indeed do something that might put others at risk. We owe you nothing."

"That's fair, Freddie. All I ask is that if you do find something suspicious, you let us know. Is that OK with you and you?" he said, looking each in the eye. They nodded.

The same marine that welcomed them was outside the door. He walked them down to the lift, then on to where he had met them and wished them a wonderful weekend. It was after seven.

"What's the plan guys?" asked Gill as Stan started the car. "Don't know about you but I have nothing on this evening, I'm hungry, thirsty and frightened."

"How about one drink and a serious talk followed by several drinks and something to eat?" suggested William.

"Sounds good to me. Weather looks OK. How about my deck followed by dinner somewhere?" asked Freddie. "Maybe High Road Brasserie? I have a friend who can usually fix me a nice table."

"Done and I can't wait to meet your friend, Freddie. My guess is that she is young, fit and has bad taste in men."

"Gill, that's harsh. But probably fair!"

CHAPTER 44

William didn't go for a run on Saturday morning. It had been a very late night. First the serious stuff over two bottles rather than one drink each. Then High Road Brasserie until it closed. Gill had the good sense to head home at that stage but Freddie came back to William's for a night cap which lasted until the sky started to lighten and the birds started singing. All in all, a good night's work and the serious stuff had been settled swiftly.

William had kicked off. "Seems to me that refusing to cooperate fully with the Fed and HMRC would be a problem. DPK would be considered unhelpful by the Fed. But more important Gill and I could be prosecuted and probably convicted. My suggestion is that we tell them and HMRC we are prepared to keep our eyes open but will not expose ourselves to any risk whatsoever."

Freddie and Gill both agreed and Freddie raised the next issue. "OK, we are all in. But one question remains: do we prioritise HMRC or the Fed or do we tell each of them what, if anything, we discover? I am reminded of what a boss told me back in the day. He said, 'Freddie, if you have to referee a fight between two gorillas, the first thing you need to do is to choose your gorilla!' I choose the Fed. They are the bigger gorilla by far. But I am happy to be outvoted. I don't like seeing you guys threatened by HMRC; they know they are placing you in harm's way. That's not how British civil servants are supposed to operate. It's simply not on."

"I prefer the Fed as well," said Gill. "That chap from HMRC sent shivers up my spine."

"Agreed," replied William. "But what about Felicity? The audit team will be wondering where she has gone. Gill, I know you won't like this but I think we need to tell them that she has been dismissed for gross misconduct."

Gill looked crestfallen. "No! We can't do that."

William looked at Freddie who nodded. "Yes we can, Gill. And I think Freddie needs to announce this as soon as possible."

At lunchtime, William was sitting in his usual booth at Balthazar, enjoying a glass of Sancerre but feeling quite nervous. It was a long time since he had been immediately attracted to someone and he wanted to make the right impression. Then Ina arrived, and she looked stunning. She was taller than he remembered and more athletic looking. Her red hair contrasted with a green blouse tucked into jeans and she wore faded Converse sneakers. He went over to greet her as she was ushered across. William brushed her cheek with a kiss and they sat down.

"What are you drinking?" she asked.

"Sancerre. How about you? What would you like?"

William realised that he sounded as nervous as he felt.

"The same please."

Ina looked around. "Yes, this place is just like the one in New York. Maybe a bit bigger."

The manager came across to say hi to William.

Ina smiled. "You seem very well known here, William."

"I guess so, I tend to come to a few places I like rather than always trying places that are new. Boring, I suppose. But I do try out new places that are owned by people I know, mainly because I get invited to the free soft launches! Seriously, I eat out a good deal and I like places like this which are full of fun and energy but where I can get a table where I can talk without shouting or being overheard. Booths like this one are perfect."

William felt a little guilty saying this as the main reason for choosing particular tables was that he was becoming a little deaf and he was too vain to consider a hearing aid.

"So, how's the new job?" he asked.

"It's a bit strange. New city, new employer. Travelling to Canary Wharf every day. The tube is packed even when I'm leaving work at seven o'clock. Some days you can't even get down to the Jubilee line platform. It's very different from Edinburgh. I'm not sure I like it so far. Not sure I will ever like it."

"Yeah, I know just how you feel," replied William. "I try and avoid travelling during the busy times. Have you inherited a decent team?"

"Too soon to know. I've got five direct reports. Two of them are Russian and seconded from head office. It's a bit disconcerting as they often speak to each other in Russian and I have no idea what they are saying. Also, I arrived in the middle of the audit and the work load is immense."

"Ah yes, I gather you have met Freddie Findlay."

"Freddie! How come you know him?"

"I'll tell you in a minute. Let's order first."

With orders taken, and a bottle of the Sancerre on the way, Ina asked again. "So, Freddie is a charming man. How do you know him?"

"Well I was a partner at DPK some years ago working on advisory projects, not audit. But I bumped into Freddie a few times and as we live quite close to each other in Chiswick and are both single, we often share a few drinks and put the world to rights. I saw him a few days ago and he mentioned the Kutzevenia audit and that he had met you. He was very impressed."

"He gave me the impression he was what my mother called a 'ladies' man'," said Ina.

"Well, I couldn't possibly say," replied William with a smile that he hoped, confirmed the impression.

The food came and went and, just like their first meeting at the marina in Chiswick, there wasn't a dull moment. William suggested a couple of glasses of Pinot Noir and they soon noticed people arriving to eat plates of sandwiches with cups of tea or glasses of champagne. The manager came over again to say he was leaving and asked if they would like another glass of Pinot Noir on the house.

"We would be fools not to," said Ina, standing up before William to shake the man's hand.

When they finished the wine, Ina said she had to leave and William got the bill.

"Next time will be on me," she said.

William's heart leapt. "Will there be a next time?" he asked.

"I very much hope so. I'll call you. Or maybe you will call me," she smiled. When they left Balthazar, William kissed Ina on both cheeks before he set off to Waterloo Station and she set off for the tube. As he walked over the bridge, the Kinks' 'Waterloo Sunset' song came to mind. He pictured Ina under the Waterloo station clock. Romantic; could this be the start of something special? Was it too late in his life to start a new relationship? How old was Ina anyway? He did his sums. She said she qualified as an accountant in 1993 when she was probably about twenty-five. That would make her around fifty. Yes, perhaps this could be the start of something special.

CHAPTER 45

It was Sunday morning and Freddie and Lesley were fast asleep in his bed when his mobile phone pinged with a text message. He got up.

"Leave it Freddie. What can be so important at this time in the morning?" said Lesley.

"It's midday," he replied, looking at his phone. "And I now have to be somewhere this afternoon. What are you doing today?"

"Well, I was thinking about giving you the best blow job you have ever had but I guess you don't have time now."

"Wrong!" he replied, jumping back into bed.

At three o'clock, Freddie got on his bike, cycled down to Kew Bridge, crossed over and set off along the towpath heading for Richmond, then on to Teddington Lock where he crossed back over and waited on the other side.

At four-thirty a motorcycle arrived and a tall, black, leather-clad figure walked up to him, pulled off her crash helmet and gave him a full on-kiss. "I've got the goods for you, Freddie. Both data sticks are fixed. The new password is Fragrant with a capital F. I thought you might find that easy to remember. One of them is completely blank. It hasn't been wiped; it's never been used but you may as well have it back. The other contains an Excel spreadsheet which I glanced at. I hope it makes more sense to you than it did to me."

Freddie took the sticks wondering what on earth he would be able to make of them if the genius in front of them couldn't understand.

"Babe, you are so kind. I owe you. And I will repay you. I know how difficult it is for you at Government Communications Headquarters and I understand why you have to be careful. But I'm now gainfully employed again so how about Venice for a dirty weekend sometime soon?"

"Name the date Freddie, arrange a business class return ticket and I'll be there. Gritti Palace I hope."

She put on her helmet, started the motorcycle and roared off. Freddie pushed his bike back over the river and cycled home in a more stately fashion. Then he called William and Gill. They agreed to meet up at six-thirty.

The three of them went over to William's office and sat at his table. He stuck one of the data sticks into his iMac and Freddie gave him the password 'Fragrant'. William looked at him with a raised eyebrow before entering it. There was nothing at all on it. He ejected it, put in the other one, entered the password and there was an unprotected file on it called Marvin Gay. William opened it and they all leant forward. It was a complicated spreadsheet and he enlarged it to fill the whole twenty-seven-inch screen on his desk.

They stood up and stared at the document. There was a list of about two hundred names. All of them looked Russian. The next column contained postcodes, most of which seemed to be in the London area. These were followed by a column with five-digit reference numbers and then three columns with more Russian names, with the same names appearing many times. About thirty names in total. Then there was a column that looked like a list of abbreviations of countries such as SWIX for Switzerland and LICH for Lichtenstein. Others such as such as JVD and AGA made no sense to them at all. Finally, there was another column with more reference numbers, this time with eight digits.

The spreadsheet was of very poor quality and William's initial reaction was that it had been put together very rapidly. The others agreed.

"This does not look like a spreadsheet created by the bank. It looks like something cut and pasted and cobbled together from a number of sources to make some sort of record. Look, you can see different fonts," said Gill. "The obvious interpretation is that Mark put this together and it's connected with the money laundering that is almost certainly going on in the bank."

"I agree," said Freddie.

"So, what do we do with this?" asked William.

"I suggest that we pass this straight to Colin and he

gives it to HMRC. Job done. Trebles all round!" replied Freddie.

"OK, but do we tell anyone we have looked at it?" asked Gill.

"I don't think so," said William. "I know it's very unlikely that anybody at Kutzevenia would get to hear about it but why take the risk. Why don't we say we have just found the sticks in the bag from Mark's locker? And we can change the password to something more sensible so HMRC can have fun getting to it."

"I can speak to Sparks first thing tomorrow and ask him to send the laptop straight to Colin when it has been opened up," said Freddie. "So our hands will be clean. But I think there are two more questions: first, do we give the spreadsheet to the Fed? Remember they are our gorilla. Second, do we keep a copy?"

"Christ! Why would we want to keep a copy? It's incendiary!" Gill retorted.

"You never know when you might need some leverage, Gill. I'm not saying we ever will. But it's always sensible to have a card in one's hand. For example, maybe that odious bloke from HMRC reneges on the deal and you guys find yourselves facing court. Having that spreadsheet up your sleeves could be useful evidence. And, back in the day, I was told more than once not to destroy evidence."

"I think we should give John Britney at the Fed a copy of the file and let Wendell know we have done so," said William. "OK, it's just my opinion but I can't see any downside. It puts the firm in the Fed's good books and it won't do any of us any harm. In fact, precisely the opposite. But let's be completely clear. We do not tell Colin or the Fed that we have a copy and we do not tell Colin we have sent a copy to the Fed. If we work this right we might just get a result. HMRC are happy, the firm is happy, the Fed is happy and last, and probably least, we may have made a small but positive impact on society. But small is probably an understatement."

Freddie went home and sent off an email to Sparks asking him to deliver Mark's PC to Colin as soon as it was unlocked and all the folders opened up. William sent an email to Colin asking for a meeting as soon as possible and Gill went off home in an Uber and breathed a huge sigh of relief. It was over. At least for the time being.

CHAPTER 46

Stan was outside at nine o'clock the next morning and they arrived at the Hilton, Park Lane shortly after ten. William's presentation was at eleven o'clock and he quietly entered the room to watch the presentation leading up to the coffee break scheduled for ten-thirty. It wasn't a hard act to follow. When the room emptied for the break, he introduced himself to the AV team, ran through his slides and did the sound test. He had been giving similar presentations for the past thirty-five years but still found himself nervous. But he liked the sensation as adrenalin moved through his system. The talk went well. He finished exactly on time, as did the question and answer session and he sat down to listen to the last speaker who was a good example of how to deliver a bad presentation. He had no passion, too many slides – most of which Willian couldn't read – no real insight, a boring voice, a boring delivery, platitudes and to put the icing on the cake, the guy over-ran by five minutes. William spent most of the time thinking about the meeting he had arranged with Colin for three-thirty.

They met in a small office and William felt uncomfortably

close to Colin as he explained that he had discovered the data sticks in the bag containing Mark's odds and ends. He handed them over to Colin.

"Who else knows about the data sticks, William?"

"Just Freddie and Gill. And we haven't tried to open them."

"Let's be completely clear on this, William," said Colin in his usual patronising voice. "You have told me, and I should tell HMRC, that the only people who are aware of these sticks are you, Freddie and Gill and that none of you have attempted to open them?"

"That's correct. And I hope HMRC will agree that we have provided sufficient assistance that they can wipe the slate clean as far as our tardy notification of the money-laundering suspicions are concerned."

"I'll do my best to ensure this is the case William, and respond to you on this point in due course."

Stan was waiting for William down in the garage and they were back in Chiswick Mall by four o'clock. No sooner had William made himself a cup of coffee, he received an invite to a conference call at five. The host was Colin. The invitees were himself and Malcolm Croft from HMRC. He dialed-in at the appointed time and, as usual with such calls, found himself listening to music for about five minutes until the others came online.

"Good afternoon, William," said Malcolm Croft. "Thank you for finding and passing us the two data sticks.

I just have a couple of questions. First, why did you take so long to find them? Second, are you sure no one tried to access them?"

"Our focus was on getting the PC. The bag seemed to be just full of the usual stuff we accumulate over time. I'm not a detective, I'm an accountant. Anyway, what's the big deal?"

"Need to know, William, need to know."

"OK, as far as your second question is concerned, I can confirm that as far as I know neither Gill nor Freddie accessed the sticks and I can tell you with certainty that I didn't. I've already told Colin that this was the case. So why are you still on my case?"

"Thanks for your time, William." And the line went dead. William had lived his life with honesty as a first principle. But on this occasion, he had no doubts that he had played his cards correctly.

CHAPTER 47

First thing on Tuesday, William went over to his office and sent a copy of the Marvin Gay file to Wendell, explaining the background and the fact that HMRC also had a copy. Then he saved the file to his iMac and another data stick. He sat back wondering about the file. What could it mean?

From the annual compulsory DPK anti-money-laundering sessions William knew that there were two types of false passports. Forgeries and real blank passports. Neither would get through passport control as the forgeries were never good enough and the numbers of any stolen blanks would ping when put into the system. But both would be good enough to meet the anti-money-laundering requirements as proof of identity when making an investment or depositing more than ten-thousand pounds cash in a bank.

The Kutzevenia issue was no longer his problem but he had become curious anyway. And it was his nature to spend time looking into anything that was of interest to him. He spent most of the morning looking at the DPK confidential 'Fighting Financial Crime' case studies on the firm's secure intranet. Most of it involved really complicated structures. By lunchtime, he started to understand the basics of how large-scale money laundering actually operated. He had a short break for something to eat and a glass of wine. Then he got back to it.

He soon found a case that seemed relevant. In 1994, a very wealthy Russian national (referred to as 'KM') founded a bank (referred to as 'AL') in Russia. Following the financial crisis in 2008, the bank suffered significant losses and was ultimately declared insolvent. The Russian state agency, the Deposit Insurance Agency (DIA), was appointed as liquidator.

Between 2011 and 2015, KM settled over nine billion dollars of his assets in a dozen discretionary trusts based in New Zealand. A New Zealand solicitor and his wife were the directors of the companies that acted as trustees. The trust assets were held largely for the benefit of KM, his partner and a number of other individuals. Between 2013 and 2016 the assets were invested in a number of companies based in the British Virgin Islands, namely Tortola, Virgin Gorda, Jost van Dyke and Cooper Island. These companies in turn invested in a wide range of high-risk, high-reward ventures including oil and gas exploration, property development and most recently bitcoin trading. The result was that the value of the original settlement increased from nine billion dollars to over one hundred billion dollars in a tax-free and under-regulated environment.

William read this and smiled. He had enjoyed two wonderful holidays in the British Virgin Islands even though the trip involved flying to Antigua, transferring to a light aircraft to fly to Tortola and then setting off to explore the islands. Once in a yacht, the other time in a very large catamaran. Both times they had visited the islands mentioned and, apart from Tortola, he couldn't recall an ATM let alone a bank. On some of the islands there wasn't even a jetty and you needed to drive your dinghy up the beach and pull it in with you as you waded ashore. The 'Soggy Dollar Bar' on Jost Van Dyke was well named. And he remembered another island when someone hosting a big table took out a credit card and the owner looked at him as if he had pulled a gun. Hold on, thought William. Jost Van Dyke. JVD on the spreadsheet. No. Must be something else. Can't be that obvious. Or maybe it can. Maybe the passports are intended to create false identities; could the list of names be for people that don't exist anywhere other than on paper – virtual clients not real clients?

William had a quick look at the DPK BVI statistics. The total population of the Islands was about thirty-thousand people. The number of registered companies about twelve-thousand. And in terms of investment into UK properties, these companies owned twenty-three-thousand properties in England and Wales; about half of which were located in London with around twelve-thousand in Westminster and six-thousand in Kensington and Chelsea. And in Green Street, London W1, fifteen of the highly desirable properties were owned by offshore companies. Then he found another document relating to an island in the Caribbean called Nevis. It was described as the most secretive island on the planet with eleven-thousand residents and seventy-thousand limited companies.

Around five o clock William received an email from Colin, copied in to Freddie, Gill, George and Daniel. 'I have just finished an update meeting with Malcolm Croft from HMRC and an officer from the National Crime Agency. I am advised that there is no helpful CCTV coverage in relation to the disappearance of our colleague. I will keep you informed.'

CHAPTER 48

Gill went to the gym first thing Tuesday, did some running on the treadmill, some weights and some thinking. She was in the Mount Street project room by 8.30 am and the wealth management team meeting kicked off on time.

Gill looked at her team. She hated lying. Even worse, she feared that she would never see Felicity again. But she put on her brave face and started. "Thanks to you all for rocking up on time. I know you were working until late last night. The good news is that we are on the last leg and we should be back at Canary Wharf next Monday to integrate our reports with the primary bank reports. But I do have some bad news. For reasons which I am not able to share I have to tell you all that the reason Felicity has not been around for the last couple of weeks is not, as I told you previously, that she is unwell. The truth is that she has been suspended as we have been looking into an issue relating to her original application to the firm and, sadly, as a result of some irregularities, we have had to suspend her employment."

Felicity was a very popular girl and the chatter started immediately. Gill let it run for a while and then decided it was time to move on. "I know how you feel and I'm as disappointed as you are. But we have to put this behind us and agree the work-plan for the next couple of days. Kathy, could you get this organised please and come and see me as soon as possible?"

When Kathy turned up they went to the little kitchen and Gill made sure no one was in earshot. "I will tell you more about this in due course. It's complicated. Bear with me, try and keep the team focused and we will talk again soon – I promise."

Gill spent the rest of the day reviewing the audit workbooks and reports and headed off home. Just before she got on the tube she got a text from Jane: 'Sorry, should have finished my shift hours ago but still on the go. Can we make it eight o'clock at the pub? I'll come straight from the shop. Looking forward to a shower later… XXX.'

She texted back. 'Looking forward to it already!'

She put on a silk t-shirt and jeans and got a cab to The Eagle. Jane was already there sitting at a table in the garden looking very butch. Hair gelled back, chains around her neck, black fingernails, thick jeans, Doc Martins, and a leather jacket over the back of her chair. Gill gasped. What the hell was this? Where was the smart, sexy girl she thought she knew?

Jane caught sight of her expression, stood up, grinned and kissed her firmly on the lips. "Sorry about this get up. I'm not releasing my inner butch, promise! I've been doing some slightly undercover stuff for the last couple of days and need to look the part. Let me get you a drink. I could do with another. It's been a long day."

When Jane got back to the table she explained more. "Actually. it's not really undercover. It's just that I have been tasked with investigating some dealers who are focusing on the LBGT community around Westbourne Park and I needed to look the part. Needless to say, LBGT is not the terminology you hear in the station. The blokes have their own language."

"How do you feel about that?" asked Gill, seeing a side of Jane she hadn't seen before and rather liked.

"I don't like it. But actually, there is no malice in it. Anyway, how has your day been? And shall we eat here?"

At eleven-thirty they stumbled back through the bar and out into Askew Road. Holding hands and leaning against each other. Laughing together and looking forward to showering together. Jane was on a three-thirty call the following afternoon, Gill had no meetings in the morning. The night was warm and about to get hotter. Heavy rap music and powerful base 'Raspberry Shit' by Pharrell Williams invaded the quiet as a car drove slowly up the street. The music stopped and the car drew up alongside them, mounted the kerb and stopped. The back near-side door opened immediately and the driver's side door started to open as well.

"What the fuck!" Gill wondered what on earth was going on. She just stared at the car. But Jane moved fast. She took two steps towards the rear door and as the man was getting out she slammed the door in his face. He fell back. She opened the door and slammed it again. He screamed. She moved to the driver's door just as the man stood up and turned towards her. She kicked out and under his crotch exactly as she had been taught. "Kick through not at." He almost doubled up with the pain. His head was close enough; she kneed him in the face and turned back to the first man who was struggling to get out of the car.

Gill didn't know what to do. She was frozen and petrified as Jane reached inside the car and pulled the guy out by his head. Then he was on his knees, but he wasn't finished, he was searching for something in his jacket. Jane stood motionless for a second, stepped back, put her weight on her left foot, inhaled and then exhaled as her right foot kicked forward as hard as possible and her Doc Martin shoe hit the man in the throat. His head went back and bounced against the car door and he fell to the pavement. The driver managed to get back into the car and closed the door. Jane made no attempt to open it. She looked completely used up and simply watched as he started the car and sped off. The incident had taken about three minutes and she was on her arse on the pavement. Over and done.

"He's getting away!" shouted Gill "And so is he!" she said, gesticulating at the other man hobbling and then running along the pavement towards the Goldhawk Road.

"I'm not fucking chasing them," replied Jane. "I think we got off lucky there. But what was it all about? They weren't muggers, that's for sure! They could have seen us as easy prey to be raped but that doesn't feel right to me either. Did you get a good look at either of them?"

"No. I was so scared. I thought they were going to rape me."

"I didn't get a good look either and I have no idea about the number or even the make of car. I'm wondering if I should call it in. If I do we will be down at the station all night looking at photos. I think we should leave it for now and I'll report it tomorrow. I still don't know what it was they were after."

Gill had a good idea but decided, for the time being, not to make things more complicated than they already were.

CHAPTER 49

William, Gill and Freddie met for a catch-up in More London on Thursday. It had to be quite late in the evening as the other two were going full speed on the audit.

Gill had booked a room with a great view of the Tower of London and Tower Bridge. William never tired of it. What's more, she had booked a room that had discrete patterns on the windows facing inwards so that colleagues or clients passing couldn't see who was dining there. She had also ordered excellent wine and William pressed the button to alert staff that service was required.

He was on his second glass when Freddie and Gill arrived at around nine o'clock. Before they could say a word, William said, "No apologies. I understand absolutely. Clients come first. Let's get your whistles wetted and sit down and relax for a while."

"I didn't mention this to you earlier because I wanted to get my head straight before telling you about what happened on Tuesday evening," Gill said. "I was having a drink and something to eat with Jane, the police woman that handled the identification when William and I went along to the mortuary. Anyway, when the pub closed we decided to go back to her place for a coffee and we were attacked."

"You were what?" exclaimed William.

"Well, yes, that's the best way I can describe it. A car drew up, crossed the kerb and two guys got out. At least they would have got out had Jane not charged them down. She slammed the door in the face of the first guy and then did the same to the driver. She was kicking them in the balls, kicking them in the neck, kneeing them in the jaw. She was like a dervish, she beat the hell out of them. One ran away; the other managed to get back in the car and drove off. It was all over in a few minutes."

"Did you call the police?" asked Freddie.

"Actually no. Neither of us got a good look at either of the guys. Big blokes is all I could say. Jane said that she should call it in but all that would happen is that we would spend the rest of the night looking at photos. Neither of us caught the number plate. She said she would go down to the station on Wednesday and report it. But you know what? Thinking about it, neither of us really thought it was a mugging or attempted rape. But if not, what?"

"I guess we all know what you're thinking, Gill. And my guess is that you are right," replied William. "Sounds to me like another abduction but this time unsuccessful. It has to be connected with the fucking passports. But the key thing is that you are safe and sound."

"I didn't move. Jane charged them down. I was petrified; I thought I was going to be raped. I did nothing."

"Gill, don't beat yourself up," said Freddie. "Jane is a

cop, trained to deal with bad guys. You are an accountant. When stuff starts going off, the best thing you can do is to stay still, or in my experience get on the ground and make yourself as small as possible and then stay still. The good news is that you and this Jane person are both intact."

"Gill, are you OK to stay and talk about all of this stuff or would you rather bail out for the time being?"

"Thanks William, I'd rather stay."

"OK, let's talk about where we are. We have reason to think that some people in Kutzevenia Bank are involved in money laundering and looking at the spreadsheet that poor old Mark put together I think I have some idea how they're going about it. I think they are creating false identities, false clients if you like. And they are setting up trusts in places with little or no real anti-money laundering processes, maybe even easily corrupted regulators and somehow washing the money and sending it back into circulation.

"But here's the thing. I think we all understand that this might be high stakes and systemic or just a couple of entrepreneurs. Whatever. Mark, Felicity and now this attack on Gill. This is serious. None of us are responsible for trying to stop this. We have done our bit. So the first question is, can we just keep our heads down and wait for the Fed or HMRC or whoever to close this thing down? After all, they both have the data key, which seems like it might be helpful."

"My vote is to do precisely that," said Freddie

emphatically. "And we should do so immediately. As I've mentioned before, industrial-scale money laundering only exists to clean really dirty money and that money is always made from crime. Serious crime. People like us are insignificant. We are no more important to them than the insects they get someone to wipe off their windscreen. And I'm not making this up. I've encountered these sorts of people in the past and I don't want to encounter them again. We have done what we said we would do for the firm. We have done what we said we would do for HMRC. And as far as the bank is concerned the audit report is pretty straightforward."

"Gill, what do you think?" asked William. "I agree with Freddie absolutely. I've never been so scared in my life as I was the other night. I have had enough of this."

"OK. Done. I will drop a note to all parties explaining that as far as we are concerned it is job done. Guess we better get out of here. It's past eleven. Can I give both you guys a lift home?" They took the lift down to the ground floor and walked across the huge foyer where Freddie had a quick chat with one of the twenty-four-hour reception team. Needless to say, it was a tall slim blonde lady. Five minutes later they were in the car heading west.

"What do you think about that attack on Tuesday night?" said Freddie, after Gill had been dropped off at her flat. "Do you think Gill may be overreacting? Could it be connected to the bank thing?"

"My guess is that it is. If the cop was not as quick off

the mark, God knows what might have happened. I hate to say this, but I think she may have ended up wherever Felicity is. Probably in the ground. I'll tell you what though, Freddie, I've copied that spreadsheet to a data stick and I'm going to put it somewhere very safe. And if push comes to me being shoved off this mortal coil, that spreadsheet will end up shafting these people – whoever the fuck they are. Stan, please drop me off at home and take old Freddie on to his house. Take care, mate. By the way, feel like killing some clays on Sunday morning then lunch somewhere?"

"Done. Goodnight, old chap."

CHAPTER 50

William cycled up to the library in Devonshire Road the next morning and bumped into Sky on Chiswick High Road at around twelve. "How about a quick drink?" he asked and within a few minutes they were in the George IV. William ordered three shots of Sipsmith vodka on the rocks just to be loyal to the local distillery. Sky went for a large Sipsmith G&T.

"Could you look after something for me?" said William, after the usual gossip. "It's a data stick which has some very confidential stuff on it. So confidential that I think someone might try to steal it from me so I'm worried about leaving it at home."

"Sure, no problem. I'm off to Oxford later on to see my wretched children and my delightful grandchildren and will be back on Sunday afternoon. Bring it round and I'll stick in my knicker drawer. Only joking; I actually have a very safe, safe. But it will cost you a drink, so how about another one? And seeing as we're here and I haven't had breakfast I could demolish a burger and chips!"

William got home at four, called Ina and left a message. "Hi, hope all is well. I was wondering if you felt like coming to The Chiltern Firehouse some evening next week, say, Thursday or Friday?" The reason that he had chosen this particular restaurant was not because he really liked it – in fact he didn't like it at all – but it was in Marylebone and Ina had told him she was renting a flat in that area for the time being. It would be convenient for her and, hopefully, she might invite him back for a coffee.

Later on, Stan dropped off Diana at the Pollen Street Social at eight where William was waiting, sitting proudly at the best table. She walked across the room, as usual her skirt just a bit shorter than one would expect, her blouse just a bit tighter. She beamed when the waiter brought a little table for her handbag. The place was buzzing as usual but the service calm and competent.

"Diana, you look absolutely lovely. Have you done something to your hair?" he said.

"Of course I have. Cut and coloured this morning. And I'm still smarting from the price and the need to tip three different people. But I'm worth it, as that annoying American used to say in the commercials. Anyway, business is going very well indeed. And guess what? My firm has been singled out as a model of diversity. I have five male escorts, as well as nine females. All charming and very fit, young and not so young, gay, straight and bi. Black and white and somewhere in the middle. The youngest is twenty-two, the oldest sixty-one and very attractive indeed."

"Tell me more. I love hearing about your business. I ought to invest in it."

"No chance! I now have fourteen client-facing employees, plus Chloe who runs the operation with her two assistants whose names escape me for the moment. Our charge-out rate is variable and ranges from one hundred pounds an hour to maybe two hundred and fifty. I take up to fifty per cent. If any of my staff wish to sell something other than company I take no margin at all and neither approve nor disapprove. Target utilisation for the client-facing staff is twenty hours a week."

William smiled. "You are starting to sound like an accountant."

"Far from it. But someone once said to me 'If you can't measure it you can't manage it.'"

William was an accountant and had been doing the sums. Diana was rightly proud of her business and loved talking about it.

"Say, on average, each client-facing employee is generating about two-thousand pounds a week. If you have fourteen, that's twenty-eight thousand a week and you get fifty per cent? Diana, that's fourteen-thousand pounds a week!"

"Yes William. But I do have overheads."

"Such as?"

"The office, which also doubles as a gossip shop, coffee shop, changing room, showers, whatever. As you know, it's in Old Burlington Street and that doesn't come cheap. What's more, it's open 24/7 because many of my escorts like to get dressed in their working clothes away from their homes. Plus I employ Chloe and the assistants and have research costs."

"Research costs?"

"Of course. Even though new members need to be sponsored by an existing member, we have to research them very carefully before we can allow them access to our website. And that website costs quite a bit, I can tell you."

"Maybe you should think about charging for membership to cover the cost."

"William, for heaven's sake. Do you take me for a fool? Membership is five-thousand pounds a year. And I have about one hundred members, many of whom never use our service. By the way, you are looking a good deal more relaxed than lately. What's new?"

"What's new is I think you should pay the bill this time."

"It would be my pleasure," replied Diana. "But seriously, what is new?"

"I walked into a situation in the firm that really had nothing to do with me. But I got involved and it turns out that we're probably dealing with criminals. Scary stuff. Way out of my experience. And, indeed, my pay grade. Someone died, another person I cared about is missing."

"Cared about? Or care about, William? Present tense or past tense?"

"I'm sorry to say it looks like the latter; but it's now all in the hands of the authorities and the senior guys in the firm and I'm just grateful to be out of it and sitting here with you and the prospect of a free dinner."

"There's no such thing as a free dinner, as you will find out when you take me back to your place!" She stood up and smiled at the two men at the next table who had been listening intently to the conversation.

"Have a nice evening gentlemen, here is my card if you want to get in touch."

They were back in Chiswick Mall by eleven and as Diana sat down on the sofa in the first-floor living room. William adjusted the Lutron, put on his 'night club' playlist and sat down beside her with his feet on the coffee table. "Let me guess what you would like, Diana. First, a large glass of a top-notch Pinot Noir; second, a couple of lines of excellent coke and third you would like to make mad passionate love to me."

"Correct on first and second but wrong on third. I paid for dinner, it's down to you or should I say you down on me and making the mad passionate love."

As always, Diana used the attic guest suite overnight. When she arrived downstairs the next morning, William was up and about. Breakfast was in the back garden. She called a cab at about ten and was off.

"Saturdays are always frenetic. My team come and go, if you see what I mean. And William, last night was pro bono." He waved as the cab drove away but she was already on her phone. He walked back inside, shaking his head. She was making over a million pounds a year. And she made it look easy. Most of the partners in DPK were making less than that and making it look almost impossible.

CHAPTER 51

The weather was dry but cloudy on Sunday. William did his usual run to Putney, picked up the papers and read them over his breakfast, showered, changed, got his guns and cartridges out of the cabinet and set off for Northolt in the MGB. His top was down in spite of the weather and he was ready to do battle with Freddie. And Lizzy as it turned out. They decided to shoot for pheasant with the clays being launched from the high tower. William preferred the higher, slower clays and scored the highest. Lizzy was second and Freddie was a less than well-mannered loser. "I've been practising for grouse. The season starts soon."

As they were walking along the path back to the club house for a drink, Lizzy stopped by a bench to talk to a friend. Freddie looked back and noticed a young couple who had just arrived. As he watched, he saw the girl aiming her shotgun directly at William.

"Down Will, down," he roared, pushing William down and throwing himself on the grass.

"What the fuck!" cried William. "What's happening?"

"A girl over there was pointing her gun at us. I thought we were goners."

Freddie looked up. The couple were staring at them

with amazement. He got to his feet and walked swiftly over. "What on earth do you think you're playing at, pointing your gun at us?"

"I wasn't," she replied. "I was pointing it at the tower."

"Well, we were standing between you and the tower. And you must know that you never, ever point a gun anywhere near anyone. I bet it was the first thing someone told you before they even allowed you to hold a gun. If not, it should have been."

"Well. it wasn't loaded."

"That's not the point. Many people have been killed with 'unloaded' guns. If you are not shooting, you hold the gun broken, like we are holding ours. Then everyone knows it's safe. You scared us to death."

When they got to the club house, Freddie spoke to the manager and pointed the couple out to them so he could have a word with them. "You know William, I could use a stiff drink. What with Mark and Felicity gone, I actually thought she was going to kill us. A twelve bore at fifteen yards could really mess you up. Perhaps I'm getting paranoid. Anyway, I'll have three shots for medicinal purposes. Same for you? Lizzy is driving."

After the drinks and a salad each they decided to meet up later at Freddie's place. William called Sky and she decided to come along.

The evening was hot and cloudy; thunder seemed imminent. They were back on Freddie's deck and by 8 pm were pretty wasted. It seemed to William that it had been months ago that they were last here together. But when he worked it out in his dazed head he realised it was only three weeks since Felicity had seen the blank passports. 'What three weeks' he thought. 'Thank God it's over.' When he passed the data stick unobtrusively to Sky it felt like the final paragraph of a short story.

There was no music, no planes. Not much conversation. Plenty of white wine in the fridge in Freddie's parents' shed. Plenty of red around as well. No wind to disturb the remaining coke on the glass-topped table. Lizzy rolled the occasional joint and passed it around. Sky's hand was on William's thigh, moving upwards. 'There's life in the old dog yet,' he thought, almost saying it out loud by mistake. Freddie and Lizzy were snogging like a couple of teenagers. William felt at peace for the first time since they were last on this deck.

"Those fucking kids," said Sky, taking her hand away from William's crotch and looking at a text on her phone. She turned on her posh voice. 'We were very concerned about you driving after drinking at lunchtime. We worry about you having an accident and also the example you are setting for your grandchildren. Hope you got home OK. PS Please don't use the C word in front of them again. We have mentioned this before. We don't like Trump either but don't feel it necessary to sink to his level. Love you' "Love you. Love me! Jesus Christ."

"Cool down, babe," said Freddie. "Put this between

your lips. And I mean the joint not the part of my anatomy I know you would prefer!"

"FOF," said Sky. "In other words, fuck off Freddie. Just give me the joint!"

CHAPTER 52

Sadie owned an incredible penthouse flat in Docklands with views right across London. Three bedrooms, one of which was converted to a gym, three bathrooms and a massive living room. Her roof terrace included a small plunge pool and she was relaxing in the warm water when one of her phones rang. She could tell it was Peter Carby from the ringtone and she leapt out of the pool to answer it.

"Hi."

"Hi to you. How are you? It's ages since we talked. Is your cottage available over the next few weeks? And are you?" he asked.

"Both."

"Excellent. I have been asked to organise something which is right up your street. Could we meet up this evening around six o'clock at the place where we met last time?"

"I'll be there." said Sadie and went back to the pool.

If the penthouse was huge, sophisticated and calm with wonderful views, Sadie's cottage in the country was the complete opposite; tiny, scruffy, dark and surrounded by bushes and trees. That was why she had bought it. She only visited it when she needed it for business and her ownership was via a limited company that wasn't connected with her in any way. Just as well, given the contents she kept there. Apart from guns and ammunition, the spare room contained all she needed to extract information from any man or woman that a client might deliver: knives, saws, canes, whips, a taser, a cattle prod, a small electricity generator, ropes, plastic ties, a soldering iron, pliers, a blowtorch and a vice.

In the cupboards there were drugs to send the patient to sleep for a while and drugs to send them to sleep forever. There was also a large first-aid kit; the last thing she wanted was the patient dying too soon.

The work was done in the bathroom which was lit very brightly so that the videos would be professional quality. It constantly surprised Sadie how many clients wanted evidence. Her track record was a hundred per cent and she had no doubt it would continue as she was an expert interrogator. What's more, she enjoyed the work; every minute of it. Her favourite clients were a married couple a few years ago. They took a long time to die and she really enjoyed making sure that each of them saw the other in agony. Apparently a copy of the video was sent to the children. Sadie didn't ask why. In fact, she never asked why. And that would be the case when she welcomed her next guest.

CHAPTER 53

William walked into One Lombard Brasserie to meet Lionel. The place was buzzing as usual. Lionel was sitting in a booth with a client and it was clear lunch number one hadn't been a dry affair. There was an ice bucket with some white wine and a decanter of red wine. As William approached, there were guffaws of laughter and much coughing and napkin waving. He couldn't help himself from smiling.

"William, William, lovely to see you. Have you met Hannah?"

"No, I haven't but I have certainly heard your name many times, Hannah. Lovely to meet you."

"Call me Pal. Everyone does, apart from my lovers. And what they call me is a closely guarded secret."

Pal was a living legend in the Lloyds insurance market. She wasn't a small person by any means, and was one of a very small number of powerful women in one of the last bastions of male domination. William was really pleased to meet her. But he was also relieved when she said, "Lovely to meet you, William, but I'm dying for a fag, then I have to get back to the office and I need to be in The Lamb by four, so I'm off." She lifted herself out of her chair with some difficulty, picked up her glass and swallowed the rest of the wine, kissed Lionel on the forehead and walked surprisingly swiftly to the door, acknowledging several people who spoke to her as she passed.

"Would you?" asked Lionel.

"Would I what?"

"Don't be obtuse William. Would you… I don't know what the current phrase is but would you have sex with her?"

"Would I what? Lionel, you rascal. The only reason you asked me that question is that you want to. Or you already have! By the way, why is she called Pal?"

"Her name, William, her name: Hannah Renner, both names are palindromic. Shortened to Pal!"

"The things one learns! Can I get something to drink now? Unlike you, I am hungry and thirsty. Or maybe you are as well."

"Pour yourself a quick glass of this excellent Chassagne-Montrachet William, order some food and I will make you very happy."

William ordered his lunch.

Lionel looked left and right and over his shoulder, as if to check there was no one within listening distance, as was his habit. "William, I have a message from Wendell. He is very pleased with the information you have provided. The Fed is very pleased – at the highest level. We are all good. Wendell will ensure that you and this Gill person are well rewarded. Extra profit share for you, swift partnership for her, and Freddie will have his previous history wiped clean. Colin has confirmed that HMRC and the NCA are deploying significant resources on the death of Mark and the disappearance of the grad – Felicity? – so we can relax. Incidentally, he told me all of the folders and files on Mark's laptop have revealed absolutely sweet FA. I hope that makes you happy. And now, here is a small present from Wendell, the present to seal the deal. Gevrey Chambertin 1er Cru Les Champeaux 2003 Domaine Denis Mortet. Please take a glass. I've tasted it and it's perfect."

It turned out to be an epic lunch, even by Lionel's standards, and the place was full of people eating dinner by the time they left. William fell into a taxi and it was eight o'clock when he got home. He went straight to bed.

CHAPTER 54

Tuesday morning. It was sunny and already very warm. When William returned from his run his gear was soaked and he decided to use the outdoor shower by the side of his office. He punched in his code to unlock the door into the garden. When he finished showering he punched in the code to unlock the office door, grabbed a towel, dried off, put on a robe, walked over to the house, punched in the same code backwards, into the kitchen for breakfast. Something was troubling him. But what was it? Was it darker than usual?

He thought back. It was something when he was drying himself. Something unusual, out of kilter. The light? Yes! Normally when he opened the door there was more light because he usually left the door into his office at the top of the stairs open and it must have been closed this morning. Had he closed it? Was he becoming paranoid like Freddie? Obviously! Tina might have closed it when she cleaned the room yesterday. He might have closed it. That was more than possible. Maybe he went over there after lunch with Lionel; he remembered getting into the cab but not much else. Perhaps it's time to cut back a bit on the drinking? That thought came and went quickly, as did the closed office door.

William had a client meeting that afternoon. When it finished and he switched his phone back on there was a message from Ina. 'I'd love to go to the Chiltern Firehouse. I've walked past it many times. Eight o'clock on Friday would suit me very well indeed.'

Light traffic meant he was at the restaurant fifteen minutes early. As usual, the place was packed but he was shown to a good table. With a Sipsmith vodka ordered, he had a look at the menu. Then Ina arrived, bang on time. She gave William a kiss on both cheeks and then they were seated.

"What an amazing place. That lovely little courtyard. That lovely looking doorman. But they certainly pack people in; I'm glad we are sitting here."

"What would you like to drink?" asked William.

"I'd like a glass of champagne, if that's alright."

"Of course."

When the order was being taken William asked for another vodka.

"So how was your week?" he asked.

"Well, I've been arguing with your pal Freddie for some of it. As you know you guys do a management report which points to things that you believe we should do, and it's some of the content where we're not in agreement. Nothing really critical and it's all well-mannered. Freddie is a good guy to work with and totally professional. I had heard some stories but… no problems at all so far. The only contentious issue is the size of our financial crime team. Freddie contends our staffing is less than fifty per cent of that in equivalent banks. My colleagues do not agree. I think maybe Russian banks take a different approach. But Freddie reminds me that we are authorised in the UK. Anyway, enough of that. How about you?"

"Well I had a fright last weekend when I was with Freddie." William went on to talk about the girl pointing the twelve bore and clay pigeon shooting generally and somehow moving on to his Monday morning DPK new joiner presentations. The food and the wine were gone very quickly. It was 9.30 pm and the place was getting even more noisy.

"Would you like another glass of wine or a coffee?" asked William.

"I would but perhaps not here. But before you get any ideas – and please don't take this amiss – when I suggest that my place would be more relaxing it does not mean that sex is on the agenda. It isn't." William raised his right eyebrow:

"As if."

"As if indeed, William."

Ina's flat was a few minutes away, in Chiltern Street. It was on the second floor of a mansion block and was compact to say the least. The living room was sparse with an L-shaped settee and a couple of modern chairs which didn't look too comfortable. William sat on the settee. It wasn't yet dark outside but Ina switched on a couple of lights and set about making the coffee, glancing out of the window, pulling the curtains and straightening some cushions.

"Before you say anything William, this place is not to my taste and it's not my furniture. The deal I got included six months' rent paid by the bank on the basis that I should have sold my place in Edinburgh by then. I have already got a potential buyer so I'm now seriously looking in London. And I have to say that whatever I buy will be a lot smaller than my place in Edinburgh which is a three-bedroom, two-bathroom apartment in the New Town, with high ceilings and massive bay windows looking over the Dean Village."

"Which areas in London are you looking?" he asked.

"Well, seeing as I shall be working in Canary Wharf I'm thinking of the Elizabeth line, so maybe West Ealing. Or closer, maybe Southwark. I don't really know. But I'm not interested in places like Wandsworth or Clapham or Battersea or Balham; they all seem full of young families and that's not my thing. Obviously."

"Why obviously?"

"That's a charming question, William, but at my age the thought of a young family is both physically and mentally somewhat unattractive and probably impossible."

Willian realised that he was already getting serious about this relationship when he found himself pleased with her answer. Children were the last thing he needed.

They talked a lot about their own family histories,

some sad tales, some wonderful. Confirming what they both knew which was that every life contains bits of both. Another cup of coffee, another glass of wine and William called a cab. He was glad that he hadn't asked Stan to hang around as it would have looked ostentatious.

She took a step closer, laughing nervously, and reached past him to lift up the latch on the door.

He could smell her perfume. A hint of lilies.

He wasn't sure what to do. With other women it was so much easier. Diana, for example. He knew exactly where he stood with her and what she wanted.

She leant towards him, expectantly. He moved forward so they were only inches apart and gave her a kiss. A proper kiss. She pressed herself into him. Making a move had been the right decision.

And he was gone.

CHAPTER 55

Saturday morning. A rest day for William. He knew that if he exercised every day he would injure himself and he enjoyed a lie in from time to time. As he lay in bed he thought about the evening with Ina and their kiss and found himself reliving the experience and imagining what might have happened later. He felt his cock harden.

When he finally got up it was raining pretty hard and he welcomed that. His lawns were dry and brown, Stan had been down to the allotment almost every day for the past few weeks to get water from the standpipes, which was a pretty exhausting task. People were saying it was almost as bad as 1976 when standpipes in every street were planned and a minister for drought was appointed. Dennis Howells was his name and the day he took office it started raining and didn't stop for weeks. William remembered it well.

There were a few emails on his iMac including one from George Price which was sent yesterday. He opened it up immediately. It was copied in to Gill and Freddie. 'William, just to let you know that I understand that the matter we discussed is no longer a potential problem for the firm. As a result, I have closed my file. Best regards, George.'

'That's good,' thought William, 'one more sign that's it all over.' Next was an email from Gill, in response to George. 'Glad I'm not crossing paths with him again. Have a good weekend.'

Then Freddie's response to George. Just, 'See U Next Tuesday.' William knew what he meant by that. And it wasn't a pleasant term.

The first thing that went wrong was when William looked at his BT phone and internet bill. Not that the bill itself was unusual. He downloaded it to his desktop but when he opened up 'Finder' on his iMac and went to file it he couldn't find the folder named 'Bills' let alone the sub-folder marked 'Utilities'. More to the point, the entire folder marked 'Documents' seemed to have disappeared. William knew he must have screwed up something and set about trying to find it. First, he went to Spotlight and typed in 'bills'. Nothing found. It was time to restart the iMac, that usually worked. But this time it didn't. All his documents were still hiding somewhere.

He checked his email folders. No problem there, thank God. He kept trying to find the documents but gave up and decided to go over to the house and see if all was well on his MacBook. It wasn't. No folders. Nothing in iCloud. So, he went back to his office and called the Apple helpline. After going through the somewhat trying procedure, he was talking to a reassuring Irish voice within a few minutes of dialing.

"My name is Dan. Please give me a number where

I can call you back if we get cut off." Then "What's the problem, William?"

"I've lost all my files!"

"Don't worry, we will get them back for you. Where were they when you last used them?"

"In a file marked 'Primary Documents' on iCloud and on my desktop."

"Right then, maybe you could allow me access and we will fix this for you. I'm opening iCloud Drive. Please log in."

William did as he was told. The guy asked him to accept the Apple pointer which went straight to Settings. William clicked as requested. Then Advanced and then Recently Deleted Items. And there was his Primary Documents folder. He clicked on it, then on Restore as requested.

"That should do it. Let's wait a few minutes and check all is OK. By the way William, this process only works within twenty-eight days. So be careful next time."

"Thank you Dan. Much appreciated."

William made himself a large drink. He knew, he absolutely knew, that he had not deleted the folder and files. It must have been someone else. He'd read about malware that could be downloaded accidentally and which could move files and threaten to delete unless a payment was made. Maybe he would get such a note. Or maybe it was a hacker, just having fun. Or maybe someone got into his office to do it. But how? The back gate was always locked, the door into the cottage was always locked and no one knew the login passwords for his computers. And why? That was easier. The obvious suspect was Kutzevenia. Maybe they suspected he had copied the spreadsheet that was on the data key to his computer and were trying to remove it. Even if they had, he had another copy on his own data stick that was safe with Sky. No one could know that. But he needed to talk to Freddie. Perhaps this wasn't yet over.

Chapter 56

Gill and Jane were seeing each other whenever they were free. They had become a couple. And on that Saturday night they went to Zedel for an early supper then walked to She Soho for cocktails, Jane's favourite bar. Expensive, exclusive and very sexy. In spite of many offers to come partying, they left when it closed at midnight and went back to Jane's for cheese on toast and a bottle of Shiraz.

"I didn't want to say this in the bar, babe, but I have some news about that guy Mark. He's been put on the back burner. No more active investigation at the moment."

"Are you sure? Why?"

"Sure I'm sure. No one is assigned to the case. There's no pressure from anyone; no kids, no relations, no pressure from his employers, what are they called, DRK?"

"No, DPK!"

"Anyway, the bottom line is that bosses have decided there are 'More important cases on which to focus our scarce resources'. All of my cases are domestic or gang-related and it's not rocket science to get a result."

"Let's have a shower and go to bed, Jane. All that stuff is over for me as well."

Freddie and Lesley were also out early that evening. They met at Bar Boulud underneath the Mandarin Oriental and opposite Harvey Nichols where she had been doing some shopping and then experiencing something that to Freddie sounded like cryotherapy at 111 CRYO.

"Sorry," he said, "could you take me through that again?"

"Well, it's about freezing your body. Like they do to dead people who want to be stored in a freezer until a cure is found for whatever it was that killed them. But not exactly like that, obviously."

"You mean cryogenics?"

"Yes, well, whatever! It was a great experience. You get asked a load of questions about your health and stuff like your blood pressure, allergies, etc. Then you go into a changing room and you take off your clothes and jewellery and put on tiny shorts and a kind of sports bra plus a face mask, gloves and slippers. No selfies going on there, I can tell you. Then you end up in front of this door into a chamber which is minus ninety degrees centigrade."

"Fuck off, Lesley!"

"No, you don't understand. This is serious stuff. When you go in, you are told to exercise continually and they monitor you all the time. Anyway, as soon as I was in there my heart rate felt like it was going through the roof, my legs and arms felt like they were burning with the cold and I could see frost on my skin. Even my hair was frosty! Then a voice said 'One minute to go' and after that I was out of there. I can tell you it was quite a relief. But I felt great."

"Why Lesley? Why did you go through all that that?"

"It's very good for you. It's been tried and tested in the US and the UK and the benefits are well documented: muscle relaxation and recovery. Premier Division football clubs and top rugby clubs provide the facility to their players. Apparently, some are doing three or four sessions a week. You should try it." Freddie shuddered theatrically.

"Don't think that's for me. It might damage my libido forever. You wouldn't like that would you?"

"Haven't really thought about it, Freddie. Don't look at me like that! I'm only joking, well, half joking at least. Can we order now?"

CHAPTER 57

Sunday morning. William jogged to Hammersmith picking up his papers as usual. It was only eight o'clock but already twenty-three degrees and there wasn't a cloud in the sky. The front page of the Sunday Times splashed 'Hottest August day in a decade' and he was confident that this wasn't fake news. It was probably an understatement, given how hot he felt. He decided to take his classic MGB to Annie's rather than walk and enjoyed the short drive with the top down. As he turned into the side street he saw Freddie sitting at an outside table and waved.

Annie's was a brunch institution near the river in Chiswick and almost always packed, but William and Freddie were in no hurry and were both happy to down a couple of Bloody Mary's and chat before their food arrived. Avocado on toast for William. Full English for Freddie.

"OK, William, what's the problem this time?"

"It seems to me that the bank problem might not be solved entirely. First, the attack on Gill. I think that it probably wasn't a coincidence. Second, I had a bit of a shock yesterday. All the files on my iCloud had been deleted."

"What!"

"Yes, the entire folder. And I am one hundred per cent certain that I had not deleted them. One hundred per cent. Now the good news is that you can recover deleted files within twenty-eight days. So that's not the problem. The problem is, who did it?"

Freddie swallowed the last remnant of his breakfast, looked sadly at his empty Bloody Mary glass, and gestured to the waiter for two more.

"OK. My thoughts on who is responsible, in no particular order: the bank, the bank, the bank or some third-party cyber-crank. The next question is how. Clearly the crank by hacking, possibly the bank by hacking or, maybe, by breaking in. I guess we could get someone to have a look at the online history but sophisticated hackers take pride in leaving no trace unless they want to leave you a message.

"How about someone used your MacBook or your iMac? They would need to have physical access and to know your device password, your iCloud user name and your iCloud password. Who could know what they were?"

"Well, no one."

"What about Stan or Tina? Have you ever logged on when they might have seen what you entered? Maybe when you use your MacBook, which I have seen you use on the kitchen table? And do you use the same password for each device?"

"You already know the answers – yes and yes."

"And do either of them know your entry codes to the

office building and the back door into the garden?"

"Yes and yes again!"

"What's more, both Tina and Stan are often in your kitchen and may well have seen you enter your password to open it. And it's always lying around somewhere in the house. So, we have two prime suspects, William."

"But why? Why would they want to delete my files?"

"I'm not suggesting they deleted your files. I'm suspecting they helped someone else – probably the bank. As to the why, there are usually three reasons. Blackmail, sex or money. Sometimes a combination of all three. And if I was a betting man, I would put my stake on Stan."

"I know you don't like him but I think you are probably wrong. Stan owes me. I helped him get back on his feet. I pay him a decent wage. He has a free flat. And his job is pretty easy, to say the least."

"I appreciate that, and you're probably right. But if not Stan, then Tina."

"No! That's even less likely. She doesn't need money, her husband makes a fortune and she has looked after me for nearly twenty years. She is as honest as the day is long!"

"In that case we are back to the cyber-crank or the bank hacking into your system. The good news is that I have a contact who can help."

"Would this by any chance be the same contact that cracked the data keys' security?"

"Perhaps, William, perhaps. In any event, I will need to borrow your MacBook for a few days."

Brunch went on until about one o'clock then William drove very carefully home, promising to deliver the MacBook later that evening. Freddie went down to his shed, retrieved his second phone and arranged a meeting for ten o'clock that night after William had delivered his laptop. At eight-thirty he put the phone in the back of his shorts, the laptop in a Harrods carrier bag and walked to Kew Bridge railway station. He stood on the platform for ten minutes waiting for the train, looking carefully at other people arriving. When the train arrived, he got on board and a few minutes later he got off when it stopped at Barnes Bridge station where he sent a text. Then he walked onto the footpath by the railway line heading back to Chiswick. Halfway across the bridge he looked around but couldn't see anyone behind him and just one person coming towards him. As their paths crossed the carrier bag changed hands.

CHAPTER 58

Monday morning. It was hot again. Very hot. There were delays on the Central line. But Kathy Stobart was relaxed about being a little late. The Kutzevenia audit was all but finished and she had no other engagements in her calendar – at least for the time being. Freddie had indicated that his feedback would be very positive which would be helpful in getting the promotion to senior manager which she was chasing, and the weekend had been great, especially her second date with her colleague Tom. But the heat started to get to her as she walked towards East Acton station and it was even hotter inside

She looked at her watch as the train approached: 8.55 am. She felt the cooling air ahead of it. Then a hard push in her back and she was in that air, then she was on the track, then under the train, then gone. The CCTV recorded the exact time of her death as 8.55 and twenty-two seconds.

Passengers all along the Central Line were stuck for hours. 'Person under a train' or 'Passenger action' they heard as they stood and sweated and swore. "Why do these people always do it on Monday mornings?" they asked each other. "What a selfish way to kill yourself." That was Kathy's epitaph.

Jane called Gill at lunchtime. "Are you free for an early drink?"

"Is the Pope a Catholic? Usual place at 5.30 pm?"

"Done!" And by 5.35 pm they were sitting in the garden of The Eagle with a cold bottle of Picpoul de Pinet and some crisps.

"So, how was life at the sharp end of law enforcement today?"

"Pretty gruesome as it happens. I spent most of the morning looking at CCTV of a girl falling, jumping or being pushed under a train coming into Shepherd's Bush station. Gruesome got replaced by frustration pretty quickly because the platform was so crowded it was almost impossible to see what happened. Of course, everyone at the station hopes it was an accident or a jumper; we've got enough on our plates as it is."

"What do you think?"

"Well I think it might have been a push. But looking at all the CCTV before and after I haven't found anyone looking likely, nor has the guy working on the same videos. But you know, none of that really felt so awful because just after I called you I had to sit in on the interview with the train driver."

"Christ, you poor thing. What a day. What a horrible day. What do you want to do?'"

"I want to go home, have some cheese on toast and drink some Shiraz and cuddle. It worked OK last time."

Jane had two days off the next day and Gill had nothing serious to do in the office given the audit was closing down so they didn't get out of bed until after eleven. As they set the table for breakfast, Gill switched her phone back on. There was one voicemail. And it was from William. "Gill, I'll get straight to the point. Kathy Stobart has had an accident. She was hit by a tube train on her way to work yesterday. Nothing suspicious; crowded platform, you know how these things happen. I'm really sorry to tell you that she died instantly. I've just heard about it and I'm on a train to Bristol. Could we meet up later? I'll have more information then. I'll be back about five."

Gill fell into the chair behind her. Phone on the floor. Head in her hands. Tears of sadness, fright and terror in her eyes, she wailed, "No. No. No! Fucking hell! What's happening? Oh fuck, oh Christ. What's happening? Fucking hell!"

Jane grasped her from behind. "Gill, babe. What is it? Who called you? What is this about? You're frightening me. Tell me what's going on. Stop crying and tell me what is going on!"

"I don't know!"

"So tell me what you do know, babe, and let me tell you something first. I think I may be falling for you and nothing you tell me now is going to change that!"

Gill was silent for some seconds. She started from the beginning. Jane listened intently, just asking a few questions from time to time. When she finished, Gill started crying again and Jane went and made some coffee. She sat down. "I don't blame you at all for not telling me about this before. In fact, I've been wondering a bit ever since those two guys tried to attack us. My sense was that they were after you specifically. I don't why I thought that, it just seemed that way. Do you think the police have joined all this up? The Mark guy, that Felicity, now Kathy?"

"I've no idea. All I know is that HMRC and others are on the case and I think it's a lot bigger than DPK."

"Do you think you are in danger?"

"Well it looks like it, doesn't it. Felicity told Kathy about the passports. After all Kathy is – Christ, I mean was – her boss. And Felicity told me."

"Gill, you might be right. I'd like to say that I can find out what law enforcement are doing but I don't think I would have much success in that department. The NCA tend to focus on money laundering, organised crime, cybercrime, child sexual exploitation, modern slavery and stuff like that. We only get involved at the end of the process when it's time to confront the bad guys. The question is, what are we going to do about this? How about a drink while we think? And how about a hug before we have the drink?"

"Right," said Jane as she topped up Gill's glass. "You are going to meet William later on. How about you ask him if he would mind if I tagged along? Maybe three heads are better than two and I will have a very different perspective on this than you accountants."

"I'll ask him but he may wish to keep it in the family."

"That's not a problem, we are almost family now are we not?"

"Of course. And thank you," said Gill.

CHAPTER 59

Gill called William at 5.30 pm. He immediately agreed that Jane's perspective would be valuable and suggested they meet up at his place at seven. When their cab drove down Chiswick Mall, Jane looked astonished. When it pulled up in front of William's house her jaw dropped. "What is this? Does he have the whole building?"

"Yep. Crazy, isn't it?"

They went through the house to the back garden and sat together while William went to get some drinks.

When he came back, Gill was first to speak. "Jane and I have decided that now would be a good time to take a decent holiday and I shall be telling my counsellor that I shall be taking three weeks leave at the beginning of next week."

"I think that's an excellent idea. But tell me, is this because you feel threatened given Kathy's death?"

"Yes and no. I think I am at some risk and can't imagine anyone is going to give me protection. But I also feel I need a holiday. I have no current client commitments and I want to spend some quality time with Jane."

"And I want to spend some quality time with her," added Jane.

"So, you guys are off. From my perspective, I think any risk to you, Gill, is a remote possibility. You know nothing that could create a problem for the bank. If I were you I would try and forget about the whole experience. As far as Freddie and I are concerned, we are even further removed, in that the bank can't possibly know that we have had sight of the spreadsheet that Mark created. Last but by no means least, we know from Colin that HMRC and NCA are on the case. And the good news is that those guys, plus the firm, are happy with our contribution. You've been listening intently Jane and you're new to all of this. What's your perspective?"

"I agree with almost everything you have said, William, but bad guys are not always that logical. Most of the time they are pretty stupid. And very bad guys do not hesitate to get rid of people just in case. In other words, if they have any doubts they wouldn't think twice about taking you, or Gill, off the board. And Gill is one hundred per cent correct. There is no way the Met would even consider providing any semblance of protection in this situation. NCA might, if you actually had any valuable evidence. But you don't. Do you get what I'm saying?"

"Yep. Guess so. But I'm not going to lose any sleep about it."

"Good for you, William," replied Jane. "I think that's the best approach. By the way, this bottle seems to be empty!" They all laughed.

William disappeared and came back with another

bottle of white wine and one of red. Then went back into the house and reappeared with a tray containing plates, cutlery and napkins.

"Can I help, William?" asked Jane.

"That would be kind."

When the two of them were loading more trays, this time with pasta and salad, William spoke softly. "I know you will look after her, Jane. But here is my card. Any worries about her safety, let me know immediately. Any worries at all. Gill is very special to me."

"I will, William, and same goes for me. Here is my card. It has my mobile and the nick number. Now, let's celebrate." And celebrate they did.

CHAPTER 60

William decided to ask Ina to lunch and thought about this carefully. First, he emailed Freddie to see which Saturdays or Sundays he and Lesley could make. Then he walked over to the house and asked Tina if she could help out and if so which dates she could do. By the end of the day, he had two Saturdays and one Sunday which would work, so he called Ina and asked her to lunch. They agreed the following Sunday and called Lorna to see if she and Alex were free and Freddie and Lesley could also make it. Job done.

Apart from a couple of client meetings William had time on his hands and he made some good progress with his book over the next few days. Now that the problems were over, he found it much easier to concentrate. But when Freddie called on Friday afternoon he was quite glad to be distracted.

"Would now be a good time to bring back your MacBook?"

"By all means."

Freddie arrived by bike. He walked in and took the MacBook out of his backpack. "Here you go, old chap. It's pushing five so how about a sharpener? And then I'll tell you what's what."

They sat down in William's office. Drinks were poured and Freddie spoke. "No one has hacked into your files. If someone has gained access it's because they have impersonated you. That's the bad news. The good news – if you can call it that – is that there is no evidence that anyone has gained access."

William breathed a sigh of relief. "But files were deleted."

"Yes but that doesn't mean they were read. And you have restored them. So, the question is the one we discussed a few days ago. Who and why? Seems to me that we need an answer to this. I assume you have heard about Kathy Stobart?"

"I have heard the news. Terrible. And too much of a coincidence to be an accident. But let me take you through a conversation I had the other day." William summarised the evening with Gill and Jane, leaving out the girls' relationship and the excesses of the evening but Freddie's frown suggested he was troubled.

"So, the girls are off on holiday and it's you and me facing the music?"

"I'm not sure there is any music to face, Freddie."

"Well, if there is, my bet is we will face it quite soon. In the meantime, I'm looking forward to lunch on Sunday, if only to see what Ms Ina Maclean looks like when she lets her hair down. She is pretty straight-laced at the bank. I won't give the Russian word some of them use to describe her but it's like the opposite of a Baked Alaska which is hot outside and ice cold inside."

"Well Freddie, old chap, if I ever find out I shall not be telling you. I'm not a kiss and tell sort of bloke as you know."

Saturday morning was bright and breezy. William ran up to Richmond Park and instead of following the path he went off piste, following narrow deer tracks across the grass and through the woods. At one point he became completely lost. He loved the feeling of being outdoors in wild country, sometimes stumbling and once falling. He laughed out loud. What could be better than this? Then he jogged back home, looking forward to a shower and breakfast and anticipating the lunch party the next day. Of course it would be fun but what he hoped was that it might be an opportunity to get much closer to Ina.

The lunch was over. Tina had finished most of the washing up and gone off home. Freddie and Lesley had set off for a swim in his pool and Alex and Lorna's taxi had just left. William and Ina were upstairs in the living room lying together on the huge settee, listening to Beach House playing quietly. She put her hand on his thigh. "What a wonderful lunch, what nice people and what an extraordinary house. I'd love to see more of it. Where do you sleep?"

Later on, when William was awake and Ina was asleep, he was happy. He had been very nervous, not because of his body – he knew he was in very good shape and the tan from his recent holiday in Santorini still looked pretty good. He just wasn't used to sexual seduction. But Ina seemed to understand this and had taken the lead. It had worked out very well for both of them. And when she got up and told him his shower was too big for one person, it was even better.

CHAPTER 61

It was Monday morning. Six weeks since he had taken the call from Gill and heard about the passports. Mark dead, Felicity probably dead, Kathy dead and Gill assaulted. It felt like a fucking nightmare to William. But on the positive side, he had met Ina. It was the first time he had fallen for someone since Ryoko. That was more than forty years ago and he still touched her photo almost every day. Ina would have seen it as she walked through his dressing room but didn't mention it. He respected that. But maybe it was time to move it to somewhere else.

Another talk to the new intake at DPK. Stan was waiting outside to drive him there. William got out of the car in Tooley Street and strolled into More London. In spite of all the tragedies and uncertainties, he still loved the place. As usual, the DPK reception was full of energy. Photos on the weeks' new joiners. Slogans on the screens: 'You can make a positive contribution to colleagues, to clients… to the world'. And he knew that was true.

Downstairs in the auditorium he delivered his talk with no less enthusiasm than six weeks ago. He asked and answered questions. He told the intake the truth as he saw it. Made sure that they recognised that they were the product and understood that this was both a massive benefit and that being part of a 'Big Three' firm was a great credential but also carried great responsibility. But, at the back of his mind, he was remembering last night.

CHAPTER 62

Julian Harper had worked in the City and in politics for twenty years. He had loved the cut and thrust, the dog eat dog, the opportunity to apply his intellect and to leverage the formidable network his parents had provided, plus his personal network via Eton and Jesus College Oxford. He described that time as "dish dash dosh old chap. With the emphasis on the dosh!" But even though the dosh had survived, the dish had stayed on in St Barth's and his dash had evaporated. But he had never been as happy as he was at this moment, walking through his woods with his two pugs. He had sold the house in Balham, south London, for one-point-two-million pounds and bought the ten-acre wood for about ninety-thousand pounds, and the tiny cottage next to it for one-hundred-and fifty-thousand. He hadn't made up his mind what to do next.

He knew that the folk in the village nearby thought that a single man with a couple of pugs called Joan and David had to be gay. He wasn't but didn't care what they thought. And whenever he visited the pub they couldn't be friendlier. He was content. He had no partner but plenty of friends; not least his pugs. Brave, inquisitive, but often incontinent; he loved them for their faults as much as their spirit. But that day, with the autumn dawn sunlight slanting through the trees and lighting his path, they were squabbling like an angry couple. And then they disappeared.

Julian followed their direction and came across a path. It was hardly a path, just some leaves, bracken, shoots and grass that had been worn down. He was intrigued having never been that way before. He walked on, hearing the pugs chattering to each other again but sounding a little subdued. He walked further. And stopped. Something seemed wrong. Something seemed out of place. A shiver ran down his spine. What was it?

He looked around, trying to work out what was worrying him. Nothing to be seen but the pugs were silent. That had never happened before. He walked on. There was still no sound from the pugs. And there they were. Standing next to what looked like a hastily covered mound. What looked like a place where something might be buried. Where someone might be buried. And close by, in the bushes a petrol can. This looked serious.

Julian thought for a while and decided to called 999. The operator asked him to accept her request to track his location and sent him the link to his phone. She then took his personal details and instructed him not to move. When he told her about Joan and David she said to forget about them for the time being and explain more about the mound. Which he did, hoping that he wasn't mistaken. Praying he wasn't about to make a fool of himself. She ended the call. Within a few minutes, Julian got a call from a man identifying himself as DI Clarke who repeated all the questions the 999 operator had asked plus some others. How big was the mound? The DI also instructed him not to move. He didn't.

The DI called again and reminded him not to move. Half an hour later he called yet again and explained that they were going to get his exact location by using a drone. Ten minutes later he could hear it hovering overhead and he moved forward slightly so that its camera could spot him. A few minutes later he had a call from a breathless policeman asking him to tell him how to get to him without going near the mound. When the policeman arrived, he took a good look at it and got on his radio. Julian couldn't hear what he was saying.

Julian, Joan and David stood still and silent having been told for the third time not to move. Eventually reinforcements arrived. People dressed in white paper coveralls with blue covers over their feet. A huge tent. Lights inside and out. A pathway marked out by stakes with blues light on top. Still cameras, video cameras, computers. The constant sound of phone calls and texts. Julian asked if he could take his dogs home. The answer was no.

Shortly afterwards, DI Clarke came over and introduced himself. "Sorry for this inconvenience. One of my officers will escort you back to the main path and take you home. He will have a lot of questions for you, please bear with us. We need you to stay in your house and not mention this incident to anybody. The last thing we need at this stage is the media descending on us. I will be along to talk to you as soon as possible."

By the time Julian got home, the pugs were chattering away so he fed them. He offered the officer coffee and made a cup for himself. Then the questions started as the policeman went through a form which Julian guessed was used irrespective of the situation. Full name, address, contact numbers, date of birth, place of birth, national insurance number, family members, dependents, employer and employer's address, any previous convictions, religion, when did he buy the cottage, why did he buy the wood? The questions went on and on. He did his best not to be irritated and finally they were over. This time when he offered the guy a coffee he accepted it.

DI Clarke arrived at around lunchtime and stood reading the completed form carefully and then reading it again. Julian spent the time making himself a couple of cheese sandwiches and ate them sitting at the kitchen table. Then the DI started asking questions. How often did Julian walk in the woods? Were the pugs always with him? Had he seen any strangers or vehicles in the area over the past few months? Had he ever walked in the woods with friends and family and so on? When he had finished, Julian thought he might be entitled to ask the DI a question.

"Is it a grave? Is someone buried there? When can I go back to my wood?"

"I'm afraid I can't answer those questions at the present time but we will inform you when you can go back to the wood. I imagine it will be in three or four days. And please remember, in the meantime, you must not tell anyone about this incident. If you do you could be prosecuted."

CHAPTER 63

Julian did as he was instructed and told nobody. But the following afternoon the press arrived at his cottage door and started swarming all over his wood, pressing hard against the police tapes and trying to get a shot of what everyone assumed was a grave. He told them the wood was private property but they just ignored him. By the time it got dark there was rubbish all over his previously pristine paths. It broke his heart.

The press were there again early the next morning. They had discovered that Julian had actually come across the grave and reported it to the police. Somehow, they had also discovered his telephone number. It had to be a police leak. They kept calling. They kept ringing his bell and hammering on his door. They were knocking on his windows and taking photos through them into his living room and kitchen. It was a nightmare. He complained to the police officer who had taken up station outside his front door but she said there was nothing she could do. The pugs were panicking; barking all the time when they weren't whining. Twenty-four hours ago, he was living his dream. Now he was living in a nightmare.

He took Joan and David to his office upstairs and

connected to the BBC news programme. After a few minutes, he saw his cottage and his wood on the screen and then DI Clarke standing in front of a police station with a microphone in front of him and some papers in his hand. It looked like he was about to make a statement. Julian turned up the volume.

"I am Detective Inspector Clarke of Thames Valley Police and I wish to make a short statement regarding the discovery of a possible grave in a privately-owned wood near Amersham. We are at a very early stage in our investigation but I can confirm that we believe that two people are buried there and we are working on the assumption that they were murdered. We expect it will take some time to identify the victims and will structure another briefing in due course. At this time, we will not be taking any questions. Thank you."

Julian put his head in his hands. Two bodies. Murdered and buried in his lovely wood. How could this have happened? What should he do? He had no idea at all. The pugs looked at him and seemed to know how upset he was. He looked back and cried.

Back at the station, DI Clarke briefed his boss, DCI 'Bunny' Field.

"The thing is that what we have in there is a pile of shattered bones and two cans of petrol. There was another can left nearby. It looks like whoever killed them threw them in there, hit their bodies very hard and repeatedly with something like a sledgehammer or a spade, poured petrol over them and set light to them. All the bones are muddled up. Forensics have yet to even work out the sex of the victims but it looks like a man and women. Forget dental records, we are talking individual teeth."

"When do we get back the DNA, Clarke?"

"Tomorrow. We may not get a ping but we will at least know their sex."

"Any joy around the site?"

"Well, we have footprints that don't match to Julian Harper but they don't look promising. They are not recent. We are talking weeks not days."

"Prints on the petrol can?"

"Sorry, no sir. However, there is some good news. It looks like a vehicle was involved. We have tyre tracks close to the site, both coming and going. And they are in quite good shape."

"OK. Anything else?"

"Yes. The guy that owns the wood, the guy that found the site, is pretty upset. He wants to know how his name address and telephone numbers got out to the press within twenty-four hours."

"Do we know who leaked it?"

"I have my suspicions sir and will let you know if I can confirm them. And there is another thing. The guy wants to know when he will get his wood back."

"And?"

"Forensics reckon two weeks. We are talking sieves

and the hole is only big enough for one person to be in there."

"Tell him a few days and let's see how we go."

Twenty-four hours later DI Clarke knocked on DCI Field's door. "Boss, we have a bit of a result on the grave. We have identified both victims."

"Bloody hell, that is what I call a result. How come?"

"All pretty simple actually. We have the DNA. One male, one female. The male is on the system and has been in and out since he was about fifteen. He's a legal immigrant from Russia but finished six years for GBH at Brixton last year. His name is Pyotr Vorobyov. We have a current address in London and I've been in touch with the Met to have someone go around there. I doubt that it is current but worth a shot."

"What about the female?"

"Her DNA is not in the system but we have her name and date of birth."

"What! How come?"

"Forensics found a bit of metal in the hole. A bit bent and blackened but the writing was clear."

"Writing?"

"Yeah, the metal was a plate which was inserted in her arm to fix it properly when it was broken as a result of an accident. When they do this, they engrave the plate with some details. We traced this back to a private hospital near Kingston, Surrey, and they have just emailed us to say that the plate was put into the arm of one Felicity Strange who was recently reported as missing."

"Well done, Clarke. Well done!"

"Thank you, sir. It's nice to pull the rabbit out of the hat. Now all we need to do is to find out who put the bodies there. By the way, we might have a lead. There is an NCA flag on the female's file."

CHAPTER 64

The last reporters had drifted off when it started to get dark. Julian decided to take the dogs for a walk and have a drink in the pub unless it was full of media people. Thankfully the car park was empty. However, when he got inside, he found the pub was packed and the TV was on. People were talking loudly and trying to hear it at the same time. The pugs started barking and he decided to go back home. But the landlady, Paula, leaning on the bar in her usual place, caught his eye and beckoned. He found a space opposite her.

"Stay for a pint, Julian. Have a chat with Jerry over there. He has been around almost as long as this pub. Tell him what you saw and he'll spread the word. Everyone else here will talk to you as if nothing has happened. And pass me those leads, I'll take those excuses for dogs around the back and give them something to chew on."

Julian took his pint and another over to Jerry, conscious that almost all of the customers were following his progress. Jerry was in his usual seat and dressed in a bright white shirt, scruffy jacket and tie, worn-out cords and highly polished brown boots.

"Cheers, Julian. Thank you. I gather you have been

having some excitement in that wood of yours. Lunchtime today this place was packed with journalists, photographers and who knows what. By God those people like a drink. And the noise! Phones ringing and pinging. All of them speaking so loudly. And the louder it got the louder they had to speak. Not my cup of tea, that's for sure. Anyway, if you want to talk about it I can promise you none here is going to share anything with them!"

"Well actually there isn't much I can tell you. I was walking the dogs at the north end and I came across what looked like something was buried; you could see the mound. It looked suspicious so I called 999 and finally the police turned up. Lights, a tent over the hole, loads of yellow tape, phones ringing, radios chattering. Must have been at least a dozen people. So much for my wood. It will never be the same."

"Julian, woods don't have memories. Only people and maybe some animals. This time next year that area will look pretty much like it did a few days ago. The year after, it will have grown over. A couple of years later you probably won't be able to find the site – if you were foolish enough to look for it. Bear in mind that your wood has been there for a thousand years. Human beings and animals have been conceived in it, born in it, lived in it, died in it and buried in it. Who knows what might lie under it? I know it must be upsetting but it will all pass. But if you can't get over it then just let me know. I'll buy it off you. But don't expect to get the ninety-thousand you paid!"

"How do you know how much I paid?"

"Walls have ears Julian, perhaps trees do as well. And seeing as you are paying, yes, I would like another pint if you will join me. By the way, a couple of boys asked me if they could clear up that mess those people left around your cottage and I said that would be OK. Is that OK with you?"

No journalists were at Julian's door the next morning and he was able to eat his breakfast in peace watching the news. The 'Grave in the Woods' story was now relegated to the 'News, weather and travel where you are' section and that suited him just fine. He took the dogs for a walk in the woods far away from the grave site and sensed a little peace returning. But that evening the story was making the headlines again following a press conference earlier that day. It was DI Clarke again, this time speaking from an office.

"Good afternoon. I will now update you on the discovery of the grave in the woods. We do not intend to provide the exact location now or any time in the immediate future. What I can tell you is this. As previously stated, the grave contained two bodies.

"We have been unable to contact relatives of either of the victims of these tragic murders so we have decided to release their names and ask anyone who could possibly help to contact the number which will be at the bottom of the screen. Any information will be kept confidential.

The two victims are Mr Pyotr Vorobyov aged thirty-nine from Lewisham, London SE1 and Ms Felicity Strange aged twenty-four from Belgravia London SW1. We should say that at this stage that we have no information that suggests that the two victims were connected in any way. I will not be taking questions."

CHAPTER 65

At the same time that the press conference closed, William and Ina were just fifty miles away, each enjoying a glass of champagne. They were in seats 2A and 2C on the BA0346 to Nice for a long weekend that William had arranged as a surprise.

Ina still had no idea where they would be staying and what they were going to do. William had simply said that, hopefully, it would be warm and no smart clothes were required. Two hours and two more glasses of champagne later they were landing at Nice Cote D'Azur. By 1.30 pm they were sipping champagne in Le Petit Maison and trying to work out what to share from the menu. They chose well and had a great time.

The car collected them at 3.30 pm and less than an hour later it stopped where the road to St-Paul-de-Vince finished. Ina looked confused as she looked at the somewhat scruffy bar on her right. They got out of the car and their driver picked up their bags. Ina glanced at William and he pointed at a nondescript door on their left then pointed to a small gold-covered statue of a dove above the door. "Look, A Golden Dove. The Golden Dove. La Colombe D'Or. I hope you like it. Let's switch off our phones and enjoy the weekend."

And they most certainly did.

When they were on the flight back they agreed that they would get a cab at Heathrow, drop William off at home and then Ina would take it on to Marylebone as she had an early meeting the next day. They snuggled together all the way to Chiswick and William waved goodbye as the cab went on its way. "What a fantastic weekend. And it's only nine o'clock," he mused.

He let himself into the house, picked up the usual junk mail on the doormat and made himself a Grey Goose and tonic. Then he took some bread and cheese out of the fridge. He opened up his MacBook and the BBC news channel. He clicked on the weather first as was his habit. Then the headlines: 'Brexit', 'Brexit' and then 'Woodland Grave. Bodies identified'. He hadn't been following the story. But clicked anyway. 'Pyotr Vorobyov and Felicity Strange.' What? How? Why?

He switched on his phone to call Freddie. There were ten missed calls, four voicemails and six texts. Selfishly, William's first thought was 'thank God I had my phone switched off'. After all, there was nothing he could do. Then he felt guilty and listened to his messages. 'Had he heard the news?' 'What should we do?' There was a message from Daniel to all partners; 'I will be sending you all an email on Sunday morning which will be going out to staff on Sunday afternoon advising them of this tragedy but making no further comment. This matter is in the hands of the police and we do not expect any DPK staff or partners to be advancing theories about what might or might not have happened.'

William ignored all the other messages apart from one: 'Mr West. Excuse me for contacting you directly and over the weekend. My name is Alastair Chubb and I am a partner with Chubb and Chubb in West Halkin Street SW1. I have been given your number by Thames Valley Police in connection with the death of Felicity Strange. I contacted them following the announcement of her death as I have her lifetime power of attorney and I am an executor of her will. Could you please call me on the number from which I am calling you?' William pressed five and left a message on the voicemail. Then he called Freddie who answered immediately. "William, I'm on my way!"

CHAPTER 66

"Well I guess that's it. But what do you make of it Freddie?" asked William after they had discussed the police statement. "What on earth was Felicity doing with this Russian chap? Could she have been involved in some way?"

"No idea, but I very much doubt she was involved. This stuff started way back before she was with the firm. She was loaded, with a mews house in Belgravia, and she was as innocent as could be. I just can't see it."

"But Freddie, it must be connected to the blank passports. She saw them!"

"Let's leave it to the police. By the way, do you have any Southern Comfort William? I think I need some to cheer me up."

"Yes, I do. And I need cheering up too. I was really, really fond of Felicity and in the very back of my mind I still held a hope that we might see her again. And you know what? I got a call from a chap who says he was her solicitor and who wants to talk to me. But I'm sorry Freddie, I wish I knew what happened to her."

"William. Trust me. I know how you feel. I have lost people I cared about as well. Of course, I know that you lost Ryoko. It was tragic and I know how much she meant to you. But don't confuse caring for, or loving someone who you lost, as guilt. There was nothing you could have done that you didn't do for Ryoko and of course the same is true of Felicity. But I think I may be able to help. My pal – let's call her Angela – who managed to decode those two data sticks has some information which she is willing to share. To be specific, she said that we needed to know exactly what we were up against. How about my place tomorrow night about eight if everyone can make it?" suggested Freddie.

"I don't like the sound of it but I'll be there," replied William.

The following evening, Gill and William arrived at eight, and ten minutes later Angela came straight in through the back door. She was wearing jeans and a hoodie and dark glasses which she kept on. Her untidy hair was also covering part of her face and her voice was soft and somehow a bit muffled. She smiled shyly as Freddie brought out a couple of bottles of wine and some glasses and then spoke. "I trust Freddie completely and he tells me that I can trust you guys as well. But I am not going to give you my real name or tell you who my employers are. Let's just say GCHQ for the time being. In case you don't know, that is Government Communications Headquarters to give it its full name. What I can tell you is not good. To put it bluntly, you are in serious danger if the person laundering this money finds out you have the data keys I got decoded for you. And I will be in serious shit if my employers ever even suspect that I have met you!"

Angela took a sip of wine and leant forward. "First of all, I need to tell you that my employers suspect that the name of the man responsible for the money laundering that you accidentally uncovered is Jorge Perez. It's a very common name in Mexico. But he is far from a common person. He is, in fact, the main launderer for Los Zetas."

"Los Zetas?" William asked.

"Yes. They are one of the big drug cartels in Mexico. Nothing like as large as the Sinaloa but pretty dominant in the Florida Gulf, including the border with the US on that side. Their revenues are around fifty billion dollars a year and most of the money gets cleaned by Jorge and his teams.

"The cartels are notorious for their violence, as you know. Putting people in barrels of oil and boiling them, pushing a tyre over their shoulders and setting light to it, etc. But the money launderers tend to be a little more sophisticated. Jorge is an exception. It seems he gets off on it. There are some videos on his file and I have copied them onto this stick. Freddie can you put it into your computer. And guys, you might want to have another drink as you look at this. It's not pretty. There is no sound; just as well I think."

The video started. It was a little blurry but clear enough to see.

"The man on the left of the three chaps leaning on the fence is Jorge. We don't know who the others are."

It looked like a paddock but there were no horses, just four or five dogs. Quite small dogs, but angry, highly muscled creatures. They all seemed to be barking. The camera panned past Jorge and focused on a middle-aged couple and two children. One, a boy of about ten, another a girl of about fifteen. She was naked with blood on her thighs. A bored looking man was pointing some sort of automatic weapon at them. The couple looked petrified, the girl had a vacant expression. One of the men with Jorge walked into the shot, picked up the boy and casually threw him over the fence. Gill screamed. William gasped. The dogs were on the boy in seconds, snapping at him, taking bites out of him. Then he was on the ground, rolling around. They could hardly see his little body for those dogs. William couldn't take it anymore and rushed to the lavatory to be sick. Gill closed her eyes and put her hands to her face. Freddie had his eyes fixed on Jorge as if he was filing away the man's face for future reference. He was still looking at him when the camera panned back to the paddock. There were pieces of four dead bodies.

"Jesus Christ," sighed Freddie.

"There's more, I'm afraid. Do you want me to tell you?"

"I guess so," said William as he sat back down.

Angela spoke in a monotone. "Jorge likes to rape. Boys and girls, men and women. Front and back bottom.

No one lives to complain. He prefers rape to normal sex. He enjoys torture. His favourite methods are a red-hot poker; on the skin and in the orifices, pliers and worse. If he is after information rather than gratification it's the traditional water-boarding."

"Jesus Christ," gasped William. "This is unbelievable!"

"Sadly not," replied Angela. "But let's move on."

"The file confirms that Jorge arrived at London Heathrow about six days ago. Purpose of visit: business, ninety-day visa, staying at Browns Hotel in Albemarle Street, London W1. Here is a copy of his landing card. He pinged at immigration because of his known relationship with Los Zetas but no further official action was taken. Here is his passport photo. Quite good looking, don't you think?"

"Jesus Christ!" said William. "Who apart from us could know about the data key?"

"No one on my side, that's for sure," answered Angela. "If anyone knew I had helped you, my arse would be grass. And, if all goes well, given that the only witness to the blank passports is sadly dead, there is no reason why Mr Perez could have any concerns. So, my advice to you is let's keep it that way."

They talked for a while. William felt lots of questions were asked. Few were answered. Angela didn't seem in a hurry to leave; she said she had somewhere to go to later. This suited both William and Gill, they were both intrigued by her and wanted to know more. Freddie said,

"I have to do a call with the New York office so I'm off to my study upstairs but I'll be back down about 10.30 pm, so make yourselves at home. William, you know where everything is."

"Angela, what is your connection with Freddie?" said Gill, as soon as Freddie had left the room. Angela looked at her watch. "It's not really confidential but it is quite personal. I think I need another glass of wine before I spill the beans. I'll give you the long story. But if you ever read in a book about my meeting with Freddie you would think it very far-fetched." She looked both of them in the eye and smiled "Are you sitting comfortably? Then I'll begin."

CHAPTER 67

"I was born in the UK but my parents moved to Australia when I was about ten. I grew up as the stereotypical Bondi Beach girl with one exception. I was, and still am, a geek. But I embraced technology with the same enthusiasm as my friends embraced sport and surfing. That's not to say I spent my youth in a dark bedroom looking at screens. The geek stuff was in addition to the fun stuff. And there was a lot of fun on the sand.

"Anyway, I was working in IT for an insurance company called AMP in Sydney and when they offered me a job in Dubai, I jumped at it. But after a year or so I was bored silly and I applied for a few jobs in London. It was just as the term 'cyber security' was being bandied about and I responded to an advertisement from a company called Control Risks that specialised in this stuff. It was a great place to work and much, much more interesting than you can imagine." Angela took another sip of her wine.

"For starters, a chap called David Walker was one of the founders. He was previously SAS and in the early days so were many of the recruits. Other founders were some of the very good and great of UK military and the Lloyds of London insurance market. And their specific areas of expertise: personal security, cyber security and dealing with the complex facets of kidnap insurance. By the time I joined, it was a global organisation with a very sophisticated and profitable business model. I loved it.

"I must have been there a couple of years when I met Freddie. He stood out as a bit of a character and that's saying something in an organisation that has more characters than most. He was known as a serial womaniser who had just got divorced from his third wife. She was much younger than him; in fact, about the same age as his daughters and the marriage didn't last very long at all. The rumour was that Freddie had started an affair with her mother!"

Gill looked shocked. William laughed out loud. "Why am I not surprised!" he said.

Angela carried on. "I was introduced to Freddie by one of the senior guys. We were tasked to collect a civilian who had been kidnapped in Oman and taken over the border to Yemen. To avoid suspicion, Freddie and I were to act as a couple on holiday and my role was to play the part and look after the civilian when we picked him up."

"Why you?" asked Gill.

"I had picked up a bit of Arabic in Dubai, I could read maps and I'd passed the advance security driving test. Apparently, the guy was being held in the back of beyond. No one told me who he was, how much would be paid and how things would be organised. But it all sounded as if it was pretty much routine. And it did start that way."

Now Angela was on a roll. "Kidnap and ransom insurance was, and still is, very secretive. If people know an executive is insured then it increases the likelihood of them getting captured. And, equally, companies do not like the word getting out that they pay ransoms. So, Freddie and I really needed to play the part. But just to be clear, we were not talking spies, guns or any of that stuff. We were talking about insurance and paying claims. A bit like Prudential and Aviva. But a bit more complicated.

"Freddie and I had a brief meeting," Angela continued. "Actually, very brief! He told me that it would be hot for a few days in Muscat as we waited for the details of the collection to be organised and that we would be staying at the Chedi Hotel. He told me to look at the website and pack accordingly. Also, to bring some warm clothes as we would be going into the mountains to make the collection and it could be pretty chilly up there at night in February. And he told me to ensure I packed trainers, sweatshirt and sensible underwear; maybe running shorts and a sports bra."

"Sensible underwear? Sports bra?" asked Gill, "What! Why?"

"That is exactly what I asked! He said that it was possible but unlikely that the kidnappers might want to search us very thoroughly. He said, 'I always plan for the worst.' That's when I had second thoughts. But it was too late.

"A couple of days later, Freddie and I were collected

from the office and dropped off at Terminal Five. I had a business class ticket for the first time in my life! Fast-track security and then on the train to take us to the club lounge just by the gate for our flight. Freddie started pouring himself some astonishingly large vodkas and I had some lovely red wine from the massive selection. On the plane there were flat sleeper seats; mine was perfect but Freddie is a foot taller so I guess he wasn't as comfortable. Either way, he seemed to sleep better than me. The next thing I knew was that we'd arrived in Muscat and the sun was shining.

"We were at the front of the queue at immigration but it still took some time to get through. When I wheeled my luggage into the main concourse I noticed that Freddie was carrying two soft bags but didn't give it another thought as we walked towards the taxis. Then Freddie strolled towards a man with a sign with the letters FF on it and we were led to the car park and a black four-wheel drive SUV hire car. Thirty minutes later we were checking into the Chedi. And a suite with two bedrooms. I was quite relieved as I had wondered how that might all work."

William looked at her. And she smiled. "Seriously. No problem. He asked me which one I preferred.

"It was a fantastic hotel. Modern Arabic. Trendy with lovely gardens and pools. One of the pools was a hundred metres long and I had a relaxing swim before lunch. Freddie joined me but he was powering up and down like an Olympic champion. Seriously, I have never seen anyone swim so fast; and don't forget I was a Bondi Beach girl! I asked him how he did it and he told me that when he was in the Royal Navy he had to pass a swimming test every three months to keep his job. He always referred to being in the Royal Navy but everyone in the firm knew he has been in the SBS before joining."

"SBS?" interrupted Gill.

"Special Boat Service; like the SAS but navy not army. Tough guys. And I found out how tough Freddie was a couple of days later.

"We had a fantastic dinner by the pool that night. Very dark with fire pits. One of Freddie's friends from his navy days joined us. He had a large Hermes bag and Freddie gave him the entry card for our room and he left the table. 'Just delivering the maps and some other stuff,' he said. Anyway, he was back within five minutes or so and was charming company. But we knew we had quite a long trip in the morning so it wasn't a typical Freddie 'Let's have another drink affair'.

"There were two maps in the bag Freddie's pal had delivered to the room, plus a satellite phone and a first-aid box. 'First aid?' I asked. 'Yes,' said Freddie. 'We are going into the unknown. One can't be too careful.'

"We looked at one of the maps before breakfast and it all seemed very straightforward. Our destination was the Alila Hotel in Jebel Akhdar, about three-thousand feet above sea level. Apart from the hotel, the area looked completely uninhabited.

"Freddie asked me to pack my stuff but I said I thought we had planned to come back, after the handover. 'Yes,' he said, 'that's the plan. But who knows what might happen. So we keep our options open. We are not checking out; just exploring as couples on holiday often do.'

"So we took everything out of the suite and took off for this Alila Hotel. The journey time looked like three, maybe three and a half hours. And the first two hours were very boring. Dual carriageway, sand, rocks, boulders and no small talk from Freddie. But eventually, after we had stopped in a small town and filled up the tank, he spoke.

"He said, 'Before we get back on the road, could you grab that first-aid box for me please and open it. Thanks. Now if you lift up the tray with the bandages and stuff you will find a heavy package. Could you lift that out, put it in your lap and replace the rest of it. Excellent. Thanks. Now I need to ask you a favour. If you don't want to grant it, no problem. And the favour is that you forget what you are about to see.' I nodded, I don't know why. Freddie opened up the package and placed the contents under his seat, started up the SUV and off we went."

"What was in the package?" asked Gill.

"I promised then not to say but it makes no difference now," replied Angela. "And, anyway, I bet you can guess. It was a gun. I said, 'Freddie, is that a gun?' And he said, 'Yes, it's a gun. And to be specific, it is an Israeli military Desert Eagle semi-automatic handgun and it is notable for chambering the largest of any magazine-fed, self-loading pistol bullets. It is loaded with eight. We won't need more than that. It's a category killer. In fact, I'd be surprised if we need it at all. But we plan for the worst scenario."'

"He had a gun?" asked William. "A gun?"

"Yes. I'd seen shotguns before but never a handgun designed to kill people."

"What did you say?" asked Gill.

"I said, 'Freddie, I thought this was all routine.' He didn't reply as we joined the dual carriageway again but then he seemed to relax. He told me that the ransom was two-million US dollars. He said, 'The kidnappers know that if they mess us around they won't get it. Sure, they can kill civilians. But all they get are dead bodies. No money. This is the eighth delivery I have handled and I have never encountered any serious challenges. And bear in mind that back in the day we were handing over cash rather than authorising an online transfer. But all my training in the Royal Navy assumed that shit happens. And we need to prepare for the worst. Hence the gun. It could get me fired if word got back to the firm. But it could also keep us alive if things go wrong. But please just forget about it for the time being.' And I did.

"Half an hour later, when we had turned off the dual carriageway, I told Freddie to expect another turn off to the right and there it was, a signpost for the Alila Hotel. Just thirty klicks to go. But it took more than an hour! First there was a checkpoint to make sure we had a four-wheel drive vehicle. Then a casual military checkpoint.

And then countless hairpin bends as we climbed up the very steep road to the mountains. It was a pretty scary journey. Very bleak, huge drops and quite a narrow road with some big lorries coming at us regularly. Needless to say, Freddie drove fast.

"When we approached the hotel, it blended into the landscape. We could hardly see it and it didn't look that impressive. But when we actually arrived, the views were amazing, the place was amazing. It was out of this world. The firm had booked a villa right on the edge of the cliff. We were looking down at mountains and valleys. Very private, not overlooked at all. Freddie explained that one option might be to bring the civilian back to the villa after the exchange; a doctor would be waiting for us in any event. Alternatively, we might go straight back to Muscat. I asked why we would need a doctor and Freddie grimaced. He said, 'The only certainty about this exercise is that the guy will be in very bad shape, physically and mentally. I've seen the video the kidnappers sent; he already looked pretty fucked up and that was about ten days ago.'

"We had a quick lunch and then sat out on the deck of the suite looking down over the lower mountains and Freddie finally explained what was going to happen. Hopefully, tomorrow morning, he would get a call on the satellite phone giving him the coordinates for the meet; probably two or three hours from the hotel. Still in Oman, not Yemen. The firm had insisted on that. We would then set off and he anticipated that we could be followed by one of the kidnap crew just to ensure we had no back-up. One of my jobs was to use the other map we had been given to check out other routes from the meet in case there was some sort of emergency. Then he got really serious.

"He said, 'Angela, I need to talk to you about the protocols for tomorrow. These are not suggestions, they are orders. First, our code. If I mutter the number one it means a high level of danger, two is moderate and three is low. Basically, there is no need for these guys to have guns but they often carry them so that would only be a moderate increase in risk. Also, these guys often chew a leaf called quat and it can create unpredictable behaviour. You will notice that as they tend to spit it out. Again, only a moderate risk. But quat and guns together, that's a high level of risk. That's a one!'

"Then he said, 'Second, and please remember I just want to prepare for the worst, your safety. If I shout run, you don't look around, you run. You don't worry about me, you don't worry about the civilian, you run to the SUV; zig-zagging, not in a straight line. The keys will be in the ignition, the SUV will be pointed at the exit. Take a look and if I'm down drive off. And don't look back.'"

"Good God!" said Gill. "What happened?" Both she and William were on the edges of their seats. Angela smiled. "I told you that if this was fiction it would be a tall story but I can tell you what actually happened. Shit happened!

"We got the coordinates on the phone at 6 am the next

morning. The meet looked to be about four or five hours away. We were told to be there by twelve-thirty. Looking at the map, I could see there was some sort of trail but no sign of any habitation anywhere near. The SUV was parked right outside our villa, we loaded it up with all our luggage and plenty of water and set off about 7 am. For the first couple of hours the road was OK but after two turn offs it was just a dirt track with some serious rocks littered about. Then it was mainly rocks with a bit of a track between them. We hadn't seen any other vehicles for more than an hour. And as we approached the destination we climbed quite steeply. Freddie muttered that if we had any protection it would easily have been spotted.

"As the coordinates pinged on the GPS, Freddie turned the SUV so it was sideways to the track and ready for a swift exit. We got out and two really scruffy guys emerged from behind some rocks about one hundred metres away. They had scarfs around their necks and over their heads. They carried rifles, and as we got closer we could see that both of them were chewing energetically. Freddie whispered to me 'One', smiled and walked over to them, holding the phone in the air. I followed him and heard him say, 'I have all the account details. I'm authorised to transfer two-million dollars as soon as we see that our man is alive and well.'"

Angela leant forward, looking Gill and William in the eyes. "The two guys were bouncing around, smiling then frowning, looking all over the place, fondling their rifles but Freddie was still smiling. They came over to us and gestured that we should put up our arms. It was just a pat down, not a strip search, thank God. They were pretty brusque and they smelt awful, like a kind of rotten food smell and the guy patting me down had the worst teeth I have ever seen; broken, missing and stained. His eyes were red, his clothes were filthy. It was all I could do not to be sick."

CHAPTER 68

Angela poured herself another glass of wine and sat back in her chair.

"What happened next?" asked William.

"One of the guys made a gesture and some kind of jeep emerged from the other side of the rocks. It stopped, the driver walked around to the passenger door and dragged out a body. At least I thought it was a body. To say my legs wobbled would be a major understatement. But then the body's legs kind of twitched and I realised it was alive. I looked at Freddie. He was still smiling. And he made a sort of gesture, as if to say, may I look? Then he walked over, stared the guy in the face and nodded at the guys with the guns. No words had been spoken by them so far.

"The guy from the jeep with his gun over his shoulder took a piece of paper from his pocket and gave it to Freddie. Freddie looked at it, then looked at the guys with the guns. And he looked again at the guy from the jeep who I think said 'Stay'. But my Arabic was by no means perfect. Then Freddie asked me to have a closer look at the civilian and I have to say that he looked terrible and smelt even worse than the kidnappers. But he was alive, if you could call it that. So, I nodded to Freddie and he did his thing with the satellite phone. Then there was a very tense few minutes until the guy from the jeep gave us a thumbs up and the deal was done. At least I thought it was.

"Freddie and I lifted up the civilian and tried to help him walk to our SUV. I glanced at him again. It was awful. He had a scrappy white beard, filthy matted hair, red eyes and he was drooling. His clothes were ripped and filthy, probably the same as he was wearing when he was taken. He smelt of urine and, pardon my language, shit. He seemed to be trying to talk but only uttered a few hoarse words which made no sense at all.

"When we were about halfway back to the car I heard a noise like a really loud pneumatic drill banging away and some things whistled over my head. Freddie shouted, 'Run,' grabbed the civilian, threw him over his shoulder and took to his heels. In spite of carrying the man he was going faster than me. Another even louder repetition of the noise and something hit my arm but I carried on and saw Freddie had nearly reached the car. Then I tripped. I was in the dust. On the ground. Another banging and what must have been a bullet hit the rock a few inches from my hand. And I thought that's it. That's me. Gone. I was completely and utterly terrified. Frozen with fear. Eyes closed. I knew I was going to die. I knew! Then I heard someone running and Freddie arrived. Picked me up and threw me over his shoulder. More loud drilling, banging. I kept my eyes closed and prayed. The next thing I knew I was dropped on the ground. 'Stay down. You are safe,' said

Freddie calmly as he opened the car door and grabbed the gun from under the seat. 'Stay down,' he repeated.

"I heard a couple of clicks as he stood up and then two shots in quick succession. Freddie looked at me. 'It's over. You can stand up now but keep your head below the roofline. I need your help. No hurry. No panic. It's over.' I stood up, looked through the windows and saw two of the guys lying on the ground about twenty metres away, rolling around and muttering. One of them screamed something in Arabic. I couldn't make it out. The third one was partially protected by a boulder a little further away. Freddie smiled at me. He smiled as if the last five minutes had not been full of terror! He said, 'Angela, I knew your Arabic would come in useful. Now is the time to put it to the test. You will have to shout to the guy behind that rock. So here we go.' He shouted, 'I could kill you now but I don't want to.' I tried my best to translate but didn't know if I made any sense. 'You will see I have not killed the others, just one shot to their legs. But they will bleed to death if they do not get help.' Again, I did my best. Then, 'Throw down the gun and you will not be harmed.' Not sure if it was my translation but the guy just stepped out and blasted away at us. I dropped to the floor and had no idea where the bullets went but Freddie didn't even duck.

"He gave me a broad smile. 'That went well didn't it? Not. Let's have a look at your arm.' 'But what about that man?' I asked, still terrified. Freddie responded with, 'He's no threat. An amateur like the others. They were carrying

AK 47s. None of them had extra ammunition and they were all on full-automatic. His thirty rounds are gone. I could see from the shape of the magazines they were using that they weren't carrying more. And do you see how high he was shooting? Amateur. Just as I said! Mind you, one of them managed to nick your arm. Just as well we have our first-aid kit.' He took it out, cleaned up the wound and wrapped some sort of bandage tightly around it."

Angela pulled up the sleeve of her hoodie and pointed to a small scar on her left arm. "There's the proof. Then Freddie said, 'Now you can help me. You will find some compression bandages in there. I need you to wrap one tightly around this. It's just a nick but we need to stop it bleeding.' He lowered his trousers and blood was leaking out of his left thigh. He told me to make the dressing as tight as possible and then to put another tight dressing on top of it.

"Ten minutes later we were out of there. Freddie insisted on driving; it was an automatic so he didn't need his left leg. I sat in the back with the civilian who was crying one moment and trying to talk the next. He must have tried to say 'thank you' twenty times. Freddie made a call on the phone and told me that the plan was to return to the villa at the Alila and a doctor would be waiting for us to arrive and let him in. He also made another call. Something like, 'This is Freddie. Task completed. Package collected intact. Please advise extraction in due course.' The rest of the journey was uneventful but hot. We decided on open windows rather than air conditioning due to the awful smell coming from our passenger."

"So that was that," said William.

"Not exactly, I'm sorry to say," Angela replied.

"When we pulled up outside the villa the civilian woke up and asked me 'Where are we?' I explained that we were at a private villa at the Alila Hotel in Oman and that a doctor would be arriving to check him out. Five minutes later there was the doctor, along with a nurse. He told us to give them a couple of hours but Freddie mentioned my arm and his left thigh might need a look before the civilian. So, he went first and came back twenty minutes later with a clean pair of trousers. And then the doctor just cleaned up my arm, put on a new bandage and asked when I had last had a tetanus injection. I told him it was so long ago I couldn't remember so the nurse took me into one of the bathrooms and stuck a needle in my bum. Then it was the civilian's turn.

"'Follow me!' demanded Freddie and we walked to the main hotel, sat on the terrace, necked some serious drinks and ate some snacks. I can't remember for the life of me what we ate and drank. I think I was still in some sort of shock. Freddie leant forward and looked me straight in the eyes. He said, 'You did bloody well, Angela. You did exactly what we agreed. I know it was pretty terrifying and, to be honest, I didn't expect there would be such a drama. I have no idea why they started shooting at us. But we planned for the worst and it all worked out OK. The thing is, we need to re-write the script. The firm does not allow people to engage in firefights, as you know well. So, basically, we need to report that it was all routine or we will both be in serious trouble. Me, because I produced the gun. You because you didn't phone home to report it. But if you want to do that now I won't blame you at all. Think about it and let me know in due course.'

"It was about six and getting dark when we went back to the villa. The civilian was sitting on the sofa wearing one of the hotel's fluffy robes and looking almost human. The doctor was completely relaxed and in good humour. He said, 'This patient is severely malnourished and dehydrated. He is five kilos underweight and has a number of mild bruises and abrasions. I've given him a couple of injections to boost his immune system and given him some throat capsules as he has not been using his voice for some time. As you can see, my nurse has helped him shower and shave. She has also attempted giving him a haircut but my advice to her is not to give up her day job!'"

Chapter 69

Angela continued. "There were a few more things, important things. After the doctor had gone, Freddie sat beside the civilian and asked, 'So Simon, how are you feeling?' He didn't wait for a reply. 'Louise knows that you are safe and well. Do you want to call her now or wait a while? It's early evening in the UK and I'm sure she will be very pleased to hear from you. There is a phone in your room, which is through that door over there.' Simon thought for a moment, went to the room and closed the door. I asked Freddie, 'Why didn't you tell me his name before?' He replied quietly, 'Using a name makes it kind of personal. And I've learnt that in this business, personal can lead to poor decisions.'

"Less than ten minutes later Simon came back into the living room. It was clear he had been crying but he looked quite a bit better. Freddie asked him if he wanted a drink and would he like to eat something in the room or go to the restaurant. Simon looked down at his bathrobe and for the first time uttered a coherent sentence. 'Actually, I would like to eat with ordinary people but I'm not sure this is appropriate attire.' Freddie didn't say a word but left the room for a moment. Simon and I exchanged puzzled looks then Freddie came back in carrying one of the soft cases he had brought with him.

"He put it on the floor in front of Simon telling him 'I think you might find some clothes and other stuff here that will work, although they may be a bit loose so I took the precaution of suggesting a belt be included when Louise packed it for you.' Simon was a bit stunned and said, 'You went to see Louise?' And Freddie said, 'Yes, I did. I wanted to let her know I was going to bring you home.'

"And," said Angela, "that's when I fell in love with Freddie."

Gill smiled. "So?"

"So, we went to the restaurant and Freddie organised a quiet table in the corner so Simon wouldn't find the noise too overwhelming. And he restricted us to one bottle of wine." "Blimey that's a first," interjected William. "Yes, but sensible in retrospect," replied Angela. "Freddie got a call during dinner and laid it all out: Simon's chairman was on his way to Oman and would be picking him up at about ten the next morning. They would be going to the British embassy in Muscat where a temporary passport would be provided and then travel to Heathrow. On arrival they would be met by someone from the Home Office for an informal chat and then driven home. Freddie and I were booked on a flight the following day."

Gill had said little during the dinner but, in her usual way, she had listened intently. "So, Simon went to bed early in his room and…?"

"Freddie and I went to bed in the other room," replied Angela. "Neither of us wanted to sleep on the couch. We were completely and utterly knackered. The three of us had breakfast on our wonderful terrace. Simon was in much better shape and kept saying 'thank you, thank you.' And Freddie said, 'If you really want to thank us, could you do us a favour?' Simon said, 'Of course. Anything.' 'Then please don't mention the firefight. Tell everybody that we just walked to the car with no drama at all.' Simon asked, 'Why not? You were heroic!' Freddie explained, 'Well, the thing is that we are not allowed to carry guns. If my bosses knew about it I could get fired.' 'OK. Consider it done,' poor Simon croaked.

"We met Simon's boss in reception. Lots more thank you, thank you. And then they were gone. We spent the day on the beach and by the pool and had a lovely long lunch and a sleep in the sunshine. Freddie's pal joined us for dinner and came back to the villa with us to collect the first-aid kit and, I assume, the gun. We had a couple more drinks in the bar and, Gill, we retired to our respective suites! We are now nearly at the end of my story.

"Freddie called me over the weekend. He said, 'Hi. All OK?' I said 'Yes'. 'That's good,' he replied, 'but sorry to say that the grateful civilian has fucked us over. To be more accurate, fucked me over. An executive assistant in the firm, who I am close to, tells me that he told the guy from the Home Office about the gun. To be fair to him, those spooks are adept at getting to first base very quickly.

The bottom line is that the Home Office has contacted the bosses and they have no option but to fire me.'

"In fact, they didn't," said Angela. "Freddie took a resignation letter into the meeting and confessed all. He left that day. But they sent him a serious bonus in due course. Without that gun, the two of us and the civilian would have been killed. Not a great result from anyone's point of view. Especially ours! Anyway, as you know, he then went on to Lloyds of London for a while, specialising in K&R insurance, joined DPK and became a partner. I was headhunted by GCHQ about a year later and we have kept in touch. End of story! It's time I went, I think."

"Are you going out of the front door or the back door," asked William with a smile.

"The back door seeing as you ask. My dinghy is by Freddie's ladder and if I stay any longer the tide will be too far out and I'll have to drag it into the water and get muddy. By the way, please don't repeat 'That's when I fell in love with Freddie'. I don't want him getting the wrong idea."

The man himself came down stairs a little later and helped himself to a drink. He looked at them both and smiled. "I bet she has been telling you about that kidnap payment we did. Actually, it was the best thing that has happened to me. After all, if I had stayed with the previous outfit I wouldn't have met you guys. Or maybe I'm wrong. If I hadn't met you guys I wouldn't be worrying about some sadistic Mexican nutcase raping me and then throwing me into a field full of rabid dogs."

"How do you know they're rabid?" asked William.

Freddie looked at him with astonishment. "I'm not sure that is an issue, William. Seems to me that catching rabies would be the least of my concerns!"

CHAPTER 70

9.30 am at Thames Valley HQ and DCI 'Bunny' Field was back from holiday in Tenerife, face red with sunburn, still unhappy about his golf scores, tired from the late flight home and impatient.

"Right Clarke. What have we got on the bodies in the wood? Anything you can tell me?"

"We have made some good progress, sir. As you know we identified Pyotr Vorobyov aged thirty-nine from Lewisham London SE1 and Felicity Strange from Belgravia London SW1. He has form; she was a smart wealthy graduate trainee in that DPK organisation. We have got right down in the dirt and the footprints suggest two men and one woman were present at the site. We have also recovered one bullet from the grave which has a trace of the woman's DNA. Our current hypothesis is that the woman was shot and dumped in the grave and that Vorobyov was dumped in there as well."

"Before or after?"

"Impossible to tell, sir. But things have moved on quite quickly. The NCA think her death might be connected with a money-laundering scam and the Met are involved."

"Why the Met? Why not us?"

"NCA boss. It's connected to a major financial crime. Money laundering."

Bunny was getting hopping mad. He stood up from his chair, ignoring the pain from the sunburn on his back and let rip. "What the fuck! Not again! We do all the fucking work and you let them take all the credit!"

"I'm not sure that's fair boss," responded Clarke.

"Damn right it's not fucking fair. I'm off for a few days' holiday and you are just giving away our collars to the Met. Are you looking for a job up there? Is that the reason? What other good news do you have for me?"

"Well the guy," Clarke looked at his notes again, "Julian Harper who found the grave in his wood. He seems to be doing OK."

"Oh thank you so much. You have made my day. The bloke with the pugs is doing fine. Thank the Lord! Let me summarise: we have two murders with no clues and the bloke who found the bodies is OK. Great! And how about the dogs? Is their happiness high on your list of enquiries?"

"Well, yes, I mean no sir, if you put it that way, sir. But I do have one serious line of enquiry that I'm pursuing."

"Pray tell, Clarke. Are your enquiries related to finding out what dog food these fucking animals like to eat?"

"No, sir. We know a car was involved in the murders and I think we can be sure it took Strange from her house to the murder scene; some of the way, if not all of the way. I've arranged for all the number plates that were pinged in her area to be collated and I have distributed the data to the entire Met, with the instruction that any stolen or dumped cars or vans are fed into the data to see if we get a match. If we find a match we may have Strange's DNA and if that matches we are off to the races."

"Yeah, I get that but why the Met? Why not Manchester or wherever?"

"Well we know that Vorobyov came from London so the other guy might be part of the same scene. Anyway, are you OK with this, sir?"

"Yep. But I'm not holding my breath. What's next on the agenda?"

CHAPTER 71

Sun shining, a decent run and a healthy breakfast. By 8.30 am William was heading for Chubb and Chubb. He had no idea why the solicitor wanted to meet him. Had Felicity left him some money in her will? No way. Hopefully no way! Was it about that horse? Could be. No problem, unless she had left it to him in her will. No, he didn't think Felicity had that sort of sense of humour. Something to do with DPK? Some information that might help the police? All these ideas and questions passed through his mind and the journey was fast. When he got to West Halkin Street he was ten minutes early but decided to ring the bell anyway.

The door was opened immediately and he was shown into a meeting room that looked like it hadn't changed in centuries. There were shelves full of old books, pictures of old men, no pictures of women, no obvious technology. How did Felicity have a relationship with these people?

Then Alastair Chub came into the room. He looked exactly as William imagined he would: suit, tie, waistcoat, grey hair and reassuring smile.

"Good morning Mr West. Sorry to keep you waiting."

"No problem at all," William stood up and they shook

hands. "Please call me William." His instincts told him that Alastair was probably an OK bloke.

"Coffee, tea, glass of water?" asked Alastair.

"A black coffee, no sugar please." The solicitor left the room for a moment. When he returned he sat down opposite William and put his elbows on the table, frowned a little and said, "Seems like we might be working together on Felicity's behalf."

William wondered what was going on. "I don't know what you mean by that."

"It's not a long story, William. I will save you the details, but Felicity's parents, Kit and Sarah, their parents and their grandparents and their great-grandparents have been clients of Chubb and Chubb for many, many years. Wars, illnesses and unfortunate marriages – to say the least – combined to leave poor Felicity with a very substantial inheritance when Sarah died. And she had insisted beforehand that Felicity became a client of Chubb and Chubb so as to protect the legacy."

"OK, but what on earth has this got to do with me?" asked William.

The solicitor looked a bit nervous, a bit embarrassed. He cleared his throat. "Ah, well, Felicity appointed you as her second executor."

"What? No way. Why?" William was shocked and puzzled. "Do I have to do it? You are the executor. I assume you will be down in the detail. What do I have to do? I mean, I was an executor when my wife died and when each of my parents died. But I knew them. I knew what they would want. It wasn't a problem. But Felicity? Why? There must be many people more suitable."

"William, what I suggest you do is read this letter that Felicity left for you. Take your time. Let's talk again in a few days. We need to discuss the funeral arrangements and many other matters. In the meantime, I think it would be appropriate for me to share some information with you. I mentioned that we have looked after the family for generations. Sadly, tragically, Felicity was the last survivor and she was very wealthy. There is the small house in Belgravia, a very large house on the Wentworth estate where the tenant is a Japanese bank paying around twenty-thousand pounds a month rent. Twenty-thousand pounds a month. And Felicity also had a substantial investment portfolio. We are looking at an estate of over twenty-million pounds and Felicity's will requires both you and me to dispose of these assets. So, again, I suggest you take this letter and contact me after you have read it. I have no idea what it contains."

Alastair stood up. "Just one more thing. The police have been kind enough to return the items they removed from Felicity's house when they were seeking to find relatives and any other helpful information. They needed to change the locks. Here are the keys. I haven't been there. Perhaps you might like to consider how we could dispose of any personal belongings. Oh, and one last thing. I promise you this will be the last thing. I insisted that she made a will and she insisted she didn't want to. The net result is there are no beneficiaries named in the document."

"OK, I need to think about this. Of course, I will read the letter and I will get back to you. But please keep the keys for the time being."

CHAPTER 72

William walked around the corner to Motcomb's wine bar and ordered a large glass of Chablis. Then he took a good look at the envelope Alastair had handed to him. Cream, Smythson. Then he pulled out the letter. Again Smythson, with what he assumed was Felicity's address printed on the top. He was looking at the other side of Felicity, the side she had kept hidden from colleagues. The rich side. It was a short letter and in longhand:

Dear William,

This is a strange letter to write as the only reason you will read it is if I have died before you. And with all due respect that is rather unlikely. But that boring Mr Chubb insisted. So here we go:

I would very much like you to be my executor alongside Mr Chubb. You know me and he doesn't. In fact, you probably know me better than anyone else. I have no partner at the moment; actually, I have never had a serious partner! And I have no living relatives or even close friends.

Since I was an intern at DPK, when you gave me

some very valuable advice over that lunch at Cote, I have achieved my objectives and that is mainly down to you. I trusted your advice completely.

I have no idea what is the right thing to do with all my money if I die before you. But I know you will make the right decisions.

Love
    Felicity

PS
    Don't miss the other piece of paper in the envelope. It has all my passwords and stuff.

William read the letter again. And again. He ordered another Chablis and a double espresso. He couldn't really picture Felicity's face. He tried to remember what she looked like when they had the coffee after she rejoined the firm. Or even when they met up with George in Partnership Protection. But then, somehow, he did remember. Not the Felicity of a few weeks ago but the intern Felicity, the lunch at Cote looking over the river at Hay's Galleria and writing down her commitments on the piece of paper he gave to her.

Gill called at about two. She was meeting Jane to go to the theatre later but was not under the cosh and could meet up at five. They agreed to have a quick drink in Bar

Americain in Zedel. William left Motcomb's and walked up to Piccadilly and along to The Royal Academy, using his Friend's card to look around and then have a coffee in the Keeper's House. And as he walked down the stairs at Zedel, leading to Bar Americain, the rope was being removed from the entrance. Just like at Motcomb's, William was the only customer when he arrived. He ordered a Sipsmith vodka on the rocks and took out the letter again. As he finished reading it for the fifth time, Gill arrived looking every inch like a successful DPK partner. He stood and they air kissed.

"Just a coffee for me, William, if that is OK with you."

"Of course. But why so?"

"Jane has got us tickets for 'The Ferryman' at 7.15 pm and the thing lasts for three and half hours with a fifteen-minute break."

"Don't worry, you will love it; especially the goose, the rabbits and the fecking kids! Seriously, it's great. Ina and I loved it. However, I need you sober and I need your advice. I've been to see the solicitor who is the executor of Felicity's will and, apparently, she has named me to be an executor."

"What? You, executor? Why you? There must be people closer to her. Friends, relatives, whoever!"

"The solicitor gave me a letter from her and it seems there is no one."

Gill sighed. "Poor Felicity. How sad. Anyway you said you wanted some advice. What's up?"

"Well, should I do it?"

"Do what?"

William was feeling exasperated. "Be an executor of course!"

"William, I can't think of any reason why you would not want to carry out Felicity's wishes. She had you pegged as a sensible bloke, which you are. She certainly didn't expect that you would actually have to do this. Christ, she was in her twenties and you are, what, approaching your seventies! But here you are and there she is and do it you must."

"Yes, I thought you would say what you just said and you are right. But could I ask a favour? Could you help? Could you come with me to help sort out her stuff? And could you help me decide what needs to be done?"

"Of course, William. I'd be happy to. Just let me know when suits. Now I'm off to meet up with Jane and have a bite before three hours and thirty minutes inside the Gielgud Theatre."

William left Zedel and took the Piccadilly line tube to Hammersmith. He was home within the hour and drinking a large Sipsmith vodka five minutes later. He had a lot of thinking to do, particularly around Felicity's estate. But he came up with an idea before he had even finished his drink.

It went without saying that the vast majority of the estate, if not all, should go to charity but deciding which one would be difficult. Perhaps the best approach would be to set up a charitable trust and donate the income from the underlying investments rather than donate the whole estate at once. It could last forever. And maybe the Wentworth house could be transferred together with the twenty-thousand pounds a month income. Actually, thought William, why don't I move my charitable trust money into it? We would be looking at a serious sum which would enable us to get some decent fund managers and maybe an external trustee to sit alongside Chubb & Chubb and me. Enthusiasm took over from concern. The Strange Charitable Trust. What a great name. Time for another drink and something to eat.

CHAPTER 73

Ina came to Chiswick for dinner with William the following Friday. He wanted it to be romantic and sexy. He had decided that tuna Niçoise outside in the back garden would work well and desert would be homemade cookies with his special ingredient. Cannabis. She arrived straight from work and went upstairs to shower and change. He sat in the living room, looking through the windows which were open to a faint breeze.

The tide was running out and a couple of eights were making the most of it; moving swiftly downstream, making it look a lot easier than it was. A Port of London police boat heading in the opposite direction slowed to reduce its bow wave. He turned around when he heard Ina come in. She was wearing a colourful silk dress and high-heeled sandals.

"You look absolutely lovely. No bra?" he asked.

"Correct. No bra. And no knickers either. No need for you to raise that eyebrow, William. When I was at work I was suitably attired."

"How about a drink?"

"Scotch on the rocks please."

William got the barbecue started and streamed

some music. He chose his 'Old and Lovely' playlist which included artists like Jackson Browne, Crosby Stills and Nash, Carole King, James Taylor, Colin Blunstone and J. J. Cale. There were speakers over the table but the volume was low enough to hear the birds as dusk fell; the tinkling of the rill and the hum of the traffic on the busy A4. It was a wonderful dinner.

Later on, it was time for cookies and coffee.

"Did you make these, William?"

"Yep. I made everything this evening. Do you want another?"

"Thanks."

"How is the flat hunting going?" asked William. "Where are you looking?"

"Well, I'm assuming that I will be working in Canary Wharf for the time being and there are some great places out there. But I think I would feel a bit cut off."

"What's your price range?"

"Somewhere around £1.5 million I guess. That would leave me some room to spend some money on it. I don't have much in Edinburgh that I would want to bring down here. No great memories that's for sure. Could you pass the cookies please?"

"I don't think you should have another."

"What? Are you calling me fat, William? I'll have you know that I'm the same weight as I was at twenty-one. I think I'll have two more!"

"It's not about calories Ina, it's about the cannabis in

them."

"Say again!"

"We are talking about cannabis not calories."

"Cannabis?"

"Yes. I know that you don't smoke weed because you don't like smoking and I know you don't like me smoking it. So, I thought I could do both of us a favour by cooking some cannabis cookies. And if you eat too many, heaven knows what might happen."

"What might happen?"

"Well, you might fall asleep which is not what I want to happen."

Ina giggled. "What do you want to happen?"

"Let's leave all this stuff here, lock the door, go upstairs and I'll show you."

The next morning, William popped out of bed, put on his dressing gown, cleaned his teeth, went down to the kitchen and started making scrambled eggs. By the time Ina came downstairs, the buttered toast was in the warming drawer and the eggs needed just a minute more. Ginny pulled up in her car ten minutes later.

Ina kissed William. "I'll call you when we're on our way back from golf, probably about three. Any chance of finishing those cookies later on?" And then she was gone. It was pouring with rain.

When Ina returned she was on great form. "We had a

great game in spite of the rain. I parred three holes and got a birdie. Ginny parred three as well. The course was pretty empty so we weren't held up standing in the rain. Lunch was fun too but Ginny only had one glass as she was driving so it fell on me to polish off the bottle."

"Poor thing," replied William. "It must have been hard work. Do you want to have a nap?"

Five minutes later Ina was fast asleep on the sofa. And so was William. It was dark when they woke up and Ina left.

Willian got a text later: 'Loved my first taste of your cookies last night. Hope you enjoyed your first A levels.'

CHAPTER 74

Monday morning and William woke up at 5.30 am feeling alive and well. He was looking forward to checking out the allotment. No need to shower or even wash his hair. All of that could wait until he got back. He put on his gardening clothes, taking them from their special place in his dressing room. T-shirt and jeans, all leftovers from when they were part of his wardrobe. One of his pals used old suits for the same purpose. William wasn't quite that eccentric. But his gardening Converse shoes were twelve years old and had been dipped in the sea in the BVIs when he had fallen out of a RIB.

It was just after six. He stuck his keys and his phone in his pockets and cycled to Dukes Meadows and down Riverside Drive. It took about ten minutes. As he approached the gates he had a good look around to see who was already there. One of his allotment neighbours had a Lincoln Town Car of all things; another had a Bentley. The actress immediately next to him had a bike and the barrister on the other side had no visible signs of transport. But when everyone unlocked the gates and entered the allotment they became just gardeners.

When William unlocked the gate, pushed his

bike through and started to close it, he noticed an SUV approaching and slowing down. For some reason it didn't look like an allotment holders' vehicle. When two big men in suits stepped out of it while it was still moving, William's instincts told him to run. But somehow he realised that he had to lock the gate first. He slid the bar across, put the padlock into it, clicked it closed, grabbed the bike and ran with it. Then jumped onto the saddle and aimed for the gate at the other end of the allotment. Thank God someone had left that gate unlocked.

William didn't give anything a second thought apart from the need to cycle fast and cycle where cars couldn't follow. He pedalled hard, up towards the river then right along the towpath and over the footpath across Barnes Bridge railway line and then right along the south side towpath towards Chiswick Bridge. He was cycling as fast as possible along the path, slippery from a recent high tide. Not for one moment did he think he was mistaken. He knew the guys were a real threat. But why? And how had they known where he was? He kept on cycling hard, trying to work out his next move. He passed underneath Kew Bridge still thinking hard and pushing towards Richmond and the police station.

The closer he got to Richmond the more he worried about what he would say to the police. More importantly, how would they react? He was unshaven, in his very scruffy, sweaty gardening clothes, and probably wide-eyed and looking a bit crazy. He needed to convince them he was legitimate and really needed help. But what help? How could they help him? If those guys could find him at the allotment they could find him anywhere. And what did they want? It had to be about the passports. William thought carefully about his presentation; more carefully than any presentation he had given before. More carefully than when he had presented to two-thousand people at a conference last year. This time his life might depend on convincing someone.

He knew where Richmond police station was, left his bike outside, and went in. There was a uniformed officer sitting behind a glass screen who beckoned him forward. "Good morning sir. How can I help you?"

William swallowed. "My name is William West. I appreciate that what I am about to say is going to sound pretty strange but I am being chased by some people that want to injure me." His tone was measured as he looked straight into the policeman's eyes. "I need your help."

"Could I see some ID please, sir?"

"I'm really sorry but I have no ID. But I do have my phone if that is of any help."

"OK. Please take a seat and I'll get someone to help you." The uniform closed the screen and made a call, had a few words and put the phone down.

"Someone will be with you shortly."

William felt safe in the police station and wasn't too concerned that it was thirty minutes before a young chap in very casual clothes appeared.

"Mr West, would you like to come this way please?"

They sat in a room, very similar to the rooms William had seen on TV when murder suspects were interviewed.

"Now, could we start from the beginning please."

Thirty minutes later and William thought he had done a good job explaining the whole thing and his current predicament. But he wasn't sure he had convinced the officer.

"OK. I think I get this, sir. As I'm sure you will appreciate, it will take some time for us to interact with the other agencies and ensure we fully understand the situation. We have your contact details and will get back to you as soon as possible."

Chapter 75

William was nothing if not resourceful. He knew that he was safe where he was. No one knew where he was and no one was about to invade Richmond police station. But what to do next? His palms were sweaty; he was breathless; his heart was still hammering; his head was whirling. He tried to calm down and think rationally. Stan! He called. Voicemail!

"Hi Stan; I need your help. I'll explain more later. What I need you to do is to get some things for me and come and pick me up. Go into the house and get my credit cards and cash. You will find them on the dresser in my dressing room. Could you also get a pair of chinos and a sweatshirt plus a pair of boxer shorts and socks from the cupboard please. Finally, when you get this message could you text me and I will tell you where I am? Many thanks."

When he left the police station, William was pleased to see that his bike was still there. Just to be careful, he turned off the main road as soon as possible, cycled down to the river and rode west along the towpath, where no car could follow him. He took his time to conserve his energy and started to relax a little.

William cycled up to Ham, into the park and turned

right. He was at the car park within fifteen minutes and finally relaxed. Sitting on one of the seats near the playground area he closed his eyes for a moment. He listened to birdsong, feeling the warmth of the sun on his face and enjoying the solitude after the earlier drama. Then, from behind, slow heavy footsteps that stopped. Before he could turn round a hard hand gripped his shoulder and another slapped him so hard on his cheek he fell off the chair and crashed his face into the ground. Lying there, completely shocked, he stared up at two men. They seemed to be smiling. He knew he had to run, he knew he could outrun them. He scrambled to his feet and the larger guy kicked them out from underneath him. He crashed to the ground again. They pulled him up and the smaller man spoke. He had a London accent and a calm voice.

"Take it easy, William. No worries. I have a taser. My colleague has a taser. You have fuck all. And you are coming with us. Now!"

"What? How come? How did you find me?" asked William desperately.

"The phone, dickhead, the phone. We have had your phone for weeks. Now get in the car next to my colleague and shut up."

The car left Richmond Park and headed towards the M4. No one spoke. William started to become very worried indeed. No panic yet but he could feel it building. The men had made no effort to conceal their faces. They looked to be in their thirties, one of them had a beard. He tried to remember how they looked in case he managed to escape. But it seemed they were completely unconcerned about him knowing where they were taking him. They hadn't even tied his hands or blindfolded him. This looked like a one-way trip. He was no hero but he was a rational man. His whole career was based on logic, honesty and an ability to confront clients with the realities they were facing and encourage them to take the tough decisions that would enable them to survive and, possibly, prosper. But this was different. It was clear that they were not about to kill him; they could have done that in the park. So, they needed him alive. But for how long?

Then they were heading west on the M4. William knew the road well and as the familiar signs went past and London was left behind, he knew he had made a serious mistake. These guys must be after the data stick. What else? But how could they know? And what could he do? Had he just put it in his safe he could have given it up to these guys and maybe, just maybe, they might have let him go. Probably not. But a slim chance. But he had not hidden it. He had asked Sky to hide it.

William decided he was kidding himself. He was letting himself down. First, that option no longer existed. Second, whatever the cost, he was not going to let these people loose on Sky. Even if she gave the data stick up immediately, which would be the sensible thing, they would probably make her disappear. Third, he needed to act before it was too late. Neither of the guys were wearing seat belts, maybe he could somehow get the car to crash and then escape? He wasn't wearing a seat belt either, but did that really matter? Police would arrive, an ambulance would arrive, it must be worth the chance. And if he died, so what? He was near the promised 'three score and ten'. He was going to leave a great deal of money to people and causes that really deserved it. And whatever happened, it couldn't be worse than what these guys might do to him to find out where the data stick was.

As that terrifying thought went through his mind, the driver indicated left and slowed down as they approached a roundabout. William knew he had to do something. But what? Maybe he could do something when the car was moving slower. Maybe grab the driver and cause the car to crash. Even if no one got hurt but the car was too damaged to drive, that would be a result. So how might he do it? The guy in the passenger seat pointed at a side road on the left and grunted. The driver indicated and slowed down. William sat back, tensed and sprang forward, reaching for the driver's head. Before he even made contact, the taser hit him in the neck and he collapsed sideways into the footwell.

CHAPTER 76

Freddie was worried. He had called William first thing on Monday and left a message. There had been no response all day. It was very unusual. So, the next day he cycled over to Chiswick Mall to see what was wrong. Tina was there and she was even more worried. They both knew William was reliable and predictable. In a sense, a bit boring at times. It was inconceivable that he would just go off the grid without explanation.

"What about Stan?" asked Freddie.

"He hasn't seen him either," was the tearful response.

"OK Tina, leave this with me. Give me your mobile number. Here's mine. Let's keep in touch."

Freddie was not a man to fool himself. Underneath the womanising, carefree, burning the candle and snorting the coke at both ends character was a man that had been there, done that and brought back the blood-stained t-shirt. Mark, Felicity, Kathy and now William. He was probably next on the list so this was self-preservation as well as finding a friend. But first things first. He needed to report William as missing, so he got on his bike and set off for Richmond police station. He wasn't surprised to be kept waiting. He wasn't surprised to find himself struggling to explain the situation to a detective constable. But he was extremely surprised to hear, "Oh yes sir, I remember Mr West. He came in here with a story about being followed."

"He came in with a story. A story? What do you mean by that?"

"He said someone had attacked him and was following him."

"Well what did you do?"

"What could we do? Put him in a cell? Offer him police protection? What would you expect us to do?"

"Yes, I understand. Sorry to be so aggressive but the guy has actually disappeared without a trace and all his cash, credit cards and everything are left behind so I think something serious has happened to him. And what you also need to know is there are ongoing cases relating to a couple of his colleagues."

"OK. Can I ask you for a statement and would you like a cup of tea or coffee?"

Freddie spent the next hour and a half explaining as much as he could regarding the passports, Mark, Felicity and Kathy, without going into too much detail about the spreadsheets and the data key. He mentioned the involvement of HMRC and the NCA and it was from that point that the DC started to take him really seriously.

"So, what happens next?" Freddie asked.

"We will liaise with the other agencies and join up the dots. Feel free to call me any time. Here is my card. I have your contact details and will let you know if there are any developments."

When Freddie left the police station he looked at his watch. He had been in there three hours and ten minutes and it had felt like a complete waste of time. Who to speak to next? Partnership Protection? No. Colin in QRM? No. The Fed? No, they had no jurisdiction in the UK. He had no idea what to do. So often in his life he had let people down. Let down people he cared about. And he feared he was going to let William down as well. If he was looking at his face in a mirror he would have spat at it. He walked up the road to the nearest pub and got so pissed they had to call him a cab. Another bicycle lost.

CHAPTER 77

William's nightmare was over. He had dreamt he was tied up in a bath with a mad woman talking about a data key and threatening to torture him. It was horrifyingly realistic. She had a saw in her hand; he could almost feel the pain. And there was real pain as he slowly came to. Dull but persistent pain in his foot. He opened his eyes. He was in the bath, he was tied up and he was naked. Then he screamed. He saw his little toe resting on a piece of gauze in the middle of his chest. Just lying there. It had been part of him since he was born and now it was gone. That made him incredibly sad. His eyes welled up with tears. Then sadness turned to anger but anger soon gave way to fear. He thought he had been scared when the guys picked him up in the park. He remembered his fear as he tried to crash the car but couldn't remember what happened next. But here he was, naked in a bath looking at his little toe. Petrified.

"Ah, our hero awakes." A voice from behind that he recognised only too well. The little old lady who had sawed through his toe until he fainted then finished the job when he came to. He thought she looked and sounded like Miss Marple on TV but he knew now she was evil incarnate and fucking crazy.

"Sorry to disturb you, William, but I need to use the lavatory. I'll just switch off the video for a moment. Normally I wouldn't dream of doing this in front of anyone. I'd be embarrassed just to have a pee. But of course, you're not anyone. You're a corpse. It just so happens not yet. Anyway, I hope you're not embarrassed." She spoke as she defecated noisily.

"Anyway, bodily functions are the least of your problems. Let me wipe my bum and get down to it."

She stood up. "I'll just switch the video back on then it's time to put things in perspective. So, let's start with a simple question. Where is the data stick?"

"Can I have some water please?" William croaked.

"Of course. I'll just pop downstairs." William tried to think fast but his head was whirling and she was back in moments with a glass of water that she put to his mouth.

"Take it easy. We don't want you drowning yourself. Mind you, if you are stupid you might find yourself very close to it as I have my own special version of waterboarding. Anyway, the simple question: where is the data stick?"

"I am a very rich man, if you let me go I will pay you one million pounds within twenty-four hours."

"William, let me be clear, at some stage my client will have the data stick. Then, if I so decide, I might continue my work on you until you are begging me to end your life. That's when we might get to the issue of the million pounds. Think on that. Now, where is the data stick?"

William sighed. "It's in the Malmaison Hotel in Leith. In room twenty-one on top of the cabinet containing the TV."

"Thank you, William, that was quick. Excuse me one moment."

She was back in the room within ten minutes.

"I'm reliably informed by my colleague that you haven't been to Edinburgh in the last month. I didn't take you as stupid, you must know we have had a tracker on your phone. What do I need to do to ensure you are going to be honest with me? Maybe I should show you what might happen if you carry on playing silly buggers. Let me tell you about my tools. Some can be carried in plain sight, some would need some imaginative explanations if they were discovered.

"William, have a look at this. It's a normal metal nail file. I carry it with me all the time. It's very useful. Let me show you. So, here is your cock. Let's have a look."

She flicked it with the nail file. "Not circumcised and shrivelled with fear. Tiny. I could apply an electric shock and I may do so later. In the meantime look at this."

She gently inserted the head of the nail file into his foreskin and then wiggled it around. He screamed. She gently pushed it further in, maybe an inch. He screamed louder, "Stop, just stop!" A little further. "Please stop, please."

"OK William if that's what you want." She pulled the

nail file out roughly and quickly. He didn't scream, he fainted. And came to with a bucket of water being chucked in his face.

"I'm quite attached to this nail file. I once used it to remove a stupid lady's eye. It took just a few minutes but of course I had to put her head in a vice first and it was a bit challenging logistically. Anyway, I digress. Here is how we shall proceed. It's important that you understand and remember the rules; particularly when things get messy. Rule number one: you have to die. Rule number two: you must not lie to me again. Rule number three: if you lie to me and waste my time I will punish you faster than you can say 'I can't say'. Do you understand?"

"Yes."

"OK. Now just to be fair I think I should tell you about some of the other tools I have with me. I get quite excited just thinking about the pain I can inflict with them. First, I have designed and built a three-legged structure which is portable and can be assembled in about twenty minutes. Basically, it's used with a winch to haul you up in the air by your hands or your feet. If it's by your hands which are strapped behind your back, the torture is called 'strappado' and it dislocates your shoulders. In my experience, very few people are able to withstand it. If I winch someone up by their feet I use a cane on their backside and their back. My God, you should hear the screams!

"Have a look at this. It's an Argentinian cattle prod. I usually use it on the genitals first. When I've amused myself with that approach I smear the prod with some lubricant; baby oil, cooking oil, engine oil – whatever's available. Then I insert it. Obviously with men it's the backside. With women I have to make choices. As you can see, it's a pretty sizeable prod so it hurts quite a bit when I stick it in. But the last time I used the prod it was a sight to behold. When I pulled the trigger, I thought the guy's eyes were going to pop out. It was truly intoxicating.

"Couple of other things. Waterboarding? Not my favourite. But sometimes when I have someone hanging by their feet over the bath I can't resist filling it up and lowering their head into it. Combining that with the cattle prod up the backside usually does the trick. So, what do you think about that William?"

He was completely stunned and speechless. Frightened witless by the tools and the lustful way they had been described. Wondering how he could get out of the place. He had to buy some time. People would be looking for him.

He thought swiftly and stammered, "I'm convinced. I'd rather die than suffer like that. Can you promise me that you will make it easy for me?"

She smiled. "Of course." Then she snarled. "But if you mess me around you will be praying for death."

William struggled to talk. His voice was almost a whisper. "The data key is in my locker in the DPK building. In fact, there are two data keys in there but one has nothing on it."

"And whereabouts is your locker in the building?"

"It's on the nineteenth floor."

"How will I find it?"

"You turn right out of the lift through the glass doors and walk to your right, past a little cafe, past several meeting rooms and the lockers are on your right. My number is 19386. But you need a key and you need a pass to get there. All the doors need a pass, as does the main entrance."

Sadie frowned. "Where is your key and your pass?"

"They are in my briefcase, which is in my dressing room at home," replied William, trying hard to sound as helpful as possible.

"But the pass has my photo on it. The security people don't normally ask to look at it, you just wave it at the sensor. But if they don't recognise a person they may well put out their hand for it. Once you are past the gates no one will look at the pass."

Sadie looked thoughtful for a moment. "Getting your pass and key will be pretty straightforward. The photo might be a bit more difficult." Then she walked out of the room.

CHAPTER 78

William lay there. The pain from his tied hands behind his back was worse than the pain from his foot. He had vomit on his stomach and urine on his thighs. Even though the room was full of sunshine he was shivering. His teeth were chattering. Had he made another stupid mistake. What if she got access to the building? What if she opened his locker? But how could she get access? There was no way the security people would fail to ask to see her pass. She looked nothing like a typical employee.

She came back into the room. "Looks like I will have to leave you on your own for a while, William. I have to go to London. I do hope you will be OK. I'm going to use these scissors to undo one of your hands now; please don't be silly and try and hit me or something. I just want to put this bottle within your reach so that you don't get too dehydrated. Look, I have even opened it for you. Make sure you don't spill it. I'm going to tie the other hand to your neck so please place your arm across your chest. That's it. Thank you.

"I'll probably be back tomorrow morning and if all goes to plan I should have that data key the next day. In the meantime, please don't bother thinking about how you might escape. In the very unlikely event that you manage to undo these cable ties and get out of the bath, this room is completely secure. And if you are not still tied up in that bath when I return, I will punish you. Cheerio."

The door slammed. William heard a key locking it and then a bolt sliding. He could see a window to his right and that had solid locks on it as well. But maybe he could break the glass. He realised this was probably his one and only chance to get out of the situation and he got to work on the plastic cable tie that was tying his hand to his neck. There was absolutely no give. He took a swig of the water. What were his options? None. He had no options. He drank some more water and started to feel drowsy. Amazingly he fell asleep.

When William woke up Sadie was looking down at him.

"All intact, I'm pleased to say. I hope you had a good night's sleep. The dose I put in that water bottle was enough to send a horse to sleep. And no hangover either! So, let me give you the good news. We had no difficulty getting your pass and locker key and changing the photo on the pass didn't present a problem, provided it just gets a cursory glance.

"It's about eight o'clock now and my colleague will be entering the DPK building at about 9 am, when it is nice and busy. If all goes well he will be out of there with both data keys by 9.30 am and will call me. That's when we can have that discussion I mentioned."

"What do you mean?" asked William. "What discussion?"

Sadie smiled. "Don't you remember? Understandable, I suppose. You mentioned you were a rich man and could pay me a million pounds to let you go. Well, I want that million pounds and I will let you go nicely. But if I don't get that money you won't go nicely. You will go very nastily and very slowly. Anyway, that's a conversation to have later on. In the meantime, let's keep our fingers crossed that all goes well at DPK. If not, you might not have any fingers left to cross. By the way, I detach the fingernails first."

CHAPTER 79

"You idiot. You fucking idiot."

Sadie strode over to the bath and smacked William hard in the face.

"What did you think you were playing at? How could you be so stupid? How could I have been so stupid? No data keys. Of course, no fucking data keys!"

She smacked him in the face again. "William, you have truly pissed me off. You have wasted my time and earned yourself a beating; more pain than you can imagine. I'm going to sit down and calm down before setting about you. And you had better prepare yourself for agony. Apologies; nothing can prepare you for the agony I'm going to inflict."

"Please no," William whispered.

"Fuck you!" she said and spat in his face.

Half an hour later, she came back into the room. Again, she was just wearing a bra and pants, white plastic clogs and surgical gloves; this time she was carrying some form of apparatus. She erected a structure quickly and carefully. William looked on with horror. There were three metal rods reaching almost to the high ceiling of the bathroom and then a fly wheel on top with a rope attached at one end to a manual winch, and at the other end a hook hanging over the bath. She stepped back to admire the structure, stood on her tiptoes to grab the hook and placed it under the wires around William's feet. With some difficulty she managed to release them from the taps to which they were attached, smiled at William and started to wind the winch.

As William's feet were raised, his body slid along the bath and as the winch pulled his legs straight and then higher his face smashed into the front of the bath and then hit the taps. He was swinging in the air, upside down, blood rushing to his head, spectacles finally giving up the ghost and falling into the bath. A glimpse of blood, urine and faeces and his little toe and there he was; hands tied behind his back, feet tied and close to the ceiling, naked, helpless and pretty much finished.

"This is stage one, William. Just to get 'proof of concept' as I have heard business people say. To me it means this. I am going to inflict some pain on you. It's going to hurt more than you can imagine. If you tell me to stop I will. If you tell me where the data key actually is, your punishment will be harsh but fair. But if we don't get it soon I promise you that you will be begging me to kill you within a couple of hours. But I won't!" Then she slashed with the cane. And that's when William knew that he was going to die in unbelievable pain or give up Sky. He opted for the former; he knew couldn't give up Sky, He listened to the ecstatic grunting and cried and screamed as the cane hit again and again. He was beyond any form of logical thought and welcomed oblivion.

When William recovered enough to open his eyes he was back in the bath; his back, bottom and thighs were on fire. But he somehow continued to think about how he could buy time and maybe escape. He knew that Sadie would not kill him until she got hold of the data key but an idea floated into what was left of his mind.

"Well William, that was fun, wasn't it? Please stand up in the bath, I just want to put some lotion on your back and backside. We don't want any infection, do we? Now, put your hands behind your back so I can tie them together. Good, that seems fine. Excuse me a moment."

Sadie came back in carrying a square box which she put on the floor by the bath. "What I'm going to do to you William is quite dangerous; dangerous for you, not me, of course. But I do have to take precautions. Some years ago, when I was using this device the chap had a heart attack and almost died. Very inconvenient. But I don't want you to worry, this is my defibrillator and if your heart gives out I'll be ready to assist. Ready? Here we go." And she started to wind the winch again, her face going red with exertion and excitement.

Slowly, William's arms were raised behind him and pain raced across his shoulders. He went on to his toes and she stopped winding.

"Perfect William. That's just how I want you. This takes a bit of practice but if I just raise you a bit more."

William screamed.

"And I'll lower you now. If I raise you high enough

your shoulders will dislocate. Now where is the data key?"

William was now crying again and choking. "It's in my allotment. I promise you! it's buried in my allotment. Well, not actually in my allotment but the one next to it."

"How deep?" she asked as she lowered his arms a little.

"About a foot."

"Is it wrapped in anything?"

"No. Yes! It's in some plastic."

"Tell me exactly where it is."

"It's about six feet away from the nearest shed to my allotment in among some fruit plants. Blackberry or raspberry I think. I can't be sure. I was in a hurry."

Sadie lowered his arms a little more, left the room, and came back after a couple of minutes.

"So far, so good. It's true that you have been to the allotment twice since you got hold of my client's property so you could be telling the truth. How do I find this allotment?"

"Can I have some more water please?"

He drank as much as he could before Sadie asked, "How do I get in there?"

"There is a path through the middle and my allotment is No 451. However, it doesn't have a number on it. Most don't."

"Well how the fuck can we find it?"

William took his time. "I could draw you a map which would help but there are over four-hundred plots. I could also draw you a map of roughly where the data stick is. You could always ask someone but they might think it a bit strange."

"Ask someone?"

"Yes. There are usually people around."

"I need to think about this and talk to someone," said Sadie. "I might be gone for some time. Sit down and make yourself comfortable William, I might not be back until the morning."

With that she left the room and left William with a glimmer of hope. Would she decide she needed him to go to the allotment with her? Had he said too much or too little to make that happen? If he did get the chance to go there, what could he possibly do? Lying down, back in the bath, feet and hands numb from the ties around them, soaked with his own urine and faeces he tried to envisage escape and then, incredibly, the bathroom door started to open; slowly, silently, cautiously. Stan appeared.

CHAPTER 80

William's heart leapt. Thank God.

"Stan, oh Stan! How did you find me?" He was weeping with relief.

"Where is the bitch? Are we safe? Have you called the police? Stan, thank God you are here. You have saved my life. Where is that woman? Am I safe?"

Stan looked around the room, taking in the hoist, the filthy bath, the state William was in. He swallowed nervously, not meeting William's eyes. And William knew before Stan opened his mouth.

"Sorry boss, Sadie's asked me to babysit while she goes off to meet someone."

"Babysit? Just get me out of this bath and let's get out of here. Where are we anyway?"

"Boss. I'm not here to help you. I'm one of the bad guys."

"Bad guys? Bad guys? Stan, why?"

"Money of course. £25,000, just to pretend to run after the guy that pretended to steal your phone and do some other stuff."

"Steal my phone?"

"Yeah, outside that restaurant. He wasn't a real thief.

He just ran around the corner and handed the phone to a bloke to put an app on it or something and then he hit me a bit to make it look real and I came back the hero. I also had to listen to conversations in the car and tell them about you telling your pal Freddie that you had hidden a data stick somewhere safe and later on deleting all the files on your computer."

"Why Stan? Why?"

"Money! I've always been a bit of a gambler; poker mainly. And I've had a run of bad luck, online and over the table. I needed some cash to get me straight but I kept on losing and I kept on borrowing. You can guess the rest."

"Why didn't you tell me? I would have lent you the money. I would have given you the money. But it's not too late."

Stan didn't meet William's eyes. He just stared into the corner of the room.

"You know that they are going to kill me, don't you Stan. And look at me. This is just the beginning. That Sadie is a fucking nut case who gets off on torturing people. She's going to torture me until she gets her hands on that data stick and she might not stop then. She loves the job. You've got to get me out of here. You know I'm rich. I'll pay you a hundred-thousand. You know I'll keep my word."

"You must be joking. These people don't fuck around. We are talking Russian or Eastern European gangsters. I don't want to end up in a bath like you with acid poured all over me."

"Are they that ruthless Stan?"

"You bet they are!"

"Well why do you trust them? Ruthless guys don't take risks. You are a risk. They could take you out of the picture and save twenty-five-thousand pounds at the same time. Think about it Stan. And when you are doing your thinking, bear this in mind. Yes, you deleted the files but they are in the Cloud, Stan. In the fucking Cloud. It took me about thirty minutes to restore them. I wonder what your new pals will think when I tell them that. Stan, just help me get out of here and you will have a life and I will pay you a quarter of a million. I'll pay you whatever it takes!"

"Sorry boss"

William got virtually no sleep that night, he hadn't eaten for more than twenty- four hours and had little to drink. His foot still ached and he wondered if it was infected. His back hurt like hell every time he moved. And he was sweating, even though the room was cool. Time and time again he tried to persuade Stan it would be sensible for him to help the two of them to escape. But Stan just sat there, staring at the wall.

When daylight finally arrived, Sadie came into the room, still in her outfit of bra, pants, surgical shoes and face mask.

"Thanks Stan. See you later. Good morning William, I trust you slept well."

He didn't reply.

"Poor Stan. Greed and naivety, not a good combination for survival, let alone success." She smiled.

"Today is an important day for you, William. If you are lucky, it will be the last day of your life. If you are unlucky you will wish it was.

"I've decided that we need to investigate your allotment claim and, sadly, I think you need to come along. The reason I say 'sadly' is that allowing you to get out of this bath, where you will in due course die, presents a degree of risk. And if you are just wasting my time and exposing me to risk, then you know what the penalty is for that, don't you? My winch and cattle prod will be waiting together with some even more interesting devices."

William said nothing.

CHAPTER 81

Sadie came back wearing jeans, trainers and a scruffy t-shirt. Stan still wouldn't meet William's eyes.

"Well William," said Sadie. "Stan knows exactly where your allotment is. So, we don't need you to come with us. But we have decided to take you on our gardening adventure so you can show us exactly where you buried the data stick." William said nothing.

"Stan, help William out of the bath and put these clothes on him. No need to clean him up. He is, as they say, a dead man walking."

They had to half carry William down the stairs. The early morning sun almost blinded him as they shoved him into a SUV. This time the seat belts were all fastened. Sadie was in the front passenger seat, William in the back with another guy who pointed to his taser just in case William hadn't noticed it. Stan drove. William had no idea of the time but guessed it was nine or ten when they arrived at the allotment. A Lincoln Town Car was parked near the gate and he recognised it. Eddie, the eccentric Italian was there. And his allotment was between the footpath and William's plot.

The gate was locked as usual.

"Where is the key?" asked Sadie.

No one replied until William spoke. "I've got no idea."

"Fucking hell Stan, why didn't you tell me the gate would be locked?" she asked.

And then Eddie came walking down to the gate. William's heart sank. "William, how are you? Who are these guys?" he asked as he unlocked the gate.

"Er, just friends who want to have a look. Thanks Eddie," as Eddie opened the gate for them. "No need to lock, we shall only be a couple of minutes."

All four of them walked in.

"William, that was very sensible. I'm beginning to believe you. I hope you're not going to let me down or that brief shoulder exercise will become something much more painful. Perhaps a cattle prod up your arse might remind you of the posh boarding school I bet you attended – until, that is, I press the button."

They arrived at Eddie's allotment and navigated the aqueducts he had built from bits of drainpipe and guttering so he could irrigate his plot via the standpipe.

Then they were at William's immaculate plot with Stan's new raised beds and everything in its place. William was amazed that only a few days ago he had thought this was important. He pointed to the overgrown space next to his plot; overgrown with weeds. Artichokes gone to seed, collapsed runner bean poles, couch grass everywhere, some empty manure bags on top and around a massive rhubarb plant. He decided to point at the bit that looked the most difficult to access.

"You will need a fork; there's one in my shed. Stan has a key." They all looked at Stan who looked at the ground.

"Well, you could break in," said William. "The side windows are only Perspex."

There was a shout. "Will, good to see you. How are you? Actually, you look a bit peaky if I may say so. Who are these good people?"

"Friends, Barry. Just wanted to look at the allotment. Sorry to say that yours is looking like it might not pass inspection in September."

"That's why I'm here, old chap. Anyone want to help me tidy this lot up?"

"We were just leaving," said Sadie. And they did.

Eddie had left the gate unlocked and they were soon on their way back. "We are coming straight back here tomorrow morning before any more of these fucking gardeners are out of bed," said Sadie. "William, you are going to point out the exact spot where you buried that stick. Stan, you are going to get a fork, collect us, drive us here and dig the fucking thing up. And you," pointing at the other guy, "you with the unpronounceable name. You will get a gun, and be ready to shoot any early birds. And I'm talking two legs not two wings. Got that?"

"Yes," he replied. "I already have a gun. And if this fucking farce continues for much longer it will be pointing at you."

Back at the house, Stan and the other guy went up to the bathroom with Sadie and William. "Right William, take off your clothes and put your hands behind your back." He obeyed and winced as Sadie put the wires around his wrists and manoeuvred him into the bath. "OK, you guys can fuck off. If we want to get back to Chiswick early tomorrow morning we are going to need to leave by 5.30 am so be here on time. Don't be late."

They left and Sadie looked down on William intently.

"I think you are being very sensible telling me where that stick is, William. At least, I hope you are. I'm not entirely sure. You are an intelligent man and I'm asking myself if I might be missing the point. Why would you not have given the location of the data sticks immediately? Why take the pain?"

She stood beside the bath, looking down on him and abstractly tapping her fingers on the enamel.

"Were you hoping that someone would come to your rescue? Were you trying to buy time? What do you care about this stick? Why not give it up?"

"I don't want to die," he whispered, tears in his eyes.

"Well, if the stick is found where you say it is, you are going to die tomorrow William."

She frowned and looked at him intently.

"Of course there is another reason why you might be misleading me. Perhaps it's not a case of where it is, but who it is. Perhaps someone else has it."

William met her eyes and didn't blink.

She shrugged. "Anyway, we will know the answer tomorrow. Because if the stick is not there my guess is that you may have given it to someone you care about. Someone so important that you are prepared to be tortured on their behalf. So, let me tell you this: poor Stan, poor naïve Stan, has told me all about your close friends, where they live, what they do. If necessary, I shall keep you in that bath and bring them down here to join you, one by one until I get that stick. Sleep well."

CHAPTER 82

Freddie was getting even more anxious. He had spoken to Tina and checked out the house. It was obvious that something bad had happened. He had called Stan and he'd said 'William must be away'. But that couldn't be right. More to the point, tomorrow was August 12th – the 'Glorious Twelfth – and the two of them had accepted an invitation to shoot grouse at a very prestigious estate in Yorkshire. Should he go or should he stay in London? What could he do? The police had been alerted. After the meeting at Richmond police station he had provided all the information they had requested plus a couple of recent photographs he had found when looking thorough William's things. In the end he sent him one more text. 'See you at the butts, I hope!' But he didn't expect a reply.

Freddie needed to be at the shoot in time for breakfast and he wouldn't miss it for the world. Full English, plus kedgeree followed by toast and marmalade all served by their host's staff. His alarm went off at 4 am. After a quick shower and shave he put on his shooting gear; thick socks, Viyella shirt, brown corduroy trousers and tweed jacket. Nothing to scare the birds.

He carried his packed suitcase downstairs, collected

his Barbour jacket and cap, waterproof over-trousers and boots. Even in August it could be pretty chilly, probably raining in Yorkshire, and the floors in the butts were always wet. He stowed everything away in his Range Rover and went back for his guns. Unlocking the cabinet, he took out his two Purdey side by sides, made in Hammersmith just down the road, and a couple of boxes of cartridges. The shoot would provide the rest. Last but not least he put the hip flask he had filled the previous evening in his shooting bag, alongside his phone and binoculars. He was all set for bagging those birds as they flew towards the guns; low, seventy miles an hour, skittering all over the place as if they knew that they had to make themselves difficult targets.

"Let the battle commence," he said out loud as he started the engine.

As he was about to leave his drive and turn into Hartington Road, William's car went past with Stan driving and someone else in the front passenger seat. He just caught a glimpse but it wasn't William. What the fuck! What was Stan doing at this time in the morning? Without a second thought he pulled out and followed the Mercedes. In Freddie's previous life he had been instructed on how to follow cars without alerting the driver. This was exceptionally difficult when there was just one vehicle following; three would be ideal. But 'we are where we are' was a phrase he had heard many times, so he stayed well back, looking for any sign that Stan might have seen him.

When they got onto the M4 he ensured there were one or two vehicles between them and was able to think.

'I should be on my way to shoot grouse and I may be on a fucking wild goose chase. If neither William nor me turn up there will be hell to pay. Two guns absent is little short of a disaster. Shall I see if I can get my phone out of the bag? No, I can't reach that without stopping. Where the fuck is Stan going? Is he somehow involved in this? I've never trusted the little shit. Why would he say William was 'away'? Let's think about timing. I'm half an hour past the M25. It's about three hours max to get to the shoot from there. And it starts at 10.30 am. It's nearly 6 am now so I can still make the shoot on time if I turn around at the next exit which is just coming up. Hold on, he's indicating left.'

Two cars also took the exit and Freddie glided in behind them. Then one followed the Mercedes as it turned left off the roundabout. Freddie did the same, staying well back. After about ten minutes the Mercedes slowed, indicated left and turned into a minor road. The car in front of Freddie continued on. He slowed down further and then turned left. "Fuck, fuck," he muttered; hands tight on the steering wheel, staying even further back, willing himself invisible. After a few more miles along the narrow road the Mercedes slowed right down. "That's it. I'm fucked, they've made me," Freddie muttered to himself. But then the car in front turned into a drive of about a hundred yards with trees and bushes each side leading to a house surrounded by foliage. Freddie continued on and pulled into a little space by the side of a road in front of a farm gate. He sensed – he knew – that William was in that house.

Looking at his watch, Freddie thought about calling his host and explaining that he couldn't make it. He decided not to. He thought about phoning the police. And decided not to. What if William wasn't there? What if there was an entirely reasonable explanation? But if he was there, what could be done? Who else might be in there? His days of derring-do were way gone. He had experienced fear, he had been injured. He had faced death and had no desire to do so again. Forget 'no desire'. He had no capability. His hands were sweaty, his forehead sweaty, his breathing already harsh. He could feel his heart beating. His hand went to the ignition key and he started the engine. Then he swallowed, switched it off and opened the door.

It was only when he had walked a couple of yards that he realised that he had left the key in the ignition and the door unlocked. He smiled, looking back in his mind thirty years or more. A thin wiry SAS instructor had said, "Freddie, for fuck's sake! You are not parking up to go to fucking Harrods. If this goes tits up, and it probably will, we will be running away from some hard cases with guns. Do you really want to be looking for your car keys at that moment? In this world, two seconds can be the difference between life and death. Actually, two tenths of a second can be. Where possible, leave the fucking engine running and the door open!"

CHAPTER 83

Inside the house, Sadie was downstairs and William was having yet another attempt to persuade Stan to help.

"Stan, you are the dead man walking. Just like me. But I can save you. I think I can save both of us. You must know you are in deep shit. You must know that these people do not leave any loose ends. You are the loose end Stan. You fucked up by not actually removing the files from my iMac. You might be encouraged to tell all to the cops in return for a smaller sentence. They know that, so of course they will take you off the board and save themselves some money at the same time.

Stan put his hands in his pockets, turned his head way and didn't speak.

"I have money, Stan. More than enough money. I can set you up with enough money to disappear and get a new life. I will pay you a million pounds to help me get out of here. And I will make sure these guys will never get to you!"

"Oh yeah. How would you manage that?"

"Money, Stan. Money. And connections!"

"Sorry. Can't be done. Let me get you out of the bath and get you dressed for the allotment."

Stan moved behind William and somehow William found himself standing up, naked, knees trembling, eyes close to tears, chest thumping, hands tied behind his back, feet damp from his own urine, dehydrated, weak from no food for two days and terribly, terribly scared. There was no way out.

Sadie came into the bathroom with a broad smile.

"Time we were on the road, chaps!" She untied the wires around William's wrists. He took a breath, turned and hit her in the face. But the blow was weak and ineffectual and he slipped as he punched.

She smiled. "I'm looking forward to the rest of the day, William. I know I said your death would be painless. I've changed my mind. When we get back here later I'm going to have some serious fun with you. The boys will be gone. Just you and me. And I'm already getting very excited. My imagination is running riot. I can't wait."

"Look," croaked William. "Let me just say this. The data stick is not important. I know for certain that DPK, the accountancy firm, has a copy of the information that's on it. And so does the Federal Reserve in the States. Torturing me, killing me, will make no difference. All the data is already out there. Why are you doing this?"

"I don't know. And I don't care. I have job to do and I shall do it. I'll enjoy doing it. And I shall get paid for doing it. I will give my client the data stick. They give me the money. End of story. End of your life. Although I have to say that my story will be more enjoyable than yours. And, imagine. Even if my clients changed their minds, you will still have to go. Otherwise you might crop up with some allegations down the line and that would have a negative impact on my business. Let's get going."

Freddie had been working his way very carefully towards the house from the side. His shooting clothes helped as they were designed to blend in with the landscape but he took no risks whatsoever. He stayed close to the ground. He remembered an ex-Indian special forces sergeant. He was as hard as nails and as smooth as silk; an iron fist in a velvet glove. It was midnight, just outside Aden, South Yemen. The back of the back of beyond. It was a handover of one-million dollars cash from a Lloyds syndicate to a bunch of stoned ragheads. Real cash not counterfeit. Freddie and Iron Fist had been tasked to get it back in order to teach them a lesson. Grabbing our guys doesn't pay! They had crawled towards the gap between the handover and the other guys' four wheel. Inch by inch. Iron Fist had looked at Freddie. His bright white teeth grinning in the dark and whispered into his ear: "Softly Freddie. Softly. Softly, softly, catchee monkey." And they did.

Afterwards Iron Fist had passed an envelope to Freddie. "We did well Freddie. Sweet as a nut. Sweet as a nut indeed. I'm authorised to give you this bonus. Be wise how you disburse it." The envelope had contained one-hundred-thousand dollars – cash.

CHAPTER 84

Freddie crawled on. Still approaching the house from the side but a little more to the front. He had smeared his face and grey hair with earth as much as he could, given the dry soil. His nose and eyes were inches from it. His hands and nails were in it. He was ten feet from the car and had no idea what to do next. Another situation came from the back of his mind. There were three of them. All SBS. All fucked up with nowhere to go. The RIB had gone, the weapons had gone. The GPS, as usual back then, was useless. "What next skipper?" whispered Freddie. The boss, a young northern guy with a thousand-yard stare whispered back: "When we know now't we do now't." And they did now't for three days until they heard a chopper. Freddie decided to push himself further into the dirt and wait.

The front door opened. Freddie did not look up or move a muscle. He heard a female voice. "Stan, get in first. You, put him in the back behind the passenger seat and make sure his seat belt is fastened then walk around and sit beside him. Any problems smack him in the face with your gun. For fuck's sake don't shoot him. Make sure the gun has its safety lock on. Now, before we have another fuck up, Stan, did you collect the keys to his allotment and shed?"

"Yes."

"Good. We'll get down there and let ourselves in. William will point us to the location; we dig up the stick and you drive us back here. Then you two fuck off and get rid of the car."

"What will you be doing?"

"Don't worry about me Stan, let's go."

Freddie was desperate to see the woman, desperate to see William, but he kept his face in the dirt. He heard the door being locked and a couple of minutes later he heard the car doors close, the car start, and then drive off. He heard it slow and stop at the road. He heard it drive away until he could no longer hear it. And only then did he lift his face from the dirt.

Ten minutes later, Freddie slowly moved backwards into the foliage. Having heard the door of the house being locked, he was pretty sure that no one was in there. But he remembered a similar situation involving another ransom delivery; this time with a female colleague.

"Is the room empty, Freddie?" she had asked.

"Yeah I'm pretty sure it is."

"Then let's get at it," she had urged.

Freddie smiled as he remembered what he had said, "Pretty sure doesn't hack it babe. I'm pretty but I'm not sure."

"So, what do we do?"

"We wait, listen and learn."

An hour or so later, they had both heard the click of a cigarette lighter and a few minutes later they smelled the smoke. Two hours later they heard snoring. Half an hour later they had walked out of the house with a million dollars. And the guy had still been snoring.

Freddie decided to wait a while in the undergrowth and then made his way backwards towards the road and his Range Rover, asking himself some serious questions. Is now the time to call the police? Would they be prepared to stake out the place? Why had William hidden the data stick in the allotment? It didn't make sense; DPK and the Fed had copies of the spreadsheets. What the fuck was going on? What should he do?

CHAPTER 85

As dawn broke and Stan was driving back to London he was thinking about what William had said and he was worrying. When he had been approached, the guy had known about his gambling debts. They weren't really serious but getting out from under was a relief. It had seemed to him at the time a no-brainer. But that was before he had met the crazy woman and her torture chamber – in a bathroom, for Christ's sake! What the fuck could he do? He thought about his options all the way back to Chiswick. Should he just make a run for it when they were in the allotment? He knew the area very well including almost invisible gaps in the fencing; surely the guy with the gun wouldn't run the risk of a shot? What about crashing the car? He had no doubt he could do that somewhere suitable. But even if he did and managed to get away, where would he go? No home, no job, no money. Just debt and an angry loan-shark.

William was also worrying but his worries were in a different league. He knew that he was in for a beating when there was no sign of the data stick and he knew that would be just for openers. As soon as they got back to the house the serious stuff would start with the fucking mad woman enjoying taking some revenge. Then she might actually start rounding up his friends and putting them through the same process. When it came to Sky, of course, she would give up the stick immediately but would she be left alive? William doubted that. How could he have got her involved in all of this? He thought of his future and all he could see was his pain, his friends' pain and his death. What could he do to change the scenario? And he thought about all the things that had seemed important to him. Spectacles matching his watch strap, socks paired so the Pringle logo was on the outside on each leg, which table to sit at in restaurants and his heart rate when he was running. Fuck me. What a fool!

They arrived at the allotment just after 7 am. There were no cars outside. William wondered why he had imagined there would be. Stan unlocked the gates and in they went. It was a lovely morning and the place was filled with the sound of birds and the smell of earth. But what used to be a place of solace to William now felt like a graveyard.

When they got to the plot and Stan had taken the fork from the shed, he gave William a look. William held his breath as Stan leant on the fork looking at the guy with the unpronounceable name. 'Now,' thought William. 'Now!'

'Now,' thought Stan. 'Now.' The fork straight into the guy's stomach, the expression on his face as he tried to pull it out, the howl of anger from the crazy woman. It all flashed through his mind. But he couldn't do it. William breathed out with a sigh.

Stan and the other guy started lifting off all the rubbish that lay on top of the spot where William had told them he had buried the stick. William kept hoping someone would turn up nearby, notice his hands were tied and call the police. No one came. And, of course, no stick was found.

Sadie's face was furious. Her anger uncontrolled. She was shaking, stamping her feet and running her hands through her hair. She looked around, went into the shed and saw the long asparagus knife. Twelve inches long with a serrated edge. She picked it up with her right hand and stood before William. "You stupid, stupid fucking idiot. I'm going to kill your friends. I'm going to extract what I can from them and then I'm going to kill them. And I'm going to kill them in front of you. They will all know that their pain – and it will be quite some pain – is all down to you. And when I spare them anymore pain and put them to death I will make sure that the last thing they see is your face." Then she pulled back her arm and swiped the knife across William's chest where blood erupted instantly.

"It's just a scratch. Don't think you are going to get off so lightly, you fucking arsehole. And on the subject of arseholes, don't forget. I warned you. You are going back in that bath and I'm going to hoist you up. But this time your arms will be raised further, your feet will be scrabbling around in the tub to try and keep the pressure off. Again, I'll stop winching at that stage and enjoy the show. Listening to you panting, waiting to hear you scream. Then I will winch a little more. And that's when you start to scream. Not too loud I hope; because what I am waiting for, what I really want to hear is the pop when your shoulders become dislocated. I can't wait for that moment. Doctors describe the injury as causing extreme pain. It's likely that you will faint.

"Of course, you are of no use to me if you have fainted, no use at all, and no fun. But I have a plan to wake you up. It might be a little upsetting. It might even give you that heart attack. I hope not. But if it does then it's not a problem because I am completely confident that you have given the data stick to one of your friends and I'm sure they will give it up quite quickly when they join us. I mean, why not? So here is the plan. I turn my winch, I hear the pop, you scream and carry on screaming; maybe you faint. And then I pick up the cattle prod and stick it up your arse. And I promise you this. When I press the button, you will forget about the pain of your dislocated shoulders. And that's when I will get out my blowtorch! Let's get back to the house and set to work."

Chapter 86

Freddie had come to a decision. He knew that the logical thing to do would be to call the police. But that wasn't necessarily the right thing to do. Would they be prepared to come out here in numbers just on his say so? Probably not. Even if they did, would they be armed? Would the bad guys use William as a hostage? Probably yes. And who knew more about hostage rescue than he did? Probably no one. Freddie's first decision was to get inside the house and see what was going on in there. There was no urgency; if those people were going back to the allotment in Chiswick it would be at least three hours before they got back. He set his phone to wake him in an hour and promptly fell asleep.

When Freddie woke it was bright sunlight. At DPK he might have appeared to be a bit casual about details, a bit of a loose cannon. But the house he was going into looked like it could become a potential war zone so he prepared carefully. Tweed jacket off, dull green Barbour on. Barbour hat on. One Purdey in his left hand, locked and loaded; the last thing to do when shooting with pals; the first thing to do when there was a chance of encountering the bad guys. The other Purdey on the strap over his shoulder.

And his shooting bag: phone, hip flask, a dozen cartridges, Swiss army knife. He switched the phone to silent and left the Range Rover as before. Keys in the ignition, door unlocked.

The best approach to an unfamiliar and potentially dangerous situation is camouflage. And back in the day, Freddie had worn it all. But here, wherever the fuck 'here' was, a different approach was required. He broke open the Purdey in his hand, as one would, and walked nonchalantly along the road and up the drive to the house. Birds singing, sun behind thick clouds, greenery everywhere. The epitome of someone's country cottage.

Without hesitation, Freddie strode up to the front door; ready with his somewhat pathetic question about where the shoot might be. But there was no reply to his knock. And no reply to his second knock. More important, there was no sound of movement from the undergrowth, trees and other foliage. He walked around to the back of the house and knocked on what looked like the kitchen window. And as he peered through it he saw a kitchen that looked like shit. Unwashed plates, cups and glasses. Dirty dishes and filthy saucepans. A frying pan with what looked like burnt mince; frozen food cartons on the draining board and pizza cartons on the floor. All of this struck Freddie immediately, none of this registered as important. Amber lights so far. He knew there were never green lights in this kind of world.

Freddie took out the Swiss army knife and set to work

silently on the back-garden door into the living room. Ten minutes he was inside. He stood still and listened for five minutes before he took a step forward and then another one and another one until he found himself at the foot of the stairs.

Freddie knew there were other rooms on the ground floor but for some reason he was drawn to go upstairs. Was it a smell? Was it a sound? Whatever it was he walked up the stairs and through the open door into one of the bedrooms. Unmade bed, clothes all over the place. Women's clothes on the floor, on a chair and on the bed. No danger here. The next bedroom was empty.

Freddie couldn't believe what he was seeing when he opened the door to the last bedroom. He gasped. "Fuck, fucking hell, Jesus Christ." Canes, knives, saws, pliers and pincers. Hypodermic syringes, rope, a cattle prod, tasers, some kind of plastic mask. Handcuffs, something that looked like a battery. And a roll of barbed wire. Boxes of pills, bottles of water and bandages.

"Jesus fucking Christ!" he gasped. "What's going on here?"

It was only when he looked into the bathroom that Freddie saw the real horror. It looked like some sort of scaffolding was leaning into the corner of the room with more ropes, a winch and a defibrillator beside it. But as he walked across to it and looked in the bath his heart sank. He could see urine and faeces; blood around the taps and plughole, what looked like William's spectacles and something else. He leant over and looked more carefully and felt vomit rising in his throat. He choked it back; his eyes watering, not believing what he was seeing. But there it was. A toe. A fucking toe! It looked like a little toe. "Oh William, poor fucking William, what have they done to you?" Then Freddie looked at his watch. It was time to move.

CHAPTER 87

They were back in the car and in the same seats, travelling fast on the M4, William was holding Stan's jacket to his chest, trying hard not to look at the blood spreading onto his trousers. In desperation he gasped, "Encryption."

"What do you mean by encryption?" asked Sadie.

"How will you know the data stick you get is the one they want?" mumbled William. "It's encrypted. It has a very complicated and secure password. When you get the data stick – and I'm sure you will in the end – it will be encrypted. No doubt your clients will access it eventually. But what will happen to you if it doesn't contain the stuff they want?"

"I'll just beat the password out of you, don't worry about that!"

"No you won't. I don't know it."

"We shall see William, we shall see. Wait until I ask which of your pals you want me to interrogate first. Ina, Gill, Sky? They all look quite appealing to me."

The car left the motorway. In the front was Stan and the guy with the unpronounceable name. William and the mad Sadie were in the back. In spite of the blood on his chest William was becoming calm and thoughtful.

Thinking about how he might kill himself to avoid the pain that he knew was coming. Thinking about death was not the end of the world. Just the end of his world. He took comfort that he was leaving a great deal more than he was given. He smiled for just a brief moment thinking of the faces of his godchildren when they saw his will.

What would the mad bitch do with his body? Might he just disappear? Would anybody really miss him? Sure, Freddie, Sky, Gill and maybe Diana. Anybody else? Yes, maybe Lionel, maybe Ina. Ina! What would she be thinking? Wondering why he hadn't called? Maybe she had left him a text or voicemail and was wondering why he hadn't replied. Maybe she assumed that he didn't want to see her again. But he did. And he wouldn't. He felt so sad that his first proper relationship for so many years would end like this. There was nothing he could do to stop what was going to happen. Or maybe there was. Maybe when he got out of the car he could just run for it. Yes, he was missing a toe and could hardly walk. Yes, his hands were tied behind his back. But why not have a go. He was a runner. Running was what he did. And if he could make it to the main road, who knows what might happen. A car might stop and help him. He could be run over. He decided to give it a go. Committed!

CHAPTER 88

Freddie was moving. He had managed to close the back door enough to make it look as if it had not been forced. Then he had walked down the road and back into the bushes, making sure that he put the undergrowth back in place as he walked backwards. Some light rain had started, dripping off his Barbour cap. It was too late to go back to his car and get the waterproof over-trousers. He looked at his watch. Too late to change anything. But not too late to run things through his mind. To consider for the tenth time what might happen and when. To run every scenario through his head countless times. Who might have a gun? What would William do? What did these people look like? The only face he would recognise other than William's would be that shit Stan.

The traffic noise from the road changed and a car seemed to be coming up the drive. Freddie dialed 999 on his mobile and whispered, "I don't know where I am but a guy with a gun is chasing me. I'm hiding. Can you get my location? I'm going to run but leave my phone behind." The black Mercedes stopped five feet from Freddie, the back door on the driver's side opened and a man was pushed out, hands tied behind his back, face banging on the gravel. Freddie nearly dropped his gun. It was William. But not the William he knew. White face, blood all over his chest. Blood around his mouth. An old man, a broken old man. Freddie readied to burst out of the foliage but hesitated. Not yet.

A huge guy got out of the front passenger seat and walked towards the door of the cottage. It looked like he had some kind of handgun. Then a small, stocky woman got out of the car, walked around the back and kicked William in the head as she walked past.

"Lift him up and take him inside," she shouted to the big guy.

Freddie smiled. There were three people standing. One gun to be seen; maybe another but not in anybody's hand. They all had their backs to him. He stood up and stepped into the drive, shotgun firm into his shoulder.

Freddie was not a hero. As he shouted, "Put down the gun!" the huge guy turned towards him and Freddie pulled the trigger on the twelve-bore. Ten feet. The guy's shoulder disintegrated, he cannoned backwards, his gun went flying. For a second there was silence. Then he screamed and rolled over and over in the gravel.

"William, down! Stay down," he shouted, and pointed the gun at Stan and the old lady standing next to him. Stan looked petrified. The lady's eyes looked mildly amused. But then Freddie stepped forward, moved his gloved hands onto the hot barrel of the shotgun, pulled it back over his shoulder and hit her head hard with the walnut stock. She fell, her eyes rolled up and she didn't move.

Ten minutes later Freddie heard the sirens and two police cars arrived. He stood still as a statue, arms aloft, gun on the floor as several armed and frightened police shouted at him, "Put your hands on your head!" Then pushed him down flat on the gravel, hands grabbed and wrists cuffed behind, tight and painful. Finally, pushed into the back of a police van. In spite of the discomfort he smiled. Job done. Not exactly what was planned for the Glorious Twelfth but a good bag by any standards.

CHAPTER 89

When William woke up he felt numb all over. The bright light above him looked familiar, the smell of antiseptic reassuring, the cool hand on his forehead comforting and then the voice. Soft, a little Scottish lilt, just like Miss Marple. He screamed and screamed again.

"Calm down, William. You have been through a very painful experience. But you are safe now. Safe. You are in Princess Margaret's Hospital in Marlow and I'm looking after you. Go back to sleep. Rest. There are people who want to talk to you but no one will until you feel up to it. Sip this water and swallow this pill. We can talk later."

Later, Freddie didn't know where William was and had some challenges of his own. But things could have been worse. First, the guy he'd shot with his twelve-bore hadn't bled out. Second, according to the police, his shot looked like self-defense so far. Third, the woman he had whacked was alive and well and the stock of his nine-thousand-pound Purdey was undamaged. Last, but by no means least, he was not held in custody and by the evening he was ensconced in Marlow's only decent hotel and enjoying dinner with Bruno, his solicitor and old friend.

"OK Freddie, before we get another bottle of this

surprisingly drinkable Pinot Noir we need to prepare for your meeting with the police tomorrow. It will be nothing like the chat you had with them earlier. Can I just ensure I understand exactly what happened when the Mercedes pulled up? The car stopped, you stood up, a man got out with a handgun. You were a few feet away from him, pointed your shotgun at him and told him to drop the gun. He raised it so you had no option but to fire and you intentionally aimed at the gun not the man. The next thing you saw was the woman reaching into the bag she was carrying. Rather than letting off the other barrel you hit her over the head with the stock of your gun and she went down. Is that correct?"

"One hundred per cent old chap. It's as if you were there watching."

"One last question Freddie, and this is bound to be asked. What on earth were you doing in Wiltshire with a shotgun in the first place?"

"Well, I have to say, that is a tricky one. Actually, very embarrassing. I committed a mortal crime."

"Freddie, are you sure you want to tell me this? You know that you can't retract later."

"No old chap, I need to get it off my chest. But there's no need to look so worried; by God you have gone a little pale.

"William and I had been invited to 'You know whose' shoot in Yorkshire for the 12th; breakfast, dinner, the whole shebang. I was leaving the house, crack of dawn, happy as Larry. But William had been AWOL for a couple of days and when I saw his car driven by that little shit Stan I decided to follow it."

"How come you recognised the car?" asked Bruno.

"First of all, it's a black S Class Mercedes and second I recognised the number at the same time as I spotted that prick, Stan."

"You knew the registration number of William's car?"

"Not all of it; just the first bit which is FF16. How could I not?"

The bar closed at eleven so Freddie woke early, and on his way back to Chiswick he called Lizzy and explained that William was OK but in hospital. She agreed to call Sky. He also called Lionel and a couple of others at DPK – last but not least Daniel and Colin; and left a message with Ina at the bank. He got back to Chiswick around ten, changed, made a few more calls and popped round to William's house. Luckily Tina was there, albeit at her wit's end. Freddie reassured her that William would be home soon and picked up some clothes from his dressing room, together with a pair of spectacles. Then he set off back to St Margaret's. When he got to the hospital and went to reception he was directed to floor eight and given an envelope for William. When he arrived on the eighth floor he was directed to room fifteen.

When Freddie knocked on the door there was no reply. He knocked again but there was still no reply. He opened the door. The bed was empty.

"Christ!" But then he heard the toilet flush, a tap running and William limped into the room.

"Have you ever seen a grown man cry?" asked Freddie. And they walked towards each other, held each other, grabbed each other and then they both did exactly that.

"Fuck this," said Freddie.

"Where are the tissues?"

"No idea, my old friend. No idea."

Then William cried and cried again. "Where am I and what day of the week is it?"

"Marlow, in a private room in St Margaret's hospital, and it's the 13th. How are you feeling? What did the doctor say?"

"I'm malnourished, dehydrated and needed two pints of blood. I've got eighteen stitches across my chest and they need to do something where that bitch sawed off my little toe."

"Sawed off?"

"Yes. Sawed off. Slowly! I wish you had let her have the other barrel. She was like some fucking Rosa Klebb!"

"Yeah, well, shooting an unarmed woman might be a tad difficult to explain," replied Freddie.

William continued. "I also have some damage to my back, my thighs and my arse but no stitches required there. They have given me a tetanus injection, pain killers and antibiotics and are going to operate on my foot tonight and, if all goes well, I can be out of here tomorrow afternoon. But I have to go to the police station to make a statement before coming back to London. Have you made a statement?"

"Only a brief one but I am off to the station with Bruno later on for the full monty. He thinks they will be impressed that I aimed at his arm not his head."

"Did you?"

"No, I aimed at his chest. Someone once told me to aim at the largest bit of the target but I missed. Lucky for him. Lucky for me. I must now be off to meet Bruno and I'll come back later. By the way, reception asked me to give you this."

CHAPTER 90

William opened the envelope and shook out a phone. His phone; scratched, no power but still threatening. Fucking Stan, acting like a hero, behaving like a shit. Coming back with a bruised face and delivering his phone with some sort of tracking device. Reporting his conversation about the data stick with Freddie in the car. 'I have put the data stick somewhere safe.' Sneaking into his office and deleting all his files. And what might happen to him? If he was lucky, a few years in prison. If unlucky then maybe a bullet in the back of his head. Either way, William had absolutely zero sympathy. He started making a list in his head. Must call Ina, must call Gill, must call Sky. Need to arrange transport for tomorrow; speak to Freddie later, must get new phone… and then he slept.

"Rise and shine. I'm back and this lovely lady wants to check you over," announced Freddie, sitting down on the bedside chair and watching the nurse take William's temperature, pulse and blood pressure before telling him that he would be given an injection to block his foot at six, be taken down to surgery at seven where he would be put under sedation for the operation and he would be back in bed by eight.

"Well, that's something to look forward to," said Freddie. "I've had that sort of sedation; best drug I've experienced."

"How was your session at the police station?" asked William.

"I think it went pretty well," said Freddie, cheerfully. "Bruno did most of the talking. They had checked that I had a licence for the guns. They had checked that I was expected in Yorkshire. They had already got Stan's story, which I think matched my account. The big guy's handgun was loaded and the safety was off. They told me that this still looked like a clear case of self-defence. Then I spent two hours writing it down – on paper, can you believe it? Paper!

"Tell you what, William, some bits of the police system are pretty good. For example, the guy had a record of you going into Richmond police station to ask for help and me going in there later and reporting you missing. But there was nothing on their system relating to Felicity's disappearance, the involvement of HMRC and the NCA even though our names and DPK would all be connected. So much for the Police National Computer! By the way, Bruno would be happy to have a chat with you and sit in on your meeting tomorrow if that would be helpful?"

"That's good. Could you ask him to come here about 9 am? Hopefully I will have recovered from your wonder drug by then."

They arrived at the police station, shown to a very basic and somewhat intimidating room and offered tea or coffee. Five minutes later, two middle-aged men walked in. One in a suit and tie, the other in jeans and a sweatshirt; they all shook hands. The man in the sweatshirt smiled.

"Good morning, gentlemen. My name is DCI Martin Brook. This is my colleague DI Stanhope. Is there anything else you need?"

"We are good, thanks," from Bruno.

"OK, let's get started," said Brook. "Do you have any objection to us recording the meeting?"

"None. I assume we will get a copy of the tape?" said Bruno.

"Yes. of course." The DI pressed some buttons. "For the tape; William West and his solicitor Bruno Gilmour are present as are DCI Brook and DI Stanhope. Messrs. West and Gilmour have no objection to the meeting being recorded."

Brook leant back, relaxed but purposeful. "Mr West; you are not a suspect in this situation. You are a victim and, potentially, a witness. If at any time you feel uncomfortable for any reason we can stop for a while. I know that you have just come out of hospital and apologise for asking you here at short notice but there are some things we need to clear up quite urgently. And Mr Gilmour, please interrupt as you see fit.

"Mr West, please tell us about the Monday morning

when you got the call from Gill Middleton and take it from there. Your colleague Freddie Findlay has already provided some background; we just want to fill in some gaps." William sipped his coffee and went through the whole thing. No one interrupted until he mentioned meeting with the guy from HMRC. He couldn't recall his name. Brook pressed him on this but he just couldn't remember. He knew Gill would as she had taken an instant dislike to him and offered to call her.

"Quick question, Mr West. Did he give you a business card?"

"No."

"Please carry on."

William swallowed and continued. He described the allotment, the chase, cycling, hiding, Richmond police station, no help there. Richmond Park, the solace of sleep, the smacks in the face. Waking in the bath. The horror, the toe, the torture, the attempts to fool the bitch. Good luck when they went to the allotment the first time; no luck the following dawn. The bitch's threats; caned back, nearly dislocated shoulders, the threat of the cattle prod. Hope gone. Nothing but pain and death ahead until "Drop the gun". Then, moments later, bang! "Down, Will down!" Head in the gravel and a man screaming. Then "Stay down Will!". The sound of something heavy hitting something hard and what sounded like a body falling nearby. Sirens, blue lights, tyres on gravel, men and women shouting. Then an ambulance.

William stopped talking. There were tears in his eyes and his body was shaking.

"Thank you, Mr West, you are doing very well. Let's take a break for a while," said Brook. "Have some water. We will be back in a few minutes, we just have a few more questions."

The DI switched off the tape. Bruno put his hand on William's shoulder. "We can stop this now if you like. Go back to London, come back another day."

"No, let's get this over with, Bruno, and then maybe you could drop me off in Chiswick Mall on your way back to Hampstead."

"Done."

CHAPTER 91

DCI Brook and the DI came back in. Tape buttons pressed. "For the tape, William West and his solicitor Bruno Gilmour are present as are DCI Brook and DI Stanhope. Messrs. West and Gilmour have no objection to the meeting being recorded."

"We are nearly finished now Mr West. I just have a couple of questions. Are you OK with this?" asked Brook.

"I think so."

"Right, I want you to tell me more about the involvement of HMRC."

"Well I know that we should have alerted them earlier as to our suspicions but it was a very sensitive situation."

"Detective Chief Inspector Brook, I'm not sure where you are going with this. William is here as a victim and potential witness. He is not in a fit condition to comment on whether or not he or DPK should have alerted HMRC earlier. If you persist with this line of questioning we will have to abort this interview."

"Understood. But could you bear with me for a couple of minutes. I promise you that there is no need for concern. OK Mr West?"

"To be frank I was relieved when we did contact

HMRC and when Colin had briefed them and when the HMRC guy came to our meeting I felt a weight off my chest. And when I heard that they had linked up with the NCA it was like 'job done' from my perspective. Although I was still very concerned about Felicity."

"Did you or Freddie have any direct contact with HMRC?"

"No. Colin advised that they required a single point of contact and he was the designated person in the firm. Why do you keep asking about HMRC?"

"The reason I ask, Mr West is this: no one in the Met police, the NCA or HMRC has any knowledge of the possibility of money laundering at Kutzevenia Bank or the disappearance of Felicity. So, either you and your pal Freddie have cooked up some kind of story or Colin has been leading a lot of people down the garden path. And we are pretty sure he has been doing exactly that."

"I'm sorry," said William, "but I can't accept that. That cannot be correct. There must be another explanation."

"Anyway, where does this leave us?" asked Bruno.

"I think it leaves you forgetting the last few minutes of this meeting," replied Brook.

"Mr West, you must not share this suspicion with anyone. Just act as normal as possible under the circumstances. And when, contrary to my instructions, you tell your pal Freddie, ask him to do the same. Thank you both very much indeed for your time. One of my colleagues in London will call you in a couple of days to arrange another meeting."

CHAPTER 92

"Didn't like that 'another meeting,'" said William as they walked to Bruno's car.

"Don't worry about it. I'd venture to say that you guys are home free. And I have to say William that I was very impressed with your recollection: 'Drop the gun.' Moments later, bang! Only a fool would wait to shoot and Freddie's no fool. Seems like you are not as shaken up as I thought you might be. But on that subject, will anybody be around at your house? Do you want some company? And how will you get in without your keys?"

"Thanks Bruno. That's kind. Can I borrow your phone?"

It was about 1.30 pm when Bruno stopped outside William's house in Chiswick Mall. William pulled himself painfully out of the car, touched Bruno on the shoulder, limped to his front door and rang his bell. The door opened and there was Tina. One look and tears flooded her face. His eyes welled up as well. They hugged each other.

"Welcome home, William. And what have you got in that filthy carrier bag?" They walked into the house and Sky emerged.

"William, you look like shit!"

"Christ, I could do with a drink!" were his first words.

Drink in hand, shoes off, feet up on the huge settee in the upstairs drawing room. Sky asked, "Why is your foot bandaged, William?"

"It's long story, Sky. The short story is that some guys picked me up and took me to a house where some mad bitch wanted to know where that data stick was. In the process, my little toe got cut off. Happily, Freddie rocked up and here I am. Can the long story wait? I seem to have been telling it for the past twenty-four hours. The good news is that all I have are some cuts and bruises."

"Do you want something for the bruises on your face? Have you looked at yourself in a mirror?"

"Well I have but these specs are so filthy I couldn't see much."

"Give them here. Christ, let me get you a top up while I clean them and you frighten yourself."

William went upstairs to his bathroom and took a long hard look at himself. He looked dreadful. He looked old and ill. He had dark bruises on his cheeks and forehead, bloodshot eyes, was unshaven and unkempt. One of his front teeth was chipped. He shaved, washed his face and undressed. The stitches across his chest looked horrifying. He didn't try to see what his back looked like. Before putting on some new clothes he weighed himself. He had lost three kilos.

Sky was in the kitchen talking to Tina. "How about

some smoked salmon and scrambled eggs with some toast, William? You look like you could use some."

"Thanks Tina, we will be over the road."

As they sat down by the river, Sky produced a sheet of paper and a pen. "You need to make a list. I'll write it down."

"What list?"

"Tasks, William, tasks."

"Why? What do you mean?"

"Don't be simple. There are things to be done. And it will do you good to be looking forwards not backwards as you are doing now. I think the first thing is call Ina."

"Ina?"

"I said don't be simple William!"

The list was long: Call Ina. Recover the car and get rid of it – too many memories. Make an appointment with HCA Private Health in Chiswick High Road for a full check-over and arrange for a nurse to come every other day for the next ten days to dress his chest and back. Make another appointment to have the stitches removed. Take his passport and other ID with him to the High Road to get a new phone. On the way, visit Stan's flat and check all is OK with the tenants. Advertise for a new 'Stan', fix a meeting with Bruno, sort out the insurance claim for the car and his Cartier Roadster which was long gone. Fix a meeting with Partnership Protection and a lunch with Lionel. What about Colin? Could the cops be correct?

Tina came into the garden with the food. "Coffee or wine?"

"Both please."

"Red or white, Sky?"

"Red please, although nothing really goes with scrambled eggs, does it?"

"I need these eggs and they are just how I like them and do you know what?"

"What William?"

"I've lost three kilos over the past few days!"

"That's wonderful, William. Truly wonderful. It's a shame the weight loss makes you look like an old man. But it's wonderful that your vanity has returned so quickly!"

"Sky, I love you so."

"I know you do, darling. But don't forget who is top of your 'To Do' list."

Tina returned to the riverside and took away the plates.

"Another?" she asked, pointing at the almost empty bottle.

"Why not?" said Sky. "We don't have to finish it!"

Sitting in the August sun, watching the tide roll out, William began to feel himself again. The terror and pain he had been remembering already looked a little blurred, like soft focus. The screaming was less loud. And when Sky asked for the long story he took a sip of his wine and told her everything.

CHAPTER 93

"Wake up Mr West. Mr West!" William opened his eyes. It was two days later and his new phone was telling him it was time to get up. He had a busy day ahead: 9 am he had the nurse coming in to change the dressing on his stitches. 12.30 pm: lunch at Bruno's offices just off Fleet Street. 3 pm: a meeting in More London organised by George Price, the Partnership Protection guy. William didn't know who else would be attending; and finally, drinks with Freddie and Gill at 5.30 pm for a general catch-up.

Of course, it was Addison Lee, not Stan, outside the house five minutes early at 11.25 am. The traffic wasn't too bad and William spent the time changing some of the settings on his iPhone X. He arrived at Bruno's office at five-to-one and was shown into a meeting room with a table set for lunch and offered a glass of wine.

Bruno arrived before he had taken a sip. "Good to see you William! You're looking a lot better than last time we met. How are you feeling?"

"Not bad at all, Bruno, but I'll be glad when my chest and back are all healed up and I can get back to doing some exercise.

"You know Bruno; every time I come to your office

I'm reminded that your charge-out rate is even higher than mine. But at least the hospitality is first class."

"William, don't be unkind. And, anyway, you won't need me after today so you can stop worrying about costs."

"What do you mean?"

"I mean that the police are not going to charge Freddie and HMRC are not going to take any action against you, Freddie or Gill Littleton in respect of your delay in reporting your money-laundering suspicions. I think they may be present at the meeting at More London this afternoon and you will be able to hear it first-hand."

"That's great news, Bruno. Thank you."

"My pleasure, William. I will always be here if you need me. I don't think the meeting at three will be too challenging although it sounds like a cast of thousands will be there."

"So, who will be there?"

"I'm not sure William. But you will be among friends as far as I am aware. Now let me tell you something else. That Sadie woman, that 'mad bitch' according to Freddie, has done a runner. As you know, she was suffering from severe concussion and was in the same hospital as you were. But unlike you, there was a police officer outside her room twenty-four hours a day."

"Fuck me!" William didn't know what to think.

Bruno continued. "To say that DCI Brook is not a happy chap would be a significant understatement. Apparently, the officer doing the 2 pm–10 pm shift observed two orderlies wheeling a gurney along the corridor and thought nothing about it as they passed him. The next thing he saw was the face of a nurse who had just removed a tranquilliser dart from the back of his neck. They're not sure exactly what happened but the current theory is that the two orderlies put the woman on the gurney, took the lift to the ground floor and simply walked out of the ambulance staff exit, loaded her into a private ambulance and drove off."

Bruno poured William some more wine. "The police have CCTV of what appears to be the vehicle in question leaving the hospital but they lost track of it after a few minutes."

"Good God! Can somebody just do that? Spirit a criminal out of a hospital and drive off into the blue? That's crazy. To think that the bitch has got away with it. It's just not fair!" William felt really let down.

Bruno nodded his head. "Agreed. I was looking forward to my day in court. And my fee!"

"What about the guy with the gun?" asked William. "Don't tell me…"

"No, no problems there. He is still safe, if not sound, in the Princess Margaret Hospital with an armed officer plus a back-up outside his room. He was in intensive care for forty-eight hours but the bottom line is that they had to amputate his right arm from the shoulder and he has also lost his right ear."

"Serves him bloody right."

"Agreed. The bloke is going down for a long time. He is an illegal immigrant from Ukraine and he's been in prison more or less all the time since he was twelve. He is the main suspect for two murders and he is going to be shipped back there as soon as possible. But they have matched his fingerprints on a table to that partner – Mike's? – house who was thought to have committed suicide but was actually found to be murdered. He might go on trial here first. God knows! Anyway, let's have a coffee and get a cab to your office."

CHAPTER 94

When Sadie woke up she found herself lying on a sofa in a large living room with a man sitting opposite her in an armchair.

He smiled. "The angel awakes. How are you feeling?"

"Not bad. Who are you? Where am I?"

"I am the guy that hired you, Sadie, and this is a house that I use from time to time. Please call me Peter." He was tall, middle-aged and dressed in blue jeans and a light blue cashmere pullover. He sounded well-educated and calm.

"We have removed you from the hospital and we had to shoot you with a tranquilliser pistol to ensure minimum fuss. There are no after effects but you may have a bit of an ache in your arm where the dart hit. It's nothing to worry about."

"Thank you, thank you."

"No problem. Would you like a cup of tea or coffee or something stronger?"

"Tea would be wonderful. Thank you."

He came back with the tea.

"Sadie, tell me what happened. What went wrong?"

"To cut a long story short, I got a call letting me know the parcel was on its way and he was delivered to

a chat with the client. I guess it won't surprise you that there is no fee on the table. After all, you know what the rules are."

"Yes, I know the rules."

"Good. Anyway, before we get down to the details I'd like to introduce you to my other two guests. They are down in the billiard room."

Peter opened the door and they walked along a corridor and through a door leading to some steps down to a cellar. It was a large room with a full-size billiard table in the middle illuminated very brightly by a traditional light fitting above. Two people were playing snooker. Sadie looked around. The room was warm and charming, probably converted from a coal cellar or maybe some sort of utility room. There was an old furnace in the corner with dusty bags of coal leaning against it. One of the snooker players swore as an unintentional cannon broke the silence.

"Let me introduce you, Sadie. Say hi to Antonina."

"Hi." Antonina didn't look up, just played her shot.

"And this is Arseny." He didn't look up either, just walked around the table looking at balls and considering scenarios.

"Peter, tell me what is going on here please. If I am not welcome here just give me some clothes so I can change out of this hospital gown, give me some money so I can get back to London and let's call it quits. We have both invested time and money in the William project and we have nothing to show for it. We are professionals. We know that sometimes things happen which are out of our control. Can we just move on please?"

"Sadie, I wish it was that easy. I truly do. But I have a problem that I need to share with you. In fact, I have two problems, but they both amount to the same thing. The first problem is my client. His name is Jorge Perez. He is a brutal man with an even more brutal family. And he has associates that are always looking for weaknesses. He wants you dead. The second problem is my reputation. If the market gets to hear that someone I hired fucked up, then my brand will be tarnished or maybe even destroyed. You failed. You broke the rules. So, I have to take some action."

"You mean you are going to kill me? Then fuck you Peter or whatever your name is. Go ahead. I'm not afraid of death, I have dealt death. Just get it over quickly!"

But the quaver in her voice and the shaking of her body told the truth.

"Sadly Sadie, it's not as simple as that. You disappear. So what? We kill you, cut off your head and send the photo, so what? My client needs to see someone suffer for this fuck-up otherwise he might appear weak. And I need to show potential clients what happens to people who fuck up projects or I shall be out of business. To cut to the chase Sadie, we have to make a movie for Jorge. One that rocks his boat. A movie that clearly demonstrates that I do not suffer fools gladly. And, of course, you have to be the star."

"How much? How much money to turn this around?"

"Come on Sadie, don't grasp at straws. You have dished it out and enjoyed it. Now you have to eat it. Antonina, Arseny, finish that game and let's make the movie."

CHAPTER 95

The camcorder had more than four times the pixels of a standard HD product and the sound quality was excellent as well. But Antonina was a true professional so extra lighting and microphones had to be set up. There was no hurry. With movies like this it wasn't easy to get a second shot.

Sadie was shivering in spite of the warmth of the cellar and wondered what she could do to stop this happening. She wasn't tied up and no one seemed to be focusing on her. As she tensed, Peter spoke without even looking at her. "The door upstairs is locked, there is a key. It's not in my pocket or anywhere you could find quickly. So, don't waste your time thinking about it."

"I need a pee."

"That's the funniest thing I have heard for a long time. You will pee Sadie, don't waste your time thinking about that either."

As Antonina set up the camcorder Arseny unrolled a sheet of thick plastic which covered and overlapped the billiard table. Then he attached plastic cable ties to each of the four corner legs of the table. He stepped back as Peter inspected his work.

"All good?"

"All good."

Arseny and Antonina lifted Sadie off her seat and Arseny ripped the hospital gown off her shoulders. They pulled her and carried her to the table as he shouted at them. Peter held her legs as they tied each hand to the corners and all three of them were needed to hold her kicking legs and tie her feet. Even when tied she was arching her body in an attempt to escape. Shouting, screaming, swearing but not crying. Yet. Camcorder ready, microphones ready to hear her but not Peter. Balaclavas on. Thumbs up all round.

"Wait. Stop! Sadie, I think we need to do a sound test. It may be a little uncomfortable but please bear with us. In the meantime, you might like to look at that old furnace heating up in the corner and all that ancient ironmongery. Talking of heating up, here we go with the sound test."

Peter placed a steam iron on Sadie's stomach. "Sorry if it's a little cold. It will heat up shortly." She started screaming after five minutes, then it was squealing. Nothing could be worse, until Peter pressed the button for steam.

Antonina had a water spray which she used on the burns and the screams became sobs. But when Peter took the poker out of the furnace and touched it on each of her breasts the sound was horrifying.

"Close up on the face Antonina?"

"Yes."

"Good. Now from above. My hand in this thick glove

holding these pliers which are gripping this red-hot metal rod. I want you to track it from here between her feet, slowly moving upwards until it is right between her legs. The scream died quickly as Sadie passed out. When she woke she just muttered, "Kill me, please kill me now."

"OK Sadie, if that's what you want that's fine. I think we have got enough."

Sadie found herself on the floor of the cellar with Peter kneeling beside her.

"Sadie, you are going to die soon. But to be honest, I don't know how soon. You see, the thing is that I watched this programme on the BBC a while ago. It was about Catholics killing Protestants. Not in Northern Ireland but way before that. It was something to do with Guy Fawkes. All a bit boring. I think the series was called 'Gunpowder'. But one bit caught my imagination.

"The Catholics, at least I think it was the Catholics, were trying to get some sort of confession before they killed the Protestants. Or it might have been the other way round. Anyway, one chap was hung, drawn and quartered in graphic detail. I think I recall steaming intestines sitting on his chest but maybe I imagined it. But as for the lady, it was quite terrible. But don't worry, it was after the watershed. They laid her on the floor, just like you are now, and stuck a sharp stone under her back. Then they took this old metal door and put it on top of her so just her head, feet and hands were uncovered. And do you know what they did next? They started putting more and more stones on top of that door until she confessed – or whatever.

"We have these two pieces of metal which we are going to put under you on each side of your back. They are a bit sharp so it might be a little uncomfortable. Then we will put the old door over there on top of you. That will be a bit more uncomfortable. And then we will start loading all those bags of coal over there on top of the door and we shall see how many it takes to grant your wish. We thought about carrying out the experiment while you were on the table but we weren't sure it would take all the weight. But I'm assured we can still get good sound and vision down here. Sorry I won't be able to see how things work out in real time but I have a meeting to attend. But l promise you, I will see the movie in due course. Goodbye Sadie. Sorry that you broke the rules."

CHAPTER 96

Bruno and William arrived at More London just before 3 pm and William signed Bruno in. They went up to the tenth floor and into one of the large meeting rooms with views over the Tower of London and Tower Bridge. All the seats were occupied apart from two. William was startled to see that Wendell was sitting at the head of the table. He stood up, towering above everyone; six feet six tall and slim. "Good afternoon William. Great to see you. Welcome Bruno, good to meet you. Grab a coffee take a seat and let's get this meeting going."

Wendell leant forward. "I think some introductions might be in order so I will kick off and we will go round the table. My name is Wendell Gunn. I'm the head of DPK global financial services."

Next to him, Daniel grunted, "I'm Daniel, the boss of the UK FS business."

Then, "I'm William West, DPK FS Senior Adviser."

"I'm Bruno Gilmour of Gilmour Lovell and Partners and I'm here as William's lawyer."

"Colin Taylor, Head of DPK FS Quality and Risk Management."

"George Price, I run Partnership Protection for DPK."

"Good afternoon, I'm DCI Martin Brook, Thames Valley Police."

"DI Craig Stanhope, Thames Valley Police."

"I'm John Britney from the US Federal Reserve."

"Jackie Starling from the NCA, South Eastern Division."

And finally, sitting next to her, "I'm Freddie Findlay and I'm the partner responsible for the Kutzevenia Bank UK audit."

"OK, thanks for that guys; let's get started," suggested Wendell. "First things first, this meeting is on the record. However, it's not being recorded. Christine Sanderson, sitting over there in the corner, will make a note of any decisions made and will circulate it internally. Those of you who are not DPK may of course make any notes that you wish. OK? Second, I have discussed this whole issue with our Managing Partner, Diana Patel, so I am speaking on her behalf as well as mine. Any questions before I get onto my first agenda item?"

"Why isn't that chap from HMRC here?" asked William.

"Good question and very timely. Perhaps I should cut to the chase."

Wendell stared at Colin Taylor. "Colin, let me tell you and everyone else here what we know. We know that you have misled the firm to an extraordinary extent. We know that you did not advise HMRC at any stage. We know that the gentleman that you introduced to us as being from the HMRC was in fact some sort of stooge. We know that you did not report the missing graduate – Felicity Strange – to the police and also suspect that you provided her address to some people intending to harm her. We are also pretty sure that you gave the same people the data stick that William passed to you. And that these very same people are probably responsible for the murder of one of our colleagues, namely poor Mark Lawson, and the imprisonment and, I can hardly bring myself to say this the…" Wendell stopped and swallowed. "The imprisonment and torture of William to find the whereabouts of the original data stick. But what we don't know is why on earth you did this."

William couldn't believe his ears. There must be some mistake. Colin? Colin! The man responsible for managing the firm's risks. The man everyone trusted to maintain the integrity of the business. This couldn't be true. "Jesus Christ," he said aloud. "Colin, tell me this isn't true!"

Colin looked down. "I have nothing so say except that I shall be speaking to my lawyer and will respond in due course."

"I need to interrupt," said DCI Brook as he stood up. "Mr Taylor, please listen carefully. I am arresting you on suspicion of perverting the course of justice and aiding and abetting grievous bodily harm and money laundering. You do not have to say anything, but it may harm your defence if you do not mention when questioned something you later rely on in court. Anything you do say may be given in evidence. My colleague DI Stanhope will now take you to a local police station and you will be able to contact a solicitor in due course."

DI Stanhope asked Colin to stand and placed handcuffs on him saying, "Sir, this is standard operating procedure."

CHAPTER 97

Wendell spoke. "Christine would you be good enough to escort DI Stanhope and our ex-colleague to the express lift? I believe a car is waiting for them in the visitor's space. In the meantime, let's have some more coffee and, hopefully, make some decisions."

Five minutes later they were ready to resume and Wendell asked George to lead off.

"It will not surprise any of you to know that the Partnership Protection Team has been focusing on events in the US and Russia as well as the UK. We have been in daily contact with the Federal Reserve via John and with several officers of the Central Bank of the Russian Federation. We have also been in direct contact with Pavel Lapshin who, for those of you that don't know, is a DPK Global Client Service Partner and with Andrey Zaitsev who is the Chairman and CEO of Kutzevenia Bank. It seems to me that we are in a fairly good place.

"First, our audit has not identified any evidence of systemic or comprehensive money laundering across the bank generally, although we will be reporting in our management letter that the AML resources and processes are not currently fit for purpose. Andrey has already established a project to make them best in class globally. Second, the US, UK and Russian regulators have taken a very deep dive into the wealth management business and will be making a number of arrests as we speak. It's all pretty small beer; maybe a couple of hundred clients creating false identities in the UK to take them completely off the grid. The data that Mark Lawson captured was very helpful; we estimate that about £2 billion might be confiscated. Sadly, not one UK resident is involved, so no payback to HMRC."

"What about the fucking thieves, George?" asked Daniel in his usual blunt fashion. "Any of them UK residents?"

"Well," replied George. "The police are on the case here and they have a strong lead to whoever got hold of the blank passports. Incidentally, they were only useful for creating the false identities; they wouldn't pass muster across passport control as the missing numbers were already in the system."

"Thanks, but how are we going to play this? How are we going to do, what do you call it, 'Reputation management'?"

"Good point, Daniel. I've discussed this with my global colleagues and with the guys in the Big House," replied George. "And we believe we have a good story. First, we need Colin to resign rather than be fired. I don't think that will be difficult. We have plenty of leverage whatever his motive. So, let's say that's a given. Second, we agree a press release with all the constituencies. And we tell the truth."

"That's a pleasant change!"

"All right, Daniel. Let's move on," suggested Wendell giving him a sharp look to wipe the smirk off his face.

"So, this is what happened," announced George. "We were delighted to win the Kutzevenia Bank contract against strong competition and commenced our first audit in February of this year. Freddie Findlay took over the lead when, sadly, Mark Lawson passed away. During the course of the audit the DPK team identified the possibility that the wealth management business based in London could have wittingly, or unwittingly, been laundering money, probably the proceeds of crime. The relevant authorities were notified and we understand arrests were made.

"The chairman and CEO of Kutzevenia, Mr Andrey Zaytsev, has expressed his gratitude to DPK and pledged to redouble his efforts to ensure that the bank is best in class in terms of anti-money-laundering processes governance. In the UK, the Financial Conduct Authority has notified Kutzevenia bank that a Section 166 Skilled Person's Report is required in order that an independent assessment of current AML processes and governance is provided. Has anyone any comments?"

"How are we going to play this for internal consumption?" asked Daniel.

"Well, what were you thinking?"

"Maybe something about the team? Freddie could do

with some good internal PR given his history. And then there is William. People often ask what he's been doing since he retired and why are we paying him all this dosh. Maybe we could big him up some way? And that lady who was number two on the audit, Gill something. Could we fast-track her into the partnership?"

Wendell smiled at Daniel. "I think those are excellent ideas in principle and I'm happy for you to take them forward as you see fit. Any other comments or questions, John? I'm conscious you haven't said a word. Anything you would like to contribute?"

John smiled and looked at everyone around the table. "Well I would like to add my thanks to the team. It's a great result from our perspective. These things are always complicated but we now have a line of sight towards some very powerful people in the US, Mexico and Honduras. When I say powerful, I'm talking about three or four of the main players in the drug business. Losing a billion dollars would be no big deal to them but if we can nail them in money laundering you might even get a text from the White House, or from the golf course!"

"Jackie? Bruno? Freddie? William? John? Are we done?" asked Wendell. "No comments? Good, then we are done. I have another meeting at five then a dinner so I shall say goodbye all. And William, take care down at your allotment. From what I have heard, it sounds like a dangerous place to be!"

William texted Gill: '5.30 pm at Baltic.' Thirty seconds later he received an emoji of a glass of red wine. He noticed Freddie talking to the lady from the NCA and gestured five fingers, then pointed down. Freddie arrived in reception nearly ten minutes later with a broad smile on his face. "I got her number!"

CHAPTER 98

William woke up at 8.30 am on Saturday morning feeling pretty good. His stitches were finally gone, his cracked tooth had been capped, his nightmares had stopped. And when he went for a run, he didn't notice that he was missing his little toe. The only cloud on the horizon was the lunch he had arranged with Ina. They had spoken on the phone, exchanged emails but not met since he got back from hospital. First, he just didn't feel up to it, then Ina had flown off to Russia in connection with the money-laundering scandal. He guessed his name might have cropped up over there and wondered what her reaction might be.

They had arranged to meet at Balthazar again. It seemed the right place to have what might be a serious conversation; a conversation that might re-kindle their relationship or maybe draw a line under it. William was in no doubt that he wanted the former but when she arrived and he rose to kiss her she turned her head so he kissed her cheek and not her lips.

"How nice," she said. "We have the same table as the first time. Anyway William, I'll have a glass of whatever wine that is that you're drinking and you can tell me what you have been up to and why you just cut me off and didn't even reply to my texts and emails."

"I thought Freddie had called you and explained what was going on."

"Well he called but really to let me know you were OK. He said you would fill me in due course. So now is your chance. I know it's something to do with the money laundering that was discovered in the wealth management business. Thank God that was all going on way before I joined!"

"Let's order and I'll explain."

After they had ordered their food and a bottle of the wine and they were drinking, William started. "Some of this might not sound credible but I promise you it's true. I'll just provide the headline and maybe we could go into the details later. Some of the stuff is not really suitable for a discussion over lunch." Twenty minutes later he sat back.

"All pretty horrible. Thank God Freddie pitched up when he did. Anyway, I'm now back to my usual self and went for a lovely run this morning."

Their food came along but neither William nor Ina had much of an appetite. Eventually William asked, "What about us Ina? Are we still good?"

"I think so but I wish you had told me about the passports and your suspicions."

"I don't think it would have been the right thing to get you involved, it could have been dangerous and anyway I promised the head honcho that I wouldn't tell a soul apart from Freddie. But let me apologise and let's have a drink. I feel like a glass of red."

"Well I feel like a whiskey."

"Excellent, they have a list as long as your arm."

Later on, Ina looked William in the eye. "You asked me are we still good. I think we should get a cab back to your place and see if we are."

CHAPTER 99

Sky called William. "What are you doing this evening?"

"Meeting you, I hope," he replied.

Sky came to William's an hour or so later. It was the first time they had spent an evening together since they had met when he had just come out of hospital.

"First things first William, here is the bloody data stick. I know where I would like to stick it!" William took it and looked at it. Such a tiny thing to have caused him so much pain. What should he do with it now?

"I'll be back in a moment, Sky," he said, and went downstairs to where Stan had kept his tools. He picked up a hammer and a pair of pliers and went back upstairs.

"Let's take a bottle over the road and have a couple of drinks before dinner. The sun's come out. By the way I've booked La Trompette, I hope that's OK."

"Of course it is. But what the fuck are you going to do with that hammer?"

They sat down in their usual seats. William took one sip of his wine and then stood up, picked up the hammer and pliers and walked over to the paved area of the garden. Then he took out the data stick, pulled it apart with the pliers and smashed it into little pieces with the hammer shouting "Yes! Yes! Yes!" as he did so. Then he picked up all the pieces and threw them as far as he could into the river. He came back to Sky. "That's just how I would like my ashes scattered when I pop off. I hope you will look after that for me."

"Don't say that, William. You may be far too old for me but there's life in the old dog yet. And on that subject, how's it going with Ina?"

"I saw her on Saturday and am seeing her again at the weekend."

"Sounds like it might be serious. Could she be the one?"

"She might be. Anyway, let me top you up. The cab is coming in ten minutes and I'm feeling a bit peckish. I forgot to have lunch!"

Over dinner, Sky told William about her new boyfriend.

"I met him in the library; he works there."

"He works in the library?"

"Well not exactly, he's on work experience."

"Work experience? How old is he?"

"I'm not sure. I haven't asked. And he hasn't asked me either. I don't know, maybe thirty. Or perhaps a bit younger. He's incredibly fit and training to be a football coach."

The wine arrived, William tasted it and, when their glasses were filled, he frowned. "Sky, I'm sorry but what is a trainee football coach doing working in Chiswick library?"

"To be honest William I haven't asked. We don't talk too much really. When we are together we spend most of the time in bed. Actually, not in bed but you know what I mean."

"Spare me the details, Sky. They will make me feel even more inadequate. But the age difference? I mean, I know you are incredibly attractive and sexy but I'm twice, maybe three times the guy's age. How do you manage to pull all these fit young men?"

"Well this one says he really gets off on MILFs."

"OK I get that. And who could blame him? He's a lucky guy."

William tucked into his food, silently congratulating himself for not suggesting that Sky probably fell into the GMILF category.

CHAPTER 100

William woke up at ten o'clock on Thursday morning. He felt he deserved a lie in and the rain on his window confirmed that would be a good idea. Later on, as he was eating his breakfast and thinking about the weekend, he suddenly remembered that Ina was coming and he hadn't organised anything at all. But did it really matter? He decided it didn't. He had plenty of food in the house, fresh and frozen, and he knew she was playing golf with Ginny on Saturday and having lunch at the club.

Gill had sent some dates for Felicity's funeral service in Knightsbridge and the celebration of her life in the event space at More London. William replied that he could do all of them and wished her a good weekend.

In the end, the weekend was easy. Ina arrived at about seven-thirty and wanted an early night as she was being collected by Ginny at eight in the morning so they walked down to the Old Ship and ordered fish and chips and a bottle of Chablis. The next morning, William insisted on giving Ina a decent breakfast. And as he was washing up and she was on her way to Royal Mid-Surrey he suddenly stopped. Was this like married life and was this what he wanted; washing up and waiting for his wife to come back from the golf club? Maybe it was. It wasn't what he had planned. But of course, he hadn't planned anything.

They went to The Glasshouse in Kew for dinner on Saturday night. When they got back to William's place the tide was all over the road. William took his shoes off, crossed the road and put them on the steps then went back and carried Ina over the water.

"How often is the tide this high?" she asked as they reached dry land.

"Not very often. But I kind of like it. It's the sea showing who is in charge."

"The sea?"

"Yes, the sea, the tide and, of course the river doing battle with it. That's why there is that strong glass alongside the railings; the tide has got that high in the past. I'm going upstairs to get some dry socks."

"I'll come with you. I think it's time for the bio-oil massage on your scar and who knows where else. How about bringing some champagne?"

On Sunday morning, they took the MGB to Richmond Park and walked all the way round then drove back to the house where William prepared kedgeree.

"How's the house hunting?"

Ina was a bit reticent. "I haven't been looking too hard to be honest. It's been pretty full-on in the office. First, we had three people charged with the money-laundering thing so we have been looking to replace them. Then, yesterday, the FCA advised us that three people with control functions were having their approvals removed and I think that is because the police think they were involved. One of them reports directly to me. To be honest I didn't like or rate the guy but it's just one more challenge."

"Why don't you come and stay with me for a while?" was on the tip of William's tongue but something stopped him saying it.

Instead, he said, "What about looking in Richmond for a house or a flat? It's very close to the golf club, you like the park and there are some fast trains to Waterloo; get on the Jubilee line and it would be about an hour door to door."

"Provided I'm still working there."

"It's convenient for most places in town. But are you thinking of leaving?"

"I don't know, I need to sort myself out. Maybe when I go up to Edinburgh tomorrow I'll have some time to think about myself. Anyway, it's time for a drink."

They had a lovely lunch at the kitchen table, then read the papers, listening to William's Sunday playlist of calm classical music. But soon it was time for Ina to leave and they arranged to meet the following Monday evening when they would both be back. They hugged and kissed when Ina's car arrived outside and, as usual, William told her to take care and waved her off. It was time for him to pack; he was off to Club la Santa in Lanzarote the next afternoon to try and recover his fitness.

CHAPTER 101

When Willian got back from Lanzarote there was a letter from Alastair confirming that the service for Felicity would be held on the coming Friday morning at the Church in Belgravia that Gill had suggested, and it contained some papers for him to sign in respect of his role as executor. William found he could now think of Felicity without the feeling of massive sorrow and sense of guilt. The second letter was from the Crown Prosecution Service with a witness summons alerting him of the dates when he was required to attend as a witness at the Old Bailey and a list of the accused, including Stan. It also stated that a meeting, or meetings, in advance of the hearings might be required and explained how he could claim his expenses.

He turned on the outside heaters, put on some quiet music, rolled a joint and sat outside in the dappled light coming from the heaters. Life was good.

Lizzy called. "About the celebration tomorrow night, Freddie has called to confirm everything. He is bringing Lesley. Are you sure Ina can't make it?"

"Sadly yes, she has to run a team event which includes a dinner."

"Well, he said to tell you that it's going to be smart. Not smart casual but smart, although ties are not required. He's going to make all the arrangements and we need to meet at 6.30 pm in a bar called Mr Fogg which is just off Berkeley Square."

"Yep, I think I know it. Shall I send a car for you and you can pick me up?"

"Yes please; say five-thirty and I'll ping you when we are close. Should be a fun evening!"

At five o'clock the next afternoon, William was looking at himself in the mirror in his dressing room. He thought he looked smart and stylish and that made him uncomfortable. He liked his clothes to be unremarkable. He didn't like them to make a statement; it was a work thing. When meeting someone for the first time he worked on the premise that one never gets a second chance to make a first impression. And work had been so much of his life for so long that it was also his personal preference. But tonight, he was wearing one of his two statement suits. This one Gucci. It was jet black with some grey flecks which exactly matched the grey silk shirt with a button-down collar. Black Ferragamo loafers; the Gucci ones would be too much of a cliché. And of course, black spectacles and a black leather strap on the Cartier Tank watch that he wore on occasions such as this.

Lizzy didn't ping him, she rang the bell. She looked fantastic; short Chanel skirt and some sort of silk blouse with an awe inspiring multicoloured jacket and some very, very high heels.

"Hi babe, it's time to party!"

"Lizzy, you look wonderful! But can you walk in those shoes?"

She skipped down the steps as he was locking the door. "Your carriage awaits sir!"

As they settled down in the cab Lizzy turned to William. "How is it going?. How are you? Really."

"It's good. I'm fitter than I've been for ages, work is good. Ina and I are getting quite serious."

"Bloody hell, Will. Serious?"

William spoke slowly. "I can't remember the last time I felt this way. In fact, I don't think that has happened since Ryoko… Sure, it's been a long time and anyway Ina may not feel the same way. I'm seventy soon and she's fifty-eight."

"Don't be fooled Will, women never tell men their real age! I have never been that daft. Well, maybe once. But never again."

"She didn't tell me. We went away for a weekend at Columbe D'Or and I had a look at her passport."

"How romantic," she said, rolling her eyes. "Seventy years old. God. But don't worry, Will. Seventy is the new fifty."

"I sincerely hope not! Fifty? What is fifty? It's working your balls off; work, work, work. More and more responsibilities. More and more pressure, sometimes stress. No time to keep fit, no time to have fun. It's still paying out shedloads on the kids, the mortgage, Christ knows what else. And then lying awake worrying that you're not putting enough into your pension. I've seen it Lizzy and so has Freddie and most of my pals. Not for me. Seventy is the new seventeen."

"Seventeen?" gasped Lizzy. "Seventeen?"

"Yes!" replied William. "Think about it. Seventeen. No working your balls off, no responsibilities, no pressure. Stress? What's that? Time to keep fit if you want to. Which you won't want to. No money worries, no alarm clock. And lots of sex, lots of drugs. What's not to like?"

"Acne? Stupidity?"

CHAPTER 102

"Bloody hell," said Lizzy as they walked into the bar. I get it, Phileas Fogg. Around the world in eighty days. Not exactly subtle is it. But I like it all the same. Can we sit over there?" she asked the man who greeted them.

"Of course, madam, will it be just the two of you?"

"No, we will be eight shortly," she replied.

"The table will be yours until 8.30 pm."

"Perfect. Thank you. Can I have a look at the drinks menu?" asked William. It came within a minute. "Would you mind waiting for just a second?"

And then, "May we have a magnum of the Moet & Chandon Brut Imperial Rose please and could you bring the bill at the same time?"

By the time Freddie and Lesley arrived the bill was paid and William and Lizzy had almost finished their first drink. When Gill and Jane and Sky and her toy boy turned up and all the glasses were full, Freddie proposed a toast: "Here's to us, living a life that most people could not dream of!" They clinked their glasses.

"Freddie, what's the plan?" asked William.

"Well, I thought dinner at Hakkasan and then some fun at Annabel's."

The dinner was great and they walked up the street to the club. Lizzy paused near the reception desk and stared at the picture opposite. "What are you looking at?" asked Freddie.

"Now, look, guys I may be a bit pissed. But I didn't get to where I am without knowing my stuff. And I am here to tell you that you are looking at a very expensive painting. This is Picasso's muse and/or lover, Marie-Therese Walter. He was bonking her when she was about seventeen and he was in his forties."

"Of course. You are correct madam," interjected the man who was standing beside the painting, and probably ensuring no one walked out with it.

"Mr Caring has a substantial collection and it's one of his favourites. But he has renamed it Annabel."

"He has renamed a Picasso?" Lizzy queried.

"Yes madam. Mr Caring pays great attention to detail."

"Pays a great deal of attention sums up the man," said William. "I read that he has spent about fifty-five-million pounds on this place."

"Well, can we get to a bar and see if it is money well spent?" asked Lizzy.

In fact there were three bars in the club and of course they had to try them all and they got separated quite quickly. Freddie realised that he had drunk quite enough when he started seeing double, and as he stumbled towards the gents he nearly bumped into a swarthy chap coming out. He mumbled an apology but the man just scowled at him. Freddie thought he recognised him but couldn't remember where they had met. In fact, the next day he couldn't remember much about the evening until he saw his Amex charges.

CHAPTER 103

The sound of Tina vacuuming the stairs woke William on Thursday. He knew it must be after ten because that was when she usually arrived. His head hurt. And he was lying on the top of his duvet, still wearing his statement suit and silk shirt. Thank God, his Ferragamo loafers were on the floor and there was no sign of Lizzy. Was this early stage dementia or just half a bottle of champagne, two bottles of wine and a few cocktails? He hoped it was the latter as he went back to sleep.

'I'm getting too old for this,' thought William again as he tried to remember exactly what had happened the previous night. Lizzy turning up looking very smart and the cab journey to Mr Fogg was completely clear, as was the magnum of champagne, the walk to Hakkasan and most of the meal. He also remembered them going into the new Annabel's and a completely over-the-top bar which somehow looked perfect. They had discussed at length what to drink and in the end, he remembered they each had something different. For some reason he had a Southern Comfort with ice, a drink he hadn't tasted for years. It just seemed right at the time. But his head suggested that it probably wasn't.

The club had been quite crowded but not too noisy. Until the disco. What was that all about? God he'd been dad dancing with a very young complete stranger. Actually, grandad dancing more likely. Then there was another bar and he thought another restaurant. Did they have another meal? Or was it a dream? The girls. He remembered them coming back from the powder room. "Guys you wouldn't believe what it is like up there. It's like this bar on acid. It's like a complete fantasy. You must go and have a look." 'Please God we didn't try,' thought William. He tried to remember what happened next but it was a total blank.

He went into his wet room and turned on all the nozzles in his shower so he was blasted front, side and top. Then he reduced the heat slowly until it was as cold as was bearable. By the time he had dressed he started to feel a bit better but he was grateful he had nothing in his calendar other than the Felicity event later on.

He met Tina in the kitchen. "No run or gym this morning William?" she asked with a knowing grin. "Can I get you something to eat? Maybe a Bloody Mary? Drink it with a couple of Nurofen Express and you will be right as rain shortly. Always worked for me when I was running my pub."

"You know what, I think I will," replied William. "And I'll make myself some toast and honey. But first things first, I need a couple of glasses of water."

It was nearly twelve when William walked over to his office

and made himself a cup of coffee. As he was drinking it he went through Felicity's things again and looked at her passport photo to try and bring her back to life; to try and get the essence of her. But like all passport photos her face was unreadable. He carried on looking, just to see if anything would give him some sort of help in the talk he knew he would be asked to make at the event later on. Nothing at all spoke to him except the scruffy piece of paper containing the objectives she'd written down at the lunch in Cote so many years ago. In the end, he decided not to prepare anything at all and just told himself no platitudes!

He arrived at More London at 5.30 pm even though the event was scheduled for six. He knew that Felicity's colleagues, friends and anyone else who had heard about free drinks would arrive very promptly and he didn't relish the prospect of walking into a crowded room. He liked to be there first. And apart from Gill, he was. She came over and they air kissed. "William, you look surprisingly well!" and off she went to see the catering manager.

Chapter 104

By 6.30 pm the event room was pretty full and fifteen minutes later Gill stood on the miniature stage so she was head and shoulders over everyone. People were still talking so she waited for the noise to die down and eventually stop. Then she counted down five seconds before she spoke.

"Hi, I think I recognise almost everyone here. But in case you don't know me, I'm Gill Littleton and I was Felicity's counsellor and her team leader. I just wanted to thank you for coming along this evening to share some drinks and anecdotes. This is not a time to mourn or anything like that… But it's certainly a time to count our blessings."

Gill wanted to say some more but she didn't know what to say and she started welling up. "And let me now introduce William West who would like to say a few words."

"Thank you, Gill."

He stepped up to the stage, with hardly any idea about what he was about to say. But there was no hesitation.

"Well, I don't recognise many of you. And if this is a typical DPK drinks event, I won't be surprised if you don't recognise each other tomorrow." There were some small chuckles around the room.

"Anyway, the reason I wanted to talk to you this evening is that I think we all have a lesson we can learn from Felicity. And I would like to share it with you." William waited a few seconds.

"I met Felicity about four years ago. She came to the firm as an intern and ended up sitting near me. All I knew is that she was sponsored by a very senior partner. Of course, that couldn't happen nowadays…"

William looked out at the people with his eyebrow raised. The chuckles were louder and a voice: "Of course not!" The chuckles turned to laughter.

"It wasn't that long ago that Felicity joined the firm and asked me for a coffee. then she showed me a piece of paper. A piece of paper on which I told her to write down her objectives; all sorts of stuff. It now had a tick against every one. And it had travelled the world." He took it out of his pocket. "And here it is. So what do I have to say about Felicity? She inspired me. And I hope she will inspire you!"

William wasn't surprised with the applause. But he was a bit surprised by the number of people who came up to him afterwards and wanted to learn more about Felicity. It seemed she had been somewhat of an enigma and hadn't made that many friends. But now she was gone, everyone wanted to know her. The only person who actually did know her was the guy from the stables. Gill had invited him and when she introduced him to William it was clear he was a bit uncomfortable and ready to leave. William understood and took him over to the bar for a chat. And when it was time for him to go, William took him down to the ground floor and showed him the way out of the building.

By nine o'clock the atmosphere in the room was typical. People shouting to be heard and other people having to shout louder so that they could be heard. Those who chose not to drink; the rest becoming increasingly incoherent. Gill came up to William and they found a quiet space in the corridor.

"Good job, Gill. Well done. Want to get out of here and have a quick bite?"

"God yes. See you downstairs in five?"

"Done."

CHAPTER 105

Friday morning. And it was a perfect autumn day. Alastair Chubb was outside the church when William arrived. Gill turned up on time and the guy from the stables arrived shortly afterwards. The service started at 10.30 am and finished ten minutes later. William passed an envelope to the vicar discreetly. Alastair suggested that William and Gill should walk back to his office with him.

As they walked along, William asked a question which had been troubling him for some time. "Is there something we need to bury or ashes we need to spread?"

Alastair answered swiftly. "We do have some ashes. Is there anywhere you would suggest we spread them?"

"How about Hyde Park?" suggested Gill.

"Well I'm not sure one can get permission to do that," replied Alastair.

"Why not leave it with me and Gill, if that's OK. Where are they anyway?"

"Actually, they are in my office so you can pick them up now if you wish."

At 12.30 pm, William and Gill were walking down Motcomb Street having spread the ashes in Hyde Park and probably broken some rules. They were grinning like a couple of guilty school children when they walked into Motcombs. A bottle of champagne, some toasts to Felicity and some excellent smoked salmon sandwiches and they were finished.

"See you on Wednesday, William; have a good weekend," and Gill was gone. William was home by three.

Out of respect, William had worn a suit and tie to the service earlier so he went upstairs, shaved, showered and changed into beige chinos and a blue cashmere sweater. He also swapped his grey spectacles and watch strap for blue ones, tapped the photo as he left the room and went to check that the bathroom in the suite that Ina used was fully stocked; which of course it was.

William waited until six before making himself a drink. In the meantime, he had taken some smoked salmon and chicken out of the fridge, prepared a salad, mixed the dressing and scrubbed the baking potatoes. He had also put the glassware on the table outside and switched on the outdoor heaters. Music was next; he put on a playlist called 'Dinner 3'; it was more than four hours long; everything was set.

William was standing on the steps when Ina came into view; straight back, brisk stride, smiling as she towed her small case behind her. He waved and went up to meet her. They hugged and kissed in the road, and walked back to the house where they hugged and kissed again.

"I'd like a drink and then a shower if that's OK with you."

"Of course, what would like? Sipsmith gin and tonic?"

"Yes please. But go easy on the tonic!" They both smiled at the familiar phrase.

"How was your week?" William asked.

Ina put her feet up on the coffee table, leant back and sighed. "Pretty tough seeing as you ask. The good news is that I had a positive meeting with the FCA, and we are in good shape to file the accounts as planned. The bad news is that I've spent most of my time interviewing for both the roles I need to fill and so far, the candidates have been underwhelming to say the least. One of the problems is that HR are so scared of being accused of some sort of bias that they don't rule enough people out. And I end up interviewing someone completely unsuitable just because they are gay, or trans or Muslim or old or whatever. Don't get me wrong, I would never rule out such people but I wouldn't rule them in just to cover my arse."

William listened happily. He loved hearing people get stuff off their chest and he thought the best time to do it was a Friday evening with a drink in hand and a friend by your side.

"By the way William, I saw Freddie in the office this morning. Seems like your celebration was pretty glamorous."

"Yep, it was quite a night. I can't even remember what we were celebrating."

"Maybe an early celebration of your seventieth birthday?" Ina smiled mischievously. "I thought you told me that you were sixty-five."

"I don't think I have ever mentioned my age, you must have dreamt it. Anyway, isn't it time for your shower?"

Ina was back in less than an hour. She was wearing black leather trousers, with a silk top and a sweater hanging off her shoulders.

"Ina, you look lovely. Just lovely. Glass of wine or another gin?"

"The latter please. What are we having to eat? As usual I'm starving!"

"Smoked salmon first and then tandoori chicken with a baked potato. Hope that's OK."

"Sounds perfect. Hope it's a decent-sized potato." It was. And the conversation and wine flowed beautifully.

It was ten-thirty. The music playing in the background had been constantly interrupted by the planes flying into Heathrow but that hadn't worried either of them.

"That was a great dinner William. And please note that I left a bit of potato."

William felt a little worse for wear but laughed anyway. "How about a coffee?"

"I'll get it," said Ina. "I want a tea and you never make it quite right. Nespresso or instant?"

"Nespresso please, the green one," said William, relaxing into his chair, listening to a track by the Cocteau

— 428 —

Twins, and remembering the author Ian Banks writing that if you thought you could recognise their lyrics you were either stoned or drunk.

Ina filled the kettle and switched it on. She pressed the button on the Nespresso machine to heat up the water and took a couple cups and saucers from the cupboard and an Earl Grey tea bag. Then she went to her handbag, which she had deliberately left in the kitchen, and took out the envelope she'd put in the bag the previous night. Carefully, she placed it on the edge of one of the cups and, fingers trembling, poured the powder into the cup, placed it by the Nespresso spout and pressed the button. As William's cup filled she made her Earl Grey tea. She was back at the table within five minutes. William took a sip of his expresso and winced.

"Is that OK?" asked Ina.

"It just tastes a bit bitter."

"Maybe I used the brown pod not the green one you like. Shall I change it?"

"No don't bother, it's fine."

William took another sip. "Yes, it's fine."

William shared out the remaining Shiraz and finished his coffee. It had been a week since they had been to bed together and Ina was looking at him as if to say, 'What are we waiting for?'

He felt himself stiffen as he thought about it. No need to wash up, no need to tidy up. Let's just go up. But then, as he thought about it, he felt some palpitations in his heart, as if it was beating far too fast. And then colours. The colours around the table, around the heaters, around Ina. Every colour seemed to change. Was he having a heart attack? A stroke? What the fuck was going on? He looked at Ina. She was smiling, as if oblivious to what was happening to him. Just a tiny bit of concern on her face. She looked at him carefully and said, "William, I think I should take you upstairs."

The last word he remembered was "revenge!"

Sweat, heat, pain. White lines on a black lacquer table. Skin, smelling of an unknown scent. Heart pumping, lungs close to burning. But he wasn't running. He was lying down. Ina, in sexy underwear, looking down on him. Going down on him. His nose in a patch of red hair. Panting. Two people panting. Climax.

Felicity. On a grey horse, riding into fire. His toe, sitting on his chest. Grey and bloody. His poor toe! Freddie rising up like Lazarus from his tomb, the rustle of the branches, the explosion from the barrel, the silence before one man screams. A kaleidoscope of colour morphing into a bar in Annabel's. Light on the water, lights on the table, lights starting to permeate the blackness. A soft Scottish voice again. A familiar voice. 'Revenge, William. Revenge.'

Chapter 106

As his dream turned to reality, William knew that his left arm was trapped. He couldn't feel his fingers. Everything was numb. Panic set in. Fuck! But then he realised that his right arm seemed free. Yes, he could move it. What had happened? Where was he? It felt like he was in a bed with a duvet on top of him. He was. And it was his own bed! Ina was fast asleep and lying on his left arm. Fear was replaced by relief and confusion.

Ina woke up as William pulled his arm from underneath her. She turned and smiled at him. "Well that was quite a night! I got my revenge and the best sex ever. Three times in one night."

"I never knew I had it in me," replied William.

"You didn't. I put it in you. Revenge is sweet. I was paying you back for the cannabis cookies. You fed them to me without warning and said they might add some spice to the night. Which, as I hope you recall, they did. So, last night I returned the favour by crushing two Viagra tablets and putting them into your coffee. Maybe it was a bit of an overdose as you seemed a bit off to start with but after that you were like a guy in a porn movie – not that I've ever seen one of course. Anyway, I read somewhere that the reason they can keep at it for so long is that most of the chaps are gay."

"Why?" asked William. "Why did you think I needed Viagra?"

"Need is not the word, I just wanted to stretch the boundaries a bit and it worked like a charm. So, lover; how was it for you?"

"Pretty fantastic, seeing as you ask! How did you get the pills?"

"Men can get them from some pharmacies now without prescription so I had to persuade my pharmacy pal in Wigmore Street that my partner was far too shy to come along himself. He made an exception this time but I don't think we need to trouble him again unless you feel the need!"

CHAPTER 107

William met Lionel for lunch at Scotts. The first time he had been back there since his phone had been stolen. At least he had thought it had been stolen. That bastard Stan!

"How is your pal Freddie?" asked Lionel.

"Last time I saw him was in Annabel's last week," said William.

"Annabel's?" Lionel exclaimed. "I thought the place was closed!"

"All done up now in a house close by. What a place. What a palace! Has to be seen to be believed. Richard Caring has truly pushed the boat out. Having said that, to continue the analogy, I was two sheets to the wind when we arrived so my memory of the occasion was far from perfect. Don't even know how I got home; I was three sheets by then. I remember Freddie was on fine form. The guy is irrepressible and I'll never forget he saved my life."

"You know what, William, it might not be the first time Freddie has saved a life. And back when he joined the firm, there were plenty of rumours around his back story and some suggestions that he hadn't left all that SBS derring-do stuff behind."

"Come on Lionel, tell me more."

"William, this is just a rumour about a rumour; so please don't dwell on it," Lionel whispered. "And please don't mention it to anyone else, in particular Freddie. Have you heard of Group 13?"

"Group 13? No."

"Well, it is rumoured to be a secret cadre of ex-SAS, SBS and military intelligence operatives, with a remit in the same shadowy realm as 'The Increment', i.e. deniable covert actions such as assassinations. Both units are rumoured to be run via the Foreign Office, through the SIS. And the rumour is that Freddie is still connected to these guys."

"Fuck me," gasped William, much to the surprise of the sommelier approaching with the remnants of the first bottle. "You are joking, aren't you?"

"No. But it's just a rumour. Most people think the whole outfit is made up. Google them and you will see."

"I most certainly will!" replied William.

CHAPTER 108

Julian was walking Joan and David through his wood to have a look at the memorial. He had thought twice about allowing it to be placed before saying yes. He was now pleased that he had; it reminded him how lucky he was to be alive and it looked exactly right; plain oak and beautifully carved. 'Felicity Isabell Strange. Rest in Peace.' He often wondered what people would make of it in the years to come.

On the way back, even though he was almost half a mile from his cottage, he could smell the wood smoke from his chimney. It seemed to be reminding him that winter was waiting. A cold breeze drove the message home and he was glad to get inside and get warm. As was his habit, he switched on the TV and made himself a cup of instant coffee and settled down to watch the news. It kicked off as usual with politicians arguing with each other, then it was yet another gang-related murder in London followed by the FTSE 100 having reached an all-time high.

Julian sighed, looked at his watch and decided to go to the pub. Then he grabbed the remote control and turned up the volume as he heard the name Felicity Strange. A middle-aged man in a suit and tie was standing outside a building and, behind him in uniform, was the policeman that had interviewed him after he had found the grave. "And Frank Meadows has pleaded guilty. This was a heinous crime, killing and burning the body of an innocent twenty-five-year-old trainee accountant and also burning his partner in crime. The investigation by Thames Valley police and the conviction of this cold-blooded killer marks the end of an intensive and imaginative investigation and I would like to congratulate Detective Inspector Clarke and his team on a job well done."

'Well,' thought Julian. 'How on earth did they manage that? Christ knows. Better get down the pub and spread the news.'

CHAPTER 109

When Freddie opened the email, his first thought was 'How did he get my address?' His second, 'What the hell does he want?' The address was a no-brainer: Linked-in or whatever online. Or maybe he just hoped there was only one Findlay in the UK firm, which there was. But 'what does he want' was a different matter. Yes, they had worked together in the Royal Navy and Control Risks and yes, their paths had crossed a few times afterwards but they were never friends. In fact, there was something about Peter Carby that Freddie didn't like. He read the email again.

'Hi Freddie,

Hope all is well with you. I have been in the Middle East for a while and have just returned to Blighty. I wondered if we might catch up. It would be to our mutual benefit.

Could you call me on the number below when you get a moment?'

'Mutual benefit' thought Freddie. But old comrades are old comrades, so he made the call. Peter answered immediately and when Freddie announced himself he sounded overjoyed. "Freddie, Freddie, old chap. How nice to hear your voice! How on earth are you?"

"Very well indeed, thank you Peter. How's it going with you?"

"Pretty damn good, Freddie. Pretty damn good!"

"So how can I help you?"

Peter lowered his voice. "There is something I would like to discuss with you face to face, I'd rather not talk about it over the phone. Nothing shady or anything like that, I promise you."

'Promise' thought Freddie. A promise from Peter was worth less than nothing. But his curiosity was piqued.

"Can we meet?"

"OK, Peter, where and when suits?"

"Somewhere in West London would work best for me as I'm renting a flat in Chiswick at the moment."

"That's a coincidence," said Freddie, "that's where I live. Why don't you come round to my place, say tomorrow or Thursday?"

"Thursday and done," said Peter. "Is 6.30 pm OK?"

"Perfect. I'll email you the directions now." Freddie sent the email, sat back, made a couple of calls and headed home.

Just after six-thirty on Thursday, Freddie's doorbell rang. He hurried to open it and there was Peter, soaking wet. He looked bedraggled, befuddled and nothing like the man Freddie had known back in the day. But Freddie was a kind man. "Come in old friend, let me take that coat." Peter shuffled out of it. "Come in, come in," said Freddie feeling sad about the way his former comrade looked and regretting his doubts about the man's veracity and motivation.

Freddie took Peter into the living room. "Have a seat. What would you like to drink? I have Chase and Sipsmith vodka in the freezer and almost anything else. Was it absinthe that you liked in the sand pit? I can't really remember."

Freddie was warbling a bit and knew he sounded nervous. He also knew why he was nervous. Peter hadn't said a word since he had arrived. It seemed that whatever he had to say wasn't good news.

They sat facing each other. Freddie couldn't help noticing the worn-out damp rubber-soled shoes that Peter was wearing and the frayed damp turn-up on his cheap trousers. It was clear that he was in what Freddie's mother used to call 'straitened times' and Freddie was considering how much he should donate.

"What can I get you?" he asked.

"Nothing for me at the moment, thanks Freddie. And to be honest this is not exactly a social visit."

"OK. What kind of visit is it? How can I help?"

Peter seemed to wake up a bit; to show a little more energy. He leant forward. "The thing is that you have fucked me up, Freddie. Fucked me up right royally."

"Hold on mate," was Freddie's response. "I haven't seen you for years. How come I've fucked you up?"

"Shooting that guy, Freddie, taking off his arm and shoulder and putting Sadie into a coma."

"Sadie! Who the fuck is Sadie?"

"Freddie, how many women have you put into a coma recently?"

"OK. I get that. The bitch that tortured my pal. But what's that got to do with you?"

"She worked for me, Freddie. That's what it has to do with me."

"She worked for you? What the fuck! She worked for you! Peter. Are you sure you don't want a drink? I'm going to get one for myself."

"No you are not," said Peter as he reached into his jacket pocket and produced what Freddie recognised as a nine millimetre Glock seventeen, a highly effective short-range handgun. Freddie knew immediately that he would need to play this carefully. He seemed to wobble on his feet then he sat down heavily.

"Oh fuck! Fuck! What's going on here?"

"You don't need to know, Freddie. It's all over for you. Just get down on your knees and let's get this over with."

"For fuck's sake Peter, just tell me!" Freddie was calm but needed to look scared, to look like a victim. Not difficult when a handgun is pointing at your face. He cast his eyes around the room as if he was hoping to find some sort of weapon, watching Peter's eyes, his mouth, his fingers, not yet on the trigger. "Tell me why. Please Peter. Why?"

"OK Freddie. A two-minute heads up and then you are history. I tasked that guy you shot and that woman you clubbed with getting some data that belonged to my client. Your actions prevented that recovery and caused my client some inconvenience. I attempted to ameliorate the downside by demonstrating to my client how I dealt with sub-optimal staff and, trust me, it was quite dramatic. She took an hour to die and was screaming every second. So, count your blessings. You won't even hear the bang. My client is Jorge Perez. He is a very brutal chap. But I thought he would be satisfied once he watched the video of Sadie's punishment and all would be well going forward. However, as you know, some pictures of your so-called heroism emerged in the press. Unfortunately for you, Jorge recognised you having the time of your life in Annabel's recently. And it irritated him, so he asked me to remove you. Simple as that. Needless to say, failure is not an option from my perspective. You know how it is Freddie. Clean shot to the head."

"What the hell are you talking about?" said Freddie. "I don't know how it is. I've never killed anyone in cold blood. You don't have to do this, Peter. I have money. Plenty of money. Enough for you to get lost in the world and have a good life."

"I do have to do this." Peter picked up a cushion.

"This might soften the sound. And anyway, after you are dead and I've taken the photo, I'll be out of here with everything I've touched wiped clean within a couple of minutes. I don't think your neighbours will be hearing anything anyway. And nor will you."

Peter was holding the gun in his right hand. It was pointing down and it seemed to Freddie that it was being held quite loosely. As he was once again searching for options he saw movement behind Peter but kept his eyes firmly on the gun. "Kneel down, for Christ's sake!" said Peter, gun in one hand, cushion in the other.

There was a moment's silence, then came a very loud voice. "Armed police. Drop the gun." Freddie threw himself sideways to the floor and Peter turned around to see two uniformed policemen in the doorway pointing Heckler & Koch carbines at him. He stood totally still then dropped the Glock and put up his hands.

Jackie Starling came into the room as Freddie was getting to his feet.

"Can I have a drink now?" he asked. "And couldn't your guys have come in a bit earlier? I was getting a bit worried."

"Of course you can have a drink," she replied. "I'd like to join you but I'm on duty. You did well, Freddie. And I'm sorry I doubted you when you called and suggested that this Peter Carby might be a real player. The video is perfect. It's a slam-dunk confession. If we had intervened earlier it might not have been quite so simple."

"Where is he now?" asked Freddie.

"He's in your hall being searched."

"Thanks," said Freddie who walked straight out to where the handcuffed Peter Carby was standing, looking helpless.

"I'm sorry Freddie; it was you or me!"

"I know," Freddie replied. "Don't feel bad about it, Peter. Feel bad about this." Then Freddie pulled his right leg back and kicked Peter as hard as he could in the balls. "You must be a complete fucking idiot to think I wouldn't realise you were up to mischief. And think on this, dickhead. I would have been able to take you down even if it was just one on one." Peter collapsed on the floor. And that was when Freddie kicked him in the head.

Then he looked at the two cops who were picking Peter off the floor. "You didn't see that did you?"

"What?" they both replied.

"Good. But if you ever do see something like that and want to learn; the trick is to aim through the balls not at the balls. Have a nice evening!"

CHAPTER 110

William was watching TV when Freddie called him at eight o'clock.

"William, what are you up to?"

"Nothing old chap; just watching a crap programme and reflecting on being nearly seventy."

"Can I come round? I have just had an incredible experience I want to share and maybe cadge something to eat."

"No problem at all. I was about to sort something out for myself anyway."

They sat at the kitchen table and Freddie took him through the whole event. The call from Peter, his call to Jackie Starling, the arrangements to have the two policemen in the house, the positioning of the cameras disguised as mirrors and the two armed cops practising walking silently from his study to the living room doorway. Then, the arrival of Peter.

"I actually felt sorry for him until he produced the Glock."

"A fucking gun?"

"Yes, a real fucking gun. Even though I knew the police were there I nearly wet myself – or worse. But the guy is a professional; he kept his finger outside the trigger guard so at least I knew he wasn't going to shoot me by accident.

"Peter told me that he had organised those guys to grab you and had that mad bitch torture you. By the way, he also told me that she had been tortured and killed and he thought that would pacify that money-laundering nutcase who was after the data stick. It did for a while. But apparently, he saw me that night when we were in Annabel's having fun and that irritated him. So, he told Peter to kill me. Can you imagine the headstone on my grave: 'Frederick Findlay Rest in Peace. He died because he irritated some bloke he had never met'. Freddie paused, shook his head and frowned.

"What's up?" asked William.

"What's up is that I am a fucking idiot! I have met the man; I barged into him at Annabel's. I thought I recognised him but I was pissed and anyway he was very blurred."

"Well you were pissed!"

"Yes, but that's not what I meant. He was that guy in the video Angela showed us. The guy with those fucking dogs and the kids. How could I be so stupid!" Freddie got up and walked around the room muttering to himself. Then sat down, calmed down and took a sip of his wine.

"Why did the cops wait so long to come into the room?" asked William.

"I don't know. They said they wanted some sort of confession from the bloke. You know, I was getting a bit scared. And I was so relieved afterwards I didn't ask. Tell you what though, when Peter was handcuffed and standing in my hall, I kicked him in the balls harder that I've ever kicked anyone before. Literally, it lifted him of the floor and he fell down in a heap. I kicked him in the head, then I felt great – although my foot hurts like hell! How about another bottle?"

"Tell me something, Freddie, do you think the guy is still irritated and might organise another attempt?"

"I asked Jackie about that. She is not down in the detail but he is, as they say, a 'Person of Interest' to the NCA and she reckons it is unlikely. The NCA and the Fed are about to recover nearly £2 billion of the money that passed through Kutzevenia Bank. And she thinks the guy will have enough on his plate dealing with the people whose money it was to worry about you and me. She told me his customers may be second tier in terms of size but they are up there with the big boys when it comes to violence. In any event, let's keep tonight under our hats. I don't want people worrying."

What Freddie didn't say was that when Jackie used that word 'unlikely' a switch went off in his head. 'Unlikely' didn't do it. He wasn't about to spend the rest of his life looking over his shoulder. And he had already decided that he would have to act. 'Unlikely' had to change to 'impossible'. And the sooner the better.

He knew that killing the guy would be challenging. But that wasn't the problem. Not getting caught would take very careful planning. And he would need some help. Angela! He smiled. "Why the smile Freddie?" asked William.

"I was just thinking about Jackie. She was really pleased with the result this evening and said she couldn't thank me enough. I nearly said that a quickie would be thanks enough but didn't know whether I'd get a snog or a slap."

CHAPTER 111

William and Ina had dinner at La Trompette again followed by more drinks at home and some coke which led to a very late night. It was nearly ten o'clock when William woke up on Saturday morning. No sign of Ina. Just as he was going back to sleep she came in wearing jeans and a cashmere sweater, looking as if she had spent the last twenty-four hours in a spa.

"Rise and shine William. I think we have brunch in High Road Brasserie at twelve followed by some shopping. You can have a kip later on before cooking me dinner. Bloody Mary or orange juice?"

They had a very relaxing day, lunch at The River Café walking down the Thames, crossing at Putney Bridge and crossing back over Kew Bridge holding hands and chatting about everything and nothing. Ina fell asleep on the sofa. He stood, looking at her, thinking of all the lovely times they had spent together and made a decision. If it felt like the right moment; he was going to suggest that she moved in with him.

At 6.30 pm, William was chopping onions for a shepherd's pie, carrots and broccoli for the vegetables and scrubbing potatoes for the topping. He had decided Shiraz rather than a posh Claret and a white Rioja to go with the starter which was going to be smoked mackerel with horseradish that he had found in the fridge and that was still days away from its best before date. Ina arrived during the chopping. She was wearing some kind of cashmere pyjamas and looked perfect.

It wasn't the most romantic time of the evening but as they were cleaning up in the kitchen William went for it. "Ina, I've been thinking. I know that you have been looking for somewhere to buy and even though prices have fallen a bit you haven't found anywhere you like. I was wondering, would it make sense for you to move in here with me? I'd like that a lot."

"William you are so sweet and so kind but I'm not sure you would like that. You have your own way of doing things; it's all organised. You like it that way. And actually, so do I. I love the way we are now. I like it that we have dates. I miss you when we aren't together but I also like to be on my own from time to time. And I know that you do as well. Yes, I know I have my own suite here but it's not the same as my own place. Maybe one day. But for the time being I want to carry on dating. And remember what you said the other day: Seventy is the new seventeen. And seventeen is far too early to settle down."

William looked a bit hurt or maybe it was relief on his face. Ina stood on her toes, put her arms around him and whispered in his ear, "Do you remember what else you said about seventeen? Sex, drugs and rock and roll. Let's go upstairs and get into the sex and drugs."

CHAPTER 112

Monday evening, Freddie was in the shed at the bottom of his garden retrieving his burner phone and calling Angela. "Where are you?"

"Cheltenham, but I'm on my way back to Richmond shortly. I'll be home by nine."

"Can I come to you?"

"OK but bear with my paranoia; be careful and come in the back way."

Freddie was very careful. He walked all the way to Turnham Green tube station and was certain no one followed him. When a Richmond-bound train arrived he waited until the last moment to get on board. Fifteen minutes later he opened a gate into a garden and knocked on the back door.

"Babe," he said. "Any chance of a drink?"

"Yes. And I think you are going to need one. But only one, I have a lot of information you are going to want to remember. As you asked, I have had a good look at our pal Jorge the money launderer and murderer. He has a Platinum Amex card. I can now gain access to his spending very quickly as they text cardholders immediately when a charge is made. I can get to see that, no problem; the amount and the merchant. For example, I can tell you that he spent two hundred and fifty-one pounds thirty pence at Sexy Fish last night before spending another one hundred and seventy at Annabel's. He spends a lot of money around Berkeley Square. He also spends loads on hookers.

"One piece of bad news. I've been able to access his hotel's system and it looks like Jorge is paying for two bedrooms; one nearly the most expensive, the other bottom of the range."

"Bodyguard?" interrupted Freddie. "But why's that bad news?" he asked innocently.

"Fuck off Freddie! How long have I known you? You wouldn't be asking me to take these risks unless you were serious about something."

"Well," he said firmly, "the thing is that I don't want to spend the rest of my life looking over my shoulder. The guy knows where I work, he probably knows where I live. He could have another contract on me as we speak. I don't think I have an option. And from what you've told me he's got it coming."

"Here's something else that you might like to know Freddie. Jorge and his pal are now booked BA business class to Miami a week tomorrow. If you want to meet him you'd better get organised. I'm happy to help if required."

"Will you be here tomorrow?" asked Freddie. "If so, same time, same place?"

"Done. I'll leave the back gate open."

Freddie took a cab from Richmond station and was home in fifteen minutes. He had already made a plan. He poured himself a proper drink and started poking the plan from every direction. He nodded to himself. It would do. All he needed was some luck with the tides and some rain. He went online to the tide tables and started his calculations.

CHAPTER 113

The next day, Freddie had all the Amex charges for Jorge over the past two weeks, and a recent photo. All he needed to know was which venues his target might visit and when. Of course, that was impossible to predict. But he knew he would get a text the moment that Amex sent their text to Jorge as he paid his bill. The range of restaurants was formidable. Freddie knew them all: Isabel, Gymkhana, Cecconi's, Scott's, Sexy Fish, Mortons, Hakassan and Novikov. Apart from Gymkhana, they all had doormen, but the bruiser outside Novikov looked like the only real threat.

Getting a chance to deal with Jorge at short notice was going to be challenging. But at least most of the places were close to Berkeley Square and it tended to be fairly quiet late at night in the middle of the gardens, so he could wait there until he got a text from Angela telling him which place the man was about to leave. Freddie's working assumption was that when he put the guy down he would become a suspect; even the prime suspect. Why? No reason. But it had been drummed into him when he first joined the service: 'Freddie, plan for the worst-case scenario'. And that is what he intended to do.

The main challenge was getting to the location and getting away without being identified. Where were the safe spaces? He called in sick at DPK and started pacing the streets around Berkeley Square and beyond. He paid special attention to CCTV cameras and places where he could be invisible. He reconnoitred the surroundings during the day and at night, wearing thick glasses and a hoodie, and went into town using a travelcard purchased with cash from a machine rather than using his Oyster. One day he did some gardening. He took a spade and a fork from the shed and dug up a couple of large shrubs. He put them to one side then deepened the hole. When he was happy with the depth, he put the shrubs back in and spread the extra soil across several other beds.

Freddie discovered that there were thousands of CCTV cameras in Mayfair and that most were positioned above head height. He also discovered that there were over two hundred in Green Park tube station alone. But, apparently, no cameras at all in the middle of Berkeley Square itself. On Thursday morning, he went to his shed and made a call with his phone from the hidden space.

"Babe. I have a plan. Just let me know when and where the hammer drops tonight and I shall be there." The forecast was for rain all night, the tide was going to be right and the mission was on.

Freddie put the phone in his pocket. His usual phone would be staying home that evening. There were two bags in the shed space and he pulled out the smaller one. The larger one contained his Desert Eagle 50 semi-automatic handgun. It was heavier and more powerful than he needed. There was always the small chance that a semi-automatic might jam but, in any event, he knew it was best held in two hands and his plan required a free hand.

The smaller bag contained a Ruger LCR revolver wrapped inside a chamois pouch. A very light hammerless gun with a short barrel. It was the perfect weapon for his purpose as it would fit into a pocket and could be drawn without snagging on clothing. It was already loaded with five +P high-pressure hard-hitting rounds. He walked back to the house and cleaned the gun and the ammunition thoroughly. Then he went down to Kew Bridge station and purchased an all-day all zone travelcard using cash for the machine.

Freddie dressed for action at 7.30 pm. It was completely dark and raining a bit. He put on a wig that he had bought some years ago for a fancy-dress party when he went dressed as a tart. He had cut it shorter so now it made him look a bit like a hippy. Then, the thick-lensed spectacles perched on his nose to add to the disguise and also to make his eyes less distinct in any confrontation. He knew that eyes could give too much away. He put on a plain sweatshirt and jeans, a scruffy grey raincoat, dirty trainers, and a wide-brimmed hat to keep off the rain. Underneath the raincoat he wore a bright blue showerproof zip-up jacket with a MetLife logo.

Going downstairs, Freddie switched on the TV and

some lights, grabbed some skin-coloured latex gloves from the kitchen and picked up an old collapsible umbrella. Then he put a large Harrods plastic bag in the outside pocket of his overcoat and a blue baseball cap in the inside pocket. Finally, for the third time, Freddie checked that the Ruger was on safety, slid it into the right-hand outside pocket and pulled it out a couple of times to see how it felt. It felt fine.

He went out of the back door and stood still for a couple of minutes, going through the plan, making sure he hadn't forgotten anything. Satisfied, he locked the door, walked down through the garden, put the bag for the Ruger back in the hidden space, closed it down and picked up his wellington boots which he swapped for the trainers. He laced the trainers together and hung them around his neck. It might look strange but no one was going to see them. Then he climbed down the wooden ladder at the front of the deck, opened his umbrella and walked along the dark and muddy foreshore. Taking this route was vital as leaving the house by the front door would have set off the motion-sensitive lights and activated his CCTV. That could create a problem should the police for any reason think he might be responsible for what was going to happen. Plan for the worst-case scenario!

CHAPTER 114

When Freddie got to Kew Bridge he walked up the slipway and through the small arch. He could hear some noise from the One Over the Ait pub nearby but no one was out and about. He swapped his wellingtons for the trainers and hid the boots behind some scrub. Then walked along the towpath, and up to the main road via the alley that emerged opposite the Music Museum. He crossed the street and walked the few minutes to Kew Bridge station, assuming that any CCTV would record that he had come from the east not the west. And he kept his umbrella up until the train pulled into the platform.

Having changed to the Victoria line at Vauxhall, Freddie got off at Green Park. Then he walked towards Berkeley Square, taking his time, looking around but making sure the hat and the umbrella were concealing his face from any CCTV. The umbrella and coat were also keeping him warm and dry. He found some cover under a tree close to the middle of the square and waited. And waited. Freddie was used to waiting but it was almost two hours before he got the ping. 'Amex charge £220.12. Scott's.' He couldn't run, it would attract too much attention. There just wasn't enough time to get to Scott's from where he was standing. He walked up to Park Lane, hailed a cab and asked to be dropped off at Kew station. He retrieved his wellingtons and carried them home. He slept like a log.

The next day the forecast was rain again. Freddie followed the same process, wore the same clothes, carried the same gun, walked along the foreshore but took a different route to Berkeley Square. He found a spot at the top of the square facing Mortons. The ping came at 10.23 pm: 'Amex charge. Mortons.'

Freddie didn't hesitate. He stood up and walked swiftly across the grass towards Mortons. Hat pulled down, umbrella up, thick glasses on; he was confident that he was unrecognisable. He saw Jorge and then another man that had to be the bodyguard, and walked towards them across the street. He pulled out the Ruger, but before he could line it up on Jorge a cab pulled up and they stepped into it. He could hear their laughter. It pissed him off, but he was pleased that no one had taken any notice of him.

On Saturday evening, it was really pouring with rain. Freddie was cleaning the Ruger when he realised that this was the night he would have to deal with Jorge and his bodyguard as the foreshore would be flooded the next night. And anyway, he just felt that tonight was the night. These hunches had come to him before and they had seldom failed him.

He was completely relaxed in his now battered and

soaked hat, his damp coat and his thick-lensed glasses as he walked down the garden at 8 pm. Again, he put on his wellingtons. Again, he climbed down to the foreshore and walked along to Kew Bridge station. Same routine: travelcard bought with cash earlier in the day, change at Vauxhall. When he got out at Green Park he walked straight down Berkeley Street. Everyone was heads down, trying to avoid the puddles, umbrellas up and walking as fast as they could.

Freddie walked past Novikov, down to Berkeley Square and found a bit of shelter opposite Sexy Fish. Mortons and Scott's seemed unlikely; Jorge had already been there on Thursday and Friday. But who knows? Maybe Hakassan tonight? No! For some reason he was convinced it would be Sexy Fish then Annabel's. The rain carried on battering the streets. The trees in the square provided little protection. No nightingale sang. There was no noise or movement from Freddie either.

After a long couple of hours, a ping: 'Amex charge, £280.35. Sexy Fish.' It was 11.12 pm. Freddie smiled, shook off the water from his cap and pulled it down as far as possible. He put the umbrella in his left hand and strolled over the road to the HR Owen showroom across the street. He looked around. Left, then right, checking the reflections in the glass. He walked slowly towards the restaurant. Hat down? Check. Umbrella up? Check. Safety off? Check. Just another guy trying to stay dry on a Saturday night.

Jorge was lighting a cigarette on the pavement. His bodyguard seemed relaxed, but was looking left, right and centre, carefully as per standard operating procedure. Freddie checked for any innocents in the line of fire then shot him in the face. The back of the guy's head splattered red all over the wall behind him as he fell backwards like a puppet with broken strings. Jorge knew what was coming and put his hands to his face as if to stop the next bullet. It went through his palm and into his right eye. The two shots were so close together, several witnesses reported that only one shot had been fired.

CHAPTER 115

Freddie had seen there were a couple of guys with rickshaws outside Sexy Fish. They threw themselves down on the pavement as he moved towards them. Another person did the same. Freddie knew that no one with any sense confronts an armed man. But of course, there are always heroes, so he ran as fast as he could with his umbrella extended above his head angled to deflect the CCTV along the route he had chosen.

First of all he swerved into Bruton Lane next to the restaurant. Then he pivoted right into Barlow Place where he shoved the raincoat, the glasses and the wig into the Harrods bag and put on the baseball cap. He was now an American tourist in a bright blue jacket with a Harrods bag. He turned right at Bruton Street, walked up to Bond Street then up Conduit Street to Regent Street where he joined a group of people huddled under their umbrellas at a bus stop. No sirens yet. A bus arrived and he joined the people under the bus shelter waiting to get on but then stepped sideways between the bus and the pavement, took off the baseball cap and mingled with people getting off and walking down the street.

Minutes later, Freddie got on another bus, stepped off

at Oxford Circus and took a bus back down Regent Street, getting off near Piccadilly Circus. Then the tube to Kings Cross where he walked past the station's cab rank and got a passing cab to Brook Green in Hammersmith. The traffic was worse than he had calculated and he started to worry when he looked at his watch. He walked down to The Broadway, and it seemed to take ages for an empty cab to appear. At last one arrived. Was it too late, should he change the plan? He decided to stick with it and got out at Staveley Road in Chiswick. Then he walked as fast as he could through the suburban streets to the apartment block development at Kew, through the landscaped gardens and hurried down to the towpath and through the arch.

Freddie was breathing heavily as he looked for his wellingtons in the dark and his heart sank when he saw that the tide had nearly reached the scrub where he had hidden them. He knew he was now going to have a battle with the river; he couldn't think of any way he could avoid it. He put his trainers around his neck and walked carefully down the slipway to the river. He stepped off and the water was halfway up his boots. This was fucking serious!

Ten minutes later, water was splashing into his wellingtons. His feet were getting very cold and the boots were getting heavy. The tide was coming in at four of five knots, the rain had increased, no moon, no lights. He told himself: 'You are not fucked, you will not try and get up the bank and onto the towpath, you have been in worse places just press on.' But he was hardly making any progress and the water was now above his knees and his boots were full. The phrase 'Fill your boots' came into his head. Whatever the fuck that meant. They were so heavy he thought about taking them off but his head still had some remaining logic. 'How would he manage to get them off? No way you could stand on one leg in this current. And the foreshore is littered with stuff that could rip your feet to pieces.'

Freddie realised that he was no longer moving forward. It was all he could do to avoid falling backwards. In spite of everything, he smiled as he imagined his ex-SBS pals laughing. 'Freddie Findlay, drowned in three feet of water.' He looked around and saw the slipway of the boat club near his house. He took his eyes off it, stared straight ahead, crouched down lower in the water and used his hand without the carrier bag as well as his legs to push through the water. Five minutes later he was dragging himself and the bag up the ladder and onto his deck.

CHAPTER 116

Freddie was lying on his back. The rain had stopped and there was a little moonlight. He guessed he had passed out for a moment; he could still feel his heart hammering so it couldn't have been long. He looked at his watch. 2.30am. He was soaked to the skin, teeth chattering, completely exhausted. But he knew there was work to be done. He took off the wellington boots and all his clothes then walked up to his back door, let himself in and grabbed the strong string and the pair of scissors he had left by the sink. He went back to the deck and tied a few feet of the string to the Ruger and wiped it carefully. Freddie hesitated. He knew the danger of keeping it. But he also knew how hard it would be to replace it. And 'who knows,' he thought, 'I might need it again.'

Naked, legs apart, bare feet on the floor, cold moon flitting through the clouds, Freddie stood firm on his deck over the river and thought the thing through, remembering all he had been taught. And he started to whirl the gun around and around his head, holding tight to the string, letting out the length, slowly letting the string slip through his tired hands, whirling and whirling until he thought it was at maximum velocity. Then he let go. The gun flew high into the middle of the river, opposite his neighbour's house.

Then it was time for the trainers. Freddie tied them together then stuffed in the socks, the latex gloves and the phone. He found a couple of stones in the garden path and jammed them in as well. It was a repeat performance. Tie on the string; round and round, faster and faster, then Freddie let the trainers fly. They landed in the middle of the river. Result! When he got back to the house, he wiped the floor where his damp feet had muddied it, put all his clothes, including the coat and the wig into the washing machine at forty degrees. He then looked to see what he would have been watching on TV if he had been home, and checked out a couple of programmes. Then he had a long, hot bath, scrubbed himself thoroughly and went to bed.

CHAPTER 117

Freddie's alarm woke him at 7 am. It was still dark. He put on jeans and a sweatshirt, took everything out of the washing machine, grabbed a spade from the shed, lifted up the plants he had pulled up from the flower bed, buried the clothes, replaced the plants and spread the excess soil around. He brushed the spade clean before putting it back. When things had settled down he planned to take everything out and dispose of the stuff more safely. Before going back to the house, he used the garden hose to clean off his wellingtons. He was eating his breakfast and watching a repeat of last night's Match of the Day when the doorbell rang.

No panic. Freddie had planned on the basis that he might be a suspect, or even the prime suspect. Of course, he might have made some sort of mistake. Of course, there might be some CCTV issues. But there couldn't be anything that would stand up in court. And even then he had an excellent lawyer. But when he opened the door his confidence took a turn for the worse.

There were two young men standing on the doorstep in casual clothes. The elder of the two held up an ID card.

"Good morning. Mr Findlay?"

Freddie muttered, "Yes."

"We have a couple of questions for you, sir. May we come in?"

"What questions?" asked Freddie.

The reply came with a smile. "To be precise Mr Findlay. Have you found God? Would you like a copy of Watchtower?"

"No thank you, but have a good day." He closed the door softly and smiled.

Later that morning, Freddie had another coffee and thought very carefully about the previous night, wondering where or how he might be exposed. His own security system would prove he hadn't left the house. He wasn't too concerned about CCTV or any identification. And even if he could be connected to the location in some way, so what? It would be just circumstantial evidence, and that wouldn't hold up in court. Anyway, there were bound to be a number of people with motives on which the police would be focusing. And how much resource would they allocate when they discovered who the victims were? Not much was his guess.

CHAPTER 118

Monday morning. December 1st.

Julian was in his cottage. The 'Mayfair Murder' was on the news. 'Thank God I've left London he thought.'

Joan and David both snuffled at the same time to show him they agreed.

Ina was in the office early even though there had been a long lunch at William's yesterday.

Freddie was reading a text that had just arrived from a phone he didn't recognise. It said: 'Relax, for the time being. I look forward to working with you again in due course.'

Jackie Starling was smiling as she put down the phone.

William was running off his hangover prior to going to DPK and his Monday morning presentation.

DCI 'Bunny' Field was in his office listening to DI Clarke. "It's a scandal, sir. Those murders of the businessman and his assistant in Mayfair are the ninety-sixth and ninety-seventh this year."

"They weren't murders, Clarke. They were hits. Take it from me, the victims weren't a businessman and his assistant; they were a drug dealer and his bodyguard. Now, what have you got for me on that fucking domestic?"

Acknowledgements

I really enjoyed writing this book; so much so that it was nearly 50,000 words longer than it is now! Many thanks to Rebecca Carter who encouraged me to get a professional editor and many thanks to Louise Buckley who was that editor. The team at Spiffing Covers have been the icing on the cake.

Last, but definitely not least, I would like to mention my wonderful partner in crime Jenny Yamamoto. Without her this book would not have been written.